FALLEN

From behind I heard quiet movements as the security men readied their weapons. They weren't pointing them at the figure . . . yet. I raised my voice, speaking clearly and loudly. 'I am Mage Alex Verus of the Junior Council. If you are an enemy of Mage Drakh, Mage Crystal or the other Dark mages who operated this facility, we will assist you. If you side with them and against the Council, you will not be harmed should you come peacefully. Step into the light and make yourself known.'

Silence. Seconds ticked away. Then the figure stepped forward.

It was a boy in his twenties, as Anne said. He looked quite ordinary, but my hackles rose the instant I saw him. There was an aura around his form; it was faint and hard to see, but the shadows were clinging to him a little more than they should, hinting at something larger and darker behind. I recognised that pattern and I knew what it meant, and all of a sudden I wasn't interested in talking any more. 'All units,' I said quietly into my communicator. 'Defensive formation. Prepare for enemy summons.'

The boy swept his gaze over us, looking down from the top of the stairs. Futures flickered as he made his decision, but I didn't need to scan them to know what was going to happen. 'Why do you all keep coming?' he said to no one in particular. His voice sounded wrong, older than it should have been.

By Benedict Jacka

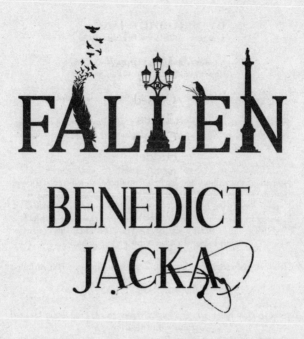

FALLEN

BENEDICT JACKA

orbit

www.orbitbooks.net

ORBIT

First published in Great Britain in 2019 by Orbit

1 3 5 7 9 10 8 6 4 2

A CIP catalogue record for this book is available from the British Library.

ISBN 978-0-356-51112-2

Typeset in Garamond 3 Lt Std by Palimpsest Book Production Limited,
Falkirk, Stirlingshire
Printed and bound in Great Britain by Clays Ltd, Elcograf S.p.A.

Papers used by Orbit are from well-managed
forests and other responsible sources.

MIX
Paper from
responsible sources
FSC® C104740

Orbit
An imprint of
Little, Brown Book Group
Carmelite House
50 Victoria Embankment
London EC4Y 0DZ

An Hachette UK Company
www.hachette.co.uk

www.orbitbooks.net

'You don't have to do this,' Anne said.

We were in Canonbury, one of the districts within Islington. It's one of London's upmarket areas – not on the level of Westminster or Chelsea, but a long way from cheap. London has a lot of places like Canonbury, old expensive terraced houses crammed into winding tree-lined streets, with small parks in between where people walk their dogs. For the most part, mages don't visit them. It's true that mages are more common in cities, but there are close to ten million people in London, and that's enough to dilute the mage population pretty heavily, even if they wanted to spread out, which they don't. So they cluster, and the areas in between fall off their radar, to the point where the average mage knows about as much about the residents of Canonbury as the average resident of Canonbury knows about mages. It's symmetrical, I suppose.

Right now we were standing under a sycamore tree, looking across the street towards a house on the other side. It was a July evening, with the sun setting behind the rooftops, and the air was still and warm. From around us, voices and chatter drifted up, the sounds of traffic coming from the main roads nearby. Anne had led me here by a roundabout route, taking a path down an old canal lined with benches and willow trees. It had been a pretty walk and I'd enjoyed it, but I had the feeling it had been a delaying tactic.

'Neither do you,' I told her.

'Yes I do,' Anne said. '*You* don't have to.'

'Would you really prefer to go in on your own?' I asked. 'Anyway, look on the bright side. You're not going on trial this time.'

'That's what you think.' Anne thought for a minute. 'How long will we have?'

'Until we get the go signal?' I asked. 'Call it about a twenty per cent chance for the next hour, forty per cent for one to two hours, twenty per cent for later and twenty for never.'

'So that's a forty per cent chance of being stuck here all night.'

I leant in and kissed the side of Anne's head. 'Come on. Are we really going to come this far, then turn around and leave?'

Anne sighed. 'I suppose not.'

We crossed the street and walked up the steps to the house. It was on the large side for a terrace, with bay windows. Anne rang the bell and as we stood waiting, we heard footsteps approaching from the other side.

The door swung open, light and noise spilling out into the summer evening. From down the hallway I could hear the sound of chatter and raised voices. The woman who'd opened the door was in her fifties with greying hair, and wore an evening dress and a pearl necklace. 'Oh good, you're here. We were starting to think you wouldn't make it. Alex, wasn't it? Do come in. Anne, the coats are going in the hall.'

I sat at the dinner table and felt out of place.

There were seven others in the dining room. The woman

who'd greeted us was sitting at the head of the table, presiding over the meal. At her right side was her husband, a thin, melancholy-looking man currently focused on drinking his soup. Occupants three through six were the two daughters and their partners. Number seven was Anne.

'. . . just can't understand how anyone like that can get elected,' the younger daughter was saying. 'I mean . . . no? Just no?'

'Well, it's lack of education, isn't it?' the boy who'd come with her said. 'The funny thing is that they're voting against their own interests. You'd think they'd be able to see . . .'

It was odd to think that this was the house that Anne had grown up in. Well, one of them. According to Anne, when she'd first been placed with the family, it had been in Finchley – they'd moved to Canonbury when she was twelve so that the elder daughter, Elizabeth, could go to a better school. That had been fourteen years ago, and apparently they'd been living here ever since.

I looked around at the dining room. Most of the walls were taken up with shelves, with plates and bowls mounted upon them, well spaced. There were several chests of drawers, all covered with white lace tablecloths. Despite its size, the room felt cramped. It didn't really feel like a room for living in, one where you could stretch out and put your feet up: it was a display room, every piece of glass and china arranged for effect. A partition led into the living room, and a door at the side opened into a hallway containing the stairs and the entrance to the kitchen.

The older boyfriend was talking now. He was English, with short brown hair and narrow glasses, and looked to be a good five to ten years older than his fiancée. '. . . real problem is that people aren't listening enough to experts,' he was saying. 'Instead they're being influenced by private elements in the media. All these billionaires who can just manufacture fake stories. I mean, we try to do the best we can to provide a more balanced view, but . . .'

'It must be very difficult,' the mother said sympathetically. Her husband sipped his soup.

Anne and I had been a couple for a year now. I'd suggested meeting her family more than once, but Anne had put it off, and now that I was here it wasn't hard to see why. My time on the Council had gotten me into the habit of paying attention to social hierarchies, and on reflex I'd found myself analysing the other people around the table. The mother was the head of the household, and both the elder daughter, Elizabeth, and her fiancé, Johnathan, apparently had her approval. Elizabeth wore an engagement ring with a large diamond, positioned prominently. Neither the mother nor Johnathan wanted me here. In the case of Johnathan, the reason wasn't hard to guess: he considered himself the alpha male of the group and I was an intruder. The mother's issues were less obvious, and I suspected they were something deeper, something involving Anne.

The younger sister apparently held less favour in her mother's eyes, judging by the choice of seating. Neither she nor her boyfriend had been paying attention to me so far, but I knew that when trouble started, it would come from her. As I formed the thought, I couldn't help but smile. *Trouble.* What a dramatic way to put it.

'Why don't you ask Alex?' the younger daughter said brightly.

Johnathan had been in mid-flow; the question caught him off-guard. 'What?'

'Well, you were just saying that the government ought to do more, weren't you?' the younger daughter said. According to Anne, her name was Grace. 'Didn't she say you work for the government?'

'More or less,' I agreed.

'So what do you think the government should be doing to cut down on populism?'

'Come now, Grace,' the mother cut in smoothly. 'We shouldn't ask him to talk business at the dinner table.'

'No, that's fine,' I said. 'The first answer would be that it's a loaded question.'

'What?'

'You're assuming that populism's a bad thing that needs to be stopped.'

'Isn't it?'

I shrugged. 'Most of the time, when someone says "populism" in that context, they mean "something that's popular that I don't like". If they like it, they call it "democracy" or "representation". It isn't the government's job to promote your opinion at the expense of everyone else.'

'But come on, now,' Johnathan broke in. 'You have to admit that so many of our recent problems have been because the government hasn't been stepping in.'

'That's one way to look at it.'

'Don't you agree?'

'Actually, the majority of my work these days revolves around solving problems originally caused by the people I work for.'

Johnathan paused; obviously the conversation wasn't going the way he'd been expecting. The other people at the table had fallen silent, watching our back and forth. The only one who wasn't looking at us was Anne.

Johnathan tried to rally. 'I suppose the core of the problem is the recent trend of anti-intellectualism.'

'Is that what you'd call it?'

'Of course.'

'So you think the issue is . . . what? That people don't respect cleverness enough?'

'Not just cleverness,' Johnathan said. 'Expertise, depth of knowledge. Wisdom, even. Instead they end up following people who promise them easy solutions.'

'Well, there's definitely some truth to that,' I said. 'I have to spend a lot of time trying to explain to people that the situation's more complicated than establishment bad, rebels good. And there's a real danger of getting demagogues in a situation like that. People are so focused on the establishment that they don't notice that they're being duped by the ones who are claiming to be on their side.'

There were several nods. Johnathan was about to speak, but I kept going. 'But none of that really explains where the animosity towards the establishment came from. And it's a mistake to chalk that up to anti-intellectualism. They don't think that the people in charge are stupid or uninformed. They just don't trust them. Big difference.'

'So you'd say that the problem's a lack of communication?'

'You mean that the problem is that the government hasn't done enough to get its message out?'

'Yes, exactly.'

I nodded. 'Then no.'

'What?'

'The people I'm dealing with think the establishment doesn't care about them because, for the most part, the establishment doesn't care about them. Stepping up the propaganda isn't going to make much difference.'

'It's not propaganda.'

'Whatever you call it, if you keep saying one thing and doing another, people eventually notice.'

Johnathan tried to think of something else to say. The mother cut in. 'Which department did you say you worked for again?'

'It's usually security work.'

'You mean you're part of the police?' Elizabeth said.

'Not exactly,' I said. 'I can't really go into details.'

'Because if you told us, you'd have to kill us?' the younger boyfriend said.

I smiled politely at the stale joke. There were several laughs. 'Guess we'd better be careful what we say around you,' the boy said. 'Might be being recorded.'

'You don't need to be so melodramatic,' Johnathan said. He was trying to keep his tone light but there was an edge to his voice. 'He probably spends all his time sitting in meetings.'

'A lot of my days are like that.'

'Well, has everyone finished?' the mother said. There was a murmur of agreement and she looked over. 'Anne, I think it's time to bring the dessert in.'

Anne nodded and rose to her feet. I didn't look after her as she left; Johnathan's last words had stirred up memories. *Meetings . . .*

The Keeper briefing room was ugly, peeling paint and cheap tables. The chairs were uncomfortable enough that most of the people in the room had chosen to stand, forming a loose circle. Blinds had been pulled down over the windows, and the only light was coming from the illumin-ated map at the centre of the room.

The map was a projection, three-dimensional and sculpted out of light, and it showed a section of landscape a little over a square mile in size, the hills rising almost to waist height and the valleys falling to the level of my knees. The bulk of the terrain was covered in trees; most of the rest was undergrowth or open field. There was only one building, low-slung with two long wings. From above, and at this scale, it looked quite small.

'The Order of the Star's current plan is to attack in a pincer,' I said. As I spoke, I channelled through the focus: translucent blue arrows appeared on the map, sweeping down from east and west towards the mansion's two wings. 'They'll gate as close as possible to the edge of the ward radius, then move in. Constructs will be on point, with security forces in the second wave and guarding the flanks. Primary objectives are here and here—' Green dots appeared in the wings. '—with secondary objectives spread through the ground and first floors.' Lighter green dots appeared as I spoke, covering the building. 'The goal is to take the above-ground sections of the building in the initial surprise attack.'

'Excellent!' Landis said. Tall and lanky, he was half-leaning on one of the tables. 'Wonderful thing, optimism. Might I enquire what the plan is should they fail to do so?'

I smiled slightly. 'Director Nimbus didn't feel it necessary to go into the details.'

There were various noises of displeasure from around the room. 'Correct me if I'm wrong,' one of the other Keepers said, 'but I thought you were on the Junior Council.'

'Correct.'

'Doesn't that mean you outrank Nimbus?'

'Also correct,' I said. 'However, he demanded field command for this operation, which the Council granted. Director Nimbus also made the decision for the primary attack force to be drawn from the Order of the Star, holding Shield Keepers in reserve. Which is the reason we're here.'

'Director Nimbus can't find his own arse with both hands and a map,' a third Keeper suggested.

'Didn't quite hear that,' I said, and looked around the circle. 'Opinions?'

The Keeper who'd pointed out my rank crouched down, studying the landscape thoughtfully. The light projection fuzzed around his legs. His name was Tobias, and he was a dark-haired man in his forties who, for reasons best known to himself, wore a large Stetson hat. 'Don't like it,' he said.

'Reasons?' I asked.

Tobias pointed down at the landscape. 'Too far from the entry point to the target, not enough cover. Easy crossfire.'

'With surprise—' another Keeper said.

'One never wants to depend entirely on surprise,' Landis said. 'Drakh has unfortunately proven quite skilled at anticipating attacks in the past. Which regretfully leads me back to my earlier question as to the presence or otherwise of our backup plan. I do hope that we're not it?'

'Unfortunately, I rather suspect we are.'

Tobias nodded as if he'd been expecting it. 'Of course,' another Keeper said. 'Wouldn't be a job for the Order of the Shield otherwise, would it?'

'Why don't we just blow the place up?' someone asked.

'Because the objective isn't to destroy the mansion,' I said. 'The Council want Richard Drakh, alive if possible.

Secondary objective is to recover any strategic intelligence and imbued items within the building.'

'Ambitious.'

'For what it's worth, I agree with you. However, the Council has decided that our operational objectives are to take the mansion intact.'

'Lovely,' Landis said, rubbing his hands together. 'Any chance of backup?'

'After a fashion,' I said. I activated the focus, and a pair of aircraft appeared at head height above the mansion, circling lazily. They were small and sleek, grey-coloured with swept-back wings. 'The Council has – reluctantly – exercised its influence. A flight of Panavia Tornados from the RAF, armed with Paveway guided bombs, will be on station when we launch the attack.'

'Didn't you say the Council wanted the place intact?' Tobias asked.

'I managed to convince them that the risk of the attack failing was high enough that it was worth preparing a backup plan,' I said. 'Needless to say, this option should be considered a last resort. It'll be a pain in the neck for the Order of the Cloak to cover up, it'll cause significant collateral damage, and most of all, from the Council's point of view, it'll mean we'll have no idea whether Richard Drakh or any of his cabal are dead.'

'I don't think we need to bomb the place to know the answer to that,' Tobias commented.

'We have been telegraphing this attack for a pretty long time, yes,' I said. 'Still, those are our orders. Any other questions?'

I looked around the room. A couple of the Keepers shook their heads.

'Then let's get ready,' I said. 'We'll be moving out in a little under one hour. Operation is scheduled to start at ten-oh-five.'

'Into the bloody breach again,' someone commented.

I smiled slightly. 'Let's hope it's not as literal this time. Look on the bright side. In a couple of hours, this war might be over.'

'And how exactly—?'

'Alex?'

I snapped back to the present. Anne was standing next to me, holding a tray. 'Would you like some?'

I stared for a second, then shook off the memory. 'No. Thanks.' The dessert was something white and creamy. I hadn't noticed her bring it in.

'. . . women's healthcare is so bad in this country,' Elizabeth was saying. 'I had to wait nearly two hours for an appointment and I didn't get a proper interview until I saw the doctor. It could have been an emergency and they wouldn't have known . . .'

'Johnathan?' Anne asked, moving around.

'Oh, I really shouldn't.'

'Come on, Johnathan,' the mother said with a smile. 'You can't come all this way and not try some. I insist.'

'Well, I'd love to, but . . . I hate to be a bother, but is it chilled? Anything lactose-based really sets off my allergies if it's at room temperature.'

'Oh, that'll be fine,' the mother said. 'Anne will put some in the freezer and check on it every few minutes. Then you can have it once it's cool.'

I looked at her in disbelief.

Anne caught my eye before I could say anything: she

gave a tiny shake of her head and I held my tongue. Anne disappeared into the kitchen.

The rest of the people at the table were ignoring me now. The conversation had switched over to education and which schools were the best, and I wasn't being included. I was fairly sure it was deliberate, but I had trouble making myself care. My thoughts kept wanting to go back to last October.

The raid on Richard's mansion hadn't been a disaster, but it hadn't been a success either. The Council had 'won', in the sense that they'd been left in possession of a smoking pile of rubble. There had been a handful of prisoners who'd been outside the mansion when the bombs had hit, but as with the raid on the Tiger's Palace, none had been mages. Richard hadn't shown himself on the battlefield at all, and most of his forces had withdrawn through gates before the airstrike. I'd taken some flak for calling the strike, but not that much. It hadn't been clear who was winning or losing prior to the pullback, but if the battle had played out, the Council forces would have taken significant losses. As things were, they'd lost very few.

All the same, the Council hadn't been happy. They'd been hoping that the strike on Richard's mansion would end the war, or at least shut down his operations. Instead, Richard had simply set up shop in a new base, and one that was sufficiently well-hidden that the Council had yet to track it down. The one plus from my point of view was that I'd gained a few converts among the Light ranks. The news had got out that I'd been the one to insist on having those Tornados standing by, and that had raised my popularity a bit. It hadn't done anything to make the mages of the Council like me any more, but the security forces, and to a lesser degree the Keepers, had noticed. People whose jobs put them on the front lines pay attention to these things.

But regardless of my personal fortunes, in the larger scale, the attack had been a failure. To win the war, the Council needed to kill Richard, or force him to the negotiating table. They hadn't done it in the three months between the Tiger's Palace raid and the mansion attack, and they hadn't done it in the nine months between the mansion attack and now.

'. . . further away from London would be much cheaper, obviously,' Elizabeth was saying. 'But I don't know . . .'

'Yeah, that means you'd have to live with country people.'

'Yes, not really our sort of company.'

Anne reappeared, carrying a serving of the dessert, and set it down in front of Johnathan. 'What temperature is it?' Johnathan asked.

'It's fairly cold,' Anne said.

Johnathan tested it. 'Ah, good.'

'Will that be all right?' the mother asked him.

'Well, we live in hope, as they say! But it does look delicious.'

'Oh, thank you,' the mother said to him with a smile. 'Anne, while we're finishing up, could you do the dishes from the main course? That way the sink will be clear for the dessert plates.'

I couldn't stay quiet any longer. 'Did you send your servants home for the evening?'

The conversation at the table stopped as everyone turned to look at me. 'Excuse me?' the mother asked.

I could feel Anne's eyes on me but I didn't meet them. 'Well, you know.' I kept my voice pleasant. 'I was wondering who handles the domestic duties when you don't have guests over to do it.'

The father looked back and forth and hesitated, obviously wondering if he should be intervening. The daughters and their boyfriends watched warily. 'I really don't appreciate your tone,' the mother said.

'I'm sorry, I must have misunderstood.' I rose to my feet. 'Tell you what, since I'm not having dessert anyway, I'll go help. I'm sure we won't be too long.'

Without waiting for an answer, I turned and walked out into the hallway. The mother stared after us, but by the time she'd made up her mind about what to say, we were already gone.

Did you really have to do that? Anne asked.

We were in the kitchen washing up. The running of the tap made enough noise that it would have been hard to eavesdrop, but we weren't talking out loud; we were using a dreamstone, a focus I own that allows for mind-to-mind conversation. It had other powers too, ones that were considerably more dangerous.

Anne and I had fallen into the habit of using the dreamstone whenever we were alone, and often when we weren't. Anne's my Council aide, and we'd spent most days over the past year in and out of the War Rooms or the other Council facilities around London. I have a lot of enemies in all of them, and when you work in a place like that, you learn to be careful about being overheard.

Have to, no, I said. *Wanted to, yes.*

Anne made a frustrated noise. Dreamstone communication is expressive; you get all the emotions that tone of voice can contain, along with a lot more. *You didn't have to insult them.*

I took a plate from Anne to rinse. *I didn't insult them.*

You were being rude.

Not half as rude as them. Seriously, chilled desserts? I have literally met Dark mages who treat their slaves more politely.

Anne gave a mental sigh. *You know, after I'd been living in the Tiger's Palace for a couple of weeks, I realised Jagadev was reminding me of her. I suppose that should have been a bad sign.*

About Jagadev, or about her?

I'm not sure.

I finished with the plate, stacked it on the drying rack and took another. *What the hell is that woman's issue? I mean, I know she's not your mother, but you're still related, right?*

Not closely, Anne said. *First cousin once removed . . . I did tell you it was complicated.*

That's one way to put it.

You sound like Vari, Anne said. *He always hated her.*

So was this how you spent most of your childhood? I asked. *Being the live-in maid?*

Well, I sort of acted as a nurse some of the time too.

You're kidding.

Beth had allergies, and Grace had some problems with a skin condition, so they needed someone to stay home.

So you were the nanny to a pair of spoilt teenage girls. How the hell did you put up with this?

It was that or the foster system. I didn't exactly have much choice.

We washed a few more plates in silence. *I'm sorry*, Anne said at last. *I wanted you to have a good evening. Instead you're spending it like this.*

Trust me, I'd much rather be washing dishes with you than sitting at the table with them.

Anne smiled. *I was just thinking about how the Council would react if they could see us.*

They'd probably wonder what this strange new magical ritual is that involves plates and a sink full of water.

Anne laughed out loud at that one. We kept working in comfortable silence.

As we worked, I flipped idly through the futures, looking to see if anything caught my eye. It's rare for me not to use my precognition these days: there are very few places where I feel safe enough to relax, and this wasn't one of them. A shift drew my attention and I looked more closely. *Huh.*

What is it?

Your sixty per cent chance just came in.

Anne glanced down at the plate in her hands; it was one of the last ones. *Do you think we should finish up?*

I think between the six of them they can probably survive.

We walked down the hall to the front door. We didn't try to sneak, and as we passed the dining room the conversation stopped. 'Hello?' someone called out.

'Apologies, all,' I called back as I put on my coat. 'Something's come up.'

There was a scrape of chairs from the dining room, and after a moment Johnathan appeared in the doorway. 'You're leaving?'

'Urgent call,' I said. 'Sorry.'

The mother had appeared behind Johnathan, along with one or two of the others. 'Oh,' she said. 'Well, I'm sorry you have to go. Perhaps Anne could—'

I cut her off. 'I'm afraid that's not possible. Anne's my

second-in-command. They need her and so do I.' I paused. 'I expect she hasn't told you, but she's probably higher-placed in the government than anyone you've ever met.'

Anne shot me a look, but the expressions on the women's faces were more than worth it. I opened the door. 'What's so urgent anyway?' Johnathan asked.

I stepped out into the summer night. 'Meetings.'

2

The countryside felt peaceful after the noise of London. We were in Devon, on a hillside in a part of the county that seemed to mostly contain fields, trees and sheep. The sun had set and the sky was lit only by stars and by the fuzzy yellow glow of towns to the south and east. Up on the hillside was a farmhouse.

I like taking a little while to look over an area before an operation. I don't mean planning or recon, though I do those too; I mean finding a place with a good vantage point, sitting there and waiting. No matter how many maps I've studied, or how many projections I've seen, I never feel happy about going into a place until I've watched it for a while.

The farmhouse had peeling white paint, with widely spaced windows and slates missing from the roof, and it looked pretty much identical to any of a thousand other old farmhouses scattered around the British countryside. There was a disused yard and a couple of old barns, but according to our information, what we were interested in was underground. The buildings and landscape were clearer than they should have been: Anne had worked an effect to enhance my low-light vision.

I heard a whisper of movement behind me; it was Vari. 'Everyone ready?' I asked.

'We've been ready for half an hour,' Variam said. 'Are we going in or what? We're not going to learn anything sitting around staring.'

'Learning about things by sitting around and staring is pretty much what I do.'

'I think you do a bit more than that these days.' Variam walked up beside me. 'So it's a go?'

'Entrance is in the cellar behind a false wall. Lock's a little tricky but I should be able to handle it.'

'Enemies?'

'Can't tell,' I said. My path-walking lets me follow the futures in which I take a certain sequence of actions, discovering who or what I'll meet on the way. But the lock was tricky enough that following the chain of futures all the way through the ones that'd open it and to what was inside would have been slow. I could have done it with more time, but the benefit was marginal and there was a small but definite chance that we were on a clock. We'd been working this lead for a while and I didn't want to waste it.

'Eh,' Variam said. 'Anne'll probably spot anyone.'

'How's Landis's op going?'

'He says boring. Bodyguarding Council members is a waste of bloody time. I dunno why they keep putting us on it.'

'Just because Richard hasn't tried assassinations yet doesn't mean he won't, but you're right, it's a waste of resources. Landis is too important to be doing that kind of work.'

Landis is Variam's master, or to be more accurate his ex-master – Variam became a journeyman a little while ago and a full member of the Keepers along with it. Up until a year or so ago, a mage as young as Variam would never have been sent on a combat assignment like this without his ex-master to supervise, but with the war manpower was tight.

'Well, I doubt we'll need him,' Variam said. 'Aren't going to be any mages, are there?'

'Just traps and whatever's left of their experiments,' I said. 'Of course, if one of those traps is an alarm and they gate in some reinforcements, things are going to get interesting.'

'That's why we have you around, right?' Variam said. 'I mean, they decide to gate in, you'll be able to give us what? A whole minute's warning? Now come on, the boys are getting bored.'

I gave the farmhouse a last look and got to my feet.

We moved up through the farmyard. I was at the front, my attention split between the house looming up in the present and the branching futures ahead. Vari took the right, his movements quick and sure, his turban making him easy to pick out even in the darkness. To the left was Ilmarin, an air mage I'd worked with a lot over the past year. Anne brought up the rear, a slim presence in the darkness, quiet and watchful.

Behind us were the Council security: a detachment of ten led by Sergeant Little. I'd pulled Little out of a hot spot a few years back and it had turned into a good working relationship. Like his men, he wore body armour and carried a sub-machine-gun; to someone who didn't know better, he and his squad would have seemed like the dangerous ones. They wouldn't have been wrong, exactly, but it was the four of us on whom the mission would depend.

The standard Keeper doctrine for combat ops is to send a minimum of six to eight mages, with at least three times as many security personnel. But I'd led a lot of these missions over the past year and a half, and I'd come to prefer the speed and responsiveness of a smaller team. Two elemental mages, one living mage and one universalist gave us the tools to handle most problems, and if things did go wrong then it's a lot easier to evacuate fourteen than forty.

'Building is dead,' Anne said quietly into my ear through the communication focus. No telepathy this time; everyone else needed to hear what she had to say. Little's men were on the same circuit, which was another area in which I ran things differently. Normally Keepers have separate communication bands for Council security and for themselves. 'Nothing alive on the ground floor.'

'Basement?' Variam asked.

'Not on the first level. Can't see further than that.'

'Move up,' I said.

Little's men advanced, three moving to the door, two more sweeping around each side. The front door lock was dealt with and the security men entered.

'Ground floor clear,' one of the men said.

'First floor clear,' came a minute or two later.

If there were anything alive in the house, Anne would have seen it, but there was no point taking chances. 'Secure the basement.'

The farmhouse felt abandoned, with that particular sense a place has when it hasn't been lived in for a long while. Traces of dust rested on the furniture. I took the stairs down to the basement while Little gave orders for one of the men, Lisowski, to stay in the entrance hall and watch our backs. If trouble came from outside, we'd be counting on him to sound the alarm.

The facility entrance was behind a wooden wall. Pulling out a hidden dowel allowed the wall to swing back, exposing a circular steel door. I stepped up and got to work. The basement was cramped with fourteen of us, but no one spoke – they'd all done this before and they knew I needed quiet. Diviners are good at breaking through security: when you can see the consequences of your actions, it's easy to avoid most kinds of alarms or traps. In this case, the builders had opted to go with a technological approach rather than a magical one, using a simple access code. There are types of locks that divination doesn't help with – a fingerprint or retinal scan, for instance – but this wasn't one. (If it had been, Vari would have just melted the door to slag. Like I said, a team like this can handle most problems.)

The door clicked and I pulled on the lever. It swung open with a creak, revealing stairs down into darkness. No breeze came out, but I thought that I could smell a faint scent in the air, something unpleasant and stale.

Variam lifted a hand and light bloomed, flames that gave no heat. They flew away down the stairs, illuminating them in orange-red. In their glow I could see steps going down for maybe sixty feet before finishing in a landing.

'Light switch,' Ilmarin noted, nodding to a small panel just inside the door.

'Doesn't work,' I said absently. I was following the paths in which I ran down the stairs, looking to see what would happen. 'No power anywhere in the facility that I can see.'

'So?' Variam said after another half minute.

'I'm not picking up anything,' I said. 'Lights are off, doors are shut. Doesn't mean it's safe, but it's definitely not in active use.'

'No Crystal?'

'We weren't really expecting to get that lucky.'

Wars between mages are very different from wars between countries. When countries fight, if they want to attack into enemy territory, they have to go through the other army to do it. Mages don't. Gate magic lets strike teams appear anywhere at any time, attacking and then disappearing back to the other side of the world. You never see mages fighting to take control of a bridge or a mountain pass, because holding those kinds of places doesn't accomplish anything. When mages engage in combat, it's for one of two reasons: either they're fighting over something valuable, or one side is attacking the other's base of operations. Otherwise, if one side doesn't want to fight, they can just leave.

When it came to bases of operations, Richard's side had the advantage. The Council operates out of various facilities spread throughout Britain. They're well-fortified, but there are a lot of them, and they're valuable, public and, most of all, *stationary* targets. The Council couldn't abandon them, which meant a massive commitment of men and resources to defend them all. By contrast, Richard's side had no facilities left in Britain, or at least none that anyone knew about. The mansions of Richard and his supporters had all been attacked by Council forces in the first months of the war, and rather than stand and fight, the Dark mages had abandoned their homes and withdrawn, hiding away in shadow realms or far-distant corners of the world. And shadow realms are much harder to attack than mansions. The Council was currently working to locate Richard's centre of operations, but if he had one, they hadn't found it.

But it's not practical to put everything in a shadow realm. For one thing, shadow realms are limited in quantity, with demand exceeding supply. For another, there are some things that shadow realms are bad at. You can't run modern communications, nor anything that requires a lot of external resources or utilities. And there are certain types of magical research that can't be done in shadow realms, or can only be done in a specific type of shadow realm that the mage might not have access to. So if one of the mages on Richard's team wanted to do some R&D, they'd often have to hide it in a place like this.

There was a reason I was taking a special interest in this particular facility. Our source had claimed that this facility was being run by Crystal, a renegade Light mage who'd fled Britain years ago under sentence of death. This was the first time her name had been linked to Richard, but I had my own reasons for suspecting that there might be a connection between the two of them. And on top of that, I knew that she wanted Anne. Crystal was in possession of a flawed immortality ritual, and she believed Anne was the missing ingredient that would make it work. I didn't know whether she was right or wrong, and given that Anne wouldn't survive the process, I didn't particularly care. Crystal had made several attempts on Anne's life, and if I had the chance, I was going to kill her. The fact that she happened to be working for Richard was just a convenient excuse.

'We'll sweep the facility,' I said. 'Search room by room, make sure it's clear. Try not to damage anything you don't have to. Assuming we don't find anyone to question – which we probably won't – we're going to be combing through everything we find. Documents, computers, research. Anything that might give us a lead on where to go next.'

'Don't break the toys, we get it,' Little said. 'You taking point again?'

I nodded. 'Follow my lead.'

The facility was dark and silent, empty corridors and abandoned rooms. With no airflow or connection to the outside, it was hard to tell how long it had stood unused: it could have been weeks or only hours. There was an unpleasant metallic scent to the air that made me think of blood.

'Well, they were definitely working on something,' Variam said. The two of us were in some kind of testing chamber, with workbenches and an open space at the far end. 'Question is what.'

'Not sure.' I was leafing through some notes that had been left on one of the benches, reading by the orange-red light of Variam's magic. 'But my guess is that it had combat applications.'

'That what it says?'

'No, this is nothing but numbers.' I pointed at the open part of the room. 'But see the marks on the floor and against the wall? They look like the kind you'd use for target mounts.'

'We sure it was Crystal running things?'

'Can't see her name, but she's not exactly going to be signing timesheets. Hopefully once we've cleared this place out, we can call in a time mage.'

Variam snorted. 'Good luck. They have a waiting list a mile long these days.'

My communicator pinged and a voice spoke into my ear. 'Ilmarin to Verus.'

I put the notes down. 'Go ahead.'

'West wing is clear,' Ilmarin said. 'There are some living quarters and a kitchen; apparently this place was fitted for long-term use. All deserted, but Mage Walker believes she's found something.'

'What kind of something?'

'There's another vault door at the end of the wing. Airtight. Apparently there's someone or something inside.'

'We're on our way.'

The vault door that Ilmarin and Anne had found looked similar to the one at the entrance. It was at the end of a corridor; security men were waiting at the intersections, the torches on their weapons casting white beams that left their faces in shadow. I walked to the front, moving from darkness to light to darkness again. 'What have we got?'

'There's someone on the other side,' Anne said. Like Ilmarin, she didn't wear armour; unlike Ilmarin, she didn't have a shield. Her clothes were reinforced, but not heavily; it was an argument I'd had with her many times and one that I was yet to win. 'A boy, early twenties. He's awake but he's not moving.'

'Only one?' Variam asked.

'I think so.'

'Human?' I asked. Given the sorts of things we'd found in Richard's other research facilities, it was a very relevant question.

Anne hesitated. 'Probably.'

'What do you mean, probably?' Variam said.

'I can't sense anything abnormal in his pattern,' Anne said. 'No injuries, no signs of deprivation. He seems in perfect health.'

'Okay?' I said.

'So why is he in perfect health?' Anne asked. 'The facility's power is out. And from the look of it, he's locked in. Either they only just left and he's been in there a few hours at most, or . . .'

'Or what?'

'I don't know, but something doesn't feel right.'

I thought about it for a second, then nodded. 'We'll assume he's an enemy until proven otherwise. Give him a chance to come peacefully, but if he doesn't, weapons free. Little, have your men behind us. Cover all angles.'

'Understood.'

'Looks like I'm not getting this one open,' I said. The door was equipped with a retinal scanner. In theory Anne might be able to trick it, but those kinds of changes aren't her speciality and I didn't want to waste time. 'Vari, you're up.'

A blade of searing red ignited at Variam's hand as everyone else stepped well back. Variam pushed the blade of fire into the door, leaning into it. The metal turned red, then yellow, then white. An unpleasant smell filled the air, something like burnt oil, along with an acrid vapour that stung the throat.

Variam made a long curving cut along the left side, and a short one to the right where the lock was. By the time he was finished, the air in the corridor was hot and I was sweating in my armour. The gashes in the metal glowed red, slowly cooling. 'That should be the hinges,' Variam said, stepping back.

Ilmarin took his place. The air mage waited for Variam to get clear, then raised a hand. My hair fluttered as a breeze swept down the corridor, coalesced, then struck the vault door like a sledgehammer. With a screech of tortured metal, the door fell out of its frame, hitting the floor with a boom.

Mage lights flew into the room, orange-red from Vari, silver-grey from Ilmarin. They illuminated a wide circular chamber, stairs running up to inset rooms on the left and right. The black screens of display monitors hung on the walls, but the only movement was the back-and-forth flicker of the lights.

'Can't see him,' Variam said. He was cooling off the door, spreading the heat out of the metal so that it would be safe to walk on, watching the room out of the corner of his eye.

'No movement,' Ilmarin said.

'He's there,' Anne said. She pointed through the doorway towards the shadows to the right. 'And he knows we're here.'

I walked into the room. In the light of the spells, I could see a table in one corner, chairs overturned and papers scattered on the floor. Variam and Ilmarin followed me through. Something made a soft scrape as I stepped on it, and I paused and crouched down. It was an empty cartridge.

'Sarge,' one of the security men said quietly from behind me.

'I see it,' Little said. 'Verus?'

I looked at where Little was pointing. Ilmarin had moved one of his floating lights over next to the right wall, and in the greyish glow I could see bullet marks. 'Interesting,' Ilmarin said. 'So those would have been made by . . . who? Facility security?'

'Which raises the question of what they were firing at,' I said.

'I'm going to take a wild guess and say it's got something

to do with the thing that may or may not be human,' Variam said.

Anne spoke. 'He's moving.'

Our eyes turned to the darkness at the top of the right staircase. A figure appeared, still hidden in the shadows. We could make out its shape, but no more.

From behind I heard quiet movements as the security men readied their weapons. They weren't pointing them at the figure . . . yet. I raised my voice, speaking clearly and loudly. 'I am Mage Alex Verus of the Junior Council. If you are an enemy of Mage Drakh, Mage Crystal or the other Dark mages who operated this facility, we will assist you. If you side with them and against the Council, you will not be harmed should you come peacefully. Step into the light and make yourself known.'

Silence. Seconds ticked away. Then the figure stepped forward.

It was a boy in his twenties, as Anne said. He looked quite ordinary, but my hackles rose the instant I saw him. There was an aura around his form; it was faint and hard to see, but the shadows were clinging to him a little more than they should, hinting at something larger and darker behind. I recognised that pattern and I knew what it meant, and all of a sudden I wasn't interested in talking any more. 'All units,' I said quietly into my communicator. 'Defensive formation. Prepare for enemy summons.'

The boy swept his gaze over us, looking down from the top of the stairs. Futures flickered as he made his decision, but I didn't need to scan them to know what was going to happen. 'Why do you all keep coming?' he said to no one in particular. His voice sounded wrong, older than it should have been.

'Fire,' I said into the communicator.

Variam didn't hesitate. A pillar of flame erupted on top of the gantry, casting the room in hellish light. From behind, the sub-machine-guns stuttered out three-round bursts.

The fire receded to reveal the boy standing unharmed. A translucent black shield was flickering around him; bullets were still hitting it, their impacts marked by flashes of black. He spread his arms wide.

'Hold fire, hold fire!' I called. 'Cease fire on the primary target, watch the sides, we have summons. Four on the left, two on the right.'

The darkness at the sides of the room seemed to writhe, figures stepping out of the shadows. They were man-sized, thin and spindly with arms too long for their bodies, and they darted forward along the walls. They were hard to see, the eye wanting to shift away, but unlike the boy they didn't have shields. The nearest one fell as bullets tore into it; the one behind staggered into cover.

From past experience, I knew that the things killed with their claws: as long as the men could hold them at range, they should be safe. Little was already directing his men into a defensive box, overlapping fields of fire holding the creatures at arm's length. Two were down and the remainder were pinned, unable to advance. Something new showed itself in the futures and I turned.

The boy was still holding off Variam's attacks, but he was focusing on Little's men. He raised one hand and a dark sphere soared high into the air, arcing downwards towards us.

A shield of air appeared just as the spell was starting its descent, and it detonated in a silent black flash, wind ruffling my hair. Variam growled. Another pillar of flame exploded around the boy; this time Variam followed it up with a bolt of fire that flew out like a rocket. The black shield soaked it up without a ripple. '*Fuck!*' Variam shouted. 'How is he stopping these?'

'Okay.' I'd been carrying a short-sword sheathed at my hip; it came out with the sound of metal on leather. 'Let's try it up close and personal.'

Variam glanced at me, then nodded. He took a step, his hand coming down to stretch out behind him, but before he could cast his spell I sensed something new. Without pause, I spun and dashed back towards the security men. 'Little!' I shouted. 'Behind!'

I saw Sergeant Little look up, startled; as he did the shadows behind his squad moved and one of the creatures stepped out of the wall and ripped a man open in a spray of blood. He went down with a scream and the security men whirled, their formation breaking.

Then Anne was there, running through their ranks. The shadow creature raised its claws and hesitated. Anne didn't. Her fingers brushed its body and it collapsed, the life seeming to go out of it. Anne was already kneeling by the injured man, working to staunch the flow of blood.

I didn't have time to watch; that creature hadn't been the only one to come out of nowhere. Another materialised out of the darkness right next to where I was standing. Or where I'd chosen to stand. I rammed my short-sword through its torso, twisted the blade, ripped it out. The weapon was a low-level focus imbued with a dispelling effect, designed to penetrate shields. The thing staggered and fell. One of the security men ran up next to me and emptied his magazine into it.

Looking around, I could see that the battle had turned messy fast. The formation of Little's men was disorganised; now instead of keeping the things pinned down, they were backing towards each other, guns sweeping from left to right as they tried to figure out if one would appear behind them. *Anne*, I called through the dreamstone. *Keep the men alive. I'm going to take out the summoner.*

Got it.

Ilmarin and Variam had pushed the boy back to the far side of the room. He was standing at the end of the gantry, face set in an expression of concentration, fighting with needle-thin wires of black energy that stabbed and struck. Variam was pressing him, fire blazing from one hand and a flaming sword in the other, trying to get close enough for a killing strike, while Ilmarin hovered in the air.

I sprinted around towards the gantry. It was about ten feet off the floor, and there was no stairway from the angle I was approaching. 'Ilmarin,' I called through the communicator. 'Need a lift!'

Ilmarin didn't need to be asked twice. A roaring wind picked me up as I ran, throwing me into the air in an arc aimed precisely down and behind where the boy was standing.

The boy sensed me, turned. Whip-like strands of energy lashed out, trying to cut me in half. In the instant before they struck, I found the futures I needed and twisted: one strand brushed my hair; the other glanced off my leg armour. The impact threw me off-balance and I landed awkwardly, my short-sword bouncing off the boy's shield.

The boy stared at me from only a few feet away. I was taller than he was, but somehow it felt the other way around: there was a presence behind him, like a shadow looming over his shoulders. There was a strange detached look to his eyes, as though something else was looking through them. Black energy snapped at his fingers, but he didn't attack. 'You will serve.' His voice was normal, weirdly out of place in these surroundings. 'Both of you—'

A narrow triangle of flame emerged from the boy's chest. He stood still for a moment, then the light seemed to go out of his eyes, the black shield vanished, and he crumpled to the floor.

Variam looked down at the body, his sword still burning in one hand. 'He getting up?'

I shook my head.

'Rest are dissipating,' Ilmarin called down from above.

I looked around to see that the battle was over. Little's men had stopped firing and I could hear them calling out to one another, checking to see that the area was clear. 'Verus to Little,' I said over the comm. 'That should be all of them, but sweep the area. Make sure we're secure.'

'Understood.'

I took a last look down at the boy's body and walked across the gantry and down the stairs to check on the wounded. I passed several of Little's men as I did so, spreading out to search the corners of the room. Back at the entrance, two of the men were lying up against the wall, with Anne checking over them and two others standing by looking outwards on alert. There was a lot of blood, but both of the men had their eyes open and were obviously alive.

'Nowy and Peterson, isn't it?' I asked. 'How are you holding up?'

'Could be worse, sir,' Peterson said.

'*Skurwysyn*,' Nowy said, and coughed. 'I am good.'

'He'll be fine,' Anne said reassuringly. She was kneeling next to Nowy, fingers laid on his throat. Despite the blood spattered all over it and across his clothes, the skin beneath was whole and smooth. She gave the security man a smile. 'Don't worry, Nowy, it hasn't spoiled your good looks.'

Nowy tried to laugh, but he was obviously shaken. From the looks of it, his artery had been opened; if Anne hadn't been there, he would have been dead within a minute. Instead, there wasn't even a scar, and with a few days' rest he'd be as good as new.

'Room's clear,' Little said, walking back to me. 'That should be the whole facility.'

I nodded, but Little didn't leave. 'Something else?' I asked.

'Wouldn't mind knowing what those things were.'

'Now?'

'Intel briefing was to expect Dark mages, adepts and armed security.' Little shifted his stance, feet shoulder width and hands behind his back. 'Nothing about summoned monsters. With respect to Mage Walker—' he nodded to Anne. '—we were pretty close to losing men on this. Would appreciate knowing how likely this is to happen again.'

I became aware that a lot of the security contingent were close by, hanging around the general area. Not all were looking at me, but they were clearly listening. Variam and Ilmarin were out of earshot in the corner of the room, looking through the notes on the table. It probably wasn't a coincidence that Little was asking this now, and I'd also noticed that he wasn't calling me 'sir'. Council security tend not to get told much, and he was asking me to give him something.

'All right,' I said. 'Be aware that some of this is going

to be guesswork. Also, while none of it is technically classified, you might want to avoid repeating it around.'

There were several nods, including from Little. 'That boy we just fought was possessed by a creature called a jinn. Otherwise known as genies. Wishes out of a lamp and stuff like that. The stories are true but they leave out a lot. For one thing, jinn didn't used to be bound inside lamps. Mages did that. So like a lot of magical creatures, they've got good reason to dislike humans.'

'So where's the lamp?' one of the security men said.

'Jinn don't have to possess lamps. People work too, though the jinn normally have to be invited in first. Either way, if they've got a human to work through, they can use their powers. As for what they're doing here . . .' I looked around, feeling Anne's presence behind me. She was still tending to Nowy, but I knew she was listening very closely. 'We've known for a while that Richard Drakh has taken a particular interest in jinn. They have an enormous amount of power, but there are two problems. First problem is that the power they can use is limited by the relationship they have with the human that's directing them. Being bound into an item cuts down on that power a lot. Probably Drakh's cabal were trying to access a jinn's full power by binding it directly into a host. Unfortunately for them, it looks like in doing so they ran into the second problem, which is that jinn *hate* humans. If they're granting wishes, they'll try to make sure they turn out as badly for the wisher as possible. If they're freed from their binding item and allowed to possess a human directly, they can cut out the middle man. My best guess is that they tried to keep control of the jinn, failed and after seeing how it turned out, they decided to cut their losses.'

'What about the bloody teleporters?' one of the other men asked.

'There were several orders of jinn,' I said. 'The one possessing the boy was probably middle-rank. The lesser ones were called jann. They weren't bound into items in the way that the greater ones were – not powerful enough. Somehow the greater jinn seem to be able to call them up.'

'That balls-up at San Vittore last year,' another man said. 'Were those the things that attacked the place?'

'Yes,' I said carefully. Now we were getting into really dangerous territory. 'I haven't run into any more since then.'

'Can *we* expect to run into more?' Little asked.

'That depends on whether Drakh's cabal are still going ahead with their jinn project,' I said. 'Maybe what happened here was enough to set them back. Otherwise . . .' I shrugged.

There were a few mutters, but no one asked any more questions. There was the sound of movement, and looking up, I saw Ilmarin and Variam walking over. Little turned to one side and started talking into his comm, and the other security men began to drift away.

It was just as well that Little's men had stopped asking questions. As I'd said, the attack on San Vittore last summer had been carried out by jinn – lots of weak ones and one very powerful one. What I *hadn't* said was that the bearer of that very powerful jinn had been Anne. If anyone on the Council ever found that out, Anne and I would be sentenced to death in a heartbeat, and that possibility had hung over us both like a shadow for the past year.

'It was her,' Variam said as he reached me.

'Crystal?' I asked.

'Not in so many words,' Ilmarin said. 'But several of the notes make reference to a "Dr Marianne", an alias of hers. There are also references to "conditioning" that sound very much like applications of mind magic.'

'So she's promoted herself to doctor now,' I said. 'Any clearer idea as to what happened here?'

'Not many specifics, but we can guess,' Ilmarin said. 'There are mentions of a subject who I suspect is the boy we just fought. Given those holding cells at the back, he probably wasn't here voluntarily. Presumably Crystal was there to attempt to maintain control of him after they bonded him to a jinn. It seems they succeeded at the second part but not the first.'

'Doesn't say what happened,' Variam said.

'Yeah, I imagine that by that point they weren't really in a position to sit around and take notes,' I said. 'But from the sound of it, Crystal's long gone.'

Ilmarin nodded. 'The last date I can find on the notes is eight days ago. If they haven't returned since then, I suspect they're not going to.'

Which meant that we were no closer to catching Crystal than before. *Damn.*

'Stakeout?' Variam asked. He didn't sound hopeful.

'Crystal hasn't stayed hidden from the Council for this long by being stupid,' I said. 'We can place a remote sensor, but I'm not expecting much.'

Ilmarin stretched, looking around. 'And so ends another raid, I suppose. At least we didn't lose anyone.' He glanced around. 'I wonder how many other facilities Drakh has hidden away.'

'Well, there's one less now,' I said. I didn't show it, but

I was worried. This experiment of Richard's had been a failure. What would happen if he succeeded?

It was an hour and a half later. The security men, along with my team of mages, had pulled back to a perimeter around the farmhouse. Although we were technically still on watch, the mood was more relaxed now, and several of the men were smoking. Our job was to guard the investigation team, but if anything was going to happen, I should be able to spot it well in advance.

'So how was the family visit?' Variam asked. The two of us were standing under a tree, a little way out of earshot. Up ahead, Ilmarin and Sergeant Little were in the farmyard supervising as the Council investigative team carried plastic boxes in through the front door. The contents of the facility would be packed into those boxes, then taken away and processed as evidence.

'It was . . . interesting,' I said. I glanced to the side, where Anne was talking with the two injured men, Peterson and Nowy. 'I can see why Anne doesn't go home often.'

Variam snorted. 'If I was her, I wouldn't either.'

'You met them back when you were in school together, didn't you?' I said. 'What did you think of that couple?'

'Father's a wimp, mother's a bitch,' Variam said. 'She wouldn't even let me in the house most of the time. Acted like I was going to steal her silverware.'

I laughed. 'Apparently I get higher-class treatment. I just got snubbed over the dinner table.' I thought for a moment. 'When Sagash kidnapped her, what happened? I mean, they must have noticed.'

'Oh, they noticed,' Variam said. 'Biggest thing they were worried about was that it might hurt their daughter's chances of getting into a good uni. Pissed me off so badly. Was actually what made me decide to find her myself.'

'And I used to think my parents were bad.' I looked across at Anne and wondered what it would be like growing up in a house like that. A couple of years ago Anne had told me that she liked the fact that when she was with me and Luna, she wasn't expected to look after us. It had seemed a strange comment at the time. 'That was when you ended up going to that dragon, wasn't it?'

'Yeah.'

Variam had called the creature he'd met the Fire Dragon, and it had given him a warning: that if Variam wasn't able to get Anne away from Sagash, she'd fall into darkness. To the best of my knowledge, I was the only other person Variam had ever told that to. Vari's always kept an eye on Anne, ever since I've known them. Everyone else assumes that he's trying to protect her; some assume he's got a crush. I've come to realise that it's for quite a different reason.

But Vari *had* been able to get Anne away from Sagash, and it had been years since we'd seen or heard anything from the Dark mage. 'You think that prophecy's done? I mean, Sagash hasn't shown up for a long time.'

Variam was silent for a moment. 'That jinn,' he said. 'Before I killed it. What did it say?'

'Something about how we both would serve.'

'Mm,' Variam said. He turned and walked away.

Anne walked over just as Variam disappeared into the shadows. 'Is Vari okay?'

'Not sure,' I said, looking after him. I couldn't help noticing that Variam hadn't answered my question. 'I think he's worried about something.'

'He does that a lot,' Anne said, and leant against me with a sigh. 'I'm glad it's over.'

I looked down at Anne with a smile and put my arm around her; she rested her head on my shoulder. 'You did well back there.'

'I'm glad everyone's safe,' Anne said. 'One more day without a disaster.'

'There's always tomorrow.'

3

It was tomorrow, and I was on trial for treason.

'As I said in my report at the initial inquiry,' Barrayar said, 'Solace and I were in one of the interview rooms with Keeper Caldera when we first became aware of the attack. We left and were immediately engaged by what we are now aware were summoned lesser jinn. After they were dealt with, we conferred and realised that the attack was most likely an attempt to rescue Morden. Therefore, we headed directly for his cell.'

Barrayar is on the small side, well-dressed, with a calm, polite manner that gives little away. Looking at him now, standing in front of the bench with his hands clasped behind his back, you wouldn't guess how many deaths and attempted murders he's responsible for. I've hated him for years. Maybe that was something people looking at me wouldn't guess, either.

'No,' Barrayar said in response to a question from the bench. 'We had separated from Mage Verus at the facility entrance and saw no trace of him until the events later.'

There were a moderate number of people in the court-room. Full trials are open to all Light mages, but in this case attendance had been restricted. Off to one side were the other witnesses to be called: several of the surviving staff from San Vittore, along with Solace and Caldera. Solace shot me unfriendly glances when she thought I wasn't looking. Caldera stood stone-faced and silent.

Sitting at the bench were the bench clerk, the records clerk and the coroner. Officially the coroner was the one in charge, but sitting at the back of the room were two men and one woman, and though all three had yet to speak and no one looked at them too closely, everyone knew that they were the real power in the room. They were from the Senior Council, and they'd be the ones who decided the verdict.

Technically this wasn't a trial, in the same way that technically, I hadn't been charged with treason. Officially speaking, this was a follow-up inquiry into the attack on San Vittore. But Council inquiries are generally motivated by politics, and the fact that they'd ordered a second inquiry strongly suggested that they were looking for a scapegoat. It wasn't hard to guess who they had in mind.

'Mage Verus appeared at the tail end of the fight in the control room,' Barrayar was saying. 'He claimed to have no knowledge of the creatures engaging us. At this point, Morden and Vihaela were able to override the door to Morden's cell and advance upon us.' Barrayar paused. 'I believe the details of the ensuing fight were covered at the previous inquiry.'

The coroner glanced sideways at the table where the Senior Council were seated, then nodded to Barrayar. 'The court will refer to your previous statements.'

'Thank you.'

I managed not to roll my eyes. The 'fight' had consisted of Caldera being taken out in one move, at which point Morden and his companion had walked out while Barrayar, Solace and I stood back and watched. But the real problem, and the secret I had to keep today at all costs, was that 'Vihaela' hadn't been Vihaela. It had been Anne.

'Once the conversation was over,' Barrayar continued, 'Morden and Vihaela departed. They left their summoned jinn behind, who began to press upon us.'

'And who was the "us" at this point?'

'Myself, Mage Solace and Councillor Verus. Keeper Caldera had been disabled.'

'And what happened then?'

'The three of us engaged in a brief discussion on how best to handle the situation,' Barrayar said. 'Councillor Verus ended the conversation by declaring that he was going to pursue Morden and Vihaela. He then proceeded to run through the creatures, avoiding their attacks long enough to reach the security gate and lock it behind him.'

'Locking the three of you in there with the summoned jinn?'

'That's correct.'

Well, of course it's going to sound bad when you put it like that. At the time, my only concern had been pursuing Anne. I'd figured that the other mages could probably look after themselves. I'd been right, though it obviously hadn't done much to improve relations between us.

'The rest of the battle is referenced in my previous report,' Barrayar said. 'We were able to hold out long enough for a Keeper relief force to arrive.'

'Did you have any further contact with Councillor Verus during the incident?'

'No.'

'Thank you, Mage Barrayar, that will be all.'

Next up on the witness stand was Solace. 'He just left us there!' she declared. Solace is the aide to Sal Sarque, one of my more vitriolic enemies, just as Barrayar is the aide to Levistus. She's not as smart or as dangerous as Barrayar, but she can still make trouble, and she was making trouble now. 'He could have stayed and helped but he just left us to die.'

The coroner cleared his throat. 'You claimed earlier that Councillor Verus was responsible for the attack.'

'Well, someone let Vihaela in, didn't they? There were only four mages from outside in the facility when it happened, and he was the only one who wasn't with us. We didn't see him all the time that we were fighting our way through to the control room.'

'And you believe that Councillor Verus was the one responsible?'

'Morden paid him,' Solace said. 'Gave him his chain of office. He said Verus could keep it.'

There was a stir, and a few people glanced at me. I didn't show any reaction.

'So then he went running after Morden,' Solace continued. 'Those jinn didn't even scratch him. I don't think they were even trying. Probably Verus was trying to catch up with Morden and Vihaela before they left.'

Oddly enough, Solace was quite right. The jinn *hadn't* been trying to hurt me. It was just as well that she so obviously hated me. If she'd been a more credible witness, people might have paid attention.

'I see. Do you have any further evidence to present to the court?'

Solace thought for a moment. 'No,' she admitted grudgingly. 'But he was useless in the fight, too.'

'Thank you, Mage Solace. That will be all.'

Solace went to sit down, avoiding looking at me.

The bench clerk spoke up. 'Councillor Verus.'

I rose to my feet and walked to the witness stand. The courtroom was quiet, and I could feel all eyes on me.

'I should clarify that this is an inquiry, not a trial, and you are not charged with any breach against the Concord or national law,' the coroner said. 'However, in the event of any future trial, should one occur, any statement made at this court can be taken as evidence.'

I nodded.

'Do you have any further testimony to give?'

'Yes,' I said. 'But first I would like to ask Mage Solace to clarify some points of information.'

'As this is not an actual trial, you do not have a right to cross-examine.'

'Mage Solace has directly accused me of capital crimes,' I said. Solace hadn't been as careful as Barrayar, and I'd done my homework before coming here. 'As such, I have the right to question her directly.'

The coroner hesitated. It was plain he didn't want to grant the request, and just as plain that he couldn't see a way out of it. 'Very well.'

I turned to Solace. 'Mage Solace. What kind of mage am I?'

'What?'

'What kind of mage am I?'

Solace looked confused. 'You're a diviner.'

'Can diviners use gate magic?'

'Why are you asking me?'

'Answer the question, please.'

'No,' Solace said in annoyance. 'I don't see how that matters.'

I nodded. 'When I entered San Vittore, along with you and Barrayar, the three of us were checked for contraband. Is that correct?'

'Excuse me, Councillor Verus,' the coroner broke in. 'Is this relevant?'

'I'll demonstrate its relevance shortly. Solace?'

'Yes, that happened. So?'

'The list of contraband items included focuses, imbued items and magic items of any other kind,' I said. 'All three of us were examined with magesight to confirm that we were carrying none of those things. Is that correct?'

'Yes.'

'All right. Now, you claim that I was the one who let Vihaela into the facility.'

Solace shrugged.

'How?'

'What?'

'San Vittore is a bubble realm,' I said. 'It's accessible only by gate magic, and its gate wards are heavily reinforced. This was established at the previous inquiry. So how am I supposed to have let Vihaela in?'

'I don't know.'

'You don't know?' I said. 'You've just agreed that I can't open a gate myself, and also agreed that I didn't have any kind of item that would open one for me, but you're still claiming that I must have let Vihaela into a place that's only accessible via gates?'

'Well, that's for a judge to decide, isn't it?'

'Actually, no,' I said. 'For a judge to be hearing the case at trial, there would have to *be* a trial, which, as the coroner has just pointed out, this is not. One of the things a criminal case requires is plausible means. Which means it has to be at least physically possible for the accused to have done what they're accused of.'

'Well, who else could have done it?' Solace demanded. 'You weren't there!'

'I wasn't with you, Barrayar and Caldera, correct. Do you remember why?'

Solace paused. 'I don't know.'

'After we'd passed the security screening, I asked if I could accompany you and Barrayar while you questioned Morden,' I said. 'Do you remember what your answer was?'

Solace shifted uncomfortably. 'I don't remember.'

'We could always ask Barrayar,' I said. 'Or one of the other witnesses who were—'

'Okay, I think I said no.'

'Which means you were the *reason* I wasn't with you when the attack happened.'

Solace looked angrily at me. 'Next point,' I said. 'Barrayar has stated that I rejoined you and Caldera shortly before Vihaela and Morden forced open Morden's cell door. I came from the opposite direction that Morden and Vihaela did, correct?'

'So?'

'So let me see if I'm understanding you correctly,' I said. 'You claim that I entered the facility with no magic items nor any ability to use gate magic. I then proceeded to override the gate wards on San Vittore and allow Vihaela into the facility, using some means that you've yet to explain. Having accomplished this – an opportunity that I only had because you refused to allow me to accompany you – I then *split up* with Vihaela in such a way that she ended up on the other side of the facility behind a locked cell door. Having done all this, I met back up with you. Does that sum it up?'

Solace glared at me.

'Your accusation is one of the stupidest and most incoherent things I've ever heard,' I said. 'If I'd brought a case like that to my supervisor back when I was a Keeper, he'd have asked if I was drunk.'

'Excuse me, Verus,' the coroner said. 'You're becoming overly personal.'

I could see smirks on the faces of a few of the audience, but knew better than to push things too far. 'Very well.' I turned back to the coroner. 'As to the question of why I chose to pursue Vihaela and Morden, there are two reasons. The first is I'm a diviner, not a battle mage. There's very little I can do against an army of summoned jinn. I decided that trying to locate Vihaela and Morden would be a more productive use of my time than staying in a battle I couldn't easily contribute to. Regarding locking the gate, well, Barrayar's a force mage. He could cut through the bars. The jinn couldn't.'

'You claimed there were two reasons . . .?'

'The other reason is that ever since I've known them, Mages Barrayar and Solace have treated me in a hostile manner. Given the choice between having the two of them at my back in a fight, and running into a horde of monsters, I decided I'd rather take my chances with the monsters.'

Someone laughed from the back of the courtroom. The coroner shot a frown in their direction, which he then turned upon me. 'Jokes are not appropriate to this inquiry.'

'I wasn't joking.'

'Well. Returning to the matter at hand, you stated in your initial report that you did not have any further contact with Morden or Vihaela. Is this accurate?'

'Yes,' I said. 'At the time, I was still under the impression that the only way for the two of them to have left San Vittore was via the main entrance. Unfortunately, when

I reached it, I met a Keeper relief force who told me that they'd seen no one exit the facility. I was able to direct them to the location of Mages Barrayar, Solace and Caldera, but I wasn't able to pick up the trail.'

'You stated in your report that you were unable to track Morden and Vihaela thereafter.'

'That's correct.'

'According to records, various Keepers and Council personnel made multiple attempts to contact you in that time,' the coroner said. 'You did not respond to any of the requests for several hours, and when you did so, it was to provide a brief message stating that you were otherwise occupied. It wasn't until the following day that you reappeared to deliver your report of events.'

'That's correct.'

'Can you give an account for your movements during this time?'

This was the most dangerous part. 'I hoped to trace Morden and Vihaela's route before they could cover their trail.' I looked straight at the coroner as I spoke, eyes straight and voice level. 'First I tried several staging points that I'd seen Morden use during my previous association with him. When that didn't work, I attempted tracking spells using Morden's chain of office as a focus. I was aware of attempts to contact me during this period but felt I couldn't afford the distraction.'

'You didn't consider the sequence of events important enough to report to the Council?'

'I felt that pursing Morden was time-critical and as such was the first priority,' I said. 'We now know that given the method by which Morden and Vihaela left the bubble realm, any such attempts to trace them were doomed to failure. However, I believe it was the correct decision given the knowledge available to me at the time.'

There was a pause. I saw the coroner glance towards the Senior Council table, but I didn't turn my head to look. 'Very well, Councillor Verus,' the coroner said. 'That will be all.'

I nodded and walked back to my seat. Almost everything I'd told the coroner in those last two answers had been a lie.

'The court will now consider timesight evidence,' the coroner said.

The bench clerk spoke up again. 'Mage Sonder.'

There was a pause, then one of the doors opened and a young man was escorted in, pale-skinned with black hair and an academic look. When I'd first known him, he'd been slender, with a pair of glasses that he'd fiddle with when nervous. Nowadays the glasses were gone, along with most of the nervousness. He was less slender too.

Sonder and I had been friends once. He'd joined me and Luna on our early adventures, and the three of us had formed a group to which Variam and Anne had been later additions. They'd stayed, but Sonder hadn't, and when events brought us together again, he wasn't very friendly any more.

'If you could state your name and occupation for the court, please,' the coroner said.

'My name is Sonder, and I work for the Council Home Office,' Sonder said. 'I'm also a Keeper auxiliary seconded on a semi-permanent basis to the Order of the Star.'

'You are a timesight specialist?'

'That's correct.'

'And were you assigned in the aftermath of the attack to perform a timesight scan of San Vittore?'

'That's correct.'

'Can you give a summary of the attack for the court, please?'

'The attack unfolded as described in the initial report, but further scans have uncovered some additional detail,' Sonder said. 'The lesser jinn were summoned in two separate areas marked on the fifth page of the report on figure C. Having been summoned into the facility, they then spread out, attacking facility personnel in the locations marked in figures D and E on the next page . . .'

I let my attention drift; this had been covered at the previous inquiry. Instead I tried to remember exactly where the rift between Sonder and me had come from. We'd been close once. What had caused the split?

Five years ago, I'd been hunted down by an adept vigilante group called the Nightstalkers. Sonder, Luna, Variam and Anne had got involved in the aftermath of the attack, and explaining why the Nightstalkers were after me had involved telling them some bits of my past that I wasn't very proud of. Sonder hadn't taken it well, and he'd liked the way I'd eventually dealt with the problem even less.

But while that had seemed like the obvious explanation at the time, it didn't fit so well with hindsight. In the years since then, Sonder had become a rising star in the Council, and that meant buying into the things the Council does. I was pretty sure that by this point he'd have been involved in Council-sanctioned operations that were just as dirty as anything I'd ever done, if not worse. So while that might explain why he'd avoided me then, it didn't explain why he was still doing so now.

Maybe it was more about beliefs. Sonder is a Light mage through and through – he grew up in the system and he belongs in it in a way that the rest of us don't. I mean, our group's all tied to the Council, at least on the surface – I'm a Junior Councilman, Anne's a member of the healer corps, Variam's a Keeper of the Order of the Shield and even Luna graduated from the apprentice programme. But none of us really buy into the *idea* of the Council. We've had too many bad experiences to trust it completely, and even when things are going well, we try to keep its people at arm's length. Sonder doesn't. At a deep level, Sonder basically believes that the world would be a better place if the Council ran everything. Maybe if it hadn't been the Nightstalkers, it would have been something else.

A split usually starts from something small. What had been the first serious disagreement I'd had with Sonder? I thought back to beyond the Nightstalkers. There had been something that was . . . oh. *That.*

Last night, Anne had mentioned her father's death and Jagadev. I hadn't said anything, but it had reminded me of something that I'd been avoiding for a long time. I was one of the few people who knew that Anne's parents' deaths probably hadn't been an accident, that the death of Variam's father probably hadn't been an accident either and that Jagadev – who had been Vari and Anne's guardian at the time I met them – was probably responsible for both.

Back in the nineteenth century, India had been the site of the rakshasa wars. On one side had been the Light Councils of India and Britain; on the other had been the rakshasa, ancient shapeshifters who traced their origins back to before human history. The rakshasa were immortal and powerful, but they weren't unkillable, and one by one they were hunted down. A hundred and fifty years ago, a team of mages had attacked the palace of a rakshasa lord and lady. The lady, Arati, was killed. Her husband was not. That rakshasa was Lord Jagadev, and he'd spent the century and a half since then nursing his hatred for humanity in general and mages in particular. And he'd worked from the shadows to arrange the deaths of the mages that had killed his wife, and their children, and their children's children, until as far as I was aware there were only two descendants of those families still alive. One was Variam and the other was Anne.

Or so I guessed. Sonder had been the one to dig all that information up, and he hadn't been able to find hard proof, but it had been suggestive. Sonder had been expecting me to tell everyone, and I could have done just that, but for a variety of reasons that seemed good at the time, I'd decided instead to force Jagadev into an uneasy truce. He'd leave Anne and Variam alone, or I'd go to the Council. It had worked, more or less – to the best of my knowledge Jagadev had cut all contact with Variam and Anne, and they'd been left to finish growing up in peace. But Sonder hadn't been all that happy with my decision, and over the years, I'd become increasingly uncomfortable with it too.

I'd thought about telling Vari and Anne several times, but I hadn't, and a big reason had been the likely consequences. There was a one hundred per cent chance that the first thing that Variam would do would be to go after Jagadev in a white-hot fury, and if he did, Anne would be right there with him. Their chances would be a lot better now, but no matter how the fight turned out, I couldn't see any of the consequences being good. Maybe Jagadev would kill them; more likely he'd run away and resume his secret war from the shadows, in which case he'd certainly do his best to screw up Anne's and Vari's lives out of sheer spite. And even if they took vengeance, what would it get them?

But if I was being honest, a bigger reason had been that I was afraid of how it would make them see me. I could imagine the first question – *why didn't you tell us?* – and the second – *so all these years you've been keeping it a secret?* Telling Vari would be bad, but I couldn't bear the thought of the look in Anne's eyes. Anne trusts me, and she's not one of those people who trusts easily or often. I hated the idea of letting her down.

But this wasn't going to get any easier if I kept putting it off. Back then, Sonder had looked up to me. Maybe that had been the point where he'd started mistrusting me. After all, if I'd keep that kind of secret, I might keep others. If I cleared that up, could it be a way to mend fences?

It might be worth a try.

The sound of my name brought me back to the present. '. . . read Councillor Verus's statement?' the coroner was asking.

Sonder didn't look at me. 'Yes.'

'Are your findings consistent with the evidence he's given?'

I forced myself to stay relaxed. Timesight can let you view any past events that have occurred at a location. There are a lot of things that can block it, and the wards that the Council layers on places like San Vittore make viewing those locations difficult. But difficult isn't the same thing as impossible, and Sonder is very good at what he does.

Right now, of all the people in the room, he was the one I had most reason to fear.

Sonder hesitated, choosing his words carefully. 'As I said in my initial report, the wards on San Vittore made it impossible to take a precise viewing.'

'However, you stated that you were able to trace movements.'

'Yes.'

'Are you able to conclusively confirm or disprove Councillor Verus's account of his movements?'

'Not . . . conclusively. But everything I *was* able to establish tended to confirm them.'

'Could you elaborate?'

'I can confirm that he did travel directly from the facility entrance to the interview room,' Sonder said. 'And he later travelled directly from the interview room to the wing containing Morden's cell. However, I wasn't able to clearly view the period in between.'

'Are you able to tell us why?'

'Council interview rooms have extensive ward protections. The corridors are less heavily shielded.'

'So you can't confirm or deny Councillor Verus's actions in the period leading immediately up to the attack.'

'No.'

'Hypothetically, could he have opened a gate in that period?'

Sonder paused. 'To outside the bubble realm?'

'Yes.'

'Um . . .' Sonder said. 'No.'

'I'm sorry?'

'There's no possible way he could have done that.'

A stir went through the courtroom. 'Didn't you just say

that you weren't able to view the interview room?' the coroner said.

'Yes.'

'Then how can you say what did or didn't happen inside it?'

'Because gate magic creates a signature in a wide spatio-temporal radius,' Sonder said. 'I couldn't view the interview room, but I could view the corridor it opened into, and I checked it thoroughly. So did the other two time mages brought in. We all came to the same conclusion. There's no possible way a gate could have been opened from there.'

I heard some whispers from behind. Without turning my head, I could see Solace staring at Sonder; she looked pissed off. I guess she hadn't seen this one coming. Then again, until only a little while ago, neither had I.

'Were you able to detect gate magic signatures from anywhere else during that period?'

'No.'

'Then do you have any other explanation for how Vihaela was able to reach Morden's cell?'

'At the moment, our working theory is that she entered it from the outside,' Sonder said. 'Somehow she was able to travel through the void surrounding the facility. Unfortunately she was using a shroud effect with sufficient power that it wasn't possible to view her directly.'

There was a pause. I felt the coroner's eyes flick to me, and I knew what he was thinking. If they couldn't come up with a plausible explanation as to how I could have let 'Vihaela' in, any case against me would fall apart.

The coroner cleared his throat. 'Thank you, Mage Sonder. No further questions.'

Sonder nodded, glanced at me and left. 'The court will now consider the evidence,' the coroner announced.

The murmur of conversations started up around the room. The coroner was conferring with the clerks, while off to one side Solace and Barrayar were having a whispered conversation. I couldn't make out their words, but from their body language Solace looked angry. The conversation that really mattered, though, was one I couldn't hear at all. The three Senior Council members at the back table had their heads together and were talking, their voices silenced by a magical barrier.

The Council members sitting at the table were Sal Sarque, Druss the Red and Alma. Druss I wasn't worried about: he was generally an ally of mine these days. Alma was a question mark. She's an ally of Levistus, another member of the Senior Council, and Levistus is one of my oldest and bitterest enemies. On the other hand, Alma's pragmatic, and if she didn't think this case had a good enough chance of success, she'd vote to drop it. She would be the swing vote.

The third person sitting at that table was more of a problem. His name was Sal Sarque, a dark-skinned unsmiling man with close-cut white hair and a scar running the length of his scalp. He's the de facto leader of the Crusader faction among the Light mages, and as far as he and his faction are concerned, the only good Dark mage is a dead one. He'd taken Morden's appointment to the Council as a personal insult, and though I couldn't prove it, I was pretty sure he'd been the one who'd given the order for Anne and me to be kidnapped and tortured. The fact that his previous aide had ended up dead in the process had made things worse, if possible, and given the choice I was pretty sure that he'd rather cut out the bother of a trial and just have me straight-up killed.

But for now at least, Sal Sarque was too busy with the war to waste resources sending assassins, which meant all I had to worry about was the political sphere. The futures were shifting too much for me to predict the decision, but I was pretty sure this case wasn't making it to trial. Which was good, because while Solace's claims that I'd gated in Vihaela were complete bullshit, what I *had* done was arguably worse. It's like the police investigating you for drug dealing when you've got a dead body in the basement. Sure, they might be on the wrong track, but if one person goes looking in the wrong place . . .

I'd done what I could to misdirect their attention. There was a reason that Anne wasn't in court today, and in fact wasn't in the War Rooms at all – I'd subtly nudged things so that the bulk of the attention would fall on me. I'd vehemently denied the gating-Vihaela charge, forcing them to focus on it. So far it was working, but I'd spent sleepless nights imagining one nightmare scenario after another. None of them had happened . . . yet.

The argument at the Senior Council table was still going. Sal Sarque looked angry, and it wasn't hard to guess why. At last Alma held up her hand, and Sarque fell silent, glowering. Alma glanced towards the bench and the coroner walked over immediately. He listened as Alma spoke, then nodded and returned to his chair.

'All rise,' the bench clerk instructed.

I stood. Over to my side, Barrayar and Solace did the same.

'The full verdict of this court will be contingent on the conclusions delivered in the official report,' the coroner said. 'However, the preliminary finding is that while various irregularities have been brought to light, there is insufficient evidence to issue an indictment against any of the inquiry subjects for breach of the Concord or any other capital offence. As such, pending the official report, no further action will be taken. This court is adjourned.'

Murmurs spread throughout the courtroom as conversations started up. At the back, the three Senior Council members rose to their feet and left through a private door. From his body language, I could tell Sal Sarque was pissed off, and Solace didn't look happy either. Barrayar looked calm as always, and as I watched he picked up his notes, tapped them to the table to bring them in line and left.

A couple of mages came to speak to me: one was a Keeper from the Order of the Star; the other a member of the bureaucracy whom I vaguely knew. They said various polite nothings and I responded in kind. There was a dark humour to it. When I'd walked into the courtroom this morning, no one had been willing to even meet my eyes. Now that the verdict was in, all of a sudden I was a person again. I ended the conversation as soon as I could, and walked over to the Keeper who hadn't come over.

Caldera glanced up as I approached, then looked back down at her papers. She's a woman of forty or so with a round face, red cheeks and a heavyset build with arms thick enough for a nightclub bouncer. She's a journeyman Keeper of the Order of the Star, and she's been a journeyman for a very long time. It's not because she's bad at her job, or at least not at what her job's supposed to be. But when it comes to climbing the Council hierarchy, it's not what you do, it's who you know. I'd joined the Keepers only a few years ago, and in that time I'd gone from

Caldera's subordinate, to the same rank, to being promoted way over her head. Caldera had never brought up the subject, but I was pretty sure she resented it, and it wasn't the only grudge she was holding.

'You didn't give evidence,' I said to Caldera.

'Wasn't called.'

'I guess they thought your report was so thorough there wasn't anything to add?'

Caldera shrugged.

I sighed. 'How long are we going to keep doing this?'

'Doing what?'

'For two and a half years now you haven't said a single word to me except when I ask you a question or the job demands it. It's getting ridiculous.'

'Is it?'

'Can you maybe look at me when we're talking?'

Caldera finally raised her eyes. 'Okay. What do you want to talk about?'

'Well, I *wanted* to talk about that fight we had at Canary Wharf, but it's pretty clear that's never going to happen, so I've written that off as a bad job. Right now I'm just shooting for basic communication.'

'About?'

'How about the inquiry we just had? You have a problem with what I did? Are you pissed that I left you with Solace and Barrayar? Do you not care? What?'

Caldera shrugged.

'You don't care?'

'You ran and left us holding the bag,' Caldera said. 'Same as usual.'

'Oh, come on.'

'Way I remember it, pretty much every time I've fought

with you, I end up getting the shit kicked out of me while you stay way back out of reach.'

I bit back an angry reply. What Caldera was saying was both true and blatantly unfair, given that she's an earth mage who can literally shrug off bullets. 'So is this it?' I said. 'This is how all our conversations are going to go? You avoid me until I corner you, then you make passive-aggressive comments until I go away?'

Caldera studied me. 'Where did you really go after that fight, Alex?'

'What?'

'Don't play dumb,' Caldera said. 'I know a bullshit story when I hear one.'

'It wasn't bullshit.'

'Oh? You were telling the whole truth and nothing but the truth?'

'No one in this room was telling the truth,' I said. 'You think this inquiry was commissioned because they wanted to know what happened? You think Barrayar and Solace were just being honest? It pisses me off the way you do this. They've been doing this shit for years, manipulating the system to try to get me, but when I play the same game back, oh, *that's* terrible.'

'Yeah, well, maybe if you were a little straighter you wouldn't have to play games at all,' Caldera said. 'I'm done going to bat for you. You want to keep trying to prove how you're smarter than everyone else, you go right ahead.'

'You know what?' I said. 'Screw you and your self-righteousness. I've been trying to make things up with you for years and you've brushed me off every time. Levistus and Barrayar and their team of psychopaths chased us literally to the other side of the world all for the sake of a grudge, and when that didn't work, they planted bombs in Luna's flat. You didn't do shit to stop them, but hey, better blame me, right? Because otherwise you might have to admit to yourself that the guys you're working for are just as bad as the ones you arrest every day.'

I turned on my heel and left before Caldera could answer. I could feel people watching me as I headed for the door, and that pissed me off further. I was tired of the looks, tired of the silent judgements and tired of the Council in general. I left the court resisting the urge to bang the door behind me.

I took a roundabout route out of the War Rooms to give myself time to cool off. Walking gave me time to think, and as I did I realised why Caldera's words had made me so angry. While Caldera has her flaws, she's honest, and back when we'd worked together, we'd always been straight with each other. Nowadays I couldn't do that. Dealing with the Council, I had to lie and evade all the damn time, and it was making me wonder if I was turning into the sort of person I'd always tried to avoid.

I ran into Sonder at the far side of the conservatory. He was talking to Captain Rain, an officer in the Order of the Star and my old boss. '. . . shouldn't need you on Tuesday, but this one's urgent,' Rain was saying. 'We need it ASAP.'

'I'm snowed under with timesight cases that people want ASAP,' Sonder said. 'I'll try, but no promises.'

Rain nodded. 'Whatever you can.' He glanced in my direction. 'I'd better be going.' He gave me a nod and left.

Sonder turned in the direction Rain had and saw me. He didn't look pleased but he didn't run away. 'Hey,' I said as I walked up.

'Hey.'

'Anything on our request for a scan of that facility?'

Sonder shook his head. 'I just don't have the hours. Maybe in a week or so, but . . .'

'We're almost sure it was Crystal,' I said. 'She's still on the most-wanted list.'

'Every Dark mage linked to Richard Drakh is on the most-wanted list,' Sonder said. 'You know how many of these requests I'm getting?'

You have the time to show up to inquiries, I wanted to say, but knew it was unfair. Sonder's a rising star in the Council, but he's not at the top yet. If they tell him to jump, he jumps. 'Thanks for today.'

'For what?'

'The report you gave.'

Sonder shrugged. 'I was just telling the truth.'

'That's not always the most common commodity in this business.'

'I suppose,' Sonder said. 'I'm guessing there's something you wanted to talk about.'

I wanted to sigh. First Caldera, now Sonder. 'Actually, I wanted to ask your advice.'

'Uh . . . okay.'

I started walking along the corridor, and after a moment's pause, Sonder matched me. 'Remember six years back, with that business in Fountain Reach?' I said. 'You dug up some information on Jagadev. Specifically, his history with Variam and Anne.'

Sonder looked startled. 'Oh. I did, didn't I?'

'Have you told anyone else?'

Sonder shook his head. 'To be honest, I'd forgotten about it.'

'I haven't,' I said. 'Do you think we should change that? Specifically, telling them?'

'Why?'

'It does kind of concern them.'

'Well, yes,' Sonder said. 'I meant, why now?'

'I suppose I'm starting to feel as though the reasons to keep it a secret don't really apply any more.'

'I guess.'

'You sound doubtful.'

'Is this really the best time?' Sonder asked. 'With the war on?'

'No,' I said. 'But I'm not sure there ever will be a good time.' Sonder still didn't seem convinced and I gave him a quizzical look. 'Back then, you didn't like the idea of keeping it a secret at all. You said that it was the truth and they ought to know.'

'I did?'

I nodded.

'Wow,' Sonder said. 'I guess it really was a long time.'

'So you'd rather keep it quiet?'

'I don't know,' Sonder said. 'Is there really any point digging it up?'

'Let sleeping dogs lie?'

'More or less,' Sonder said. We'd made a circuit around the corridors, all the way back to where we'd started. He pulled out his phone and glanced at it. 'I've got to go. I'm late for a meeting.'

'Okay.'

Sonder walked out, leaving me alone in the conservatory, and I watched him go. I thought about Sonder as I'd known him back then, earnest and apprehensive. He'd come across as naïve, but he'd also been the kind to value honesty above everything else. I was pretty sure that if I'd asked him the same question back then, he'd have told me to tell the truth. Maybe I wasn't the only one who'd changed.

There was another bit of information too. When Sonder had taken out his phone, I'd looked into the futures in which I'd snatched it out of his hands. Diviners have a lot of ways of spying on people; it's something I avoid doing with my friends, but as I said, Sonder and I aren't really friends any more. The message hadn't been about a meeting: it had been a request for scheduling a follow-up scan on San Vittore. Which meant this wasn't over.

I sighed and turned to leave. Fighting summoned jinn was easier than this.

4

My talk with Sonder had left me wary, and I spent the next week putting out feelers, looking for signs of trouble. But for once, I didn't find it. Rain told me that they'd dropped the case, and my other contacts confirmed that the Order of the Star was no longer investigating me or Anne. Sal Sarque still hated me, and Levistus still hated me, but the very next day after the inquiry, reports came in of Richard recruiting and training adepts in an organised force, and the Council met to discuss their response, and all of a sudden no one was talking about what had happened in San Vittore.

It was a weekday evening in Arachne's lair, and Arachne and I were alone. Once upon a time it would have been common for all four of us to meet here, but now Variam was busy with his duties as a Keeper, and Luna spent mornings and afternoons at the shop. Anne still came from time to time, but most often, these days, when I saw Arachne, it would be just the two of us, me on one of her sofas and her crouched over a table working over some dress or other article of clothing. It reminded me of the old days, when Arachne was my only real friend.

'. . . so they haven't made any progress towards locating Richard's base, or this adept training camp either,' I was saying. 'The war seems to be in another of its lulls.'

'Hmm,' Arachne said. 'From past experience those tend to end quite abruptly.'

'It's figuring out when that's the hard part.'

Arachne is a giant spider, large enough to tower over any human, with eight long legs, eight eyes of varying sizes and thick black hair highlighted in cobalt-blue. She looks absolutely terrifying, and most people would expect her lair to be a dark cave with webs holding the decaying bodies of her victims. They're right about the cave part, but the fact that it's brightly lit, furnished as a very comfortable living room and covered in drapes, tapestries, silks, bolts of cloth and clothing makes it a bit less intimidating. Even so, one look at Arachne would still be enough to make most people run screaming.

Arachne made a *tsking* sound. 'You know, I've been working on this style for so many years and I still can't get it right. It's such a simple thing but for some reason it's never quite satisfactory. I really thought I'd get the hang of it someday.'

I looked curiously at Arachne. It was an odd thing for her to say, as much for the reference to her age as anything else. Arachne is *very* old – if I had to guess, I'd put her at two thousand years plus – but she doesn't talk about her past.

Which isn't to say that I haven't wondered. I'm pretty sure that Arachne's history is tied together with the dragon that lives in the tunnels deep below. Arachne referred to it as a 'creator' once, which would explain a lot – I've met plenty of magical creatures in my life, but I've never heard of any other giant intelligent spiders with miscellaneous magical powers, which does raise the question of where Arachne came from. Arachne keeps her mouth shut on the subject, so wondering is as far as I've got.

'Oh, one bit of news,' I said. 'Anne's been checking on Karyos and she says she seems to be regenerating just fine. In fact, it looks like she's going to be coming out of her cocoon sooner than we expected.'

'That's excellent.' Spiders can't smile, but it was obvious from the warmth in Arachne's voice that she was happy. 'Do you have a date?'

'Two weeks to two months. The closer it gets, the more accurately she'll be able to pin it down. You want to be there for when she comes out?'

'I'd love to.'

Karyos is a hamadryad, a magical creature bonded to a tree. When the tree grows too old, hamadryads undergo a ritual to rebond themselves to a new sapling, disappearing into a cocoon and reemerging some time later. Unfortunately, in Karyos's case, there had been complications. Long story short, by the time we met her she'd been insane and trying to kill us, and she hadn't gone into her cocoon voluntarily. We still weren't entirely sure whether the 'insane and homicidal' part was going to carry over when she woke up.

'On that note, there's a favour I'd like to ask,' Arachne said. 'When Karyos is reborn, could you look after her?'

I looked at Arachne in surprise. 'Me?'

'Would it be possible?'

'I suppose,' I said slowly. 'With help. But I was assuming you'd want to be involved.'

'The world belongs to humans now, Alex,' Arachne said. 'The time for my kind is passing. You'll be able to teach Karyos more than I can.'

'Honestly, I hadn't thought beyond wondering if she was going to wake up and go right back to trying to kill us.'

'If your friends used the seed successfully, that should not happen. And from speaking to Luna and Anne, I believe they did.' Arachne looked at me. 'So?'

I hesitated, then nodded. 'I'll try my best.'

'Thank you. Now, other matters. How are you progressing with the dreamstone?'

'Well, I've been working on communication range. I still have a few issues with really long distances, but it seems to be getting better. I can use it to talk to Anne pretty much anywhere now. I can probably manage it with Luna and Vari too.'

'What about the subject of our previous discussion?' Arachne said. 'Creating more general messages, rather than to a specific receiver?'

'Oh right,' I said. The example Arachne had given was that of a general call for attention or for help, aimed at anyone able to listen. 'I practised a little with Anne.'

'You need to be able to use it for people *other* than Anne.'

'Fair enough.'

'Have you been practising Elsewhere combat?'

'It's kind of difficult to find anyone to practise *with*,' I said. 'About the only two I can ask apart from you are Luna and Anne. Luna can handle Elsewhere, but she doesn't like it, and I know it's asking a lot from her to get her to keep going back there. And Anne, well, she's got her own reasons to avoid the place.'

'And you've done everything you can to persuade them otherwise?' Arachne said. 'You've pressed on them the urgency of the situation? Or, if that doesn't convince them, you've searched for other teachers?'

I shifted uncomfortably. 'No.'

'When I first met you, you'd spent days at a time mastering some new application of your magic,' Arachne said. 'Or on researching a new magical item. The Alex I knew back then would have worked day and night to learn everything there was to know about the dreamstone.'

'I know, I know,' I said. 'But back then I was pretty much a hermit. About the only people I'd spend time with were you and Starbreeze. And Helikaon I guess, but eventually I pretty much stopped seeing him as well. Nowadays I have to be a politician.'

'Is it really your position on the Council that's the issue?'

'It does take up a lot of time.'

'But back then, when you did have free time, you tended to spend it on training and study. These days, it seems to me that far more of your time and attention goes towards people. One person in particular.'

I threw up my hands. 'Okay, fine. Look, this is the first time I've been in a really long-term relationship, okay? It takes up more of my attention than I'd expected.'

Arachne tilted her head, studying me.

'You think it's a bad thing?' I asked.

'No,' Arachne said after a moment's consideration. 'While you were more focused on your work back when we first met, you're mentally far healthier now. But that won't do you any good if your enemies decide to have you killed.'

'I know it sounds weird to say it, but I feel *less*

threatened than I did a year ago,' I said. 'This war is actually pretty good for me. Levistus and the rest of the Council are too busy dealing with Richard, and Richard is too busy dealing with the Council.'

'Your enemies won't stay busy with each other for ever,' Arachne said. 'But on to other matters. It's time we discussed the final use of the dreamstone: using it to enter Elsewhere physically.'

I leant forward in interest. Arachne had brought this up before, but she'd warned me off experimenting. 'How?'

'The how is simple,' Arachne said. 'Channel through the dreamstone, using it as a focus, as if it were a gate stone. Now that you've bonded with it, it should be easy. But before you attempt it, you must understand exactly what it entails.'

I nodded.

'We talk about "going" or "travelling" to Elsewhere, but when you visit Elsewhere in dreams, what you are actually doing is projecting,' Arachne said. 'Your body lies sleeping, while your mind forms an image. This is why you do not suffer physical consequences for anything that happens there. It's not *safe*, obviously, but it's very difficult for anything you meet in Elsewhere to harm you. Most people who die in Elsewhere do so due to their own mistakes.'

'Because they get lost, or send too much of themselves, yeah. So—'

Arachne cut me off with a gesture. '*Listen*, Alex. You have a tendency to jump ahead when you think you know what's coming. You need to understand this clearly.'

I looked at Arachne in surprise. I wasn't used to her speaking to me this sharply. 'Okay.'

'As you've become more skilled with Elsewhere, you've ceased to fear it,' Arachne said. 'If asked, you would probably say that it's dangerous, but not more so than some parts of our own world. You would be very wrong. Elsewhere is an incredibly hostile environment. You can visit in dreams in relative safety because only your consciousness is projected. Elsewhere is an immaterial realm, and it is utterly inhospitable to physical matter. If you travel there physically, your material form will react with the environment in a process that erodes both. Since there is much more of Elsewhere than there is of you, this does not end well from your perspective.'

'So . . . you get disintegrated?'

'More like dissolved. Imagine a sugar lump dropped into the ocean.'

'How fast?'

'Inanimate objects dissolve almost instantly,' Arachne said. 'For living creatures, it depends on their level of consciousness. A plant would be gone in a minute. A dog or cat might last a quarter of an hour. With a sapient creature such as a human, it depends on their sense of self and their facility with Elsewhere. A strong-willed and practised visitor could in theory survive for hours. But no matter how skilled or strong, the sugar lump is still a sugar lump, and the ocean is still the ocean.'

'Shields?'

'Do nothing. Or perhaps a better way to put it is that your sense of self *is* your shield. Anything you bring with you and hold close enough to your person has some limited protection. Clothes, jewellery, anything held in your hands. It doesn't last though. Don't take anything into Elsewhere unless you're prepared to lose it.'

I sat thinking for a minute. 'I see why you told me not to experiment.'

'Yes.'

'Then I've got a question,' I said. 'If Elsewhere is so horrendously lethal, what's the point of going there?'

Arachne nodded. 'Several reasons. First, the ability to gate to Elsewhere can be used as a travel technique. There are limitations, but in theory it gives you the ability to go almost anywhere. It's also extremely hard to trace.'

'You've pretty much just described gating. Which every elemental mage can do already.'

'You're not an elemental mage.'

I shrugged.

'There is more,' Arachne said. 'When you travel to Elsewhere, since you are physically present, you are subject to the principles of Elsewhere just like everything else in that realm.'

'So the rules you taught me about combat in Elsewhere wouldn't apply?' I said. 'You can be hurt or killed?'

'Yes, though it's more difficult. Your material form gives you some protection.'

'But basically, if someone else dreams themselves into Elsewhere and picks a fight with me, they're invulnerable and I'm not.'

'Yes.'

'You're making this sound worse and worse.'

'You aren't thinking through the implications, Alex,' Arachne said. 'While in Elsewhere, you are subject to its laws. *All* of its laws. Just as you can be injured, you can also be changed.'

'So someone can . . . change me into someone else?'

'Or *you* can change you into someone else.'

I had to stop and think about that. 'How would that even work?'

'You know that Elsewhere is fluid,' Arachne said. 'While you are there, your mind and body can, to a certain extent, be reshaped just as the dream-constructs of Elsewhere can.'

I sat thinking. It was a big enough idea that it was hard to grapple with. 'Healing?'

'Feasible but dangerous. Altering yourself in Elsewhere requires you to draw back the shield protecting you and allow the realm to touch you directly, which means you are walking a fine line between change and dissolution. I would consider it a last resort.'

'Shapeshifting?'

'Again, possible but dangerous. Bear in mind that the ability to create a body does not imply the ability to create a *working* body. While in Elsewhere, you can hold things together by force of will. Once you return to our world, any mistakes will make themselves felt very quickly.'

'Maybe body modification?' I said. I was thinking aloud now. 'That'd be easier than creating a new form from scratch. Reinforcement or enhancement or . . . hm.' I remembered a conversation I'd had with Anne. She'd explained that the problem with those kinds of life magic changes wasn't creating them, it was maintaining them. 'Would I need to understand bodies as well as a shapeshifter or a life mage?'

'In all likelihood, yes.'

Arachne was still watching me as if she was waiting for me to come to the right conclusion. 'Wait,' I said. 'You said *mind* and body. Does that include everything relating to your mind?'

'Yes.'

'Including your magic?'

'Yes.'

I sat back.

'It is the primary reason mages have travelled to Elsewhere,' Arachne said. 'Enhancing their own power, deepening their command over their magic. Adding completely new capabilities, gaining the power of multiple mages. All the power of Harvesting, without the side effects.'

'And it works?'

'There's no reason it shouldn't.'

I looked sharply at Arachne. 'In theory or in practice?'

'Yes, that's the issue.'

'Mages know about this?'

'It's not widely shared knowledge, but yes.'

'Okay, then that doesn't make sense,' I said. 'Let's say it works, and you really can use Elsewhere to add on powers as you like. Then where are the mages who've done it? There should be a whole bunch of immortal invincible archmages running around. I've seen the mages at the head of the Council and the Dark leaders like Morden and Richard. They're powerful, but they're not gods.'

Arachne nodded. 'I only know of a few cases where mages have attempted a transformation such as you describe. In every case, nothing was heard of them thereafter. It is possible that their transformation was a success, and in the process they chose to create a new identity. But as you say, one would expect beings of that kind to make their presence felt. In my judgement, the most likely probability is that they ceased to exist.'

'Because it's impossible?'

'The opposite. Magic is an intrinsic part of its user.

The kind of person you are determines the type of magic you can employ. So to change one's magic . . .' Arachne shrugged. 'I suspect it runs into the same issue. The ability to imagine is not the same as the ability to create a working model.'

I sat thinking for a minute. 'It sounds like a trap,' I said at last. 'Something that's just appealing enough that no one can resist looking at it and which you can't back out of once you start.'

'That's probably accurate,' Arachne said. 'A less sweeping but more feasible use of Elsewhere is in conjunction with imbued items. Since they're alive, they can be brought into Elsewhere, at least temporarily. While there, they can be changed or shaped just as a person can.'

'So you could do . . . what?' I said. 'Enhance them . . . No, that'd run into the same problems. Change them? Make them accept you as a master?'

'You've told me several times that you've always run up against the same problem with imbued items. You can resist their control, but you can't make them do what you want them to. Elsewhere would give you the power to affect them directly.'

'And it works?'

'After a fashion. It's been attempted, and survived. However, there is the obvious drawback.'

I sighed. 'Of course there is.'

'As I said, imbued items function in Elsewhere just as a person does. Which means that any item you bring there is placed on the same footing as you.'

'Oh Jesus. So *it* could try to change or control *me*.'

'Weaker imbued items would probably not have enough strength of self to be a significant danger,' Arachne said.

'On the other hand, the ones you would be most likely be interested in are unlikely to be the weaker ones.'

I thought of the most powerful item I owned, the monkey's paw. I'd got a look at what was inside it, just once. I imagined confronting *that* thing in Elsewhere and shuddered. 'With some of the imbued items I've seen, that might actually be worse than the wiping-yourself-out-of-existence thing.'

'Quite possibly.'

'The more you tell me about this, the more it sounds like a trap,' I said. 'You've just basically told me that if you go to Elsewhere you can get literally anything you wish for. Except that when you look more closely, it's got somewhere between a high chance and a one hundred per cent chance of getting you killed.'

'If it were easy, everyone would have done it.'

I sat thinking for a little while. 'So what's your advice?'

'I'm sorry, Alex,' Arachne said. 'I don't have any.'

'But you've just told me—'

'This is not a choice I can make for you,' Arachne said. 'If you take this path, it will lead you beyond the point where I can guide you. But there is one thing I can do. Here.'

Arachne reached behind her and picked something off one of her tables, manipulating it delicately with one foreleg. She handed it to me and I took it, looking at it curiously. It was a small wrapped package, about the size of a hardback book. 'What is it?'

'If you ever reach the point where your situation is truly dire, open that,' Arachne said. 'It may be of some help.'

I hefted the package. It wasn't heavy – maybe the weight of an orange. 'A new item?'

'You'll see.'

'You could just tell me.'

'Should you ever open it, you will understand why I am *not* telling you.'

I eyed the package. It was neatly wrapped in red paper, tied with a ribbon.

'Yes, Alex, I know you can divine its contents. Please don't.'

'Fine.' I set it down. There aren't many people from whom I'd take that on faith, but Arachne is one of them. We talked for another half an hour, then I left. Once I was back in the Hollow, I put the parcel in a drawer.

The Saturday after my conversation with Arachne found me, Variam, Luna and Anne all together in the Hollow. Officially it was a birthday party for Luna – she'd turned twenty-eight three days ago, but Anne and I had been called in all day to the War Rooms. But at last we'd been able to take a break, and it had been an enormous relief to finally relax. We'd spent the day under the spreading branches, laughing and telling stories. Anne had cooked on a barbecue, and we'd eaten and drank as the afternoon turned into twilight, stars coming out above one by one as the sky faded from blue and green to purple and gold. At last Variam and Luna had left, Luna stifling her yawns and holding Vari's hand, and the gate had closed behind them, leaving Anne and me alone.

I woke later that night, opening my eyes to look up at the ceiling. Moonlight slanted in through the windows, pale beams hanging in mid-air with dark shadows between. I turned my head to see that Anne was still asleep, her hair a black halo against the pillow. I propped myself up on one elbow and looked down at her for a little while, watching the slight movements as the covers rose and fell with her breath. Loving someone is a warm feeling, like having a small well-banked fire burning steadily inside you, and I'd been surprised at how strong it had grown. I leant over to kiss Anne lightly on her forehead, then slid off the futon, moving quietly so as not to disturb her. I dressed and walked outside in silence, drawing the door closed behind me.

The Hollow feels magical at night. The moon that shines down from above is a mirror of Earth's, but the stars are completely different, glowing clusters of blue and purple and gold. The only sound was the faint rustle of the leaves in the trees. The night air was cool but not unpleasant; I crossed the front clearing, grass whispering under my feet, and rounded the copse to Karyos's cocoon.

The sapling linked to Karyos's cocoon had grown by leaps and bounds. It had been only as high as my waist when I'd first seen it, and now it was nearly twice my height, its leaves and branches shooting upwards while the other plants around the clearing had barely changed. The cocoon itself was a hemisphere around the tree's base. It had grown with the tree, to the point that, from a distance, the tree looked like it was sprouting out of a very large anthill.

I rested my fingers against the cocoon, feeling the roughness of the bark against my skin. Above, the wind stirred the trees, the branches shifting gently before settling back into silence. I looked up at the stars, my thoughts moving in circles in troubling paths.

Movement in the futures caught my attention and I looked up to see a white shape appear from behind the copse, bright in the moonlight. 'Can't sleep?' Anne asked softly.

'That lifesight of yours is hard to fool, isn't it?'

'Not lifesight,' Anne said as she walked closer. She was wearing a silk robe, embroidered in flowers in Japanese designs. 'Just old habits.' She nodded at the cocoon. 'She's growing quickly.'

'What'll she look like when she comes out?'

'Like a seven- or eight-year-old.'

'No bark or roots this time?'

'Not that I can see.' Anne placed a hand flat on the cocoon. 'I can't read her mind, but her brain development seems healthy. When we fought her two years ago, her pattern looked twisted. No trace of that this time. I think she's going to do well.'

I looked at Anne, slender and thoughtful, gazing down at the cocoon, and had to smile.

Anne looked at me curiously. 'What's so funny?'

'I was just imagining her coming out of her cocoon and calling you "Mama".'

Anne smiled. 'Would that make you her father?'

'You're the one who's been checking on her every week. If anyone counts as her parent by now . . .'

'I'm not sure how good a mother figure I'd be.' Anne tilted her head. 'What *is* wrong? Something's worrying you.'

I sighed and walked to the edge of the copse, sitting on a fallen tree. 'It's that talk I had with Arachne.'

'About the dreamstone?' Anne came over. 'I thought you'd decided not to use it.'

'I don't *want* to use it. I'm worried I might not have a choice.'

Anne sat down next to me. Her figure cast a long shadow in the moonlight, stretching to merge with the darkness of the trees behind. 'Why?'

'You remember last year when I went to see the dragon that lives under the heath?'

Anne nodded.

'When I told Luna, she asked me about what it had said. You didn't.'

'I suppose not.'

'You weren't curious?'

'I knew you'd tell me if it was important. Besides, I had the feeling that whatever you'd learned, it hadn't helped.'

'That's true enough.' I sat in silence for a moment. 'I asked the dragon three questions. One was about Rachel: I wanted to know how I could turn her away from Richard. The dragon told me I had to convince her of the "truth of her fears". The other two questions were about you.'

Anne didn't reply, and after a moment I went on. 'First I asked how I could break you free of the influence of the jinn. Then I asked how I could become powerful enough to stay alive and protect the people I cared about. The dragon gave me the same answer to both. It told me I couldn't.'

'You . . . couldn't?'

I nodded.

'But that's wrong,' Anne said. 'You did break me free. Last year, in Elsewhere.'

'That wasn't really me,' I said. 'When I asked, the dragon told me that the link between you and the jinn was a function of the jinn's own power, and that I couldn't break it. And that was exactly what happened. I didn't drive it out – you did.'

'I suppose . . .'

'The dragon explained its answer to the other question as well. It told me I could stay alive, or protect the people I cared about. Not "and" – "or". And it told me that the person in question was you.'

'What are you saying?'

'I've been feeling for a long time that sooner or later, if I want to have a chance against mages like Richard and Levistus, I'm going to have to do something drastic,' I said. 'The more I think about it, the more it feels like this Elsewhere thing might be it.'

'But you said it would probably kill you.'

'And now you know what's worrying me.'

'No.' Anne put a hand to my shoulder; I looked up to see that her expression was unhappy. 'I don't want you sacrificing yourself.'

'I don't exactly want to either.'

'Then *don't*. How would it even help? You disintegrating yourself in Elsewhere isn't going to help anyone.'

'Just because I can't see how it could happen . . .'

'I don't care,' Anne said. 'You aren't allowed to travel physically to Elsewhere without talking to me first. Okay?'

'I guess.'

'No, not "I guess". Promise me.'

I hesitated. Anne was looking straight into my eyes, her expression set. 'Okay. I promise.'

I felt Anne relax and lean back. 'Doesn't it worry you?' I asked.

'What?'

'It's a draconic prophecy. From what I understand, they're never wrong. In fact, they *can't* be wrong.'

'Well, maybe this one is.'

I gave Anne a look.

'You've already said that you don't understand what dragons can do or how their prophecies work,' Anne said. 'Doesn't that mean that you shouldn't be counting on it? I mean, if you'd really believed you couldn't do anything to help me against the jinn, you wouldn't have come to Elsewhere. But you did, and it worked. Maybe this prophecy will turn out to be a technicality too.'

'Doesn't it bother you, having something like this hanging over your head?'

'I've never *not* had something like this hanging over my head.' Anne turned her palms upward. 'Sagash. Crystal. The Council and the Crusaders. Lightbringer, Zilean, Morden, Richard. And now the jinn and her. Every single day, I wake up knowing at the back of my mind that it's only going to take one thing for my whole world to come apart. Maybe Crystal and Sagash will come back and they won't make any mistakes this time. Maybe the Council will figure out what really happened at San Vittore. Maybe it'll be Morden, or Richard, or someone completely new. I used to lie awake worrying about it. I'd stay up for hours and I'd finally fall asleep wondering if someone was going to come for me in the night.'

'How did you deal with it?'

Anne shrugged. 'I suppose I just decided that what happens, happens.'

'But we can *change* what's going to happen. We can prepare. Head things off.'

'How am I supposed to prepare against all of that?'

'It's not like we've done nothing,' I said. 'You're far better protected now than you were a few years ago.

Something like that kidnap attempt back when you lived in Honor Oak wouldn't work if they tried it again.'

'I suppose.'

'You keep saying that.'

'I . . .' Anne hesitated. 'I suppose . . . deep down, I don't think it makes a difference.'

'What doesn't?'

'Any of it. Wards, plans . . .' Anne looked down at her clasped hands. 'It feels as though in the end, if something like that is going to happen . . . then there's no point fighting it.'

I frowned at Anne. 'You really think that?'

'Sometimes,' Anne said. She shook her head and stood. 'Come to bed.'

An hour later found me back on the futon, staring up at the ceiling. I needed to rest – I had an early appointment tomorrow – but the conversation with Anne had bothered me, and when I finally drifted off, it wasn't to sleep.

I wandered the landscapes of Elsewhere, feeling the world shift and change. Before this year I never would have come here so casually, but with the dreamstone and Arachne's tuition, I'd become almost as comfortable in Elsewhere as outside it. I walked through halls of marble, gleaming pillars reaching to arching ceilings. The marble halls became a ruined city, the city became a mountaintop, the mountaintop a castle, the castle a forest, the forest . . .

. . . stayed a forest. Oak and beech trees stretched up above, birds singing in the branches. It took me a moment to realise where I was, and when I did, my first instinct was to turn away.

Usually when you visit someone else's version of

Elsewhere, it's because they're in Elsewhere too. Either that or you can find them in their dreams and lead them here. But it's possible, with a delicate enough touch, to travel to a part of Elsewhere shaped by someone else's sleeping mind without waking or disturbing them. There's little reason to do it, since in most cases you'll find something vague and unfinished, like an artist's sketchbook. But Anne's Elsewhere is more real and more defined than anyone else's that I've ever met, for reasons that are both good and bad. I hesitated, on the verge of stepping back into my own dreams. There was only one other person to talk to here, and the thought of that conversation made me uncomfortable.

But what's comfortable and what's necessary are usually different things.

I followed the path until the trees fell away to reveal black glass walls, looming up to block out the sunlight. Absent-mindedly I created an opening large enough for me to pass, letting it disappear again once I was through. Inside the walls was a bare flat plaza, broken by a black tower reaching up to a cloudy sky. I walked to the tower, opened a door that took form at my hand and descended.

The spiral staircase wound its way down around a central well. White spheres glowed from the walls, set at even intervals, but the black materials of the tower soaked up the light. I kept descending until I reached a landing. There was only one door, made out of solid metal, thick and heavy. Three bolts held it shut. I slid them back one after another, then opened the door.

Inside the room was a young woman, with black shoulder-length hair and reddish-brown eyes, wearing a black dress that left her arms bare. She was seated on an iron throne, though not by choice. Manacles of black metal were fastened at her ankles, knees, elbows and wrists, holding her legs to the side of the throne and her arms behind its back. Chains disappeared from the manacles into holes in the throne, with only a link or two visible at each. A collar at her neck kept her back straight and her head against the headrest, but her eyes were open and turned towards me. 'Oh look,' she said. 'Visiting hours at the prison.'

The girl in the chair had many names. Dr Shirland called her Anne's shadow. Anne didn't use a name at all, just 'her'. I'd thought of her as 'not-Anne', but after the events of last year I'd started thinking that 'Dark Anne' might be more accurate. I'd asked her once what she wanted to be called, and she'd told me just to call her Anne. There was a message there.

'How are you doing?' I said.

'Oh, fine, fine.' Dark Anne tilted her head with the small amount of movement she was allowed. 'Sitting down here chained alone in the dark has really been a positive experience for me. I feel like I've grown as a person, you know?'

I walked across the room towards her. 'Well, your sense of sarcasm seems in good shape.'

'Yeah, because there's so much else to do. So what made you finally show up?'

'I figured I was due.'

'Or because your last chat with real-world me didn't go the way you wanted?'

'If you already knew, why did you ask?'

'I wanted to see what bullshit excuse you'd come up with. And yes, I heard all of it. Funny thing about being stuck here – I can hear what's going on outside just fine. Can't talk, can't feel, but I can sit around and watch everything my other self gets to do to enjoy herself.' Dark Anne raised her eyebrows. 'And yes, in case you're wondering, that does mean *everything*.'

I looked at her.

'By the way, you really ought to be more aggressive about—'

'You can stop there.'

Dark Anne smirked at me. 'Suit yourself.' The chains clinked as she shifted on the throne. 'So let me guess. Her whole *que sera sera* attitude didn't make you very happy, huh?'

'Not really.'

'Aww. What's the problem? Feel like you know what's best for her? She's not being a good little girl and doing as she's told?'

I looked back.

'I know, I know. You diviners are all about preparation and planning. Must be really annoying for someone to point out how useless it is, right?'

'Do you have anything useful to say, or are you just going to take cheap shots?'

Dark Anne shrugged. 'I don't know, what's in it for me?'

'Well, there's the little detail that anything that happens to Anne happens to you,' I said. 'So I'd say you've got a personal stake in this. Unless you think Anne's wait-and-see plan is a good one.'

'No, her plan's dumb as shit. Here's the bad news: you aren't going to change her mind.'

'What makes you so sure?'

'You really haven't figured it out?' Dark Anne cocked her head. 'Let's put it another way. Who do you think I am?'

'You're the side of Anne that Anne can't or won't deal with. Aggressive, ruthless, self-centred. You told me you were born in Sagash's shadow realm, but that wasn't really true. You were always there.'

'Well, well. Someone's been talking with Dr Shirland.'

'I answered your question,' I said. 'Now answer mine. Why do you think Anne won't change her mind?'

'Not won't, can't,' Dark Anne said. 'Think about it. According to you, I'm the evil side of Anne that's all nasty and ruthless, not like the real Anne, who's all sweetness and light. So here's a question for you. Which one of us do you think's better at fighting to stay alive?'

'You think it's you.'

'Of course it's me, you frigging idiot. I am the side of her personality that got split off *specifically* to handle life-and-death situations. Except that instead of doing that, I'm chained up down here in the dark where I can't reach anyone or do anything, while Little Miss Perfect gets to run the show. And now you're like, gosh, her decision-making when it comes to all this dark and scary stuff doesn't seem all that good any more. Hey, I wonder whose fault it is. What do you think, Alex? Who's the reason things ended up this way?'

I raised my eyebrows. 'You're blaming me?'

'You and her.' Dark Anne leant forward. 'When I get out of here, she's first on the list. You? You're number two.'

'Yeah, with an attitude like that, I can't think why she'd want you locked up,' I said. 'You played the poor-little-me act last year too. Remind me, what was the first thing you did when you got free?'

Dark Anne shrugged as best she could. 'So I cut loose a little.'

'Do you even understand how much damage you did in those few hours?' I asked her. 'It's been a year and we are *still* trying to deal with the consequences. And when I say trying, there's a really good chance it's not going to work. The instant they find out who was really responsible for those murders, what do you think's going to happen?'

'Stop whining.'

I stared at Dark Anne. 'You know how many people died because of what you did in San Vittore?'

Dark Anne didn't answer.

'Eighteen. It would have been more but for the response team.'

'Not like I did anything to them.'

'Oh, don't even start,' I said in disgust. 'You were the one who summoned those jinn. Not Morden, not Richard. You. If you're seriously going to say that's not your responsibility, then I'm done talking.'

'That one was the jinn's idea, actually. I guess all those lesser ones used to be his servants or something.'

'Which means they did what you told them.'

'Yeah, and the men there all worked for the Council, and they did what *they* told them. I'd given them the chance, they'd have shot me just as fast.'

'They're still human beings. You know the Council has an entire department for coming up with stories to tell the families of the men that die in their service? I went down there after the attack. Copies and copies of letters to relatives. I don't even know what kind of explanation they had to come up with for that many deaths at the same time.'

'They knew the risks, didn't they?' Dark Anne said. 'They were prison guards. Not exactly a goody-two-shoes kind of job.'

'I don't understand you,' I said. 'Anne will work for hours with her healing magic to save the life of someone she doesn't even know. Meanwhile, you're personally responsible for nearly twenty deaths in as many minutes, and you just shrug it off. I know she's the empathic one, but don't you have *any* of it?'

'So what about *you*?' Dark Anne said. 'Because the way I remember it, you've killed *way* more people than that. What about the Nightstalkers? Or that raid you did on that Light mage in Scotland, Belthas or whatever his name was? We weren't there but Luna told us the story. What was the body count on that again?'

'There's a difference between fighting because you have to and fighting because you want to. Both of those times you're talking about, I was pushed to my limits. Last year in San Vittore, you weren't. You could easily have neutralised them without having to—'

Dark Anne gave a loud sigh and rolled her eyes.

I broke off. 'I'm sorry. Am I not holding your attention?'

'Bored.'

'You have something better to be doing?'

'No, which should just emphasise how *boring* this is.' Anne leant forward slightly, the chains clinking as she shifted. 'Why do you do this?'

'What, talk to you?'

'No, turn conversations into some kind of ethics lecture. I mean, I actually *like* you, and when you start on this

I still want to beat my head against a wall because it hurts less. Blah blah right and wrong blah responsibility blah. Okay, Alex, harsh truth time, you listening? You've never changed anyone's mind with this stuff. Ever.'

'I've—'

'No, not even then. Either it's someone like Luna, and she's already going to do what you tell her, or it's everyone else, and they don't care what you say. Think about it. When have you managed to argue someone into thinking you're right and they're wrong?'

'It's not like I keep records.'

'You haven't! Because no one cares! Yes, people listen to you, but they listen because they think you're scary and competent. The times you've made some Dark mage or adept punk back down, you think it was because you convinced them? They back off because they think you're dangerous. And that's the only reason anyone *ever* pays attention to the words coming out of your mouth.'

I looked back at her. 'Well,' I said after a moment, 'you're making me realise one thing. Anne *is* right to keep you locked up down here.'

Dark Anne narrowed her eyes. 'For now.'

'For now?' I asked. 'I hate to break this to you, but Anne's stronger than you are. The reason you were able to overpower her back then was because you had the jinn backing you up. One on one, for all your tough girl talk? You can't match her.'

'Like I said,' Dark Anne said. 'For now. Some day she'll need me.'

'Seems to me she's doing pretty well on her own.'

'Please. You only think that because you've forgotten

what I can do. If I'd been in that research facility, I'd have taken them all down solo.'

'Which isn't going to happen, because of how badly you screwed up last year,' I said. 'Anne is not giving you control again. Ever. Long term, you want to get out of here, you have exactly one way to do it.'

'Which is?'

'Merge with her,' I said. 'Become one person again. Seriously, do you realise how insane you sound? You can't keep this up for ever. Sooner or later the two of you are going to have to work something out that doesn't come down to locking the other in a dungeon.'

'I don't know. Sticking her in here and seeing how she likes it seems pretty good to me.'

'Which you can't do without the jinn,' I said. 'Which you can't call back.'

'She can.'

'Right, Anne's going to go to the super-powerful eldritch entity that's already possessed her three times and invite it back for another try. Are you really that stupid?'

'Maybe not now,' Dark Anne said. 'But like she was saying, we've got a lot of enemies, haven't we? Sagash and Crystal, Morden and Richard, all those Light Guardians and Crusaders. Not to mention all of your new best friends on the Council. Some day things will get bad enough and she'll be desperate enough. Maybe not this month, maybe not this year, but it'll happen. You think Anne's so pure and innocent, but you don't know her like I do. When things really go to hell, she'll do whatever it takes to survive. Until then? I can wait.'

I gave Dark Anne a look, then turned and walked away.

'I'm not going anywhere, Alex,' Dark Anne called after

me. 'Someday we'll be face to face again. And I won't be so nice next time.'

There was more, but the closing door cut off her voice. I started the long climb up the spiral staircase, alone with my thoughts.

5

My talk with the two Annes left me feeling uneasy. For the next few days, I turned it over in the back of my mind, trying to come up with something I could do.

Nine days passed. I lived in the Hollow, travelling to the War Rooms each day with Anne. There was plenty to do: the war was still on a slow burn, and there was no sign of anyone on the Council plotting a move, but there were the usual problems that needed to be managed, and they kept me busy. Arachne stayed at home in her lair, and I visited her twice more. Luna kept working in the Arcana Emporium, and Variam was busy with his work as a Keeper.

Tuesday the eighth of August started like any other day.

I woke up next to Anne and we went outside for our morning workout. For me the focus was on fitness, calisthenics and resistance work with a few martial arts forms. For Anne it was hand-to-hand training; she was getting better, though she still wasn't as aggressive as I knew she could be. Once we were done, we headed back to change and to discuss the day's work over breakfast. The current issue was once again the adepts – with the news of Richard's new training programme added to the existing steady trickle that had been joining him, the Council was considering various heavy-handed responses. I didn't like any of them, but coming up with a viable alternative that I could sell the Senior Council on was tough. After that I made some calls, while Anne gave Karyos her daily check-up, and once we were both ready we gated via staging points to the War Rooms.

Morning at the War Rooms meant meetings. I delivered a report to Druss the Red, after which I had to take part in a long, frustrating interview with a task force of Keepers from the Order of the Cloak. Anne had some tricky nego-tiations with Lyle and Julia, the aides to Undaaris and Alma. We met up again over lunch to compare notes.

Afternoon was a full Council session. While Anne waited outside, I met with the Senior and Junior Councils in the Star Chamber. The first two hours was reports – finance, security, public relations. It was tedious, but while my position was much better these days, it wasn't secure enough that I felt safe not showing up. Next on the agenda was long-term strategy, which devolved into an hour-long argu-ment between Sal Sarque and Bahamus. Neither was able to sway enough members for a majority, so the decision was postponed until next week. Finally came military announcements.

'. . . and they report that the cargo was talocan filaments,' Bahamus finished.

I pricked up my ears. 'Sure about that?' Druss asked.

'The German Council wasn't able to secure a sample,' Bahamus said. 'But I've read the report provided by their universalists, and they were quite thorough. It seems over-whelmingly probable.'

Druss frowned. 'What the hell's Drakh up to with those?'

'Not exactly a mystery,' Sal Sarque said. 'Some ritual.'

'Bloody expensive way to do a ritual.'

I listened closely. Talocan filaments are a type of infused

component with some unusual properties that make them valuable for high-power magical rituals. They don't get much use since they're so awkward and time-consuming to make, which, as Druss had pointed out, made them expensive. Richard would have needed to put in a lot of work to get so many.

'Do we have any indication that Drakh's cabal are planning any rituals that would benefit?' Alma asked.

Bahamus shook his head. 'They've been quiet for almost a month.'

'Yeah, and I don't like it,' Druss said. 'We were expecting retaliations over that facility, but we haven't had a peep. Why?'

'Council intelligence thinks he may be suffering a manpower shortage.'

'What bloody manpower shortage? We haven't taken down anyone from his inner circle all year.'

There were five members of the Senior Council present today: Bahamus, Druss the Red, Alma, Sal Sarque and Levistus. The first two were more or less my allies, the last two were definitely my enemies, and Alma was somewhere in between but closer to the latter. Druss, the one who'd been speaking, was a big, powerfully built man with a thick beard.

'We've had multiple reports that Drakh's forces are having issues with morale and momentum,' Bahamus said. His manner was steady; in all the time I'd known him, I'd never seen him lose his cool. 'Remember, the pressure is on him in this war. He needs a constant stream of victories. A stalemate serves our interest, not his.'

'I'm afraid I can't share your optimism, Bahamus,' Alma said. 'In case you've forgotten, we are supposed to hold authority over all of magical Britain. A stalemate does not help our image at all.'

'That ship sailed a long time ago,' Druss said. 'Anyway, it doesn't matter. Right now we've got a breather and we should be using it to go on the attack.'

'You're the one who's been telling us how dangerous Drakh's forces are.'

'Which is why I don't want to sit around while he lines up a punch.'

'We've discussed this,' Bahamus said. 'Our offensive operations have consistently played into Drakh's strengths. If we can hold out long enough, the Dark mages of Drakh's coalition will fall to infighting as they always do.'

'That'll only happen if Drakh shows weakness.'

The argument between Bahamus and Druss started up again, and I sat quietly and listened. Nowadays much of my time was spent on these disagreements, figuring out who to support and why. It wasn't fun, but I'd come to learn that politics, at least in the Light world, mostly came down to having enough people on your side.

'Enough,' Alma said at last. 'This is getting nowhere.'

'We can't just keep sitting on our arses,' Druss said.

'Without knowledge of Drakh's base of operations, there's no way for us to launch an attack,' Alma said. 'Have you made any progress on that?'

Druss was silent for a moment. 'No.'

'Then as far as I can see, we're going to have to table this,' Alma said. 'I think we'll adjourn.'

The meeting broke up. Sal Sarque moved to speak with Druss, the two of them talking quietly in one corner, while Alma met two other Junior Council members. I rose and stepped to one side as Bahamus approached me.

'I've spoken to the others regarding your proposal for the adepts,' Bahamus said. 'They're leaning towards supporting it.'

'Including the amnesty?' I said.

'Alma isn't keen on that part.'

'It doesn't matter if she's keen, it's essential! There's no way we can possibly convince the adept community to be neutral unless it comes with a promise that we aren't going to come after them as soon as we're done with Drakh. She *has* to see that.'

The adepts had been one of the thorniest problems in this war. In the run-up to hostilities, Richard had worked hard to sway the adept community to his side, and unfortunately for the Council he'd had a fair bit of success at it. Adepts are both less powerful and less organised than mages, but one thing they have on their side is numbers – depending on how you count them, there are between ten times and a hundred times as many adepts in Britain as there are Dark mages and Light mages put together. Even if only a few per cent of them were fighting for Richard, that was a huge pool of manpower and resources that he could draw upon. I'd been doing what I could to win hearts and minds, but it was hard work, especially with mages like Alma, whose idea of diplomacy was to give someone a warning before crushing them.

'Well, I'll try to convince her.' Bahamus paused. 'On another note, don't spread this around, but we've completed the timesight analysis of that facility.'

'Finally. What took them so long?'

'Overstretched. Sonder has been busy on some other project. In any case, it seems as though it was a more important base than we realised. Drakh himself had visited it more than once. It looks as though its destruction may have significantly set them back.' Bahamus paused. 'You've been doing good work, Verus. Keep it up.'

I smiled slightly. 'Glad to know you feel that way.'

'Once we're done with this, I'll see if we can get your membership on the Junior Council made official. I know you've become a de facto member with everything that's happened, but an announcement would help solidify things.'

'It . . . would, actually. It would help a lot. Do you think—?'

A voice spoke from across the table. 'Bahamus.'

Bahamus turned. The man addressing him looked to be in his fifties, though I knew he was older, with thinning white hair and odd eyes that were so pale they were almost colourless. His name was Levistus, and he was quite possibly the worst enemy I had.

'You are needed for a closed session of the Senior Council,' Levistus said.

Bahamus frowned. 'Can this wait?'

'I'm afraid not.'

Bahamus sighed and looked at me. 'We'll have to continue this later. I'll contact you after the meeting.'

'All right.'

Bahamus left. Levistus's pale eyes rested briefly on me, then he turned away.

Anne was waiting outside the Star Chamber. 'That took a while.'

'Usual hold-ups.'

Half a dozen other mages were scattered around, though there was a general movement out. The end of the Council meeting signalled the last phase of the workday in the War Rooms. Various mages would stay for after-hours meetings, but from this point on the population would drop steadily.

Any trouble? Anne asked through the dreamstone.

Not so far. Did you hear back from the Keepers?

We kept up a mental chat as we made our way back to my office. Once there, I caught up on work while I waited for Bahamus to contact me. Half an hour passed, then an hour. An hour and a quarter. An hour and a half.

I looked at the clock in annoyance. 'What's taking him so long?'

'What'll happen if you call him?' Anne asked.

'No answer. Nothing from Druss either.'

'Are they ever going to get in touch?'

I tapped my fingers on the desk, looking ahead. Unfortunately, the futures were murky. It's easy to predict events that have already been set in motion, but it looked as though in this case, the key decisions had yet to be made. There were flickers of futures in which I had incoming calls, but all the most likely possibilities involved Anne and me sitting around for more than an hour.

'Forget it,' I said at last. 'Let's head to Arachne's.'

The sun was dipping low by the time Anne and I arrived on Hampstead Heath. The western sky was lit up in oranges and reds, long shadows stretching out across the grass and down towards the ponds below. Shouts and snatches of laughter drifted on the summer breeze. Anne and I emerged from the ravine we use for gating and touched the entry node to Arachne's cave. Arachne answered after only a moment, and we disappeared beneath the ground. The earth closed up behind us.

As always, I felt myself relax as we walked into Arachne's cave. Warm lights glowed from around the rock walls, reflecting off a hundred pieces of cloth and silk. There are really only two places I feel safe these days, Arachne's cave and the Hollow, and I've been coming to Arachne's cave for much longer. While I'm at the War Rooms – and most other places, for that matter – I have to constantly be looking ahead and watching for threats, and it's exhausting. You can't live like that 24/7, not if you want to keep your sanity.

I sprawled out on a sofa and got to work on my correspondence while Anne chatted with Arachne. The two of them have always got on well for whatever reason: usually when I introduce someone to Arachne there are problems, but Anne and Arachne seemed to fall into a friendly relationship immediately. Arachne worked away on something as the two of them talked, her legs moving more quickly than usual.

'There,' Arachne said at last. She picked up the article of clothing to hang from her front two legs. 'Finished.'

I glanced up from my keyboard to look. It was a dress, black with shoulder straps, but I was more interested in what my magesight showed me. The thing had a magical aura, and it was strong: close to my armour, if not on a par with it. The spells that made it were integrated, smoothly woven in a way that made them hard to identify, though they had the feel of living and universal magic.

'It's amazing,' Anne said.

'And powerful,' I said. 'What's it for? Wouldn't work well as armour with that much of the arms bare.'

'Thank you, *Anne*,' Arachne said with a pointed look at me. 'Not everything is about combat effectiveness.'

'Hey, I'm just saying. If you're going to wear something that'll catch that much attention, you might as well build some protection in.'

'Protection comes in different forms,' Arachne said. 'I'm glad I could finish this in the end. Balancing its compatibility with its internal growth was more difficult than I'd expected.'

'It *is* alive, isn't it?' Anne said, studying the dress in fascination. 'Who's it for?'

'Who do you think?'

Anne paused. 'Me?'

'Of course, you,' Arachne said. She laid the dress down on the table, folding it neatly. 'It needs a little more time to grow, but the spells are done. It should be fully matured in a couple of days.'

Anne hesitated.

'What's wrong?' I asked.

'It's beautiful, but . . . isn't it a lot of work for something you'd only wear on special occasions?'

'Actually, it's designed for long-term wear,' Arachne said.

'Is it an A-line?'

'More of a skater dress than an A-line.'

'Well, I've no idea what that means, but I'm pretty sure it'd look good on you,' I told Anne. 'What's the matter?'

'I'd feel bad about taking something like that if I wasn't going to use it often enough,' Anne admitted. 'Isn't an imbued dress like that really valuable?'

'Yes,' I said. 'But I'd have got you one long ago if it was just about cost. I've been trying to talk you into wearing something more protective for years.'

'If I wear something like that, everyone is going to look at me.'

'They're going to do that anyway.'

'You know what I mean.'

'What, you'd rather have something more modest?'

'Well . . .'

A chime rang out, echoing around the cave. 'What was that?' I asked Arachne.

Arachne had picked up the folded dress and was placing it in a small enclave in the wall. At the sound of the chime, she'd stopped moving. 'Arachne?' I asked.

Arachne stayed still for another moment, then sealed the enclave behind a panel. 'The perimeter alarm.'

Anne and I stared. 'The what?'

Arachne was moving to the other side of the room. I shook myself, then path-walked, looking into the future to see what would happen if I went outside. Up the tunnel, out the door, and— 'Oh, shit.'

'Who's out there?' Anne asked.

'A small fucking army.' The futures had dissolved into violence, weapons fire and spells. Lots of spells. 'Armed men and magic-users. Adepts and mages, three at least, probably more.'

Anne looked up towards the tunnel in alarm. 'What should we do?'

I hesitated. Anne and I had made contingency plans for dozens of situations, but in most cases the plans revolved around breaking contact and getting somewhere safe. Arachne's cave was the safest place we had.

A noise blared, loud and discordant. Arachne had been moving around the cave, activating devices; now she paused. 'What's that?' Anne asked.

'The communication focus,' I said. 'But it shouldn't sound like . . .'

A voice spoke from the wall, loud and harsh. 'To the inhabitants of this cave: you are ordered under the authority of the Light Council of Britain to open this door and submit to questioning. Failure to do so will be considered a violation of the Concord and will be enforced by any means necessary, up to and including the use of deadly force. You have thirty seconds to comply.'

Anne stood very still. I looked ahead to see what would happen if we didn't answer. They weren't bluffing. Actually, it was worse than that – the men outside were going to shoot first and ask questions later. When a Council team is operating under those rules of engagement, it means one of two things: either they're sure the suspects are guilty, or they don't care.

'Can you—?' Anne began.

'Talking is out,' I said. 'These guys are not here for a discussion.'

'You should run,' Arachne said.

A distant *boom* echoed down the tunnel, and I felt a faint tremor through the floor. 'What about you?' I asked Arachne.

'I will stay.'

'What? Why?'

There was a second boom, louder and deeper, and this time I felt the signature of powerful magic, earth and force. 'Alex . . .' Anne said. 'She's right, we have to go. If we're not here, maybe they won't . . .'

'They're not going to leave her alone! Anyway, go *where*?'

I heard distant voices from up the tunnel, shouts and the sound of orders. 'Withdraw into the tunnels,' Arachne said. 'The wards on this area prevent gating, but if you can travel far enough, they should weaken to the point that you can use a gate stone.'

Light flickered from the tunnel mouth and I felt a spell discharge: there was a distant yell. Arachne glanced over and made a motion with one foreleg. I felt a spell trigger, something that had been hidden in the cave's wards that I'd walked past a thousand times without noticing. With a rumble, the sides of the tunnel bulged inwards, earth and stone flowing to seal off the entrance.

Arachne stayed facing the wall and I grabbed one of her back legs. The hairs were rough under my fingers. 'If you're telling us to run, why aren't you coming?' I'd already seen that she wouldn't follow. 'Are you planning to hold them off?'

'Not precisely.'

'Then why?'

Arachne held still, not turning to face me. 'There is . . . no longer time to explain.' Arachne's voice was sad. 'There are reasons I must remain here, protections limited in time and space. In time, you will understand.'

'Understand what? I don't—' And then I cut off as I realised that Arachne was right. We were out of time.

Cracks formed in the wall where the tunnel entrance had been, spiderwebbing across as chunks of earth and rock tumbled to the floor. With a rumbling crash a breach opened, dust billowing into the cave, shields of force magic sweeping the rubble away. Men came through behind the shields, wearing helmets and combat armour, beams flickering from the lights mounted on their guns. One of them aimed at us and fired.

I was already jumping backwards, catching Anne and

pulling her to the side. We ran, falling back to the tunnel mouth at the far end of Arachne's cave that led to her store rooms and down to the deep caverns below. Once I reached the cavern mouth, I slowed and turned.

Arachne hadn't run. She lifted her front legs, magic trailing around them as she wove patterns. The men fanning out into the cavern turned on her, firing; sparks flashed as the shots glanced off, localised protective spells deflecting the bullets into the floor and walls, precise and efficient. Arachne made a flicking motion towards the soldiers, and nets of glowing light materialised out of the air, wrapping around them and taking them down one by one.

More people flooded into the cave, and this time they weren't soldiers. A ball of fire erupted, engulfing Arachne for a moment before her defensive magic snuffed it out. Arachne sent nooses of magical silk, followed by a cocoon. The nooses didn't make it through the fire shield; the cocoon did. The fire mage fell, struggling to burn away the bonds, but more and more mages were coming and they were filling up the cavern faster than Arachne could deal with them.

One of the flanking gunmen spotted me and Anne and lined up a shot. I blinded him with a flare, but more fire tracked in on our position and I had to duck back into the cave mouth. Arachne was left alone, a solitary figure in the centre of a semicircle of enemies.

An ice blast struck Arachne in the flank; she deflected it, sending a spell back at the mage with a flick of one leg. Earth magic surged and the stone beneath Arachne's feet reared and struck like a hammer. Arachne stumbled and fell. The mages around her pressed in, spells battering as Arachne's shields began to flicker and fall.

'No,' I muttered under my breath and took a half-step forward.

'Alex.' Anne caught my arm. 'Don't.'

I dug my nails into my palms. I knew Anne was right, but I couldn't stand to just leave Arachne alone. 'I can't—' I began, then stopped.

Something strange was happening in the cavern. Spells and magical attacks were still streaking in at Arachne, but they were slower to reach her. Not because they were moving more slowly, but because they had further to travel. I saw one fireball dip and fall short, though its arc should have carried it the full distance. The gunfire no longer seemed to be doing anything; it was as though the soldiers were firing into empty space. Arachne still defended, still wove her nets and spells, but she seemed smaller and smaller, a tiny shape at the centre of a vast arena. Now none of the attacks were reaching her at all.

That was when I realised the walls were moving.

The walls swept anticlockwise, rippling and turning. Men fell back towards the centre of the room like scurrying ants. The walls were brown and gold now, plated and scaled, and as I looked up I realised that the ceiling had been replaced by a starry void. I kept looking up and up, knowing what I would see, and it wasn't a surprise when I saw the draconic head, lifted on a long neck, towering above me like a mountain range.

Shouts and yells echoed through the chamber as the men fell back. Or tried to; it would have taken them ten minutes at a full sprint just to get from one side of the cavern to the other. Some of them fired at the dragon; strikes of fire and ice glanced off the scales like pinpricks. The dragon reared up, then down, its long serpentine body twisting as it reached Arachne.

Arachne was looking up at the dragon; it felt as if she was speaking, though I couldn't hear words. The dragon reached down and picked up Arachne delicately in one claw. I saw Arachne turn to look at us; for one moment her eyes met mine across the vast distance. Then the dragon was rising, soaring up into the stars and the night. As it did, space seemed to expand, reality reverting itself. A flick of its tail restored the cavern roof, blotting out the void and returning the cave to its original shape.

There was a moment of silence. The dragon was gone. Arachne was gone. All that was left was an empty patch at the centre of Arachne's lair. Anne was still there, I was still there, and so were about forty assorted mages and Council security, all picking themselves up off the floor and staring around them as they tried to figure out what had just happened.

My divination gave me a head start and I darted back into the tunnel, dragging Anne with me. Someone shouted something and without looking I threw a condenser, feeling the flash of magic behind us as it burst into a cloud of mist. We ran down the tunnel, hearing shouts fading away behind us.

'What—?' Anne managed to ask as she ran.

I don't know!

That dragon. It was the same—

Yeah, but I don't think it's coming back.

It couldn't have given us a lift as well?

We ran through the darkness. It was pitch-black but my divination guided my steps, showing me where to place my feet on the rough rock. Anne had to run blind, trusting to my guidance and her own sense of balance. Eventually I slowed to a jog, then a walk, then I stopped to listen. Silence.

I can't sense anyone, Anne said.

I can, I said. The tunnel was dark and oppressive, the weight of hundreds of tonnes of earth pressing down from above. To sight and sound, we could have been alone in the dark, but as I looked through the futures I knew that was an illusion. *They're on our trail. Keep moving.*

We kept moving through the darkness. *Do you think Arachne's okay?* Anne asked.

I'd wondered the same thing. There had been a finality in Arachne's manner at the end, as though she knew we weren't going to see each other again. But right now, I was pretty sure that we were in more danger than she was. *I think we should be worrying about ourselves. Hold up a second, I'm going to try a gate stone.*

We stopped, standing in the dark, as I took out our gate stone to the Hollow. Futures flickered out as I tried a hundred gate spells in a hundred different ways. I swore quietly, shoved the gate stone back into my pocket and resumed walking.

No good?

Too much interference. The wards over Arachne's cave were old and deep. If either Anne or I could cast gate spells, we could have tried to force it by upping the power, but neither of us was an elemental mage and having to rely on focuses was hurting us. *We'll have to go further.*

Didn't you say that the dragon lived down here?

Assuming it's still here. I looked ahead to see what would happen if we kept going . . .

I stopped. Anne bumped into me before catching herself. 'Oh shit.'

'What?'

'We're cut off.' I felt a stab of fear in my gut. The Council forces were behind us, and there was someone else ahead. And it wasn't just anyone.

'Side turnings . . .?'

'We'd have to go back, and they'd be right on top of us. Try your gate stone.'

'But you said—'

'I know. We're out of options.'

There was a moment's silence, then there was the rustle of movement and the tunnel lit up in faint green light. Anne's face became visible in the glow, set in concentration, staring down at the focus. Seconds ticked by.

'Running out of time,' I said, trying to keep the tension out of my voice.

'I'm trying! I can't get it to take!'

I was looking through the futures in which we stayed where we were. None of them ended with us escaping through a gate. 'Don't think this is going to work,' I said. 'Have you got anything else you could try?'

'If I did, I'd be trying it already!'

I took a deep breath, looked down the tunnel, then back at Anne. 'There's one thing.'

'What thing?' Anne asked, then her face changed. 'Oh no.'

'You can still call on that jinn,' I said. I hated the idea of even suggesting this, but I couldn't see any other way out. I knew exactly what was going to happen if the Council caught us, and right now, I didn't think I could stop that from happening. 'And given the other stuff it can do . . .'

Anne was shaking her head.

'You have any better ideas?'

'You don't know what you're asking.'

'No, but I know what's going to happen if we stick around!'

Anne let the gate stone drop and caught my wrist. 'No, you don't—' She took a deep breath, then spoke quickly. 'I need her help to use the jinn. And every time we've done that, she's got stronger. Driving the jinn out, locking her away that last time, it took everything I had. If I let her in again, she won't be going away. Not ever.'

I looked back at Anne. 'Well. That's not good.'

'I'm sorry,' Anne said in a small voice.

'Not your fault.' I was silent for two seconds. 'Well, I guess that leaves us exactly one direction to go.'

I took Anne's hand and we started walking down the tunnel again. With my other hand, I took out a pouch from one pocket, readying its contents. *How long will we have?* Anne asked through the dreamstone.

People chasing us are about five minutes behind, I said. *Call it about four minutes to finish the fight and get back to running.*

Who's . . . ? Anne began, then tailed off. *Oh. Her.*

Pale brown light bloomed from ahead, and a figure stepped out from the wall. She was heavyset, and her big hands flexed as she faced us. 'Councillor Verus,' Caldera said. 'You are under arrest under suspicion of—'

'Save it,' I said.

'And you, Anne Walker, are under arrest for, well, more things than I can count,' Caldera said. 'But then, you already know what they are, don't you?'

I felt Anne flinch, and I squeezed her hand once in

reassurance. 'You going to get out of our way?' I told Caldera.

'We both know that's not going to happen,' Caldera said. 'You've had this coming a long time.'

Caldera wasn't moving, and I knew why. *She's stalling*, I told Anne. *We're going to have to rush her. I'll try to distract her for you to get close.*

All right.

Three and a half minutes left. I tried to ignore the fear in my gut. Above ground in the open, I would have given the two of us good odds against Caldera. But we weren't out in the open, we were in a cramped tunnel surrounded by stone. It was the worst possible environment to fight an earth mage. 'So how many others did you bring?' I asked. 'Rain join the party too?'

'I don't need—'

Go, I told Anne, and lunged.

Caldera reacted instantly, spears of stone stabbing from the wall. I twisted aside; through the dreamstone I felt a flash of pain from Anne, but Caldera was right in front of me and I had a clear shot. I feinted with my left hand, then when she moved to block I brought my right hand up and around and threw glitterdust in her face.

But Caldera had been ready and she'd managed to get her eyes closed in time. Glowing particles clung around her eyelids, but while her vision was impaired, she wasn't blind. She backed away and I followed, reaching into my pocket for another weapon.

Caldera ignored me completely. As I lunged, she reached out over my shoulder, and light glowed as she cast a spell. As my stun focus caught Caldera in the stomach, I heard Anne cry out.

I glanced back and felt a chill. The stone walls were enveloping Anne, rock flowing over her like thick jelly, and half her body was already engulfed. I turned on Caldera in a fury. The stun focus hadn't put her down but it had made her stagger, and I hit her with everything I had, knees and fists and elbows.

It felt like hitting a lump of granite. Pain flashed through me as my blows landed, but she didn't seem to feel it. My elbow connected with the side of her head, hard enough to knock out a normal person, but Caldera only stumbled, then lifted her hand again towards Anne.

The stone of the tunnel walls rippled, pulling Anne inside it. Struggling, Anne was drawn into the wall, the stone enveloping first her body, then her head. Only when Anne had vanished completely did Caldera turn to me. Snarling, I attacked again. I might as well have tried to punch through a brick wall. Caldera took everything I could dish out, then threw a punch hard enough to break my ribs. I blocked it, but the impact threw me back.

'Seen your moves before, Alex,' Caldera said. 'Blind first, then go for the stun.'

'Let her go,' I said through clenched teeth.

'You surrender, I'll let her go. How long you think she'll last without air?'

I lunged. Somewhere at the back of my mind, I was trying to think of what I could do. Using mist or dousing Caldera's light wouldn't do much, and a forcewall wouldn't help me get Anne out. That just left my more lethal weapons, but they'd do nothing unless I could disable Caldera's protective spells.

I tried my dispel focus. It worked, but Caldera was ready for it, renewing her stone skin immediately. I got more hits in as she did, but none of them were enough to knock her out.

Caldera fell back, on the defensive but unhurt. 'No trucks this time,' she told me. She spread her hands wide. 'Bring it.'

I hesitated for an instant. There was one thing I could do. Break past Caldera, use a forcewall to seal the corridor and run. Come back for Anne later . . .

. . . there wouldn't be a later. 'It's me you want, right?' I said. 'Let Anne go and I'll stay with you.'

Caldera gave me a pitying look. 'Arrest warrant was for you both. And if I could only get one, orders were to make it her. But honestly? I'm looking forward to taking you down as well.'

I could hear footsteps from behind; we were nearly out of time. Desperately, I threw myself at Caldera.

But Caldera was stronger than me, and tougher than me, and I was running out of tricks. My blows kept landing, but they were hurting me more than her. Caldera barely even needed to block.

I kicked Caldera's leg out, but the impact sent a jolt of pain through my knee and I didn't get out of the way quite fast enough. Caldera's punch hit my thigh like a hammer, making me stumble.

I jumped back, nearly falling. 'You're just making things worse for yourself, Alex,' Caldera said.

'Screw you.'

Caldera came at me like a bulldozer, slow and heavy and unstoppable. I blocked and dodged, but I was tired now, hurt. I ducked one blow and my leg gave way from underneath me. Before I could get out of the way, Caldera stamped on my ankle, making me gasp.

'Don't get up,' Caldera told me.

I got up.

Caldera was waiting. She struck again, and this time, she finally managed a clean hit. The world flashed white, then red, then I was falling through darkness, thought and sensation fading away.

6

Pain.

I woke up slowly and unpleasantly. Lots of places hurt, but the worst was my head, jagged and sharp. I shifted and realised I was lying on a hard surface. I could hear voices around me, the murmur of conversation, someone giving orders. I tried to orientate myself. This felt like Arachne's cave . . .

Arachne.

I tried to sit up. The pain in my head became a white-hot spike and I vomited. Nausea and agony drowned out all thought for a while.

After some length of time, my head and stomach stopped hurting enough for my mind to start working again. The voices were still talking, and now added to them I could hear rustling and thumps. I cracked open an eye, moving more cautiously this time. The light hurt, but no more so than everything else, and I looked around.

I was in Arachne's lair, in one of the far corners. Council personnel were scattered throughout the cave, and it was their voices I'd heard. They were searching the place, shaking out clothing and pulling out cushions. As I watched, a security man dumped a bolt of cloth onto the floor with a thump, then started pushing at it with a boot. I wasn't up to using my divination, but through my magesight I could sense spells.

I tried to shift position and realised that my hands were

held behind my back. Cautiously, I explored with my fingers and touched cold metal. Handcuffs. I lay still, trying to think of options. No good ones came to mind, and the pain in my head wasn't making it any easier. All I could think of was my lockpicks, but I wasn't sure I had them any more: my pockets felt lighter than they should have been.

The men around the chamber were still working. There were a lot of them, but Arachne's lair is a big place, and they apparently weren't in any hurry. I tried again to sit up, and still failed, though at least I didn't throw up this time. Footsteps approached from my blind side and I held still.

A pair of heavy boots came into my vision. 'You awake?' Caldera said from what felt like a long way above.

I couldn't have answered even if I'd wanted to. Caldera hauled me into a sitting position, propping my back against the wall. Another wave of nausea rolled over me and I fought to keep myself from vomiting again. Once my vision cleared, I saw that Caldera was squatting down in front of me. She held one finger up, and pale brown light glowed from the tip.

'You see the light?' Caldera asked. She moved it from side to side; my eyes tracked it with difficulty. 'Is it blurry? Doubled?'

Focusing on the light was too hard. I closed my eyes and tried to talk. 'Why?'

'You've got a concussion,' Caldera said. 'Don't move your head around. We'll get a life mage to look at you.'

I would have laughed if I could. *I'll get healed before I'm executed. How nice.*

Caldera stayed squatting in front of me. All around, the

search continued. 'Who was it?' I said, not opening my eyes.

'Who was what?'

'Who signed the death warrant this time?'

'There's no death warrant.'

I cracked my eyes open. Caldera was looking at me eye to eye. 'What there is,' Caldera said, 'is an indictment. For you to be held for questioning.'

'Levistus finally got his four votes?'

Caldera looked at me with something like pity. 'It wasn't four. It was seven.'

The last struggling hopes within me died. I wanted to believe that Caldera was lying, but I'd worked with her long enough to know she wasn't. 'What's the charge?'

'The charge is,' Caldera said, 'that you are responsible for the San Vittore attack. Eighteen counts of murder, three counts of treason and one count of assisting in the escape of a mage prisoner. Plus assault, grievous harm and destruction of Council property, but we can probably put that aside for now.'

I closed my eyes and rested my head against the wall. It was what I'd expected. Honestly, it was what I'd been expecting for a long time.

'Going to deny it?' Caldera said.

'Is there any point?'

'Could be. Because you didn't actually do most of that stuff. Did you?'

I opened my eyes to look at Caldera. 'You think I'm innocent now?'

'Oh, you're guilty of some of it,' Caldera said. 'But the murders and the prisoner escape? We both know who did that.'

I was silent. 'You can stop lying, Alex,' Caldera said. 'We know what really happened.'

'Because of you,' I said. 'Right? You were the one to figure it out.'

Caldera just looked at me.

'How?'

'I told you,' Caldera said. 'I know a bullshit story when I hear one. I knew you were lying at the inquest. Just didn't know why.'

'And so you put Sonder on it.'

'Don't blame this one on Sonder,' Caldera said. 'He tried to duck out of it. I had to call in favours and go over his head. And in the meantime, I kept digging. Tried to figure out what really happened in San Vittore. I've been working that case for months on my own time. And I didn't find shit. You know why?'

I wasn't in the mood for this. 'No.'

'I was looking for the wrong thing,' Caldera said. 'For evidence of you colluding with Morden or Drakh, or some crime you'd done at the scene, or some back-room deal you didn't want to come out. Came up empty every time, and I couldn't figure out why. What was so important to you that you'd throw out all that smoke?'

I was silent.

'That day in the courtroom, I was about ready to give it up,' Caldera said. 'And then I remembered that there was one thing I hadn't looked into. I'd checked everything about you, but I hadn't checked the person you went in with. And when I started thinking about that, I remembered what happened a few years ago, back before you became an auxiliary. When she got snatched by those Dark apprentices, you didn't just look into it, did you? You chased them blind right into a shadow realm. And that made me wonder – maybe you weren't doing this for yourself after all. Maybe you were protecting someone.'

'Well, you figured it all out,' I said. I couldn't keep the bitterness out of my voice. 'You won, I lost, you proved you're smarter than me. Is that what you want to hear?'

'I'll make you a deal,' Caldera said. 'You become a sanctioned witness, you waive your rights and agree to give a verified confession, I'll make your sentence as lenient as I can. You still have a few friends on the Council. I'll even testify myself. I figure I owe you that much.'

'That's your deal?'

'Best you're going to get.'

I looked away.

'Alex,' Caldera said. 'Let's get real, okay? They're getting your confession. Either you give it up voluntarily, or the mind mages pull it out of your head.'

'Now who's talking bullshit?' I said. 'There's not going to be any lenient sentence. Levistus and Sal Sarque have been wanting this for years. There's only one sentence they're going to sign off on.'

'You knew the game when you sat down to play.'

'A game?' Suddenly I was furious. '*Fuck* you. This was only a game for *you*. For you this was about your job and your ego. For me it was life and death.'

Caldera shrugged.

'Where's Anne?'

'She's not your concern any more.'

'I want to see her.'

'Yeah, that's not going to happen.' Caldera looked at me. 'That offer of leniency? Doesn't include her.'

I swallowed. My throat was suddenly dry. 'What's going to happen to her?'

'You know what she did.'

'It won't happen again.' I hated how weak my words sounded, but I had to try. 'She can control it now.'

'That's not your choice to make.'

'She was possessed, she wasn't the one making the decisions. You have to know that.'

'Doesn't matter.'

'You can't just kill her!'

'That adept your team ran into in that Devon facility was possessed by a jinn too,' Caldera said. 'What did you do to him?'

We killed him. I couldn't say that out loud. 'That's different.'

'Alex, she killed eighteen people,' Caldera said. 'And those are just the ones we know about. I know she wasn't in control of her own actions. I know this is the latest piece of shitty luck in what's been a pretty shitty life. But the law says she has to go, and the law's right. She's a danger to everyone else.'

'If it means losing her, I don't care about everyone else.'

Caldera raised her eyebrows. 'You really mean that?'

I didn't answer. Caldera rose and walked away.

The men around us were still working. Some of them were starting to pack Arachne's clothing and gear away into boxes. It was the same treatment we'd given the facility in Devon. It felt a lot different having it happen to a place I'd thought of as home. I tried to think of something I could do and came up blank.

I didn't have long to wait. Caldera came back and hauled me to my feet. 'Up.'

'Where are we going?'

It was a pretty pointless question and Caldera didn't bother to answer. She just put an arm through mine and dragged me.

I craned my neck, trying to ignore the pain in my head. There were various Keepers and security men around. Few were ones I knew, and the ones I did know were all ones I recognised for the wrong reasons. They'd probably gone out of their way to pick Keepers who didn't like me. But it was Anne I was really looking for.

Then I saw her, and stopped dead. Or would have if it had been up to me. Caldera dragged me along. 'What the hell?' I said.

'Keep walking, Alex.'

Anne was being led out from one of the back rooms, and she was so heavily restrained that I could barely tell it was her. A hood covered her entire head, her arms were bound behind her in a single sleeve and her ankles were linked by a chain so she was forced to take short shuffling steps. A pair of security men directed her with rods fixed to a collar around her neck. Two more mages and four more security men formed a perimeter around her, watching with a wary eye.

'Why are you treating her like that?' I demanded.

'Because she's dangerous enough to need it,' Caldera said. She hadn't slowed down, and now she pushed me forward into the tunnel leading out. I craned my neck to try to see Anne, but I'd already lost sight of her.

'She wasn't threatening any of you! The only reason she even—'

'Take it up with HQ.'

Caldera marched me up the tunnel. I tried to reach out

to Anne, talk to her, but my dreamstone was gone. Caldera kept me moving, not letting me hang back to let the others catch up.

The difference between how Anne and I were being treated said a lot about how much of a threat they thought I was, and the bitter part was that they were right. Right now, there was nothing at all I could do to stop Caldera from taking me away. Once we got to the surface and away from the cave's wards, they'd take us through a gate, probably to San Vittore or somewhere equally bad. Once they did, I was finished. I'd have no chance of escape. I'd never see Anne again either. And there was nothing I could do about it.

Caldera led me out into Hampstead Heath. It was night and the heath was quiet, the lights of Highgate glinting from across the ponds, the park itself dark and still. The air was still warm from the evening, and trees were black silhouettes against the sky.

A Keeper was waiting for us at the entrance. His name was Avenor; I'd never liked him much, and from the way he ignored me and addressed Caldera, he didn't seem very cut up about my current status. 'Diviner's pulled out,' he told Caldera. 'Last forecast was that everything's quiet.'

'We clear for a gate?' Caldera asked.

'Got some civilians in the AO. We'll have them gone in a couple of minutes.'

Caldera nodded and pulled me up the valley and out into the woods.

Once we were twenty feet or so from the ravine, Caldera stopped and we waited in silence. The trees stood around us, just faintly visible in the reflected light from the clouds above. I tried to think of something I could do but Caldera was keeping my arm locked in hers, and her grip was like iron. My head was still spinning and my leg hurt like hell. Even without the handcuffs, I knew I'd have no chance against her, but I had to do something. I looked ahead, searching for something, some kind of edge . . .

I went still.

'Sergeant?' Avenor said from near the ravine. 'We clear?'

Caldera looked over at him, waiting. Avenor stood for a moment, tapping his foot, then put a hand to one ear, talking into his communicator. 'Sergeant Barnes. Please confirm that the civilians have been removed from the area and we're clear for gate. Over.'

A few seconds passed. 'What's keeping him?' Caldera said.

'No answer.' I couldn't make out Avenor's expression, but he sounded irritated. 'This is what happens when you count on normals.'

From the ravine, I heard the scrape of footsteps and I knew Anne was being brought up. Caldera sighed and spoke into her own focus. 'Keeper Caldera to perimeter team. Need a report on those civilians, over.'

Seconds ticked by and I felt Caldera frown. The security men at the front of Anne's detail climbed up out of the ravine, followed by the two men holding her collar poles. I saw Anne appear in the darkness, looking blindly from left to right. 'Perimeter team, report in now,' Caldera said.

'You might want to duck,' I said quietly.

Caldera started to turn.

A bolt of black energy hit Caldera in the chest. Her eyes went wide but she didn't let go of my arm, and as she fell she dragged me down with her. As I went down, I caught a split-second glimpse of a green ray lancing out of the dark, striking one of the men holding Anne's collar; he arched his back to scream and was gone in a flash of dust.

Caldera and I hit the ground, pain jolting through my head and leg. Shouts echoed through the night; there was the muzzle flash and chatter of automatic weapon fire, three-round bursts going *ratatat*, *ratatat*. A fireball burst next to us with a wash of hot air, lighting up the Council troops in hellish red. Caldera rolled, taking cover behind a tree. 'Keeper Caldera to all units, we're under attack at the cave entrance! Enemy force with battle mages. Reinforce immediately, over!'

Caldera had lost her grip on me when she fell and I'd taken the opportunity to duck away. She came up to one knee, looking around; her gaze fell upon me. 'Alex!' Caldera hissed. 'Get here! Now!'

I crouched behind a tree and looked back at her silently. Caldera's expression darkened. She rose to her feet and stepped towards me.

The night ahead of us went black in an oval-shaped pattern of space magic, masked and opaque. Caldera reacted instantly, moving to attack. A mage jumped through and walked right into Caldera's punch. He got up a shield but the impact threw him twenty feet into the trees.

Caldera held her ground, blocking the gateway. A muzzle flash strobed from somewhere in the darkness and bullets ricocheted from her skin. 'This is Keeper Caldera!' Caldera snapped into her comm. 'I repeat, we are under—'

A black-and-green shape came out of the gateway, tall and slim and moving fast. Caldera struck and the figure slid aside; it lashed out and Caldera staggered and fell back. Then I felt the signature of air magic from above, spells lancing down.

I pressed myself against the tree, but the attacks hadn't been aimed at me. I felt blades of air go whistling into the ravine and heard a man scream. Lightning flashed and in its strobe I saw more men running at me.

I hesitated an instant, weighing my options, then held my ground. Two men ran past with barely a glance; the third grabbed me and started dragging me back towards the gate. Shouts and gunfire sounded from all around us, bullets and spells flying back and forth in the darkness.

We'd made it all the way back to the gate when I caught a glimpse of Caldera. She was off to the right, engaged in a furious battle against two enemies at once; she was hurt but still upright, defensive spells a glowing halo to my magesight, and her eyes fell on me. I saw her expression twist in anger and she lifted a hand, aiming an attack, then a deathbolt slammed into her and knocked her off-balance and before she could recover, the man with me shoved me through.

I staggered through into artificial light. I was in a wide square room, the floor concrete, rusted metal hanging down from above. Looking around, I saw half a dozen men. One was focusing on the gateway; all were dressed in dark clothing and masks; several were watching me. None spoke.

'Uh,' I said. I wasn't sensing any immediate threat, but I was getting a bad feeling about this. 'Hi.'

The men watched silently. Seconds ticked away. I knew that on the other side of the gate, a battle must be raging, but there was no sound. I looked to see what the men's reactions would be if I tried to leave, whether through the gate or out of the room. Not good.

A new figure stepped through the gate and as it did, the futures changed. Suddenly there was danger, along with all kinds of chaotic outcomes, branching and multiplying from the figure walking towards me. It was hard to catch any details, but I tried to focus on him . . . her? . . . yes, her . . . and at least figure out who she . . .

Uh-oh.

The woman reached up and did something to her face. The spell masking her face dissolved, revealing another mask. It was a black silk domino, with short blonde hair hanging behind it. The eyes behind the eyeholes were blue, but I didn't need to look at them. I knew who it was.

'Hey,' one of the other men said. 'We aren't—'

'Shut up,' Rachel said as she smiled at me. It wasn't a nice smile. 'Hello, Alex.'

I didn't reply. My divination has never worked well on Rachel – she's too impulsive and too crazy – but somehow I was sure that anything I did say had the potential to go very, very badly.

'You have no idea how long I've been looking forward to this,' Rachel said. 'I'd love to tell you what's going to happen to you, but I really don't want to deal with you trying to escape. So . . .' She walked forward, taking something out from a pocket.

There was nowhere to run and no point trying. I stood my ground, staring back at Rachel. She walked up to me and pressed something to my neck, and for a second time the world went black.

I drifted through darkness. Time passed.

Gradually I woke. It was a gentler process this time. No pain or nausea, just a slow, gradual transition from sleep to consciousness. Bit by bit, I became aware that I was lying on a bed on my side, and that I was alone. I opened my eyes.

I was in a small bedroom. The bed was comfortable, with a wooden headboard, and an armchair sat against the far side of the room. Two windows were set into the wall, both covered with translucent curtains and radiating magic. There was a single door.

Experimentally I tried to move. Nothing stopped me; the handcuffs were gone. Touching my head, I realised that my injuries were too. My head wasn't painful and neither was the rest of me: it was as if I'd never been hurt at all.

I swung my legs off the bed and sat up, then stood, testing my weight on the injured leg. There was no pain or stiffness; whoever had healed me had done a very good job. Rising and walking to the window, I drew back the curtains to reveal a view out onto a winter landscape. Snow covered the grass beyond the window and the trees further back, and more snow was falling softly from a grey sky. The windows were treated with spells to ward off heat, as well as anyone trying to break through. It was all very cosy.

I didn't feel cosy. I felt horribly vulnerable and exposed. Despite the comfort of the setting, all my instincts were telling me that my position was very, very bad.

I was in some kind of safe house or fortress, probably within a shadow realm. There was about a ninety-five per cent chance that it was owned either by Richard, or by another member of his cabal. The fact that I'd been healed and left to wake up in comfort was positive; the fact that the door was locked and alarmed was not. Taken together, it looked as though I was about to be offered some kind of deal, probably the kind that carried very bad consequences if I said no.

I paced up and down. Too many things had happened too fast, and I was still feeling disorientated, like a boxer who'd taken too many shots to the head. The Council had found out about Anne. Arachne was gone. I was a prisoner, and probably Anne was too. Any one of those things was really, really bad, and I didn't know how to fix any of them. Out of the three, Arachne being gone was probably the most survivable. I didn't know how the dragon had taken her away, or where she'd been transported to, but she was alive, and probably safe. Which was more than could be said of us.

The Council finding out about Anne was a disaster. Both of us were probably already outlaws. The last time this had happened, we'd been saved at the last minute by an unasked-for favour from Morden. I didn't think we could count on that happening again. What we had done this time was much worse, and the Council wasn't going to forgive us, not ever. They were going to hunt us to the ends of the earth.

Of course, depending on the next couple of hours, the Council hunting us could be the least of our problems.

I sensed movement in the futures and steeled myself, turning to face the door. *Here it comes.*

The handle turned. Richard Drakh stepped through and shut the door behind him.

You'd never guess to look at him that Richard is one of the most powerful and feared mages in the British Isles. He has brown hair, dark eyes, a neutral sort of face with no distinguishing marks and dresses in such a way as to look as nondescript as possible. It's quite deliberate: Richard can easily catch people's attention or intimidate them, but he deliberately chooses to fly under the radar. Until he suddenly doesn't.

Richard scares me more than anyone I've ever met. It's not because he's particularly cruel or sadistic – as far as that goes, Vihaela has him beaten on both counts – and he doesn't have the invulnerability or connections of someone like Levistus. What frightens me about Richard is something much simpler. For most of my life, I've survived in a world of enemies bigger and stronger than me by being smarter than them. Richard is the one person I've never been able to outsmart.

'Alex,' Richard said. His voice was just as I remembered it, deep and commanding. 'Sit.'

I did as I was told. When I'd met Richard a few years ago, he'd been patient, allowing me to set the tone of the conversation. This time was going to be different.

Richard sat in the armchair and clasped his hands. 'I think it is time for you to learn exactly what has been going on.'

I managed to keep my voice steady. 'I would appreciate that.'

Richard nodded. 'Here is what will happen. I will talk, and you will listen. No comments or questions; you will have that opportunity later. Once you understand your position, I will ask you a question. Your answer to that question will have immediate and far-reaching consequences. As such, I recommend you pay close attention. Do you understand?'

My mouth was dry enough that I didn't trust myself to speak. I nodded.

'Good,' Richard said. 'I have been aware for many years that to fulfil my long-term plans, I would need additional resources. As you know, that decision eventually led me to the jinn, which in turn led me to the question of how to best harness their capabilities. I will not go into detail as to the research I conducted, nor the numerous dead ends. What matters is that after various failures, I decided that the crucial variable was the identity of the subject. As you are aware, jinn require a bearer – preferably a human – to utilise their wishes. The subject functions as a lens. If the lens is imperfect, the great majority of the jinn's power is wasted. The more powerful the jinn, the greater the requirements on the bearer. And the jinn I was interested in was the most powerful of all.

'The requirements in question were specific. The subject had to be a powerful mage, possessed of both strength and skill. They had to be empathic, capable of partnering with the jinn in an emotional link. And they had to be strong-willed and ruthless. As you would expect, the last two requirements caused the greatest difficulty. Finding someone who satisfied one was easy; finding one who satisfied both was all but impossible. Until I came across an almost perfect subject.'

I felt cold. I knew where this was going.

'I was interested to learn that you and she had developed a relationship,' Richard said. 'I doubt it was a coincidence. I suspect rather it was a case of assortative matching. You, after all, shared some of those traits too. Once I was prepared, I approached the two of you in Sagash's shadow realm.

'I honestly do not think that either you or Anne fully understand just how much easier your lives would have been if you had accepted that offer four years ago. At a conservative guess, it would have deterred somewhere around eighty per cent of your current enemies. You certainly wouldn't have had to deal with that death sentence, nor the constant assassination attempts, and Anne's bond with the jinn would have been made safely and under controlled conditions. But I told you at the time that it was a free choice, and I meant it. When you turned me down, I withdrew, though not without misgivings. I had no intention of allowing Anne to die, whether at the hands of Sagash and Crystal or anyone else.

'However, I watched the two of you together, something occurred to me. I'd noticed your protective manner towards your companion, and I remembered how the fate of that girl, Katherine, had been such a sticking point for you all those years ago. I could not protect Anne directly without raising suspicion – but you could. And so I decided, on that day, that you would be my agent in this matter. You would protect Anne in my stead, and because you did so of your own volition, you would be a far more motivated guardian than any mercenary.

'Of course, while you were protecting Anne, someone needed to be protecting *you*. That someone was me.' Richard smiled slightly. 'I've been your guardian angel, Alex, though you may not appreciate it. On at least three occasions that you know of, and at least two that you do not, I've intervened to keep you alive. I'm sure you must be aware of it to some extent. You're brave and resourceful, but do you really think that you would have survived this long on your own? Why do you think Morden went out on a limb to shield you? But anything you owed, you have more than repaid. Over and over again, you proved that you were the right choice. Sagash's shadow realm, the pursuit following your death sentence, the Vault, those attacks on Anne's home . . . even when those Crusader assassins abducted her two years ago. In that matter,

I admit, I was in error. I'd considered the possibility of their moving against her, but I simply did not believe that they could be so stupid. But every time, when it most counted, you were there.

'Needless to say, I was never going to allow you or Anne to be executed by the Council. Once I learned that they were moving against you at Arachne's lair, I prepared a response. We waited for them to expose themselves by bringing you outside the cave, then struck. I was sorry to hear of Arachne's departure; I always found her a fascinating conversationalist. But to answer the question that is no doubt foremost in your thoughts, yes, Anne is safe. We extracted her along with you, and she is resting in this very building. You'll have the opportunity to see her shortly.'

I wanted to see her sooner, but I held my tongue. Knowing that she was here made me feel a little better, but only a little. I was still waiting for the other shoe to drop.

'Which brings us to Anne and her current situation,' Richard said. 'Quite simply, I need Anne as a host for the jinn. In many ways, she is perfectly prepared for the role. She's honed her magical skills and power, and she has hosted it in the past. Their relationship has grown to the point where I believe she could fully utilise the jinn's power. And believe me, that power is vast. The jinn that was bound within that ring is a marid, the sultan of all of the jinn in the waning days of their empire, and it was its binding by the master mage Suleiman that ended the war. It is one of the most powerful of its race ever to exist. However, without a human lens, that power is useless. Each time that Anne has called upon the jinn, the strength of their bond has grown, and its ability to act through her has increased. If she calls upon it once more, their connection will be complete. Its full power will be at her disposal.

'Which brings us to our problem. Currently, Anne is not willing to cooperate. You can see how this presents an issue. As you know, I prefer willing servants, but I have spent considerable resources on bringing Anne to this position, and my patience has limits. She *will* take up her place as host to the jinn. The only question is how.

'I can, of course, employ force. I can threaten Anne, or use mind magic to control her actions directly. However, both of these approaches come with undesirable side effects. I believe that to reach her full potential, Anne must complete her contract with the jinn of her own volition. And I believe the key to doing so lies with you.'

I blinked at that.

'I see you're confused,' Richard said. 'A blind spot, perhaps? Well, I believe it is important that you understand. Because this ties in very much with you. Have you considered why you are in this position now? Not here in this room, but your overall situation. If I released you right now, dropped you into the middle of London, how long do you think you would last before the Council picked you up? A week? Less? You are, right at this moment, one short step below me and Morden on the Council's most wanted list. They're sending out bulletins as we speak, and come tomorrow, you will be unable to set foot in any city in Britain without drawing hunters. So I think you should take a moment to consider just how you have managed to sabotage your life and professional career so thoroughly.

'Your life has reached this point of disaster because of the choices you have made, and the choices you have made have stemmed from the type of person you have tried to be. You have attempted to be, for want of a better phrase, a "nice guy". Compassionate, loyal, a protector of the weak, et cetera. I won't address the question of how you can view yourself in this manner while having killed more people in your career than most Dark mages do in their entire lives. What matters is that nearly all of your worst decisions have directly stemmed from being too nice – or, to be more accurate, being insufficiently ruthless. Your attempted betrayal as my apprentice. Your alienation of Levistus. Your failed attempts to protect Anne from crimes for which she is self-evidently guilty. Take Levistus, since that is the most blatant. As I understand it, during the White Rose affair, Levistus specifically warned you of what the consequences would be if you acted against his interests. You ignored him, and he quite predictably responded by having you sentenced to death. You survived only due to my intervention. Let me be very clear, Alex: both your sentence and the ensuing pursuit were entirely your own fault. Levistus was more powerful than you, and you could not afford to make an enemy of him, yet you did. You then compounded your error by failing to strengthen your own position. All because you were unwilling to make the necessary sacrifices.

'Now take your current situation with Anne. Under Light laws, the Council are fully entitled to sentence you and Anne to death. A Light mage would say that you have broken the Concord and must face the penalty. A Dark mage would point out that the real issue is that the Council have the ability to enforce their decisions on you and Anne, while you do not have any ability to enforce your will on them in return. A Dark mage in such a position would have taken action to ensure that any attack by the Council would be defeated. By refusing to follow either the Light path or the Dark, you have failed at both. And once again, I am the one cleaning up your mistakes.'

Richard leant forward, resting his elbows on his knees. 'Listen to me, Alex. Your way of doing things does not work. Being nice does not work. The world is not ruled by those who are nice. The world is ruled by those who understand power and how to use it. That you are sitting here is proof of this. You no longer have the luxury of depending on me to bail you out of trouble. Except in your case the problem goes further, because this is not about you. It is about Anne.

'Anne, like you, still believes that one should be nice. In her case, however, much of the strength of that belief stems from her relationship with you. If you had not been there that day in Sagash's shadow realm, she would have accepted my offer. But you were there, and you advised her against it, and she listened, because she trusts you.

'And that brings us to the present. I need Anne to host the jinn. I cannot persuade her to do so voluntarily. Neither can Morden, nor Vihaela, nor anyone else. Except you. And that is why you are here. Because for better or for worse, you are the one person able to convince her to take this action of her own free will. So we come to the point of decision. Will you cooperate, or not?'

I looked at Richard. Richard looked back at me.

'You want me to convince Anne to host the jinn,' I said.

'I want you to *make* Anne host the jinn. The precise method, I leave to you.'

'She's not going to do something like that because I ask her.'

'Alex, you're not inviting her on a date. I'm not talking about *asking* her. Anne has been tempted by the jinn's power many times, and at present she is resisting that temptation, and the keystone of that resistance is her relationship with you. I want you to destroy that keystone. Please do not insult my intelligence by asking how. You are more than capable of solving that problem yourself.'

'If Anne calls on that jinn again, she won't be able to get it out,' I said. 'She'll lose herself.'

'To an extent.'

'There's no way she'd do that willingly. You're asking me to force her.'

'Yes.'

I took a deep breath. 'What'll happen to her?'

'She will fight on the front lines in the war to overthrow the Light Council,' Richard said. 'I can't promise she'll be entirely safe, but I fully expect her to survive. Actually, with that jinn, she'll be considerably safer than she has been with you. You will have access to her as long as it does not interfere with her duties. Provided she wants to see you, of course. Depending on the means you use to convince her, you may find it wise to allow a cooling-off period before attempting to resume your relationship. But I think she will come to understand the necessity of your actions given time.'

'Except that it won't be her,' I said quietly. 'Will it? She'll be some combination of your slave and the jinn's puppet.'

Richard held out his hands, palms upwards, in an equivocal gesture.

'What happens to her afterwards?'

'I have no objection to making some quality of life efforts on her behalf. However, the job comes first.'

I took a breath. 'Was this what you did to Rachel?'

Richard raised an eyebrow.

'That thing inside her head,' I said. I'd caught a glimpse of it once, a long time ago, while visiting Rachel's Elsewhere. Back then, I hadn't understood what it was, but all of a sudden, it made sense. 'It's a jinn, isn't it? Were you planning this, right from the start? Was she the prototype?'

'More accurately, it was a possibility I was considering,' Richard said. 'I had taken certain steps to facilitate the process, but before I could take action, Rachel linked with a jinn on her own. The results were . . . mixed, but she did provide some valuable insights about the necessary conditions in the forging of a human–jinn bond.'

'You've got one too, haven't you?' I said. 'That was what you were using in the fighting in the Vault.'

'You're stalling, Alex.'

I was running out of cards to play. 'You know the jinn isn't going to follow your orders,' I said. 'It hates humans. All of them.'

'I will take care of the jinn.'

'How are—?'

'That is not your concern. Enough questions.'

'One more question,' I said. 'What if I say no?'

'I'm afraid you don't quite understand,' Richard said. 'You *are* going to help me. Your choice is whether to do so willingly. I don't often give people second chances. I gave you two, and you turned them both down. Understand clearly that this is your last. Should you reject this final offer, there will be no more reprieves. I will take the necessary steps to gain what I need without your cooperation. You will not enjoy the experience.

'And so you come to the point of decision. Assist me, and bring Anne under my control. Or refuse, and suffer the consequences. There is no third option. Choose.'

I found myself remembering that conversation with Dark Anne in Elsewhere. She'd told me that I'd never convinced anyone with my words, that no one ever listened when I talked about what I believed in. Maybe she'd been so vehement because Anne was one of the few people who *had* listened. And that was why Richard wanted to use me now. To manipulate her, trick her or break her the way I'd done with my enemies in the past.

A terrible weariness seeped through me. I knew where this was going, and I knew the answer I was going to give. It wasn't even a choice. I wanted so badly to drag this out, buy a few more moments, and I knew it was hopeless. The edge of the cliff was getting nearer, and all I could think of was digging my heels in to slow down the inevitable.

I opened my mouth, took a deep breath. Saying the next word was one of the hardest things I'd ever done. 'No.'

Silence. I kept my eyes down at the floor.

'I see,' Richard said.

'Sorry to disappoint you.' I couldn't bring myself to meet Richard's gaze; all I could do was put some bitterness into my words. 'I guess I haven't exactly turned out to be what you wanted in an apprentice.'

'I am disappointed, yes.' Richard's voice was calm, and all of a sudden I felt sure that he'd known what my answer was going to be, known it before I said it. 'Why?'

'Why what?'

'Why refuse? You must know what the consequences will be. Why choose a course so obviously self-destructive?'

I could have lied, tried to spin a story, but if this was

going to be the end, I wanted to tell the truth. 'I've made a lot of mistakes.' I managed to look up. Richard was watching me, apparently curious. 'You're right, it is my fault that I'm here. I've made bad decisions and I've done a lot of things I'm not happy about. But there's one thing I've never done, and that's betray a friend. What you want me to do to Anne . . . it'd be taking everything I love, everything that matters to me, and breaking it. I won't do it.'

Richard looked at me, and I met his gaze. The fear was still there, but now, at the end, there was an odd sense of freedom. I didn't have to play games any more.

'That is unfortunate,' Richard said at last. He rose to his feet, straightened his jacket, then nodded to me. 'Goodbye, Alex.' He walked out and the door closed behind him. There was something final about the sound.

7

I had a brief wait before the door opened again. Long enough to see who was coming, and to prepare for the worst.

A woman walked in and shut the door behind her. 'Hello, Verus,' she said pleasantly. She was a little taller than average, with sculpted features and gold hair that fell around her shoulders. She looked maybe thirty, though I knew she was at least ten years older. She wore an expensive-looking suit, and her eyes were cold.

Cold was a good word to describe Crystal. When I'd first run into her, she'd been in charge of an apprentice tournament at Fountain Reach. I later found out that she'd been responsible for sending several of those apprentices – and who knows how many others – to be slaughtered in a blood ritual. I'd never seen any sign that she felt the slightest remorse for what she'd done. Crystal was a mind mage, a domination specialist, and her presence here meant nothing good.

I looked back for a moment before answering. 'Anne should have killed you back in Sagash's castle.'

'Anne is stupid.'

'So what did Richard promise you?' I said. 'Power?'

'Of a sort,' Crystal said. She pulled back a sleeve of her jacket to reveal a bracelet. 'I imagine you recognise this.'

'Yeah,' I said. The bracelet was thick, as long as Crystal's thumb, and made of age-darkened silver. Spiralling patterns were carved on it, and a pink-purple stone was set into the centre. Unlike some of the imbued items on the Council's list, it didn't have a name, but its description had mentioned that it acted as an amplifier for certain applications of mind magic.

'Pretty, isn't it?' Crystal said. She held it up, the stone's colour shifting as it caught and reflected the light. 'I always had my eye on this one back when I was a Light mage. The Council wouldn't let me have it. It would have made things so much easier if they had. Do you know what it does?'

I looked at her in silence.

'Domination has so many drawbacks,' Crystal said. 'You can control the target, even make them take complex actions, but you have to direct them for even the smallest things. It makes their behaviour clumsy. Stilted. You might fool a stranger, but not someone who knows the target well. This item allows you to overcome that limitation. It smooths the control and taps their memories to copy incidental details. You choose the behaviour; they carry it out.'

I thought about attacking Crystal, going for the throat. With surprise and a little time, I might be able to break her neck. But I wouldn't have surprise – she was very much ready for me – and there were guards outside ready to burst in.

'You've sabotaged my plans twice now, Alex,' Crystal said. 'Once at Fountain Reach, once in Sagash's shadow realm. I could have retired by now. Gone somewhere nice and relaxing. But you took all that away.'

'I guess we don't always get what we want.'

'Oh, I think I'm going to do quite well out of this,' Crystal said. 'If Drakh succeeds in his plan – and I have good reason to believe he will – I'll have all the resources of the Council to plunder. That's quite a step up, don't you think? But let's get down to business. When Drakh told us what he wanted to achieve with Anne, Vihaela told him that she could do it in five minutes by torturing you while Anne watched. Have you ever seen Vihaela work? She's very good. Obviously that kind of manipulation wouldn't influence anyone sensible, but as I said, Anne's stupid. And she actually cares for you for some reason.' Crystal shrugged. 'I imagine it wouldn't take long before Anne called up that jinn to make it stop. But Drakh chose my plan instead. Do you want to know why?'

I didn't answer.

'Drakh thought it was more elegant,' Crystal said. 'And it is, but that wasn't why I picked it. I picked it because this way is going to hurt you so much more.' Crystal straightened. 'I've been looking forward to this for a very long time.'

Mental pressure crushed down on me like a vice. I'd been ready for it and tried to push back Crystal's attack, but it felt like trying to push back a wave. There was no point of leverage.

I braced myself, holding my defences. It felt like holding up a circular wall, with my thoughts and self protected at the centre. But the pressure from Crystal didn't stop; it just kept mounting and mounting. There was no way for me to strike back. At least not mentally—

I took a step forward, but Crystal was already speaking a command word. A wall of force flared up between the two of us and I came to a halt, staring at her. She was only a few feet away, but it might as well have been a mile. Holding Crystal off wasn't getting any easier; it was getting harder. Already I was getting tired, and as I looked at Crystal I felt fear. She was smiling, and didn't look tired at all.

'That wall should last a few minutes,' Crystal said. 'Probably enough for me to finish the job. But if I can't, what does it matter? You can't beat me in psychic combat; all you can do is hold me off. And there's no one coming to help.'

I'd been looking frantically through the futures, trying to find one where I won. There wasn't one. In every future I could see, Crystal overwhelmed me. The only variable was how long it took. And even as I watched, the numbers were shrinking. There was no rescue coming, no reprieve that I could reach if I held out. Before long, the futures in which Crystal hadn't won would dwindle to dozens, then a handful, then three, then one, then zero.

Crystal was going to take control of me.

I was terrified of what that would mean. I fought back desperately.

It wasn't enough.

Ten minutes later, I exited the room, closed the door behind me and walked out past the guards and down the corridor. Reaching the end, I turned left. My movements were steady and normal.

Or that was what someone would have seen. The truth was, it wasn't me at all. The steps I took, the movements I made, even where I focused my eyes, were all under Crystal's control, while I watched helplessly. It was like being a passenger in the back of a car with a screen between me and the front seats. I could see and hear, but I was just a spectator. It was a terrifying feeling, like falling through a black void. Through my eyes, I watched my body go up a flight of stairs, turn into another corridor, then open a door.

The room inside was a bedroom, and Anne jumped up from where she'd been sitting on the bed. Her restraints were gone; her clothes had taken some damage, but she looked in perfect health and her eyes lit up as she saw me. 'Alex!'

I wanted to scream at Anne, to warn her. Instead I watched helplessly as my body took her in its arms. 'It's fine,' I heard myself say. 'I'm okay.'

Anne held me tightly for a moment, then pulled back to look at me, worry visible on her face. 'I couldn't tell where you were. Vihaela was here and she told me that Richard was talking to you. What happened?'

My head shook. 'It doesn't matter. Are you all right?'

'I'm fine. They just wanted to . . .' Anne trailed off and looked me up and down, frowning slightly. 'Are you sure you're okay?'

My heart leapt. *No! I'm not! Anne, it's not me. You can tell that, can't you?*

'I'm fine,' my voice said. 'Why? What happened?'

Anne hesitated and for a moment I felt hope, then she shook her head. 'We can talk about it afterwards.'

My heart sank. Anne had been scanning me with her lifesight. It's a perfect tool for diagnosing illness or injury, but it's useless against mind magic, and right now it was telling Anne that there was nothing wrong with me. 'Talk about what?' Crystal said with my voice.

'It doesn't matter,' Anne said. 'How did you get them to let you in here? What does Richard want?'

'He wants us to cooperate with him.' My body walked

past Anne, sat down on the bed facing her. 'I don't think we can get away with turning them down this time.'

Anne looked unhappy but not surprised. 'When Vihaela started talking to me, I thought that was the deal she was going to offer, or something worse. Though she didn't . . .'

'Didn't what?'

'Never mind.'

'I do mind.' My body leant forward, towards Anne. 'Something's bothering you. What's wrong?'

'She was just trying to stir things up. It doesn't matter.'

'How? What did she say?'

Anne hesitated, glanced around at the door. 'Should we be talking about this here?'

'Richard said he'd give us time to talk privately.'

'That was what Vihaela said too,' Anne said. 'Before . . .'

'Before what? Tell me.'

Anne! It's not me! Can't you tell? Crystal's imitation was good, but not perfect. My voice and words were off from how the real me would have acted: I wouldn't have spoken that way, wouldn't have pushed so far. But it was close, too close. Maybe in a calmer environment, with more time, Anne might have been able to figure it out, but here . . . I tried to reach out to Anne telepathically, link to her mind, and ran into what felt like a solid wall.

'All right,' Anne said slowly. 'Is there anything you want to tell me?'

'What?'

'Anything you want to tell me,' Anne said. Her reddish eyes stayed on me.

'What kind of thing?'

Anne looked at me for a long moment, seemed about

to say something, then shook her head. 'Never mind. It can wait.'

'No, it can't.' My voice was harsh, forceful. 'I want to hear it now.'

Anne drew back slightly, frowning. 'I don't . . . All right. Back when we first met, how much did you know about Jagadev?'

The question caught me off balance. *Jagadev? Why . . .?*

'I'd never met him before,' Crystal said.

'What about after?' Anne was watching me closely now. 'Did you find out anything?'

'Nothing important.'

Anne waited. When no further answer came, she frowned. 'Do you mean—?'

'Can you get to the point?'

'All right.' Anne seemed to brace herself. 'Vihaela said . . . she said that all those deaths in my family and Vari's, they weren't accidents. They were because of Jagadev. I mean, I knew he had something against us, but I never knew exactly why. I thought it was just that we were humans, or mages, or . . . Is it true?'

'Yes.'

Anne stared at me.

'When did you find out?' Anne said when I didn't speak.

'Probably around the time I met you.'

Anne drew a breath. 'You knew all this time and you didn't tell me?'

'Did you want me to?'

'Did I—? *Yes!*'

I felt myself shrug. 'I didn't think it mattered.'

'How could you think that? These are my *parents*!'

'I suppose.'

Anne looked at me in disbelief, then stood and walked away. She stood facing the wall, her shoulders rising and falling, before turning. 'I spent years thinking about it, after my father died. When it was my mother I was too young to remember, but after . . . I kept feeling it was my fault. That I'd done something wrong. And that was why I was in that house in Canonbury instead, with them treating me like . . . But if it *was* my fault, then I deserved it anyway. But now . . . you're telling me it was Jagadev? For two years we were staying in his house, eating his food, doing what he told us. All that time, it was *him*?' Anne shook her head. 'I know I've never talked much about my family. But you had to know how much this would matter. How could you keep this a secret all this time?'

Watching Anne's expression felt like a knife twisting in my flesh. I wanted to writhe, look away, but I couldn't, because it was true. I *had* kept it a secret, because—

'Because I'm a diviner,' my voice said. 'Finding out people's secrets and using them is what I do. And I couldn't see any good way to make use of that one.'

Wait, no! That wasn't—

Anne was staring at me. 'I thought you trusted me.'

'Yeah, well, maybe you'll know better for next time. Now how about we deal with the stuff that matters?'

'This does matter—'

'No, what matters right now is getting out of this mess that *you* put us in.'

Anne had been about to answer; now she stopped. 'That I . . .?'

'Yes, you. We're here because of you. First you picked up that jinn in the Vault, then you used it to go on a rampage against a bunch of Light mages. I haven't been saying anything because I figured that maybe I could cover it up, make it work. But you managed to be so incompetent, so *stupid* as to let slip to the Keepers that it was you. And that was why they came down on our heads.'

'What? No! I didn't tell anyone! Alex, I promise, I don't know how they found out, but it wasn't—'

'Then who else was it? There were exactly four of us there, and somehow I don't think Morden and Vihaela are on speaking terms with the Council these days. That leaves you and me, and I know it wasn't me. So who do you think it was?'

'I— I don't—' Anne faltered.

'You've destroyed my *life*,' Crystal said. 'Do you know how much I've lost because of you? I was on the Light Council. I had status, a home, a position. Now I've lost it all in a few hours, and if Richard decides he doesn't need me, I'm going to be dead. Getting involved with you was the worst thing that's ever happened to me.'

Anne was crying now. The tears in her eyes were painful to watch; the hurt and betrayal in them was a hundred times worse. *Stop it!* I screamed silently at Crystal. *Okay, fine, you win! I'll do what you want! Just stop!*

Crystal didn't answer, not in words, but I could feel her emotions. Amusement, satisfaction.

'I'm sorry,' Anne said in a small voice. 'What do you want me to do?'

'There's exactly one thing you can do that'll save us,' I heard my voice say. 'Call that jinn back and use it to get us out of here.'

Fear leapt into Anne's eyes. 'No. I can't—'

'Yes, you can.'

'Alex, I *can't*. You don't know what you're asking.'

'Why not? Wasn't that why you picked up that stupid thing in the Vault? Because it was the only way out? Well, it's the only way out now. So use it for someone apart from yourself for a change.'

'I can't! If I call it back, if I call her back, I'll be gone. They're too strong now. Please, you have to—'

'I don't care!' It was a shout this time, and Anne jumped. 'This is the *only* useful thing you can do, so do it!'

Tears were streaming down Anne's cheeks. She shook her head mutely.

'You stupid bitch!' My legs moved, carrying me close to Anne, looming over her. 'How many times have I risked my life for you now? Now the one time it matters, you can't even do this?'

'I— I—'

My hand hit Anne across the face. It caught her so totally by surprise that she didn't even flinch. She went down to her hands and knees, looking up at me in disbelief.

'Do it!' my voice shouted down at her.

Anne shook her head.

My body moved like an automaton, hitting Anne again. Inside, I was screaming, fighting. Useless. I was locked out; Crystal held the controls. I wanted to fight back, to rage, to look away. I couldn't.

Anne tried to protect herself, but her movements were weak, shocked. I knocked her arm away and hit her in the face again, this time hard enough to split her lip and send her sprawling on the floor. She looked up at me with blood at the corner of her mouth and haunted, frightened eyes. It should have made me stop, would have made any decent person stop.

Crystal made me kick her. Anne fell back against the bed.

'No . . .' Anne's voice was barely coherent. 'Please . . .'

My body reached down, hauled Anne to her feet. Her eyes stared up into mine, wide and terrified. 'I hate you,' my voice said. 'I should have left you back in Fountain Reach.' I threw her away. Anne tripped over the bed, hit her head against the wall.

I stalked around the bed towards her. Anne was lying curled up on the floor, head down, her hair hanging over her face. 'Get up,' I told her, and reached down to grab her hair.

Anne's hand caught mine.

Fire flashed along my nerves, paralysing me. As I stared down, Anne looked up at me. Tears streaked her face, but her eyes were clear and alight. 'You wanted to see the jinn?' she said softly. Slowly she rose to her feet, her eyes staying locked on mine.

I felt the pit drop out of my stomach. *Oh no.*

The room seemed to darken. The lines of Anne's figure blurred and warped, black strands spreading from under her clothes. Shadows unfolded from around her, stretching from wall to wall like wings. Anne leant towards me, and all of a sudden she seemed to be the one taller, as though something was looming up behind her, looking down on me. 'Wish granted.'

White-hot agony exploded in my hand, bursting through my body. I felt Crystal's control snap and all of a sudden she was gone. I fell like a puppet with its strings cut, my head slamming into the floor. My hand was numb and pain was flashing through my body, but I was in control again. I looked up at Anne, fumbling for the words. 'Anne— I—'

The door burst open with a crash.

Anne and I turned to see the doorway filled with people. Vihaela was there, dark and predatory, her eyes fixed narrowly on Anne, and to one side was Crystal, half hidden by the wall. And at the centre was Richard. He was ignoring me, looking straight at Anne, and in one hand he was holding something that thrummed with power.

Anne looked at Richard, and an expression of utter disgust crossed her face. 'Ah, shit.'

Purple light shone from Richard's hand. Magic reached out from him and the two women to Anne; mind, life, others. Anne's eyes rolled back in her head and she dropped to the floor. The darkness around her winked out, the black strands vanishing.

'Bring her,' Richard ordered.

Vihaela walked forwards. I tried to pull myself up but there was something wrong with my hand. 'Wait, don't—'

Vihaela flicked a hand, as if shooing off a fly. Pain and nausea rolled over me and I fell. Through clouded vision, I watched as Vihaela reached down and picked Anne up without apparent effort. She turned and carried her out. From the doorway, Richard and Crystal spared me a glance before turning away. Crystal looked satisfied; Richard's expression was harder to place. Distance? Regret? Then both were gone.

I tried to pull myself to my feet but the after-effects of Vihaela's spell made me collapse. My vision greyed, and there was a roaring in my ears. Gradually it subsided. The pain didn't. *No, Anne, come back. Please . . .*

Dimly I heard the footsteps of someone else entering the room. There was a pause; the door closed, and the footsteps drew closer. Turning my head, I saw a pair of women's shoes. With difficulty I looked up.

'Hello, Alex,' Rachel said.

My eyes slid past Rachel to the door. I couldn't make myself care about her, not now. *Have to get to Anne.* I tried to pull myself to my feet.

'Ah, ah.' Rachel gave me a shove with one foot, sending me sprawling. 'Richard doesn't want you interfering with what he's going to do to your girlfriend. Not that she'd want to see you. You saw that look on her face?'

Vihaela's spell was wearing off but my hand was still numb. I couldn't feel it, and when I tried to use it to prop myself up, it didn't work.

'We watched the whole thing on camera,' Rachel said. She pointed to the corner of the room. 'Richard wanted to make sure his investment wasn't damaged. I was just there with popcorn.' She tilted her head, looking down at me, eyes bright. 'You really beat the crap out of her. I couldn't believe she just sat there and took it. She really is a doormat, isn't she? But I guess you always liked those sorts of girls. Wait, are you crying?'

I turned my head away from Rachel, blinking back the tears. 'You are!' Rachel said. 'Look at those tears! I love it when men like you do this. You act so tough, but as soon as something goes wrong, you cry like a baby.'

I'd never hated Rachel so much as in that moment. I stared at her, too filled with pain and rage to speak.

Rachel laughed. 'Oh, you're angry? What are you going to do about it? It pissed me off so much when Richard ordered me to keep you alive, but it was worth it just to see this.' She paused. 'What, nothing to say? Come on, Alex, you're supposed to be smart, right? Tell us how this was all part of your plan.'

I didn't answer.

Rachel waited, then her smile faded. 'No, you don't have anything to say, do you? You never did, not when it mattered. It was all just bullshit.' She crouched down in front of me, her expression suddenly cold. 'You want to know why this happened? Because of you. I hope you're paying attention, because I really want you to understand this. Everything that's happened, all of this, it was all your fault. Richard gave you so many chances. He took you in and you tried to betray him. He invited you back and you turned him down. And then after all that, he still gives you a last chance to play along, and you say no again. I mean, what did you think was going to happen? You thought he was going to say "oh well", and let you go? Or maybe you thought someone was going to swoop in to save you? Newsflash, Alex. Richard *has* been the one sweeping in to save you. Doesn't work so well when you piss him off too. But I guess you never thought about that, did you? You just figured you could do whatever you wanted and it'd all work out.'

'Get out of my way,' I rasped. Anne was on the other side of that door and getting further away.

'Or you'll do what?' Rachel said. 'You still don't get it, do you? Richard doesn't need you any more. You don't get to call the shots.' Rachel paused. 'He's going to enslave her, by the way. Use that focus of his and Crystal's spells to bring the jinn under his control completely. Once that happens, you can say bye-bye to your girlfriend. She's not coming back.' Rachel extended a hand. 'Unless you want to try to stop him?'

I looked at what Rachel was holding in her open palm. It was my dreamstone.

Rachel was watching me closely. 'This is yours, right?

I took it off those Council idiots. It's supposed to be a mind magic focus, isn't it? Maybe if you had it, you might be able to do something. What do you think?'

I looked at Rachel, and even through the pain, I realised what she was doing. She wanted me to try to go through her, to start a fight. Richard hadn't given her the go-ahead to kill me, and she was hoping I'd give her an excuse.

But she didn't know what the dreamstone could do, and she didn't know that I could use it without touching it. I could reach out to Anne, talk to her and—

—what? Despair filled me as I realised how useless it would be. Arachne had told me that I could use the dreamstone to step into Elsewhere, but I couldn't manage that now, not injured and with Rachel ready to disintegrate me the instant I moved.

Maybe if I weren't so beaten down I would have tried to do something myself. But instead I reached out through the dreamstone and screamed for help, for someone, anyone, to listen and to come. It was fuelled with all my desperation and pain, and I felt barriers shatter as I threw everything I had into the call.

Rachel flinched, catching herself instantly. 'What did you—?' She glanced down at the dreamstone, then back at me in sudden suspicion.

I was swaying. The combination of Crystal's mental assault, Vihaela's spell and the drain from that call had left me barely able to hold myself upright. Seconds ticked away. Rachel stared at me, and I saw my life and death balanced in her eyes.

There was a bang from somewhere below and Rachel spun. Before she'd even finished turning, something flowed under the door and coalesced in the centre of the room. It was a humanoid figure sculpted out of transparent air, like an artist's sketch drawn in vapour. To normal vision she was invisible; to my magesight she took the form of an elfin girl with slightly pointed ears and big eyes.

She was an air elemental, one that I hadn't seen in almost six years, and her name was Starbreeze.

'Hi, Alex!' Starbreeze told me.

Rachel looked at Starbreeze in recognition. 'You?' She brought up a hand, green light gathering.

Rachel is fast. Starbreeze is much faster. By the time Rachel had finished saying 'you', Starbreeze had enveloped me and turned me and my body to air. She started towards the door, turned around, reached out to touch the dreamstone in Rachel's hand, turned *that* to air as well, then as Rachel's hand came up Starbreeze shot out back under the door and out into the corridor, taking me and the dreamstone with her. *Ooh, you got one of those?* Starbreeze asked. *They're fun!*

Starbreeze, help! I need to find Anne!

Who's Anne?

There was a pulse of water magic, and the door disintegrated in a green flash. *Ooh*, Starbreeze said in interest. *Pretty.* Rachel appeared in the doorway, eyes locking onto us, and Starbreeze whisked away around the corner and down a flight of steps.

She's my friend, she's somewhere here. Please, can you find her?

Your hand's wrong, Starbreeze said in interest.

Please, you have to help. I could feel the seconds slipping away and I was desperate. *She's been taken over by a jinn—*

Starbreeze fled, zipping down the staircase and several

corridors. I saw a mage flash past, eyes wide in surprise, there and gone. *No, wait! You need to find her—*

Jinn are bad, Starbreeze said decisively.

But you could reach her!

Mmmmmm . . . I felt Starbreeze shake her head. *No.*

From above I could hear shouts and the sound of an alarm. *Starbreeze!* I shouted. *Please!*

You're hurt, Starbreeze said curiously. *Home?*

What?

Home.

Starbreeze zoomed off down the main hallway. I had an instant to see a double door approaching at terrifying speed before we hit a barrier.

It felt like being thrown through a jet engine and out the other side. Everything went white and I was falling through space.

8

I slept for a long time. I drifted between dreams and nightmares, filled with confusion and flight and danger, but they never became clear enough for me to become conscious. From time to time I would start to swim up towards wakefulness, and each time I would resist. I couldn't remember much, but I knew I didn't want to wake up. At last I couldn't stay asleep any more and slowly, reluctantly, I returned to the waking world.

You know things are bad when waking up feels worse than the nightmares. My memory came back piece by piece, and each bit made me want to run and hide. When I finally opened my eyes, I found myself staring up at the ceiling of my house in the Hollow. Birds were singing, and it was daytime outside. It was the same place I'd woken up . . .

. . . *Jesus.* Yesterday morning? Was that all it had been?

There was a rustle of movement and I turned my head to see Luna rising from a chair. Her clothes were rumpled as though from a long night, but her eyes showed no signs of sleepiness. 'You're awake? Stay there. Don't get up.'

I tried to get up. I made it about six inches before collapsing.

'I said *don't* get up.' Luna crossed the floor quickly, kneeling beside me. 'You were in really bad shape when I found you.'

'How—?' My voice was weak, and I had to draw a breath and try harder. 'How long have I been out?'

'It's Wednesday noon. You've slept a little over twelve hours.'

It was still hard to take in. 'You found me?'

Luna nodded. 'I can tell you the story, but you want anything to drink or eat? Klara said you'd be hungry.'

I was hungry, but the thought of eating made me sick. I felt terrible; my muscles were like water, and my right hand was numb. 'Tell me what happened.'

'I'd closed up at the shop.' Luna's face looked drawn and troubled. 'Vari and I were supposed to be meeting, but I'd been waiting for— Well, it doesn't matter. Two Keepers came calling, they wanted to know if I'd seen you or Anne. One of them I didn't know, but I recognised the other, nasty piece of work called Saffron. She just kept staring while the man was questioning me, and I could feel this weird pricking, like she was looking inside me. I remembered you'd said she was a mind mage, and I figured she was reading my thoughts. So I told the truth, and when they asked when I'd last seen you both, I told them it had been a couple of days. I guess she could tell I wasn't lying because they let me go, though they warned me to call them if I saw you again.

'So they left and I called Vari. He told me that he was being held on standby and they wouldn't tell him why. Except he *also* told me there were arrest warrants out for you and Anne and that they didn't seem to care too much about whether they brought you in alive or dead. I tried to get in touch with you and Anne and I couldn't, and that was when I got really worried. Tried calling Arachne and she didn't answer either, and at that point I ran out of ideas. Just stayed in the flat, waiting for someone to call and getting more and more on edge.

'I was starting to wonder if I should go out looking when I heard a bump on the roof. I ran out and climbed up and found you lying there. I thought I saw something flitting away – it made me think of that elemental you used to be friends with – but then I was on my own. I didn't know what was going on but I knew the Council was looking for you, so the first thing I did was use a gate stone and take you here to the Hollow. Then I got in touch with Vari. I knew I couldn't tell him anything where anyone could hear, but we've worked out a code for this stuff. He sent me a message back that said help was coming, and twenty minutes later Landis showed up with this German life mage I'd never seen before. I was a bit dubious, since, you know, Keeper, but I let him in. She's been the one taking care of you. She and Landis left again early in the morning, but she's due back soon.'

Luna paused, waiting for me to answer. When I didn't, she carried on. 'What happened? I know it's something to do with you and Anne, but no one's talking. I ducked out to check the news and the police have got a section of the heath cordoned off all around Arachne's lair.'

'They found out about Anne and the jinn.'

'I was afraid of that.' Luna looked unhappy but not surprised. 'I was hoping, but . . . Where is she?'

'She's—' I took a breath. 'She's gone. Not dead, but— She's not coming back.'

'Gone where? What happened?'

I told her. I didn't leave anything out, and Luna's expression went from unhappiness to shock to horror.

When I got to the part with Anne, my voice wavered and I had to struggle to keep talking. 'I didn't want to,' I told Luna, feeling fresh tears well up. 'I was trying to

fight, but Crystal made me keep going. I couldn't stop.'
I saw sympathy on Luna's face, and she touched my hand,
her curse pulling back to let her fingers rest on mine. 'It
was Starbreeze, like you thought,' I finished. 'She must
have carried me back to the Arcana Emporium since she
thought that was my home. Lucky you were there . . .'

'Oh no,' Luna said. 'Alex, I'm so sorry.'

I'd managed to sit up at some point in the story; now
I bowed my head. 'God, this is awful,' Luna said. 'What
can we do?'

I didn't meet Luna's eyes.

There was a ping from Luna's pocket. She glanced down,
then rose to her feet. 'It's Landis. I'll be back.'

Luna was gone for only a few minutes before returning,
and this time there were two people with her. One was a
woman I'd never met before, slim and serious-looking with
ash-blonde hair. Her eyes settled on me as she walked
through the door, weighing me up.

Landis came striding through right behind her, all long
limbs and brisk movements. 'Well, well.' Normally Landis
acts like a lunatic, but he can flip from eccentric to focused
in the blink of an eye. 'So you're the new threat to national
peace, eh? Have to admit, you don't look the part.'

'It is Verus, yes?' the woman – Klara – asked. 'May I
examine you?'

I nodded. 'Go ahead.'

Klara crouched by my side and placed a hand on my
chest, studying me dispassionately. 'Alex told me what
happened,' Luna said to Landis. 'If you want to know—'

'Not at all, my dear girl,' Landis interrupted. 'I most
definitely do not want to know. In fact, I think it's very
much in everyone's interest that I know as little as possible.'

'Isn't it your duty as a Keeper to bring me in?' I said.

'Absolutely! I woke up this morning to a bulletin announcing that you and Miss Walker were to be considered high-priority fugitives to be arrested and brought in at all costs, alive if possible, dead if not. Which is why, as I said, I have no idea whatsoever as to your whereabouts. I rather think I've spent this past hour taking lunch in the Lake District.'

I looked at Klara. 'And this is . . .?'

'Of course, where are my manners? Verus, meet Klara Lorenz. An extremely talented life mage and old acquaintance. When Variam and Luna appraised me of your circumstances, I put two and two together and concluded that Miss Walker, sadly, would not be in a position to offer her services. Very fortunately, Lady Klara was willing to make a house call.'

'For which I am also not here,' Klara said in accented English. 'I am not under the authority of your Council, but I would rather this was not official knowledge, you understand?' She leant back with a nod. 'Your injuries are not life-threatening. The previous wounds you suffered were healed before I saw you. With rest, you will recover fully. Your hand is another matter.'

With everything else that had happened, I'd forgotten about that. I pulled it out from under the duvet and looked at it. Someone had wrapped it in elastic bandages that held it steady, though I couldn't feel their touch. It didn't hurt, but I couldn't make it move.

'Your body's connection in that area has been broken,' Klara said. 'There is nothing I can do.'

I didn't understand. 'The bones?'

Klara made a frustrated noise. 'Not the bones. The *Lebens* . . . no.' She looked at Landis. *'Grundmuster?'*

Landis nodded. 'Klara is referring to a concept in common parlance among life mages. Over here, they refer to it as a body's pattern. You might think of it as a blueprint.'

'Yes,' Klara said. 'Pattern. Your right hand is missing from your body's pattern. Effectively your body believes your hand has been severed. Nerves do not function; blood flow is limited. Healing is impossible. Any damage will not be repaired.'

'Can you cure it?'

Klara shook her head. 'If I had several days to work, and had the mage who had done it with me, so that I could question her . . . then maybe. Even then I would be at the limits of my skill. Your best hope would be to find the mage that did it. Assuming they would be willing to help. It troubles me that anyone would do this. It serves no function.'

Unless you just really hate someone, I thought bleakly. 'Is there anything I can do?'

'If you cannot undo the alteration, the hand will have to be amputated,' Klara said bluntly. 'Without natural regeneration, damage to the skin and flesh will not heal. Any incision will put you at risk of blood loss and infection and, eventually, gangrene. At that point, your life will be at risk.'

It was one more blow on top of too many others. It said something about my last twenty-four hours that I didn't even really feel it. I just felt numb.

'I should go,' Klara said, rising to her feet. 'I will return in two days to check on you.'

'And I should report in before anyone in the Council

thinks to ask the wrong sorts of questions,' Landis announced. 'Good luck, Verus. You can get in touch with me via Variam, but I would rather suggest you don't do so unless absolutely necessary, for both our sakes.'

I nodded. Landis and Klara left.

Luna hesitated at the door. 'Is there anything . . .?'

'I'd rather be alone right now,' I said. It was an effort to talk.

'Okay,' Luna said. 'Look, we'll figure out a way to fix this. Somehow.'

I nodded without believing it. Luna left and I lay flat on my back, staring up at the ceiling.

I felt like I'd been hit too many times in the head. I didn't have any plans, any goals. All I could manage was to keep breathing, survive one hour at a time. The numbness hadn't gone away, which might be for the best. I didn't know if I could handle the weight of everything that had happened in the past twenty-four hours.

I tried to think of something to do and came up blank. I didn't want to talk to Luna, or to Vari. A part of me wanted to go to Anne, but a larger part shrank from the idea, and even if I wanted to, I couldn't. What *did* I want to do?

Die?

I shivered at that. Not at the question, but at realising that I didn't know the answer.

I stared at the ceiling. Outside, birds sang in the Hollow, oblivious to my misery.

At last I pulled myself up on one elbow. I didn't have a plan, but I knew I needed to do something. I wished uselessly for Arachne. In the past, whenever I'd been at my lowest point, I'd gone to her. But Arachne was gone and I didn't know where.

If your situation is truly dire . . .

I sat bolt upright. The package.

I struggled to my feet and pulled open my desk drawer, fumbling until my fingers closed on something rectangular. I pulled it out and tore off the paper one-handed to reveal the contents.

It was a lacquered wooden box, hinged with no lock. I opened it to see . . .

. . . a plain white envelope.

I stared down at it. I don't know what I'd been expecting – a magic item probably. Apparently nearly all the parcel's weight had been the box. The envelope was sealed and I held it down with my elbow to tear it open.

Folded inside were two sheets of paper, covered in neat flowing handwriting. I started reading, quickly at first, then slowing as I took in the contents.

My dear Alex,

By the time you read this, I will be gone. I write these words to give you what guidance I can in what must seem a truly desperate hour. I wish with all my heart that I could do more, but this is all I have to offer. I only hope it will make some small difference.

I know what has happened between you and Anne, and have known that it will happen for some time. You may wonder how; to that I can only say that it is an aspect of my heritage. My insight into the future differs from your divination, an awareness of certain key moments and events, but from your point of view the most important matter is that I knew how and why your relationship with Anne would end. You may well ask why I did not warn you. The short and unhappy answer is that some version of these events was inevitable. I chose not to share this knowledge, preferring to let you both experience what happiness you could in the brief time available. If you are angry, I can only apologise. I hope you can forgive me.

For some time now, I have known that a day would come when you would approach me asking to meet with the dragon in the tunnels below. Once you did, a clock would begin ticking, and within a short time – two years at the very most – events would be set in motion which would lead to the end of my time under Hampstead Heath, and to Anne's enslavement at Richard's hands. From there, the possibilities split into two paths. If you are reading this letter, then events have unfolded as I have hoped. You may be hurt terribly, you may feel as though all is lost, but you and Anne are alive.

The other path was much worse. It had many variations, but in all of them, Anne killed you, with her own death following shortly after. Unfortunately, my knowledge stretches no further than this, which is why I have arranged for this letter to pass into your hands. I have no special insight as to what lies ahead. But I can still advise, and so I have written this to counsel you one last time.

First and most important is the question of responsibility. As you read these words, I am sure you blame yourself for what has happened. Do not do this. Believe me when I say (for I do not say it lightly) that Anne's fall is not your fault. Your old master set his sights upon her a long time ago, and once he did, this result was inevitable. Though I have no way to prove it, I believe that your efforts hampered and delayed his success, by giving her hope where she would otherwise have fallen into despair. But ultimately, your resources were too limited, his too great. Trust me when I say that in your dealings with Anne, you have no reason to be ashamed. You have done your best to help her, as you have helped Luna in the past, and Variam, and (not least) myself.

Now you must decide what to do, and on this matter I think I can guess the questions that will be weighing on your mind. First, an option that you may have not considered: you would at this point be fully entitled to walk away. Any debt you have towards Anne, you have long since paid. Hiding from Richard and from the Council will be difficult, but you have done harder things. If you choose to end your story at this point, passing quietly into retirement and disappearing from history, no one will blame you.

But I suspect you will choose otherwise. If this is the case, then the first course of action you have probably already considered is to enter Anne's mind through Elsewhere. If you do so, you will certainly fail. You were barely able to succeed last time with the element of surprise; the same trick will not work twice. Instead you will have to follow the plan you have considered so long. You know the risks it entails, and you are as prepared as you will ever be.

I warned you a long time ago that by attempting to remain independent from both Richard and the Council, you were choosing the most difficult path, and I am afraid this is still true. Failure will mean your death. Success may mean the same. Even if you survive, you will be very different from the man you once were. In the past you have preferred to wait and react to events; that is no longer possible. Remember the lessons you learned from Richard, but never forget that there are other ways.

I have grown close to many humans over the long centuries of my life, watched them grow and learn with the turning of the seasons, and in time, sadly but inevitably, watched them pass away. Now, for the first time, I find myself separated from one whose life still lies ahead of him. It is a strange feeling but a hopeful one. Other creatures have laughed at me for my relationships, comparing them to how humans keep pets. But I have come to see you as far more, and now, thinking of what may befall you, I feel much as a mother must when her child sets out into the world.

I would like to believe that we will meet again, but I fear we will not. Some barriers are not easily crossed. But perhaps in some other place and time, we may see one another once more, and I will hear the end of your story. Until then, know that you have my love, and my blessing. My hopes and thoughts go with you.

Farewell,
Arachne

I lowered the paper, my thoughts whirling. *She knew.* So many things made sense now. She'd known what was coming, and had been prepared for it for a long time.

A part of me wanted to be angry at Arachne for keeping this a secret, but when I looked inside, the feeling wasn't there. Maybe I could understand the decision; maybe there had been so many catastrophes now that it just didn't seem to matter. In any case, I couldn't feel resentment. I just wished she wasn't gone.

I looked back at the letter's second page. *Walk away.* It hadn't even occurred to me. Would it even matter? I'd only managed to survive this long because both the Council and Richard had wanted me alive. Now both had turned against me, and I'd been brutally reminded of just how helpless I was against their full power. Whether I ran away or tried to fight might not even make a difference.

Unless I did what Arachne had told me I needed to do. *Become a greater power.* My eyes fell on a line from the next paragraph: *. . . the plan you have considered so long . . . You are as prepared as you will ever be.*

The plan she was talking about was the one the dragon had told me, two years ago. *There are many paths, but only one that will enable you to reach your fullest potential: that which you already wielded and abandoned.* I knew what that meant.

I also knew what the price would be.

I walked to my desk and sat on the chair. Through the window, I could see the trees of the Hollow, leaves blowing gently in the breeze, the sound of birdsong drifting down from above. I rested my chin in my one good hand and looked out the window.

I sat like that for a long time.

It was maybe an hour later that I felt a gate flash. Running footsteps sounded from out in the clearing, growing swiftly louder. They raced up to my cottage and the door banged open.

Variam stormed in. 'You arsehole!' he shouted at me.

I blinked, turned with an effort. Variam was standing in the doorway, glaring down at me. 'Sorry,' I managed to say.

'You knew all this time?' Variam demanded. 'And you didn't tell us? *Either* of us?'

I just nodded. Variam's face darkened, and I saw violence flicker in the futures. I wondered if Variam would punch me. It was an academic sort of curiosity; if he did, I wasn't going to stop him.

But with an effort Variam steadied himself. 'Why?'

'At first, I just didn't want you getting killed,' I said. 'Later? Because I was afraid.'

Variam stared down at me, then strangely, I saw the anger fade from his face. 'Yeah,' he said. 'Well. That came back to bite you hard enough, didn't it?' He turned away. 'I guess we both fucked up.'

'You tried to warn me, didn't you?' I said. 'You knew something like this could happen.'

'Yeah,' Variam said. 'I stopped talking about it because I thought— oh, I don't know. That if you trusted her and believed in her, then somehow it would all work out. Stupid Disney shit. I didn't think it was going to be like this.'

'Luna told you the story?'

Variam pulled out a chair and sat down. 'Yeah.'

'The Council let you go?'

'Barely,' Variam said. 'I can't stay long, they're going to be watching me a lot more closely now. You know I had trouble at the start with the hard-liners. Gave me shit for my connections with you and Anne. That got better once you got on the Council and Anne was your aide. Now, though . . .'

Looking at Variam, it suddenly occurred to me that he hadn't suggested that he would have to cut ties with me. In fact, I was pretty sure that it hadn't even occurred to him. Just by talking to me like this, he was committing a crime, yet that didn't seem to concern him at all. 'You really are loyal, aren't you?' I said with a fleeting smile. 'I guess that's what Luna saw.'

Variam gave me a suspicious look. 'What's that supposed to mean? Never mind. What should we do?'

'Can you give me an honest answer to something?'

'Sure.'

'Do you think I'm too nice?'

Variam raised his eyebrows. 'You really think this is the time?'

'I know it sounds strange,' I said. 'But I need to make some decisions.'

Variam shook his head. 'Fine. Short answer is yes. I mean, don't get me wrong, you're tough, but you're also sort of . . . hesitant, I guess? Like what happened with the Nightstalkers. Most of the Council, all they saw was that you fought them and won. But the way I see it, you only did that after they'd tried to kill you about five times running. It was the same when we took the Hollow.'

'You think I'm naïve?'

'More like passive,' Variam said. 'It's like you always have to give the other guy the first shot, you know? Until they do, you just talk at them and try to make friends.' Variam hesitated. 'Then again, if you hadn't been like that, you probably wouldn't have taken us in. I mean, now that I think about it, I know we must have looked sketchy as hell. Anne had bad news written all over her, and I was kind of a dick. So . . . I dunno. I guess being the way you are has its good sides too.'

I nodded.

'So are you going to tell me what's up?' Variam asked.

'I'm thinking.'

'About what?'

'I've been trying to hold on to a lot of different things,' I said. 'I'm not sure I can do that any more.'

Variam frowned. 'Well . . . okay.' He glanced at his phone and rose. 'I'd better go. They're going to put me on hunting duty. Probably after you.'

I nodded.

Variam paused in the doorway. 'Sorry about how things worked out.' Then he was gone.

The Hollow felt lonely. I took a walk around the woods, listening to the birds sing in the trees. I figured I had maybe a day or two until the Council tracked me here.

Along the way, I worked out what I was going to do. Once I'd made the decision, the plan more or less formed itself. I knew which item I needed, and I knew where I could find it. To get inside, I'd need help, and to find the person who could give me that help, I'd need someone else. Once I'd figured out how to contact her, I gated out of the Hollow to one of our staging points and dialled a number into a burner phone.

The phone rang twice and was answered. A woman's voice spoke. 'Hello?'

'Hello, Chalice,' I said. 'You recognise my voice?'

Chalice is a Dark chance mage who for a while had been Luna's teacher. She's not affiliated with the Council, but she lives in their neighbourhood, and by calling her like this I was running a risk. By answering, so was she. When Chalice spoke again, it was with a note of caution. 'Yes.'

'I'm guessing you've heard the news.'

'I have.'

'A few years ago, you spoke to me about an alliance,' I said. 'Do you still feel that way?'

'That is . . . a dangerous question. You are not a safe person to be speaking to right now.'

'I know. So?'

There was a moment's silence. 'What do you want?'

'Information,' I said. 'Specifically, the location of two people. You shouldn't be at risk.'

'If the wrong people find out, I will *very definitely* be at risk.'

'Back in that café, you told me that you wanted to limit a certain person's power,' I said. 'Right now, I'm the best positioned to stop him. If you still feel the same, now's the time to show it. If not, it's best we go our separate ways.'

There was a long silence. I felt the futures dance, shifting. 'How can I contact you?' Chalice asked at last.

'This phone is active for another thirty minutes.'

'I'll see what I can do.'

I hung up and waited. Chalice got back to me with seven minutes to spare.

'Your first person of interest is still active as of recently,' Chalice said without preamble. 'I can give you a contact number. Possibly more, but that will take time. Be aware that he, like you, is currently not in the best of positions. Apparently he's had a falling-out with his partner and with her master. The second person has left the country and is in hiding. I should have a more precise location in a day or two.'

'Understood.'

Chalice paused. 'I don't know if you're telling the truth about what you'll be able to do. But if you are . . . please do your best. I'm hearing of movements from our mutual adversary that suggest he's gearing up for something. I don't think you have much time.'

I made some more calls, set things up as best as I could, then returned to the Hollow. The sky was turning from violet to purple with the coming evening, the first stars starting to twinkle far above. I sat outside and listened to the wind in the branches.

Movement in the futures made me look up. A medium-to-large fox came trotting out of the woods and slowed to a walk as it approached me.

'Hi, Hermes,' I said. Hermes had taken to hanging out in the Hollow lately, catching the occasional ride in or out of the shadow realm with Luna.

The blink fox walked up to me and stood with his front paws together, head up. He sniffed at my bandaged right hand.

'Yeah, it's hurt,' I said. 'Not getting better either.'

Hermes sat back on his hind legs, curling his bushy tail around him.

'I could do it, you know,' I said. 'Just leave. I'd have to abandon everyone. But I could probably make it work.' I paused. 'Actually, I kind of want to.'

Hermes tilted his head.

'It's because I've screwed things up so badly,' I told the blink fox. 'When things go a little bit wrong, you want to fix it. When they've gone *this* wrong, you just want to quit. I don't want to go back and pick up the pieces. I mean, I already tried once. Why would it be any different?'

Hermes looked at me.

'Okay, it *might* be different. Or it could be even worse.' I was silent for a moment. 'I don't feel like I'm much help. Maybe it'd be better for everyone if I did just leave.'

Hermes moved forward and nudged my hand with his nose. 'You want me to stick around?' I asked with a faint smile.

Hermes blinked at me.

'You think I can do something useful? Make a difference?'

Hermes seemed to pause as if considering, then blinked twice.

'You think I'm just going to fail.'

Blink blink.

'So what *are* you saying?'

Hermes looked at me expectantly.

'You think I should stop feeling sorry for myself and go do something?'

Blink.

I gave a wan smile. 'Direct and to the point.' I got to my feet. 'I'll get you some food.'

A few hours later, I got the response I was waiting for. I set up a meeting, left messages for Luna and Variam in safe channels that they'd see in the morning and returned to the Hollow to sleep.

And went to Elsewhere.

I hadn't been planning to. I knew the smart thing was to rest. I was still recovering from the past night, and time in Elsewhere isn't as restful as normal sleep. But I couldn't stay away.

I knew almost as soon as I entered the dream realm that someone was looking for me. A part of me perked up at the news, hoping against all reason that it was Anne. Maybe she'd found some way to reach out to me, she'd found out what had really happened and was coming to tell me that she didn't blame me and it wasn't my fault and . . .

It wasn't Anne.

I sighed and let Elsewhere take the form of a vast empty city, walkways and colonnades stretching between spire-topped palaces. There was a bench waiting for me, but I didn't sit. I stood out in the open and folded my arms.

A figure stepped out from between two columns. She was maybe nineteen, compact with short red hair, and her name was Shireen. 'Hey.'

I didn't answer. Shireen approached and sat on the bench. 'I'm guessing you're not that happy at the moment.'

'No.'

'You got out alive,' Shireen said. 'Better than I did.'

Shireen had been one of Richard's other apprentices, the third of four. Rachel had killed her, and when she had, an imprint of Shireen had lived on inside Rachel's mind. Somehow, Shireen didn't seem to carry a grudge. Instead, she'd been pressuring me for years to help Rachel and redeem her.

'It's not like I didn't give you plenty of warning,' Shireen said.

'Don't start.'

'Well, you have kind of been asking for it. How long have I been telling you to do something about Rachel?'

'Do not even *try* to make this my fault.'

Shireen shrugged. 'Just saying.'

'Just saying what?' I glared at Shireen, anger at the unfairness of it all boiling up. 'That this happened because I didn't work hard enough on your crazy plan of saving Rachel's soul? Although I don't know if I should even be calling it a "plan", since you've never given me the slightest clue how I'm supposed to do it. You just said "redeem her", then left me to figure out how. Not that it would have mattered if I had, since I'd still be getting screwed by the Council and Richard and everyone else. Pretty much all Rachel did was kick me while I was down. So even if I'd managed to do this completely impossible task you've tried to hang on me, it wouldn't have made any *difference*!'

'You'd have had one extra person on your side,' Shireen said. 'Couldn't have hurt.'

I stared down at Shireen. She looked back at me with no trace of guilt, and it suddenly struck me just how young she seemed. When we'd met, Rachel and Shireen and I had all been teenagers. Shireen – or this version of Shireen – was a teenager still, quick and full of energy, action without hesitation. But I wasn't.

I remembered a conversation I'd had with Luna last year. She'd told me that I was making a mistake by thinking of Rachel as Rachel; in her view, that person was gone and Deleo was all that was left. Maybe she'd been right.

'You've been setting me up from the beginning,' I said. 'Trying to get me to turn Rachel into some sort of good person. It was always impossible, wasn't it?'

'No. Alex, I promise, it was never that. There's still something left in her that's worth saving. I think that's true. It *has* to be true.'

'And I'm the one who pays the price if you're wrong.'

'Hey,' Shireen said. 'You've had the chance for a life for yourself. I haven't. All this time that you've been running around giving orders on the Council and dating your new girlfriend, I've been stuck in here.'

'So I'm supposed to get myself killed to make up for that?'

'You'll get killed if you don't,' Shireen said. 'Remember the prophecy I told you all those years back? Some day, Rachel will have to make a choice. Either she stands with Richard, or she turns against him. If she turns, he loses. If she doesn't, you die.'

'What are she and Richard doing?'

'I don't know exactly. She can hide things from me better than she could before. I get emotions, mostly.' Shireen paused. 'She's been thinking about Anne a lot, especially the last couple of days. Resentment, envy. She's getting to really hate her.'

'Because Anne's yet another person who's getting promoted over her,' I said. 'Right? First it was Morden, then it was Vihaela, now Richard's got a new girl, one who's younger and more powerful than she is.'

Shireen nodded. 'She's been feeling like that a while. I mean, she was the only one who stayed loyal to Richard while he was gone. Now he doesn't seem to need her any more.'

'Of course he doesn't. Back then she was his Chosen. Now she's just another follower.' I looked at Shireen. 'And that isn't enough to make her walk away?'

'No,' Shireen admitted.

'Luna gave me some advice last year,' I said. 'That maybe it was time to start admitting that my redemption of Rachel just isn't going to happen. I mean, by this point,

Rachel's done so many awful things that she probably can't even remember most of them. Does she ever feel bad about any of it? About all the ghosts she's left behind?'

'She buries it as deep as she can,' Shireen said. 'It's why she wears that mask. As long as she doesn't let it catch up with her, she can keep going.'

'Yeah,' I said. 'That's sort of the problem, isn't it?'

Shireen shrugged. 'I've told you the truth.'

'I get that,' I said. 'But there's something that's been bothering me about this whole thing. You keep asking me to redeem Rachel. To split her away from Richard. But you're framing it as something I'm supposed to do.'

'So?'

'I don't think that's how redemption works,' I said. 'For it to happen, you have to want to be a different person. I don't think it's something that someone else can do *to* you.'

'Well . . . you'll just have to figure something out,' Shireen said. 'I mean, I've told you enough times. You don't really have a choice here.'

'That's not very helpful.'

'Like I said. I'm telling you the truth.'

I stared down at Shireen. She looked back up at me. Time passed and I realised that Shireen wasn't going to volunteer anything more. This was what she had to offer.

'I think we're done,' I said.

'All right,' Shireen said. She rose to her feet. 'Good luck. I know it's hard, but . . . I think you can do it. Or you have to. Because there isn't anyone else.'

Shireen walked away and I watched her go. Something had been nagging at me for the second half of the conversation, something important, and as she disappeared between the columns, I realised what it was.

Shireen hadn't lied to me. Luna had hinted at it, but I'd always been sure she'd been telling the truth. But you can tell the truth and still have it coloured by your point of view. Shireen saw this in terms of redemption because that was what she cared about. Rachel was her whole world, and she wanted to make things right.

But the dragon's prophecy hadn't actually said anything about redemption. It just said that Rachel had to turn.

I filed that thought away. I couldn't see how to use it, not yet, but I had the feeling it was important. I let Elsewhere fade from around me, and fell into sleep.

9

The summer morning had a hushed, expectant feel. It was near to dawn, and instead of being a steady stream, the traffic on the nearby motorway came in fits and starts, each car announcing its presence with a rumbling crescendo before passing with a whoosh of displaced air. The sky was clear, the deep blue of the night brightening in the east into the yellow of early morning.

I arrived five minutes early, letting the restaurant door swing closed behind me. The place was empty but for a couple of workmen eating breakfast. I bought a bottle of water and sat at the far end with my back to the wall.

Kyle arrived right on time, pausing in the doorway to scan the room. His eyes passed over me without stopping. Only when he'd covered the room twice did he go to the machine to order and then come to sit at my table. 'Well?' he asked as he sat down.

Kyle is American, square-jawed and competent-looking, obviously fit. He's a space magic adept and has a complicated relationship with Cinder where he might be Cinder's property, partner, friend or all of the above. He has good reason to dislike me, since back when we'd first met I'd personally killed one of his friends and had been complicit in the deaths of several more. Then again, exactly the same could be said of Cinder, so maybe Kyle wasn't the type to hold grudges. At least, I hoped not. If he was, this had the potential to go really badly.

'No Cinder?' I asked.

'He's busy.'

I studied Kyle. He looked leaner than he had been, and there was a scar at his temple that I didn't remember seeing before. 'And you're not?'

'Busy enough that I don't have time to sit around. What do you want?'

'I need your and Cinder's help with a job.'

'What kind of job?'

'The dangerous kind.'

'So send in your Keepers and your lackeys,' Kyle said. 'Why do you need us?'

'Guessing you haven't been keeping up with the news.'

'Like I said, we're busy,' Kyle said. 'What happened, you and the Council fall out?'

'Let's just say I'm short on people I can count on.'

Kyle snorted. 'If you're coming to us, you must really be desperate.'

'This is something you're qualified for.'

'Okay, let's hear it.'

'I need to break into Onyx's mansion,' I said. 'He's got a gateway item that gives access to a bubble realm. I'm going to break into that too, get hold of the relic it's protecting, then get out.'

Kyle raised his eyebrows and looked at me. 'Just like that?'

'Just like that.'

Kyle looked back at me for a moment. There was a chime from the counter. Kyle got up, went to get his food, came back, put his tray on the table, sat back down. He took a drink from his bottle of water and tapped it on the tray. 'How many others?'

'Me and about two more.'

'That's it?'

'There aren't many people I trust with something like this.'

Kyle frowned. 'Didn't you go to Onyx's place last year?'

'Yeah.'

'Then you know who you're dealing with,' Kyle said. 'It's not just Onyx, it's his whole faction. I mean, calling it a faction is pretty fucking generous, they're more like a gang. But gangbangers can kill you as dead as anyone else, and I hung out there long enough to know that they're nasty. Mixture of thugs and full-on psychopaths. And then there's Onyx and Pyre. I know you guys on the Council don't take Dark mages seriously, but you don't want to fuck with them unless you outnumber them by a lot. And it sounds like you won't.'

'We won't.'

'What's the timeframe?'

'Probably tonight.'

'Bad idea.'

'Yeah, I know. You think it'd be a better idea to plan things properly. Stake things out, get a feeling for the area, watch them and learn their patterns. I agree. Unfortunately I can't.'

'Why?'

'Because the longer I wait, the better the chance that the Council will show up.'

'Wait, *how* bad a falling-out did you have? Never mind, I don't want to know.'

'Probably wise,' I said. 'So there are a bunch of reasons I'm coming to you guys. First, you both have history with Onyx. You know the area and you've apparently been in and out of his mansion before. You even tried to stage a rescue from the place. Secondly, last I checked, he and Pyre were your enemies too.'

'Doesn't mean we want to kick his door down.'

'I'm not expecting you to do this for free,' I said. 'I'm willing to offer you what I can. Money, favours, items. Whatever you want, as long as it's something I can give.' I looked at Kyle. 'I'm guessing you're speaking for Cinder as well?'

'Yeah, about that,' Kyle said. 'There's a problem.'

'What kind of problem?'

'Cinder's not really in a position to help.'

'If it's about payment—'

'Not about payment. You're not the only one who's had a falling-out lately.'

'With Deleo?'

'Guess news travels fast,' Kyle said. 'Yeah, with her.'

'Is this you we're talking about, or Cinder?'

'Oh, me and Deleo were never friends in the first place,' Kyle said. He touched his knee. 'She's the one who took my leg, and she'd have finished the job if not for Cinder. When he said he was making me his bondsman, she held off, but it was just holding off. Cinder was the only thing holding her back.'

'To be honest, I never really understood why those two were together in the first place.'

'Well, they're not together now.'

'Let me guess. Richard?'

Kyle nodded. 'Cinder was never happy about working for him. He wanted to go back to being free agents. But Deleo wouldn't listen, so they had a compromise. Deleo would work for Drakh, Cinder would help Deleo, but

Cinder wouldn't take orders from him directly. It was never that great a solution and there were arguments. I guess one of them finally went too far. I don't know the details – Cinder's not in the mood to talk – but he had to fight his way out of Drakh's shadow realm and he got cut up pretty badly. He's not in shape for an op like this.'

'How long until he will be?'

'Three, four days.'

Too long. 'Well,' I said. It was bad news, but there was nothing I could do. 'Guess that's that.'

'Hold on,' Kyle said. 'I didn't say no. Cinder can't do it, but I can.'

'Cinder okay with that?'

'He's not my mother.'

I hesitated. I'd fought both with and against Kyle. He was competent and resourceful, but he didn't have the raw power that Cinder did.

'From the sound of it, you aren't really in a position to turn people away.'

'If things go wrong, this is going to turn into a heavyweight fight,' I said. 'You okay with that?'

'Well, maybe I can help make sure they don't go wrong,' Kyle said. 'You know any good ways into that mansion?'

'No.'

'I do.'

I glanced through the futures, but only briefly. Kyle was right about one thing: I needed all the help I could get. 'All right,' I said. 'You're in.'

Kyle nodded.

'Guessing you're not doing this just to get back at Onyx and Pyre.'

'Pretty much,' Kyle said. 'I want a favour.'

'What kind of favour?'

'Let's just say it's something you should be able to handle,' Kyle said. 'We pull this off, I want it done. Okay?'

I looked at Kyle for a long moment, scanning futures. 'Agreed,' I said at last.

'Where are we meeting?'

'On-site,' I said. 'I'll stake out the place today. Meet me when you're ready.'

I checked in with Luna and Variam, then took what steps I could to make myself hard to track, including using an annuller and overcharging my shroud. I'd managed to stay ahead of the Council so far – from what Caldera had said, it sounded like their number one priority was Anne – but it was only a matter of time before they turned their attention to me.

The area around Onyx's mansion was forest and meadows, largely deserted. My gate landed me some distance off, and I walked ten minutes before the mansion's roof and chimneys appeared over the hill ahead. I found a good vantage point in a copse of trees and settled down to wait.

It was the third time I'd been back to this mansion, and I hadn't enjoyed any of my visits. The first time, it had belonged to Morden; the second time, it had been taken over by Onyx. For whatever reason, when Morden had escaped last year, he hadn't moved to reclaim his old home, and with Morden gone, the place belonged to Onyx by default.

Right now, there were two mages living at the mansion, Onyx and Pyre. Pyre was a fire mage with some nasty dating habits and he would be trouble, but the biggest problem was Onyx. Onyx was Morden's Chosen, and he hated me for a variety of reasons, not least because when Morden was raised to the Junior Council, he hadn't appointed Onyx as his aide but had picked me instead. I'd tangled with Onyx many times over the years and pretty much every time I'd come out ahead, it had been by outmanoeuvring him. But outmanoeuvring him on his home turf was going to be hard, and that was bad, because while Onyx wasn't great on subtlety, he was an extremely deadly battle mage. There were few mages who could beat him in a straight fight, and I wasn't one of them.

I sensed Kyle coming in the second hour. He approached cautiously from behind; I waited for him to come into view and made a movement to catch his attention. The adept changed course and approached, dropping into a crouch near to me. 'Good overlook,' he said, glancing out between the bushes.

Kyle was dressed in drab clothing that blended into the hillside, olive and dark brown. He carried no equipment; with his ability, he didn't need to. I returned to studying the mansion.

'Any movement?' Kyle asked.

'Three going out, two coming back.' A collection of flashy cars were parked in the mansion's driveway. 'No sign of Onyx or Pyre.'

Kyle grunted. 'They use gates anyway.' He glanced at me. 'You hurt?'

I'd been lying in a position that didn't require me to use my right arm. 'Something like that.'

'You weren't using that hand at the restaurant either.'

'That's because it doesn't work.'

'You're doing an op like this with only one hand?'

'Yes.'

Kyle didn't answer, but checking the futures, I saw that he was looking at me in a considering sort of way.

Minutes ticked past. Usually I like the quiet, but not today. My thoughts kept on wanting to go back to Anne and to what had happened between us, and each time I had to force away the memories. I still hadn't really dealt with it, and I wasn't sure if I could. The best I could do was focus on the job. If I concentrated on it, it was easier not to think.

Right now, though, my attempts at scouting out the mansion were being disrupted. To path-walk, you need your immediate future to be as stable as possible. Any kind of conflict or uncertainty makes it too hard to look ahead. It doesn't need to be definite either – just the potential for it. Such as the possibility of someone aiming a gun at the back of your head.

'Can you stop that?' I said without turning to look.

'Not doing anything.'

'You're thinking about it.'

'Yeah,' Kyle said, and I could feel his eyes on me. 'I guess I am.'

I twisted around to see Kyle watching me with a calculating expression. 'You thinking about getting some payback for all those years ago?' I said. 'Revenge for your friends?'

Kyle didn't take his eyes off me. 'Pretty much.'

'Way I remember it, Cinder and Deleo killed most of them.'

'Back then there wasn't anything I could do.'

'And now there is?' I asked. 'Fine. Go for it.'

Kyle frowned.

'If you're going to pull one of those guns out of nowhere

and take a shot, then fucking get on with it and stop wasting my time.'

I felt the futures sharpen, violence flickering. 'You think this is some sort of joke?' Kyle said.

'I'm about a million miles away from the kind of place where I'd be making jokes.'

'Will was my friend,' Kyle said. His voice was quiet and dangerous. 'So were the others. Give me a reason not to make you pay for it.'

'You want a reason.' I leant forward and looked Kyle in the eyes, my voice steady. 'In the last forty-eight hours, I have gone from the top of mage society to an outlaw. Ninety per cent of what I own has been taken away from me. My oldest friend is gone and is never coming back. I've been mind-controlled and forced to beat the woman I love to a pulp. I watched her look at me with tears in her eyes and beg me to stop, and I was made to keep hitting her anyway. The last thing she did before being possessed herself was to cripple me. This relic is my only chance of saving her, but I've been promised, by a creature that knows the future, that if I take it I'll pay with my life. So tell me, Kyle. What are you thinking of doing to me that's going to be worse than what's happened already?'

It was the first time I'd seen Kyle at a loss for words. He opened his mouth, looked at me, then closed it again. I turned away and we went back to watching the mansion in silence.

Mid-afternoon found Luna, Variam and me gathered in the Hollow.

'The Precursor gateway we're after is in Onyx's main storeroom,' I said, laying out a map on my desk. The map was hand-drawn and wouldn't win any art prizes, but it was accurate. I tapped a rectangular room towards the back of the ground floor. 'Here. Luna's seen it before. Vari, you haven't, so I've sketched you a picture. It's a statue of a guy in robes, grey stone, a good six feet tall. You'll know it when you see it.'

Variam studied the map. 'Two doors?'

'The second one's sealed.'

'So the only way in and out's that corridor.' Variam traced it on the map. 'And that leads to this junction . . .'

'Yeah,' I said. 'You can see the problem.'

'You mean getting boxed in?' Luna asked.

'Once the gateway is open, we'll have our exit,' I said. 'Until then, no way out.'

'Chances we can get in without them noticing?' Variam asked.

'Kyle says he knows a hidden passage that'll take us to the kitchens, and from what I can see it checks out,' I said. 'We should be able to reach the storeroom easily enough. But Luna needs to use her cube to activate the gate, and once she does, it's going to put out a magical signature like a fire alarm.'

Variam glanced at Luna. 'Sure it'll work?'

'Worked fine last time,' Luna said. 'If I were you, I'd worry less about that and more about what Onyx's gang are going to be doing.'

'Last time we did this, the gate took a few minutes to open,' I said. 'We're going to have to hold the area until it does.'

Variam studied the map. 'That corridor'll screw them if they rush us.'

'The normals and the adepts, sure. Pyre and Onyx are another story.'

'They both going to be home?'

'They were last I checked,' I said. 'Plan is to maintain surveillance on the mansion throughout the evening. Soon as we see one of them leave, we go in. If we're lucky, they both will.'

'And if we're not, they'll both be home,' Luna said. 'I've got a question. How are we going to get *out*?'

'Plan A is the bubble realm,' I said. 'It has a one-way exit system. Doesn't have to be back to the relic either. If everything goes perfectly, we'll show up a hundred miles away while Onyx and Pyre are still waiting for us to come back out.'

'What's Plan B?' Luna asked.

'Starbreeze is going to be on station. If someone gets hurt or we need an evac, she can swoop in, pick them up and GTFO.'

'Oh yeah,' Variam said, glancing out the window. 'I still can't believe you're friends with an air elemental. How'd that happen?'

'I'll tell you the story afterwards.'

'About that,' Luna said. 'Don't get me wrong, it's great to see Starbreeze again. But she's not exactly super-reliable. Does she even know what "on station" means?'

'Sort of,' I said. I'd had to explain it to her.

'And if she decides to go chase some butterfly to the Outer Hebrides?'

'I've told her that it's important,' I said. 'Really important. And bribed her and told her again it's important. But yeah, there's a reason she's Plan B.'

'I thought elementals were super-powerful?' Variam asked.

'It's her attention span I'm worried about,' Luna said.

'Once we're inside the bubble realm, things should get easier,' I said. 'There are traps and defence systems, but I remember most of them from last time. I should be able to guide us through to the relic without any trouble.'

'Yeah, until you actually pick it up.'

'You sure about this Kyle guy?' Variam asked. 'He's switched sides once before, right? What's to stop him doing it again?'

'He's got a personal stake in this,' I said. 'Besides, he's not stupid enough to try selling us out to Onyx.'

'He'd better not.' Variam glanced at his watch. 'I should check in.'

Luna watched Variam go, then turned back to me. 'Are you sure about this?'

'I know it's not the safest of plans,' I said. 'But I've been thinking hard and this is the best I can come up with.'

Luna was right to be dubious. As far as plans went, calling this one 'not the safest' was a major understatement. It wasn't that any of the steps were unrealistic on their own – we'd done things that were harder in isolation – but there was very little margin for error. If something went wrong, then the four of us would be stranded in hostile territory with enemies closing in all around. We had our magic to fall back on, but the people in that mansion could do magic too, and there were a lot more of them than there were of us.

'It's not that,' Luna said. 'It's what happens afterwards. Last time you tried using that relic, it didn't work out so well, remember?'

The last time I'd picked up the relic, its current resident, a two-thousand-year-old mind mage named Abithriax, had tried to possess me and walk out in my body. He'd come pretty close to succeeding. 'Just as well I had you and Starbreeze.'

'So what's to stop him mind-controlling you again the instant you touch it?'

'For one thing, my mental defences are a lot better,' I said. 'For another, I've got the dreamstone.'

Luna shook her head. 'You just got away from one mind mage. Wouldn't have thought you'd be so eager to go head to head with another.'

'There isn't any other choice,' I said quietly. 'My old life's gone.'

'But—'

Movement in the futures caught my attention and I looked up sharply. 'What's wrong?' Luna asked.

'Trouble.'

We walked out into the clearing and met Variam coming the other way. 'We've got trouble,' Variam confirmed. 'I just heard from Landis. Council are sending a force and he thinks you've got one, maybe two hours before they track you down.'

Damn it. 'I'm going to path-walk,' I said. 'Stay here.'

I walked off alone, and once I was isolated, looked to see what would happen if we stayed here. It took me less than a minute.

'Tell Landis his guess was right on the money,' I said, walking back to Variam and Luna. 'We've got two hours at the outside before the Hollow's under siege.'

'Can we hold them off?' Luna asked.

'Doesn't matter. Once they bottle us up, we're finished.'

'They know you're here?' Variam asked.

'Not yet,' I said. 'From the looks of the futures, I think they're using divination. Auguries and probabilistic readings. The time is what it'll take them to narrow it down.'

'I might be able to stall them . . .' Variam began.

I shook my head. 'You and Luna have to get out of here.'

'What about you?' Luna asked.

'I'm going to be playing cat and mouse.'

'On your own? At least let me come with—'

'No,' I said. 'We *can't* let them link the two of you with me. Right now, they might be suspicious, but they haven't got solid grounds to actually arrest you, and we are *not* going to give them any. You guys go to Onyx's mansion and link up with Kyle. We'll do the raid tonight.'

'While you do what?' Luna asked. 'Be a human shield?'

'While I lead them on a chase,' I said. I smiled slightly. 'Relax. The Keepers aren't going to be expecting Starbreeze.'

'Just don't play games, okay?' Variam said. 'You didn't see the mood in Keeper HQ. They *really* want to catch you.'

'No,' I said. 'I don't think I'm going to be playing any more games for a long time.' I glanced at my watch. 'Let's move.'

It was seven hours later.

Sweat trickled down my back as I leant against the wall of the service room. Brooms and mops were piled in the corner, and the far wall held a garbage disposal. My heart was thumping from the last round of sprints; now I was doing my best to stay silent and still. The weather in London had been hot; here in New York, it was sweltering.

I should have listened to Vari, I thought. *When he said they wanted me, he wasn't kidding.*

Things had started well. I'd gated out of the Hollow

without being detected, and the futures in which the Council attacked our shadow realm had quickly faded. Vari and Luna had got away without picking up any tails, and by contacting them through the dreamstone I was able to confirm that they weren't being pursued. I took a gate stone to New Zealand and set about trying to lose my pursuers.

It had worked . . . at first. By scanning ahead, I could tell in advance when the Council teams were going to be dropping in on my location, and be gone long before they arrived. For three hours I hopped around the world, gating from point to point, always one jump ahead. Somewhere around the fourth hour, though, things changed. The futures came apart and re-formed, and the Council's response times began to shrink. I didn't know what they'd started doing differently, but it was effective. Each time I would gate, I'd have less of a lead before they'd start to narrow down my position.

The last time I'd been on the run like this, I'd managed to keep ahead of the Council forces for a full month. But that time, I'd been running from Levistus and his personal troops. This time it was the whole Council, and it was frightening how persistent they were. They just didn't stop, and they could keep this up for ever.

Right now, the problem I was facing was gate stones. Without the ability to cast my own gate spells as an elemental mage could, I had to rely on focuses to travel. But each gate stone worked for only one place, and each time the Council tracked me to one of those locations, that gate stone became effectively useless. I've stockpiled a lot of gate stones over the years, but I only had so many with me, and right now more than half of the ones I was carrying were to locations that had been already compromised. Normally a gate stone being compromised isn't a big deal, since your enemies can't realistically camp out at a gate destination for days on end just on the off-chance you decide to show up. Unfortunately, the Council *did* have the manpower to camp at all my gate destinations just on the off-chance I decided to show up. Which was the reason that I was hiding in this skyscraper in New York.

I rummaged left-handed in my pocket and pulled out two gate stones, staring down at them. Both were about the size of a finger joint; one was river rock, worn smooth, while the other was cut and treated brick. *Two left.* I'd started with seven. I didn't want to go down to one, but I couldn't stall for ever . . .

Movement in the futures caught my attention and I realised the question had become academic. I looked around; the service room didn't have a lock, but there was a wedge on a shelf. I shoved it under the door and waited.

Footsteps sounded from out in the corridor, coming closer. From the futures where I opened the door, I could see that it was a man in his thirties, clean-shaven with brown hair. He wasn't wearing a uniform, but something about him gave me the feeling of a cop or investigator. His footsteps slowed as he approached my position, coming to a stop. 'Receiving,' he said. His accent was American. I could imagine him standing out there, looking from side to side as he spoke into his mike.

A moment's silence, then he spoke again. 'Nothing.' The door was thin and I could hear the man clearly. He was standing less than ten feet away. 'We have any eyes?'

Pause.

'Thought the Brits were searching ground floor up.'

Pause.

'Well, how do they know he's here, then?'

Another pause. I couldn't hear what the person on the other end was saying to the man, but it didn't make him happy. 'Confirm, moving to tenth floor.' His voice dropped to a mutter. 'Don't know why we're cleaning up their shit . . .' His footsteps approached, stopping outside.

I held my breath, keeping very still. The handle rattled. My left hand was closed around my stun focus. This guy wasn't a mage, but he could still raise the alarm. I'd have to take him out in one move.

The handle rattled again, but the wedge held. Then the footsteps were moving away, down the corridor and towards the lift.

I waited twenty seconds, then very quietly reached down to remove the wedge, opened the door and slipped out, closing it behind me. From around the corner, I could hear the man talking on his radio again. I turned the other way and moved to the stairs, my footsteps quick and soft. Once I'd made it out onto the stairwell, I breathed a little easier.

As I went up the stairs, I reached out through the dreamstone. *Luna. Situation?*

There was a little resistance, but not much. Distance didn't seem to be as much of a barrier to the dreamstone with all the practice I'd been putting in. *All good*, Luna said. *It looks like the mansion's settling down for the night.*

Onyx and Pyre still there?

Haven't seen them leave.

I reached the fourteenth floor and opened the stairwell

door quietly, stepping through into a corridor just like the one below. *Any problems with Kyle?*

He and Vari were arguing a bit, but they seem to be getting on better now. Are you safe?

Getting hunted, I said. I looked down the corridor, wondering where to hide. There was a service room on this level too, but I didn't want to pull the same trick too many times. The apartments seemed like better choices. *You and Vari have had enough time to get a feel for the area. What do you think?*

If it were just about making it in, I'd say no problem, Luna answered. *These guys are pretty amateur hour. It's what happens once we reach the statue that I'm worried about.*

You've got the cube?

Oh yeah. But you remember how long it took to open last time? It was what, three minutes? That's going to feel like a freaking month when we're trying to hold them off.

I checked to see which apartments were empty and which were occupied. A row of three along the left side showed no response in the futures where I banged on the door. They also had balconies looking out onto the Hudson River, giving me an emergency exit. *How soon can we move?*

We've been watching the lights start to go off, Luna said. *These guys stay up late though. Kyle thinks we should wait another few hours.*

I stopped in front of the apartment I'd chosen. *Okay.*

Can you stay ahead of the Keepers that long?

I'll just have to, won't I? I reached for my lockpicks. *We should . . .* I trailed off, my heart sinking. *Oh shit.*

Alex? What's wrong?

Sometimes it's the little things that screw you up. I've been picking locks for years, and it's something that

I've come to take for granted; if there's a locked door, then unless it's something really fancy, I can get through with a minute's work. Lockpicking is straightforward: you apply tension with a wrench, then use a pick on the pins.

Which takes two hands.

Problem, I said. *Give me a sec.* I searched through hundreds and then thousands of futures, looking for ones in which I picked the lock. I didn't even come close. There was no way I was getting through that door.

Change of plan. I turned back towards the stairwell, and—

—*shit*. My thoughts raced. Stairwell would draw pursuit. Lift was suicide. All that left was the service room. I ran down the corridor and slipped inside. Again I wedged the door and waited.

One minute passed. Two. I heard the sound of an opening door, along with echoes from the stairwell. The door closed. Footsteps came down the corridor, slowed, stopped.

Silence. I held perfectly still.

'I know you're there, Alex,' a voice said from outside. It was a woman this time, and British instead of American.

Caldera.

'You coming out?' Caldera said. 'Or we doing this the hard way again?'

I skimmed through the futures, looking for ones in which I was able to get away undetected. It wasn't happening. *So much for the gate stones.* I reached out through my dreamstone. *Starbreeze. Are you there?*

Hi!

I need you to come pick me up.

Mmmmm . . . Starbreeze said. *In a sec.*

Starbreeze! It's important!

More footsteps sounded in the corridor, followed by the sound of a handle rattling. 'Come on, Alex,' Caldera said. 'We need to know what Drakh's up to.'

Leaves are funny, Starbreeze said. *Look how they move.*

Please, Starbreeze. I'm in danger.

Fine . . .

The futures shifted, Starbreeze appearing in them. When she'd appear was another question. 'So let me guess,' Caldera said from outside. There was another rattle of a handle, closer this time. I could imagine her out there, looking up and down the corridor as she checked the doors one by one. 'Drakh grabbed you and now you're on the run. You're hoping to stay ahead of him and the Council as well. Sound right?'

I didn't move. Like most earth mages, Caldera can sense vibrations in the ground. It's pretty good for spotting people, but it doesn't work if they hold still. I'd seen her do this before, making noise to spook targets into running.

'It's not going to work,' Caldera said. 'The Council aren't going to stop. They're going to bring you in, it's just a matter of when.' There was the sound of another handle. She was maybe two doors down now. 'They think you were working with Drakh, by the way. You and your aide. That snatch-and-grab convinced them. But it's not true, is it? You'd never help him. I know you well enough for that. You can still help stop him.'

I felt a flash of anger. I'd watched Caldera take this line in interrogations so many times. *Hey, I know you're not really a bad guy. My bosses think so, but I know you're not like that. You didn't really mean to hurt that other guy, right? I mean, he started it, and it wasn't like you were trying to kill him.*

Why don't you tell me your side? Maybe I can help you. Now I was the one on the receiving end.

For years now, I'd been a Keeper and a Council official. Back in the old days, I'd hated people like that. It had taken me less than two days to remember why.

Another handle rattle. 'You aren't going to win a fight, Alex,' Caldera said. 'I mean, you tried that last time and I'm pretty sure you remember how that ended.'

I didn't answer. Looking through the futures, Starbreeze was ten seconds to two minutes away. *Just a little longer.*

More footsteps. Caldera was right outside the door now. I saw the handle turn, rattle. The wedge held and the handle returned to horizontal. 'I guess you're still thinking you can get out of this somehow,' Caldera said through the door. 'Outsmart everyone and get away. It's what you always do, right?' She paused. 'Know the problem with that? You're not as smart as you think you are.'

The lock on the door splintered as the door broke open, slamming against the wall. Caldera lowered her leg, recovering from her kick; her eyes locked onto me as we stared at each other from less than ten feet away.

'A lot of people have been telling me that,' I said, my voice tight and angry. 'But I do learn from my mistakes.'

'Just stay—' Caldera began, then whipped her head around.

Starbreeze zipped into the room, gave Caldera a frown, then reached out and turned me into air. Caldera's eyes went wide and she shouted into her communicator. 'Elemental! Seal the building! Seal—!'

Starbreeze sent us both flying past Caldera, down the corridor, out the window and upwards. *I don't like her,* she announced.

I'm not surprised.

We soared up into the evening sky, the lights and cars and skyscrapers of Manhattan shrinking below us. The mainland was a looming mass lit up in the sunset, while Long Island stretched off to the other side. A clear sky arced above us, the evening sun fading from yellow to blue to dusky purple. At a few thousand feet, Starbreeze levelled off and zipped away into the east.

I reached out through the dreamstone. *Luna.*

You're okay?

You know how Kyle wanted to wait a few hours?

Yeah.

Change of plan, I said. *You've got twenty minutes.*

The American coast was disappearing behind us, fading into the sunset. Above, the stars were twinkling in the clear sky, growing brighter minute by minute. It was hard to judge our speed over the ocean, but the sun was setting behind us so quickly that I could actually see it sinking below the horizon. Starbreeze is fast.

I felt Luna sigh. *So much for waiting for them all to go to sleep. At least you got out.*

Yeah, but now they know about Starbreeze, I said. Next time they'd be ready. *I want to move within five minutes of landing. Be ready.*

Will do.

I let the connection lapse and relaxed, floating on the air. There was no reason to worry any more. I'd made my choice; now it was just a matter of seeing how it would play out.

Caldera had been wrong. I knew the ways in which this night could end, and none of them involved me being brought in by the Council. In a few hours, I'd be more powerful than I'd ever been, or I'd be dead. One way or another, my old life was over.

Starbreeze sped on over the Atlantic, carrying me towards my fate.

10

Starbreeze took me in a soaring dive down through the summer night and towards the darkened countryside below. I had one glimpse of the lights from Onyx's mansion, then they were obscured by the trees and Starbreeze set me down next to Variam, Luna and Kyle. Vari had called up a small flame and its light illuminated their faces in flickering orange. Starbreeze turned me back to flesh and blood, then saw the flame and forgot all about me, leaning in to stare in fascination.

Kyle looked up at the sky, then back at Starbreeze. 'There's something you don't see every day.'

'What's the count?' I asked Vari.

'Three out, four in,' Variam said. 'Assuming there hasn't been any gating, we're looking at twenty to twenty-five combatants.'

'And six *non*-combatants who are Onyx and Pyre's slaves,' Kyle said sharply. 'Make sure you don't do that Keeper thing where you shoot anything that moves, all right?'

'We don't want any shooting at all until we've reached the storeroom,' I said. 'If we meet any single targets, we'll try to subdue them quietly. Kyle, you said you had some sedatives in your box of tricks, so keep them handy. You'll be on point with me. Vari, you're the heavy artillery. Once the alarm's raised, we'll be depending on you for cover fire. Luna, you're our way in with that cube and you can do the most while staying subtle. If Kyle and I run into trouble, do what you can.' I looked around. 'Any questions?'

'How long until the Council crashes the party?' Luna asked.

I'd been checking that on the flight here. 'We have twenty minutes clear; another ten minutes safe-ish-but-getting-risky. Anything past that, we're playing Russian roulette.'

Variam pointed. 'I think your Plan B is trying to set herself on fire.'

I turned. Starbreeze was swiping her finger through Variam's light spell with apparent fascination, the air of her body making the flame flicker.

'Starbreeze?' I said. '*Starbreeze.*'

'Hmm?'

'We're going into a bubble realm,' I said. 'Luna, show her the cube.'

Luna took out a cube of deep red crystal. Points of light sparkled from deep within as it caught the reflections of Variam's flame and threw them back. 'Ooh,' Starbreeze said in fascination. She floated over, studying the cube with her chin in her hands.

'It's the same one we used all those years ago,' I said. 'You recognise it?'

'Hmm . . .' Starbreeze said, then shook her head, her eyes still fixed on the cube. 'No.'

'Okay, you remember that bubble realm we went to back then?'

'No.'

'It was the one with the fateweaver. You remember the fateweaver?'

'No.'

'I nearly got possessed and you and Luna saved me. Do you remember *that*?'

'No,' Starbreeze said cheerfully. 'What are we doing again?'

Luna covered her eyes. 'Oh God.'

'This is our Plan B?' Variam asked.

I ignored Variam. 'We're about to go into the house over there. Once we do, we'll need you to stay ready in case we call. If we call, we'll need you to get us out. Okay?'

Starbreeze stared into the cube.

'*Starbreeze!*'

'Hmm?' Starbreeze looked up. 'Were you talking?'

'We're so screwed,' Luna said.

'If this is how you guys run your ops,' Kyle said, 'I'm starting to seriously wonder how you're still alive.'

I gave up. Starbreeze would come when I needed her, or she wouldn't. 'Let's go. Kyle, you're on point.'

We approached the mansion under the cover of darkness. Lit windows cast a scattering of light down over the grounds, bright rectangles against the black. It was past midnight and there were many more darkened windows than lit ones, but it only took one to raise the alarm. Kyle led us to an outbuilding near the mansion's west corner. It was too dark to see our footing; my divination showed me where to step but the others were less quiet and I tensed at every crack and rustle.

The door to the outbuilding creaked as Kyle eased it open. *How many people know this route?* I asked him through the dreamstone.

I felt Kyle start. *It's freaky when you do that.*

Quieter than a radio.

Kyle recovered himself. His thoughts had a distinct feel to them, organised and focused. They reminded me of Variam's, but with an undercurrent of anger, banked and smouldering. *A few of them know. Not many.*

The inside of the building was cramped, filled with rusting garden tools. Metal clanked softly as Kyle cleared a path, then there was the scrape of another opening door. There was a click and a dim glow as Kyle switched on a torch; by its light I saw him start down a flight of steps into darkness. Futures of a brighter glow sprang up, and I reached out through the dreamstone. *Don't use a light spell, Vari.*

I don't know how much I trust this guy, Variam said.

And I don't want to risk Pyre picking up your light with his magesight and wondering what another fire mage is doing in the building.

Fine.

The stairs went down twenty feet or so. Variam pulled the door closed behind us; silence closed in, broken only by our footsteps. The door ended at another door that Kyle listened at before easing open.

The door opened into a basement, cluttered with junk. The beam of Kyle's torch passed over furniture, boxes, old weapons and machinery. I could feel traces of magic from around us. This stuff had probably been Morden's, left to gather dust once Onyx took over. Distant voices drifted down and Kyle picked up the pace, a new eagerness in his movements. A stairwell at the end of the basement led upwards; Kyle went up the stairs two at a time and came to a stop at the top, against a closed door. As I followed him, I saw that he had one ear pressed against the wood, listening closely. Carefully I moved up behind him and did the same.

The voices from the other side had gone quiet, but by looking into the futures I could tell that there were two people, both female. As I listened, I heard the soft *fwump* of a gas stove, followed by the steady hiss of the flame. A cupboard opened and plates clinked.

The door was locked. *How'd you get this open last time?* I asked Kyle.

Stole the key.

Don't suppose you've still got it?

In answer, there was a flicker of space magic as Kyle opened a tiny gate to his storage space. There was a grating noise, followed by a loud click. We both went still.

Silence. There was the sound of a cupboard door from inside, followed by someone turning on a tap.

I shifted the focus of my dreamstone, broadcasting to Kyle, Luna and Variam together. It was harder than maintaining a link with only one, but I'd been practising. *I count two girls. I'm guessing slaves.*

What do they look like? Kyle demanded.

It was an odd question. Or maybe not that odd – when Kyle had told me he wanted a 'favour' I'd had a pretty good idea of what it was. *One early twenties, one late twenties. Younger one's overweight and blonde; older one's thin with dark brown hair.* I paused. *I recognise the older one. Her name's Selene.*

'Who the hell cooks meals at this hour?' Variam whispered.

'Someone who doesn't have a choice,' Luna whispered back.

Mental only, I said.

Can we go around? Variam said silently.

We don't have that kind of time.

Footsteps sounded from the other side of the kitchen. 'Hey,' a new voice called. 'Selene. Pyre wants chicken wings.'

'All right,' Selene sounded stressed.

'*Now*. And he wants you to bring them.'

'Wait . . .'

'What?'

'Can you tell him I'm with the others?'

'No, I can't.' Footsteps started up, fading away.

'Wait!' Selene called.

'What the fuck is your problem?' It was the other girl, the one I'd sensed earlier.

Selene didn't answer and the other girl spoke again. 'Stop acting like you're better than us, yeah?'

The newcomer's footsteps had faded away; now there were only two in the kitchen. It was the quietest it was going to get. *We have to move*, I said.

Let me handle this, Kyle said. He pushed open the door and slipped through.

Wait, Luna asked. *What's he doing?*

The kitchens were big, and neither girl noticed Kyle at first. The door was partially blocked by a bulky old-model freezer, its cables preventing the door from opening fully and shielding us from view. I signalled Variam and Luna to stay back and moved around the other side of the freezer.

Kyle had walked up to the right side of the room. Selene was kneeling down, going hurriedly through the cupboards. 'Selene,' Kyle said.

Selene jumped to her feet, spinning around, a hand going up to her chest. She stared at Kyle wide-eyed.

'I told you I'd be back,' Kyle said.

The other girl had been by the stoves; now she'd turned and was frowning at Kyle. 'Who are you?'

'You okay?' Kyle asked Selene.

'I—' Selene shook her head. If I peered out, I'd be able to see her; a taller-than-average girl with dark brown hair, pretty but with a drawn and miserable look. Her clothes were frayed and dirty. 'Don't.'

'You new or something?' the other girl said.

'Come on,' Kyle said, reaching for Selene's arm. 'I'm getting you out of here.'

Selene flinched back, shaking her head. 'No! You can't—' She took a breath. 'Just go.'

'No. This is different from last time.'

'Out of where?' the other girl said. She walked around a table, passing close by my hiding place; she had dirty blonde hair, cut short, and she was staring suspiciously at Kyle. 'I haven't seen you . . .' She tailed off, her eyes going wide. 'Wait. *Kyle?*'

'You have to get away,' Selene said. 'If someone sees you here . . .'

'I am getting away. With you.' He spared the other girl a glance. 'You as well.'

The other girl was still staring at him. 'Onyx and Pyre want you dead, mate.'

'I don't care what they want,' Kyle said, starting to turn back to Selene.

The other girl looked at Kyle for a second more, then I felt the futures settle as she made her decision. She drew in a deep breath for a scream. Kyle's head snapped back, his eyes going wide.

My stun focus took the girl in the small of the back. Her scream turned into a *whoof* of breath as she thumped to the ground twitching, eyes rolling up in her head.

Luna and Variam stepped out from behind the freezer. 'Saw that one coming,' Luna said.

Kyle stared at the unconscious girl, then at me. 'Why—?'

I put my stun focus back in my pocket and began channelling a thread of power into it. It would take several minutes to recharge. 'For someone who works for a Dark mage, you're way too trusting.' I nodded down at her. 'Make sure she doesn't wake up in the next ten minutes.'

Kyle shook himself and knelt by the girl's side, pulling out a syringe. Selene was looking from me to Variam to Luna, wide-eyed. 'What are you doing here?'

'They're with me,' Kyle said.

Selene's eyes passed over Variam and Luna, then settled on me with recognition. 'You're Verus, aren't you? It was after you got Morden arrested that everything went wrong.'

'Yeah, well, he's making up for it now,' Kyle said, shooting me a glare. 'Take those stairs down to the basement. There's a staircase up at the end that'll lead you out. We'll meet you there when we're done.'

'I can't,' Selene said.

'She can't,' I said at the same time.

'Yes, she can!' Kyle snapped at me.

'No, because—'

'Shut up!' Kyle stood, the syringe clenched in one hand. 'You said you owed me a favour. Well, this is it. You make sure she gets out safely, right now. You've done enough to mess up our lives already, don't you fucking *dare* back out now.'

'You should have let me finish,' I told Kyle, my voice level. 'She can't run out of here because if she does, then as soon as Onyx notices she's missing he'll kill her with that bracelet on her wrist.'

We all turned to Selene. She dropped her eyes, pulling on her sleeve to cover up the black metal bracelet that had just been visible. The movement revealed bruises on her other wrist. 'Oh yeah,' Variam said. 'Death magic focus, right?'

Kyle stared at the bracelet. 'Well . . . you can take it off, right?' He turned to me. 'Deactivate it? There must be some way—'

'Guys?' Luna broke in. 'Maybe think about having this argument later?'

'Yes,' I said, and addressed Kyle. 'And yes, I can deactivate it. With two hands and time, neither of which I have. We pull this off, then I'll do everything I can to help her. You have my word.'

Kyle looked from me to Selene, torn, the internal struggle written on his face. 'But . . .'

Variam was already moving, and he patted Kyle on the back as he passed. 'Yeah, I know, you want to be the hero. Just trust him. If he says he'll do it, he'll do it.'

Luna followed him with a sympathetic glance at Selene. Kyle took a deep breath and looked at Selene. 'I'll be back.' He turned towards the door.

'Get out of here and find a place to hide,' I told Selene.

Selene's eyes were full of fear, but she nodded. I walked past her to the door.

Onyx's mansion was big and full of corridors, but the layout hadn't changed since Kyle had last seen the place and I had my divination to guide us. We moved quickly and quietly along the halls. Shouts and laughter echoed down from above, but all the activity seemed to be in the upper bedrooms; the ground floor was empty. In under a minute, we were turning into the crossroads I'd marked on my map. The door at the end was locked. Kyle produced another key and we were inside.

The storeroom was old and dusty, piled with all sorts of junk, everything from stepladders to fishing rods. Someone had ransacked it a few times and not bothered to put stuff back where they'd found it; several crates were broken open with their contents scattered around. I could sense dozens of magical auras, but most were minor, the kind you get from items that are too old, broken or weak for mages to care about. Except the statue in the middle. *That* aura wasn't weak at all.

The statue was of a man, bearded and dressed in ceremonial robes, maybe sixty years old. His right hand held a wand, while his left was extended in front of him, palm up. His expression was confident and proud; the sculptor had done a good job of capturing his features. His name was Abithriax, and very soon I was going to be meeting him.

All right, you bastard. Let's see how well you do this time.

Variam and Luna moved into the room. 'It's not going to summon an elemental this time, right?' Luna asked.

'This time?' Kyle said.

'Council deactivated that ward when they moved it,' I said.

'They didn't deactivate *that*,' Variam said, pointing sharply at the statue. 'You see it?'

I frowned, focusing. My magesight showed me a lattice of space magic surrounding the statue, tied into the local environment somehow. 'Gate ward?' I said doubtfully. It didn't look quite right . . .

'Sink ward,' Variam said.

'Shit.'

'What's a sink ward?' Luna asked.

'Redirects gates,' Variam said. 'And the focal point is this room.'

'Which means that if we try to gate out of the bubble realm, we won't end up in the middle of nowhere,' I said, my thoughts racing. 'We'll end up here.'

Kyle frowned. 'Abort?'

I hesitated for only a moment before shaking my head. 'Change of plan. You three evac with Starbreeze once the gate's open. I'll go in alone.'

'What?' Luna asked. 'No. You need—'

'I can survive coming out into a room full of people with guns. You can't.' Movement in the futures caught my attention. 'We're out of time.'

From somewhere in the direction of the kitchens, a shout went up. 'Damn it,' Luna muttered. She shot me a look. 'This does not mean I'm agreeing with you.' She turned, pulling the cube from her bag, and slotted it into the statue's hand.

Luna's cube is an imbued item. It's powerful, but single-minded: it seems to care about Abithriax's prison, and nothing more. It's the only thing that can open the gate to that bubble realm, and Luna's the only one who can use it. As it touched the statue, light sprang up around the statue's hand, thin white beams reaching into the cube's depths. The cube responded slowly, red beams moving to answer.

'Crap,' Variam said, staring at the statue. 'You weren't kidding, were you?'

The light show was impressive even to normal vision. To magesight, it glowed like the sun. I could have pointed to it with my eyes closed from a hundred feet away. 'It's going slower than last time,' Luna said, tension in her voice.

'You told us three minutes,' Kyle said.

I was moving to the doorway, laying down a pair of gold discs into the corridor, one by each wall. 'Last time it was three minutes,' Luna said.

'Argue later,' I said curtly. I glanced over at the back of the storeroom. The second entrance was sealed off . . . probably, but there was no time to check. 'We've got incoming.'

Luna, Variam and Kyle took cover, hiding behind crates and in the corners. I stepped behind the statue. I could hear shouts and running footsteps echoing through the mansion; they weren't converging on us quite yet, but they were getting louder.

I rested a hand on the chestpiece of my armour. My armour is plate-and-mesh, an imbued item that's alive in its own way. It had been a gift from Arachne many years ago, and since then it had grown with me, adjusting itself in response to our battles. I'd put it on before leaving the Hollow. *I'm going to be counting on you*, I said through the dreamstone. The armour seemed to pulse in response.

Hurrying footsteps came down the corridor, slowing as they reached the door. From the futures where I looked out, I could see a boy in his twenties stop in the doorway, staring open-mouthed at the light show. 'What the f—?'

Kyle shot him with a taser. The adept went down, jerking. Kyle moved in with another syringe full of sedative. 'Movement,' Vari said.

'Hey!' a voice shouted from down the corridor. 'Someone's here! Hey!'

'Yo, Alex,' Variam called. 'Weapons free?'

'Knock yourself out.'

There was a *takatakatak* as someone opened up with an assault rifle. Bullets slammed into the statue, ricocheting into the walls and floor. I stayed crouched, searching through the futures. *He's twenty feet down the corridor with an AK*, I told Variam through the dreamstone. *Two of them at the moment but more coming.*

Got it.

The shooting stopped. In the sudden quiet, I could hear more footsteps converging, along with the sound of muffled voices. *He's going to advance*, I told Variam. *Five seconds.*

A pause, then the guy with the assault rifle appeared down the corridor. Through the futures I could see him, maybe twenty or so with a round face, eyes bulging a little in concentration as he advanced with his gun forward.

Variam leant around the corner and hit him with a burst of focused heat. The boy's blackened corpse hit the floor with a thump, and hot air rolled into the room, carrying the nauseating smell of burnt flesh.

Luna wrinkled her nose but didn't say anything. Running footsteps sounded down the corridor, followed by more shouts. *Guessing they won't try that again*, Variam said.

Not after seeing that, I said. I reached out to Luna and Kyle as well. *Keep your heads down, they're going to keep up fire—*

Another assault rifle opened up, along with a handgun this time. Bullets whined and chips of stone flew from the statue. I wondered what would happen if a lucky shot hit the cube and decided I didn't want to find out. *Vari, can you tell them to stop that?*

In answer, Variam chucked a fireball around the corner. I saw the red flash flicker on the ceiling; there was a yell and the gunfire cut off.

Silence fell. From down the corridor and around the junction, I could hear someone swearing, their voice muffled. Someone else was calling for backup. *What do you see?* Variam asked.

I looked through the futures where I went out and down the corridor. *I think they got the message.* There was only one guy in view, a kid of maybe twenty, dressed in combats and a leather jerkin. He was holding a handgun that looked too big for him and was peering around the corner down the corridor at the storeroom. I remembered him from my last visit: his name was Trey. *They're holding.*

Alex, Luna said. *You can hear?*

Yes.

Something's wrong. Luna sounded worried. *I think when Onyx and his guys stole the statue, they damaged it.*

I glanced up. The red-and-white lights were just visible from behind the statue, the magical signature still shouting out to everyone in range that something big was happening. I couldn't feel any sign of a gate. *Is it working?*

I don't know, Luna said. *I'm going to give it some help.* 'Vari,' she called. 'Cover me.' She moved out to the statue, putting herself in full view of anyone down the corridor.

I heard Trey shout something, but before he could raise his gun, Variam stepped out. Trey leapt for cover as Variam scorched the intersection.

'Thanks,' Luna said over her shoulder.

I got to my feet. Luna was studying the cube, frowning.

The beams of light were still playing over it, but while some had matched, the others hadn't. 'Almost,' she said, half to herself. 'Just a little push . . .' She laid one hand on the cube, the silver mist of her curse turning to gold.

I watched uneasily. I didn't like Luna having her back to the door like that. 'Make it quick.'

'Don't rush me,' Luna said absently.

Golden mist seeped into the crystal. One of the beams wavered, then intersected, becoming a solid line linking the cube to the statue. A second followed. 'There,' Luna said.

'Movement,' Variam said, not taking his eyes off the corridor.

'Luna, move,' I said.

'I said don't—'

Red light bloomed from the end of the corridor. A ball of fire roared towards us, growing and darkening as it flew, turning the carpets and light fixtures to ash. It was headed straight for Variam, and behind him, Luna. I saw Variam's hand go up as he started his shield.

I snapped out a command word. The gold discs flared into life, a plane of force materialising in the corridor, sealing it off from wall to wall. An instant later, the fireball struck and exploded two feet from Variam's nose. Flame raged, scorching the walls, trying to burn through the forcewall . . . and failing. The corridor went dark.

Think you had it? I asked Variam.

Kind of glad I didn't have to find out.

Luna hadn't turned around. 'Vari, tell that guy to keep it down, will you?'

'I'll ask nicely.'

Another fireball came flashing down the corridor,

exploding uselessly against the wall. Elemental magic can be rock-paper-scissors, and fire magic is very bad at cutting through force. 'You two, move,' Kyle said to Luna and Variam. 'You're giving him a free look at where you are.'

Variam glanced over his shoulder towards Luna, then went back to looking down the corridor.

The cube's unlocking sequence was picking up speed. 'We good?' I asked Luna.

Luna didn't take her eyes off the cube. The golden mist of her curse was still seeping into it. It had been one of the first tricks she learnt: redirecting the good luck of her curse to an external target. 'Almost.'

'Pyre's moving,' Variam said sharply.

'There!' Luna said. She took her hand away from the cube, starting to turn.

The futures changed, new possibilities flashing up. *Luna, down!*

Fire exploded inside the room. I was already ducking into cover, left arm coming up to shield my head; flames licked at me but my armour soaked up the heat. The blast lasted only an instant and was over, smoke trailing from the statue and from the wooden crates I'd been hiding behind. I looked up and my heart jumped. Variam was standing unharmed. Kyle had made it to cover in the far corner. Luna was on the floor, scorch marks on her back.

Another fire blast struck the room, and Variam flung out a hand, a shield of flame enveloping Luna and keeping her safe. As soon as it was over Variam broke into a sprint, scooping Luna up and carrying her to the far side of the room. A third blast struck, washing over his shield.

I stayed crouched behind cover, pressed between boxes and the wall. The blasts weren't hurting me, but I couldn't move. *Luna! Are you okay?*

I'm okay, Luna said, but there was pain in the message. *Vari, Kyle. How bad is it?*

'Second-degree burns,' Variam shouted. 'Need to get her out.'

'I'm fine,' Luna said. I could hear the strain in her voice. 'Just—'

Another fire blast went off, erupting from high in the middle of the room. It had the signature of Pyre's magic, but it wasn't coming from where I'd last seen him. How was he getting through the forcewall?

I hesitated only an instant, then reached out through the dreamstone. *Starbreeze. Going to need your help in a couple of minutes.*

What?

'Alex!' Variam shouted.

'I know!' *You have to get Luna, Variam and Kyle out. Like we planned. Wait for the gate to open, then get them somewhere safe.*

Starbreeze sounded confused. *You're going?*

'Verus,' Kyle called. 'How long till the gate opens?'

'I don't know!' *Not me. Everyone else.*

What?

The three people with me. Get them out of here. You just need to wait—

'*Alex!*' Variam shouted.

'Give me a second!' I was doing too many things at once.

Pyre launched another fire blast. It was a longer one this time, flames roaring through the room. Again I ducked for cover, feeling my arms and back grow warm, then hot. When it stopped, the statue was smoking and there were small fires burning across the room. None were dangerous, but they were spreading.

And then Starbreeze was there, darting from Kyle to Variam to Luna, turning them into air one after another. Kyle barely had time to flinch before all three of them were mist, swirling up along with Starbreeze. She looked at me proudly. 'There!'

'No!' I shouted at Starbreeze. 'Not yet!'

Starbreeze looked thoroughly put out. 'You *told* me.'

'I didn't— Look out!'

Pyre struck again, and this time he was aiming at Starbreeze. I saw her eyes go wide and she fled, taking the other three with her. The blast spread outward, but Starbreeze outran it, flicking out through the gap between the forcewall and the ceiling. I ducked the blast; when I lifted my head again, I was alone.

Starbreeze, wait!

That hurt! Starbreeze sounded unhappy.

Wait, the gate isn't . . . I tailed off as I realised that Starbreeze wasn't listening. I could feel her presence fading. I looked at the cube. It was still resting in the statue's hand, the beams of light still intersecting one by one, but they were barely half-done. 'Isn't open,' I said to the empty room.

A bang and a clatter sounded from the back of the storeroom. I spun to see the back door creak open a few inches, coming up against piles of clutter. 'Oh shit,' I muttered, pulling out my gun.

I could sense Variam in the distance, trying to talk to me. *Not a good time!*

Are you all right?

No! The door ground inwards a few inches, and a boy stuck his head around. I fired hurriedly, making him pull back.

This damn elemental won't turn around! Luna's shouting at her and she won't—

Too late, I said. By the time they convinced Starbreeze to reverse course and bring them back, everything would be over, and Luna was in no condition to fight anyway. *Get safe.*

The boy stepped out from behind the door, levelling an AK-47. The assault rifle roared, deafening in the cramped space, bullets slamming into the walls and chewing splinters from the furniture. The bullets went everywhere but didn't hit me.

The gun was awkward in my left hand, but I held steady until I saw the futures converge. Then I fired once. Red splashed onto the wall behind the boy's head and he dropped. I heard shouts from the corridor; they sounded like they were yelling for help. *Kyle, how—*

Pyre attacked again. Flames gouted from above, playing over the crates and shelves. I ducked behind cover, waiting for the attack to stop. It didn't. The flames kept roaring.

There were bangs and thumps from the back door. More of them were coming through, and I couldn't do anything about it. *Kyle! How's Pyre attacking?*

I don't know. Despite the situation, Kyle sounded calm and focused. *He can't put spells through a wall. If he could, he'd have done it last time we fought.*

A handgun boomed and the crate I was hiding behind shuddered. *Well, he's doing it now!*

I know, I— Wait. I've seen him use focuses, red quartz. Maybe he's got one installed in the room. Check to see where the attacks are coming from.

The crate was on fire now, and the heat was close to unbearable. My armour was shielding me from the worst of it, but I could feel my hair crisping. I searched frantically through the futures, looking for one where the flames stopped, and found it. I reared up, ignoring the pain in my hand and face, and fired blind.

There was a *crack* and I felt a flash of magic. Pyre's spell cut off, the flames vanishing instantly. Then the two boys who'd made it into the room, and who'd been waiting with their guns trained on my cover, shot at me.

One of them managed to miss. The other didn't. I didn't have enough time to dodge, and the bullet took me in the chest. It felt like a murderously hard punch. Pain flashed through me and I lost my breath in an *uff*, the impact throwing me against the wall. I hit the floor hard.

'Yeah!' the boy shouted at me. 'Get fucked!'

I lay still. I'd lost my 1911 in the fall and didn't dare reach for it. Pain was spiking through my chest and the back of my head.

There was the crackle of a radio and I heard a voice. Pyre. 'You get him?'

'We got him.'

Looking into the futures where I opened my eyes, I saw that the one talking was Trey. He was holding a giant silver handgun that looked sized for hunting elephants, so big that he needed two hands to lift it. Now that I was closer, I could see that he'd added some jewellery since we'd last met: two earrings in his right ear and a gold chain around his neck. The other boy had a bunch of face tattoos. They'd almost have looked funny except for the fact that they were pointing guns at me.

I'm going to die because Starbreeze can't tell the difference between 'two minutes' and 'now'.

'He dead?' the other boy asked.

'Right in the chest, point five oh.'

'Check him,' Pyre's voice said through the radio. 'If he's alive, keep him that way.'

The feeling was coming back to my limbs, and I knew that I'd be able to move. The bullet had struck my chest-plate; the plate had splintered and it must have drained the armour's energy reserves, but it had held. I kept still, my eyes closed.

'Looks dead,' the other boy said.

'Yeah,' Trey said. He stepped around the burning crate and kicked. Pain flared in my ankle, but I didn't move.

'What's with this thing?' the other boy said. He'd turned towards the statue, his attention off me.

'Dunno.' Trey bent down over me, poking at my face. 'Hey, I think he—'

I kicked Trey's legs out from under him and he fell onto me with a yell. I was already reaching for his gun hand, my fingers tangling in his. As Trey tried to pull back and his gun swung towards the other boy, I pulled the trigger and it went off with a boom like a cannon. The other boy slammed into the statue and slid down, leaving a blood trail.

Trey snarled and punched me in the head. We rolled over on the floor, struggling. I was taller and more skilled than Trey, but he was quick and vicious, and he hadn't just been shot in the chest. I managed to twist the gun out of his grip, but the move left me open and Trey landed a punch that made me see stars. While I was stunned he got on top of me and started pounding.

I tried to shield myself with my forearms. Trey was straddling me, his weight on my hips, raining blows down on my head. I tried to buck him off and failed, getting a blow to my temple. I felt a flash of panic as I realised I couldn't get loose. I knew counters to this position, but they needed two hands.

More blows hit my forearms and elbow. My right hand flopped uselessly, and another punch crushed it against my nose, sending a spike of pain through my face. Out of the corner of my eye, I could see movement at the forcewall, and knew the barrier wouldn't last much longer. With Trey on top of me, I couldn't reach my pockets. The boy snarled down at me and started driving hammer blows at my head, forcing me to use my one good hand to block.

With a chill, I realised I was going to lose. It was my fight with Caldera all over again. I was going to be beaten and captured, all because I wasn't strong enough—

No. Fear vanished in white-hot fury. *Not this time.*

Trey reared up, fist raised for a knockout blow, the light glinting off the jewellery at his ear and neck. I snatched with my left hand and ripped out both his earrings.

Trey screamed, clapping his right hand to his ear. His left hand fell across my face and I bit, getting a good grip on two fingers. My teeth scraped bone, and Trey scrambled off me, yelling. I let him pull me up, got the half-charged stun focus from my pocket and stabbed him with it. He went down with a crash.

I spat blood and looked up to see the last line of light from the statue merge with the cube. The statue seemed to double, an arched gateway materialising. As it did, magic surged from the corridor and my forcewall shattered, the gold discs sparking and burning out. Onyx had arrived.

I took one glance towards the door and saw Onyx, Pyre and too many people with too many guns. I darted for the statue, trying to grab the cube and get through the gate before they could open fire.

I almost made it.

Divination can only do so much. You can dodge, but that only works if there's somewhere to dodge *to*. Time seemed to slow down as I floated towards the portal, and just as I was passing through the gate I realised that between Onyx, Pyre and all the guns, it was actually physically impossible for them all to miss. I managed to avoid Onyx's force blade, the bullet that would have gone through my head, and the ones that would have taken out my legs. The fire blast and the last volley of shots hit me square on.

Pain seared through me and I fell. Behind me, the gate, destabilised from the loss of the cube and by the attack spells, collapsed.

11

Silence.

Slowly and painfully, I rolled onto my side. I was lying in the entrance room to the bubble realm, and I was alone. There was no sign of where the gate had been. My upper back and right shoulder blade were throbbing as if they'd been seared, there was a sharp pain around my lower back just next to my spine and there was something wet above my right hand.

The right hand scared me the most. I looked down.

The bandages on the hand had been scorched off. Beneath, the skin was red, and two bloody holes gaped, one in the middle of the palm and one just above the wrist. Gunshot wounds; the bullets had gone through and through. I could see white bone and had the nauseating feeling that if I tried poking a finger, it would come out the other side.

Twisting my head, I could see that the armour over my right shoulder blade had been partially melted. My armour had saved me, diffusing the heat across my back. From looking into the futures where I stripped, I could see that the skin was scorched, but no more. Finally, I reached around with my left hand to my back, afraid that my fingers would find a hole in the armour and the skin beneath, and instead found a bullet embedded in the mesh. There was blood, but the skin was unbroken. It must have been one of the shots that had gone through my hand.

I was lucky that it had: if it hadn't lost so much energy, it would have penetrated . . .

Had it been luck? I vaguely remembered my right arm twisting to shield me as I dived. I hadn't done it consciously. Maybe it had been a reflex. Or maybe my armour had moved on its own.

'Thank you,' I said quietly, and felt the armour pulse. It was damaged, badly damaged. Imbued items aren't just things, and they can be hurt or killed. The armour couldn't have much strength left.

I already knew that I wasn't being pursued, so I went through my pockets. My stock was running low: I had my gate stones and not much else. I'd lost the stun focus back in the storeroom. One of the few items I had left was a jar of healing salve, and I unscrewed it one-handed and applied it. It didn't do much – the item had never been designed to treat such severe wounds.

'Guess I should look on the bright side,' I said to no one in particular. 'I couldn't use that hand anyway.' Blood was seeping from the wounds, and for the first time I was glad for the loss of those nerves. If they hadn't been numb, I'd have been in agony.

I did what I could to bind the wounds, using what was left of the bandages and strips of my clothing. The bindings started to soak through immediately, and I remembered what Klara had told me about my hand not healing. Until I got proper treatment, I was going to keep losing blood.

Better not hang around then.

I got to my feet and looked down at the red cube. Its glow had died and now it sat silent on the floor, sparks glinting in its depths. 'I'm having a rematch with Abithriax,' I told it. 'You coming?'

The cube watched me.

I stooped and picked it up, then started walking.

The interior of the bubble realm hadn't changed much from the last time I'd seen it. Off-white walls and rounded corners gave the rooms a muted, soft feel, and patches of light shone from the ceiling. The silence was total. My muffled footsteps felt like the only trace of life in an empty world.

As I walked, I reached out through the dreamstone. *Luna.*

Alex! Luna answered instantly. *Oh, thank God.*

You doing okay?

I should be asking you that. Luna's thoughts were clear, with no trace of pain this time. *You sound hurt.*

Had a little trouble getting through the gate. I heard a faint *splat*; glancing down, I saw that drips were falling from my right hand. I lifted it to slow the bleeding. *But I'm inside and they're not. What about you guys?*

Starbreeze dropped us off when Vari wouldn't stop shouting, then she did a runner. I don't think she's coming back.

No, running away's pretty much her standard reaction when she's upset. How far away are you?

Miles. Vari thinks he can gate us back pretty close to the mansion.

A sealed door blocked my path. I searched the futures and saw that there were controls hidden behind a wall panel; I pulled it off awkwardly with my left hand and got to work. *No point*, I told Luna. *The whole place'll be on alert by now. Probably they've found the passage we used to get in. If you guys try to break in again, it'll be a bloodbath.*

Then what are you going to do? Luna asked. *If Vari's right, then as soon as you leave, you're getting dropped right back in that storeroom. They'll all be waiting.*

I could camp out in here and wait for them to get bored.

You think that'll work?

I found the trigger for the door and channelled a flow of magic. The door opened about a quarter of the way, then grated to a stop. *Not really.*

The controls weren't responding, but the gap was big enough for me to fit and I squeezed through into a corridor going left and right. *So what are you going to do?* Luna asked. *Fight your way through one-handed?*

Suppose I'll cross that bridge when I come to it.

Looking through the futures, I couldn't recognise any of the paths ahead. Apparently the cube had dropped me into a different part of the bubble realm from last time. I picked a direction at random and kept going. Luna was silent for a moment and I had the feeling that she was talking. *Okay*, she said at last. *What if we attack at the same time that you're coming out? We pull some of them away from the storeroom and you'll have a better chance.*

Yeah, they're not going to fall for that. Onyx and Pyre will send a few guys to keep you busy while they stay by the statue. Only way you're going to pull them off is to fight your way right into the mansion.

We could.

And if you do, you'll be too deep to disengage. Chances are whoever's at the front will get killed.

If we don't, you'll get killed.

I'm not letting you guys do a suicide run against Onyx and Pyre, I said. *Look, if I can get the fateweaver, it'll open up options. Maybe I can figure out a way to bypass the sink effect.*

Either way, I'm pretty sure I've got better chances of getting away solo than the three of you have with a frontal attack.

Right, Luna said. She didn't sound happy. *Because using the fateweaver to fight Onyx worked so well last time.*

Hey, I've got out of worse situations than this.

Name one.

Uh . . . I said. *Got to go. I'll be in touch.*

I kept on walking, following the curving corridors. The only sounds were the echo of my footsteps and the occasional drip of blood. I wondered if Abithriax was watching me now, and how I'd look if he was. He'd see a mage in battered and burned armour, right hand ruined, left hand holding the cube that was the key to his prison. What would he be feeling as he looked at me? Curiosity? Contempt?

'So I've always wondered,' I asked the cube. 'Why did you choose Luna anyway?'

The cube didn't answer.

'I mean, you obviously picked her out. I knew that as soon as she told me the story about how she "found" you. I was just never sure as to why.'

The corridor ended in a door. I set the cube down on the floor and took out my tools. 'I suppose you could have just bonded with the first girl to pick you up,' I said over my shoulder as I started working on the door. This one was more complicated, needing a password as well as a specific magical signal. 'But I never got the feeling that that was what you were doing. You always struck me as the kind of imbued item that has a purpose. So what was it? What were you created for?'

The locking mechanism gave way. I put my tools back in my pocket, picked up the cube and put a hand to the door. It slid open with a hiss.

The room within was a deathtrap. Mirrors covered the walls, floor and ceiling, even the backs of the doors, all tilted at slight angles. A tiny panel at the far corner held three projectors, aimed so that the energy beams they sent out would reflect over and over throughout the room in a deadly lattice able to cut flesh and armour to ribbons.

Or at least that was what they would have done if they'd been active. The projector at the back of the room was inert, and without it, the room was just a lot of mirrors. A glance through the futures confirmed that it wasn't going to activate. I walked in and took a closer look. The mechanism hadn't been sabotaged or deactivated that I could see: it had just failed.

Now that I thought about it, a lot of the systems in the bubble realm seemed to be failing. I'd been passing flickering and dimmed lights, and that door that had jammed hadn't been the only one. Maybe the entire place was finally falling apart. It had lasted for over a thousand years undisturbed, but that had been before Luna and I had broken its seals six years ago. Bubble realms aren't all that stable.

'Maybe it's because of us,' I said to myself as I opened the door and kept going. 'When we opened this place back then, we must have disturbed a lot of stuff. And no one's been doing maintenance.' I looked down at the cube. 'Was that why you showed up? Because the Council had found the statue, and you knew that sooner or later they'd force a way in?'

The cube sat silently.

'Doesn't explain why you'd pick Luna though. I mean, if you wanted the place opened, a Council mage would have made more sense. But then, if you just wanted it opened, you could have done that a long time ago. So what *do* you want? I guess maybe you want to keep Abithriax sealed, but at the rate it's going, the prison might not last much longer . . .'

No answer.

'You know, I kind of feel like I'm doing all the work in this conversation.'

I kept working my way through the bubble realm. Not all the traps were inactive, but I had my divination and my memories, and unlike last time, I didn't have a bunch of people chasing me. My hand kept bleeding. The bandages were soaked through, and I was starting to wonder if I should be worrying about blood loss.

And then, all of a sudden, I was there. The corridor opened up into a huge circular room, columns around the edge rising up into darkness. The lights set densely around the wall should have illuminated the room brightly, but only a handful still glowed, leaving deep, uneven shadows. At the centre of the room was a dais, and on the dais was a pedestal, a barrier of force shielding a small object within.

Time to end this. I checked to see that my route to the pedestal was clear, and stepped out.

At least, I'd meant to step out. Instead, I hesitated. Nothing was stopping me. I knew that I was perfectly safe, at least until I opened that barrier . . .

And that was the problem. As soon as I did, I was going to stop being safe.

Come on, I told myself. *After everything else that's happened the last few days, this should be easy. If you can make it through Richard's shadow realm . . .*

Except that in Richard's shadow realm, I hadn't been the one making the decisions. I'd just reacted to what had happened. Same with what had come afterwards. Even the raid we'd just done, in a way. Sure, I'd planned it, but the big choice had been made for me.

If I took up the fateweaver, I wouldn't be able to react any more. I was going to change, and I didn't know how much of my old self would be left.

It's not as though you have much choice.

But wasn't that how I'd ended up like this? I'd adapted and reacted, telling myself that I was doing what I had to. And in doing so, I'd let Richard and the Council set the prevailing wind. Now that wind had blown me to the edge of a cliff.

I did have a choice. I'd always had a choice. Richard had been trying to teach me that, in a way. It was just that accepting that lesson would have meant giving up things I cared about. Now it looked as though I was going to have to give them up anyway. If I wanted to save Anne, I would have to change.

In the old days, when I was struggling with something like this, I'd have gone to Arachne. I'd have asked her what to do, looked for reassurance. But Arachne was gone, and who could I go to instead? Luna? Even if she was willing, it wouldn't work. Sitting back and letting other people make decisions for me was how I'd gotten into this mess in the first place. This had to be *my* decision.

Maybe I'd been so passive for so long because, deep down, I'd been afraid of what might happen if I stopped. I'd relied on the judgement of Arachne and my friends because I hadn't really trusted my own. There's a ruthless streak inside me, something cold and lethal that Richard had recognised from the very beginning. When I'd rejected Richard, I'd rejected that part of myself as well. Except that by doing that, I'd also turned my back on the part of myself that was most decisive, most willing to commit to a choice and accept the consequences. In a way, I'd made the same mistake as Anne, burying my dark side in the hope that it'd go away.

But it hadn't gone away, and to be honest, I'd never really *tried* to make it go away. Again and again, when my back was to the wall and I was in real danger, I'd fallen back on that part of myself to stay alive. And so it had always been there, a quiet voice at the back of my mind. Vari had said that I was too passive, that I always let my enemies take the first shot, and he'd been right, but he hadn't understood that the biggest reason I did that was because I was resisting that little voice reminding me how much easier it would be to just kill them instead.

I couldn't afford to be passive any more. For a long time, I'd been pretending to be something I wasn't. It had been a holiday, and now my time was up.

I remembered Hermes. *Stop feeling sorry for yourself and go do something.*

I gave a half-smile. 'Well,' I said aloud. 'It was good while it lasted.' And I walked out.

The room had been left almost exactly as I remembered it. I could see the place where Griff had moulded the stone into chains to bind Luna, see the patch on the floor where Onyx, Rachel and Cinder had killed him. If I looked closely, I thought I could even make out a faint stain on the floor. Now that I was closer, I could see the fateweaver, half obscured by the barrier, a simple wand of ivory. There were three receptacles on the edge of the pedestal, each the size and shape of the cube. I reached out towards the leftmost one—

I felt menace from the cube, clear and threatening.

I stopped dead. All of a sudden, the futures had stopped being safe. 'You don't want me to open it?' I asked, being very careful not to move.

The cube didn't exactly answer, but the sensations changed, becoming demanding and insistent.

I thought for a second. I knew Abithriax was watching and I didn't want to speak out loud. Reaching out with the dreamstone, I touched the cube delicately, its thoughts slick and hard, like wet glass. I projected a clear image of what I was intending to do.

The cube seemed to consider a moment, then its resistance ceased. I dropped it into the receptacle. The barrier pulsed and vanished.

I started to reach for the fateweaver, then paused. I could feel my armour around me, wounded and bleeding. It had carried me this far, but it wouldn't survive where I was going. Slowly and painfully, I stripped it off, blood leaking onto the mesh from my useless right hand. When I was done, I folded up my armour and laid it on the dais. 'I'll try to get you out safe,' I told it.

The armour stirred under my hand. I straightened, took a deep breath and picked up the fateweaver. 'Hey, Abithriax,' I said to the air. 'I'm back.'

A voice spoke from behind me. 'So I see.'

I turned. A man was standing there, his hands clasped behind his back. He had white hair and a white beard, thinly streaked with red, and wore the crimson robes of a member of the Old Council. He looked exactly the same as when I'd last seen him, but then he'd been dead for over two thousand years. Or at least his body had.

'I want the fateweaver,' I told Abithriax.

'You act as though you expect me to be surprised,' Abithriax said. 'Everyone who comes here wants the fate-weaver. Do you have any concept of just how many mages have come before you? Of how many have stood where you stand right now?'

'Not really.'

'No,' Abithriax said. 'You have no idea at all. So very many. Begging and demanding, confident and fearful, brave and cowardly, all find their way here. All wanting the same thing, all thinking themselves clever enough to hide the desire burning inside. All ending the same way.'

'I imagine you haven't had too many come twice.'

'And you think that makes you special?' Abithriax looked at me with contempt. 'I was a master mage for more than two thousand years before you tried your first fumbling spell. You are a child.'

'I suppose to you, I am,' I said. 'So are you going to try to possess me again?'

'Why should I bother?' Abithriax asked. 'You shield your thoughts, but your body tells me all I need to know. Your own power is insufficient to win your battles, so you come here, expecting to make use of mine. I have no need of a weak bearer.'

'Liar,' I said. 'You aren't doing it because you can't.'

'You think those mental defences you are so proud of could withstand me at my full strength?' Abithriax said. 'I could break your mind like a twig. I choose not to. Be grateful for that, and go live the brief remainder of your life in whatever manner seems best to you.' Abithriax vanished, leaving me alone.

Or not quite alone. I could feel his presence from within

the fateweaver, locking me out of the item. I didn't know whether Abithriax really could possess me if I didn't invite him in, but he was right about the gap in our abilities. I had no way to take the fight to him.

At least, not here.

I reached out to the dreamstone in my pocket, and channelled. I'd practised this over and over again with my divination, and now that I did it for real, the spell was quick and easy. Even though I'd known in advance, it was a surprise how little power it took. You'd think something like this would be harder.

A translucent oval appeared in mid-air, hovering in front of me. It could have been an ordinary transport gate, except for two things. First, it seemed to lead into the same room I was standing in already. Second, there was a transparent barrier across the gateway, visible to magesight as a faint shimmer. It would give to pressure, but air didn't flow in or out.

I stepped through the gateway, the fateweaver in my hand, and let it close behind me. 'Abithriax,' I said again.

The fateweaver didn't respond.

He's not even paying attention. Well, that'd change soon enough. The pedestal was still there, empty in this reflection. I set the fateweaver down on it, then stepped back and waited.

Seconds passed. I bounced up and down on my toes, full of energy. I didn't feel as though I was dreaming at all: I felt more awake than I'd ever been. My vision was clearer, and vitality surged through me. I could get used to this.

Focusing on the fateweaver, I saw tiny wisps trailing upward from it, like evaporating light. I glanced down to see that the same wisps were trailing from my clothing and the wrappings around my hand. I wondered how long I'd have.

Abithriax rematerialised, blinking into existence in front of the fateweaver. He looked around, frowning. The room wasn't shadowed any more, but clearly lit in grey and blue. 'What are you doing?'

'Let's try this again,' I said. 'I want the fateweaver.'

'Travelling to some shadow realm will not change my answer.'

'But this isn't a shadow realm,' I said. 'This is Elsewhere.'

Abithriax went still.

I nodded down at the fateweaver. 'See those trails? How long do you think it'll last?'

'So this is your plan.' Abithriax studied me. 'The fateweaver will last longer than you will.'

'Possibly,' I said. 'I imagine it'll depend on our relative strengths of self. You're probably stronger as far as that goes, but then, the fateweaver isn't your natural body. I expect that'll work against you. As to who'll give out first?' I shrugged. 'I'm not sure. Want to find out?'

'Hm,' Abithriax said. 'You surprise me.'

'First time you've been in Elsewhere?'

'Please,' Abithriax said. 'I'll admit your Council has made some advances, but in pure magical theory, you have a long way to go. No, my surprise is to do with you. I remember sifting through your memories quite clearly, and you were a type I'd seen many times. Trying so hard to prove that you weren't a Dark mage. Yet now you come here willing to throw away your life and mine, just to take what you want. A Light mage would never do something so destructive.'

'I'm done pretending to be Light.'

'So I see,' Abithriax said. He looked at me a moment longer, then shrugged. 'Very well.'

'Very well?'

'I concede the conflict,' Abithriax said. 'As you have correctly surmised, I value my life more highly than you do yours, and I am unwilling to take the risks of a direct confrontation in Elsewhere. My powers are at your disposal.'

'I'm afraid that's not going to work.'

Abithriax frowned at me. 'What?'

'Don't get me wrong,' I said. 'I'd love to be able to take advantage of your abilities. There are a couple of problems I'm going to be dealing with quite soon that a mind mage would help with enormously. Unfortunately, I can't trust you.'

'It appears you do not have a choice.'

'You aren't listening,' I said. 'I told you. I want the fateweaver.'

'I *am* the fateweaver.'

'No, you're bonded to it. I'm going to do the same.'

'I have no interest in sharing it with you.'

I tilted my head. 'Sharing?'

Abithriax's face darkened.

'I don't know how many people you've possessed and thrown away over the years,' I said. 'Right now, I don't really care. But I'm pretty sure you've had this coming for a long time.'

Abithriax struck. A wave of mental pressure crashed against my mind, trying to roll over my thoughts. It was similar to how it had been with Crystal, but Abithriax was better. Faster, stronger. A true master.

But this time I could fight back. I met Abithriax's attack

with a wall of pure will and threw him away. Abithriax rallied, redoubled his efforts, and I held him off. It was a strain, but I could do it. He wasn't breaking through.

Surprise flashed across Abithriax's face, followed by concentration. The two of us stood ten feet apart, eyes locked. Abithriax tried to worm his way through my defences, and failed. I could sense what he was doing, and I started to press him back.

Then Abithriax disengaged and struck with some attack I'd never seen before, sharp-edged like a blade. My defences shattered and Abithriax's will poured in. Panic rang like a gong as I sensed him starting to take control: with a surge I threw him out, rebuilding my defences higher and stronger.

My body was feeling odd, insubstantial. I glanced down and felt a chill. The trails of light coming up from my clothes and hand had multiplied, and threads of my coat were flaring and wisping away into nothingness. Whatever Abithriax had done, it had damaged my ability to hold together in Elsewhere. I hadn't even known that was possible.

'You should not have come back,' Abithriax said.

I struck again, my will pressing in on Abithriax, and I copied what he'd done to me, bearing down on him from all directions. I saw strain flicker on his face as he fought back, but he was losing ground. I pushed against his defences, trying to seize control of his thoughts—

—it didn't work. It was like trying to grab onto slippery ice. They slid away and Abithriax used the opportunity to push me out of his mind. We were even again.

Without looking down, I could sense my clothes disintegrating. My body would be next: already the nails on my right hand were being eaten away. It didn't hurt – it felt as though I was becoming lighter, on the verge of flying. I'd probably keep feeling that way right until I evaporated.

This wasn't working. I needed to do something different.

Abithriax launched another attack. I fended him off, thinking fast. Abithriax was standing close. The last time we'd fought, I'd gone for his body . . . or what had looked like his body. But it hadn't done anything, not really. The man standing before me was only a projection. The real Abithriax was inside the fateweaver.

Abithriax tried the same trick again, withdrawing then striking with a knife-edged blade of mental energy. This time I was ready and met it with a surge of my own, blocking it. It was painful but not lethal, and I realised that it was meant as a way to break down my defences. Abithriax was a mind mage, and that was how he was thinking. Victory by domination.

I wasn't going to beat him at his own game. I needed to fight like a Dark mage.

I forced Abithriax back, but this time, instead of launching the same attack, I focused on him, straining to see. My senses felt impossibly sharp, and on some level that my magesight couldn't usually reach, I became aware of another layer underpinning what my eyes were showing. Abithriax's form was hollow, half real, but within the fateweaver there was something else. The fateweaver was a tightly woven mass of white, and wrapped around it was a spiderweb of green light, something alive that pulsed and thought.

Experimentally, I pulled at it. Green strands stretched, tearing.

Abithriax screamed. A shockwave of mental energy

lashed out, shattering my attack and my shield. I felt Elsewhere flow in, engulfing me, and frantically I threw up my defences. After only a second, I managed to stabilise, but this time I'd been hurt badly. Half of my clothes had been dissolved, along with all my remaining items; only the dreamstone was left, and the lethal wisps of light were starting to rise from my skin. The fingers on my right hand were gone and the palm was being eaten away.

But Abithriax was hurt too. He was staggering as if drunk, and the wisps of light rising from the fateweaver had multiplied. Glaring at me balefully, he attacked again, but I'd taken his measure now and I knew that here in Elsewhere, my will was a match for his. I met his domination attempt and forced it back.

Seconds ticked by. I could feel sweat on my brow, dissolving as soon as it beaded. Abithriax stared as if trying to bore a hole in me with his eyes. Both of us were past subtlety: it was will against will, each of us trying to overwhelm the other. I strained with everything I had, trying to break through to Abithriax's core.

And Abithriax began to give way. It was slow, very slow, but I could sense him losing ground. Instead of attacking, he was being forced to defend. I kept pressing and felt Abithriax slipping, bit by bit. I saw a flash of fear in his eyes: he redoubled his efforts but all it did was slow me down.

My right hand dissolved into nothingness. With its connection to my body severed, it hadn't been able to survive the corrosion. I felt its loss distantly, set it aside, kept going. Abithriax's defence was feeling frantic now. 'Wait,' his projection said.

I looked Abithriax in the eyes and kept going.

'Wait,' Abithriax said again. Again I could sense that image: a green web wrapped around the fateweaver's white. Abithriax's defences were an invisible barrier, but I was pressing inwards and he didn't have much more ground to lose. In only a few more seconds, I'd break through.

In desperation, Abithriax tried the same trick he'd used before, recoiling to lash out, but I'd been anticipating it and was ready. As his defences fell back I surged in, and for an instant I could reach that green web.

An instant was all I needed. One moment Abithriax was gathering his strength; the next his mind was ripped to pieces. His projection convulsed and disappeared, the green web fraying and coming apart. I tore the fragments from the fateweaver and scattered them.

The patches of green light drifted, dimmed, faded.

Abithriax was gone.

I staggered, catching myself. Light was rising up from my body; my vision was whiter than it should have been and I knew I didn't have much time. The wisps of light coming from the fateweaver had multiplied, and they were intensifying as I watched. The ends of the wand were glowing white, starting to dissolve. Reaching out with the dreamstone, I could sense the fateweaver's presence. It was hurt, dying. It had been dependent on Abithriax, and now that he was gone, it wouldn't survive.

Unless it had a substitute. I tried to link with the item, using the dreamstone as a bridge. The fateweaver seemed to react, but weakly. It wasn't stabilising. Abithriax had maintained some sort of mental link with the thing, but I wasn't a mind mage. The fateweaver was glowing; the item was becoming ethereal, part of Elsewhere. I stared at it, then looked at where my right hand had been.

There wasn't time to think. I dropped the dreamstone, picked up the fateweaver in my left hand and placed it against the stump of my right hand. As I did, I focused my will, reshaping the fateweaver into a new form, one linked to me.

Agony exploded in my arm. It felt as though I had a bar of molten metal fused to my wrist. I forced through the pain, disregarded it. *Join with me*, I told the fateweaver.

The fateweaver latched on, merging into me like flowing water.

Chaotic sensations flashed through my mind, insane and indescribable. I struggled to keep my sense of self, hold against the pressure. Gradually the tide slowed, eased.

The wisps of light streaming up around me were so bright I could barely see. I felt light and airy, my feet nearly floating. I snatched up the dreamstone and channelled. A gate appeared, and I flew towards it.

I burst through the gateway like a diver landing in water. Sound and sensation hit like a hammer and I slammed into the floor of the bubble realm, the impact knocking the breath out of me. Behind me I felt the gate to Elsewhere wink out. I rolled onto my back and stared up at the ceiling, moving my limbs experimentally. They were all still there. More than that, the pain of my injuries was gone. I felt better than I had for days.

I sat up, took a deep breath and looked down at my right arm.

The stump of my right wrist and the fateweaver were gone. In their place I had a new hand, white and pale as though sculpted from alabaster. Tendrils of white traced into my forearm, linking into my flesh. I flexed the fingers of the hand one by one, closed them into a fist, opened them again. The movements were sluggish, but they became smoother as I watched.

The view my magesight gave me was . . . odd. The signature from my hand was still recognisably the fateweaver's, but it had changed, less like an imbued item and more like a living creature. I couldn't tell for sure, but through the dreamstone the fateweaver seemed stable. Actually, I didn't need the dreamstone. I could sense the fateweaver, feel its presence in my thoughts.

I got to my feet and stretched. I felt refreshed, as though I'd been given a whole new body. Maybe I had. Glancing down, I saw that most of my clothes had dissolved: my coat was gone and my shirt was hanging in tatters. My trousers, made of a heavier material, had fared a little better, but still looked like they'd been attacked by a swarm of moths. Everything in my pockets was gone: I had the dreamstone, and that was it.

New hand, though. That counts for something.

I could use the fateweaver as a hand. What about its powers?

The last time I'd used the fateweaver, Abithriax had placed the knowledge of how it worked directly into my mind. The item granted the ability to determine future events, choosing what would and wouldn't come to pass. But back then, Abithriax had been the one to actually *use* it. This time, I'd have to figure it out on my own.

I looked into the futures, trying various approaches. It took me only seconds; the fateweaver's magic felt very compatible with mine. From a quick glance, it didn't seem as though I'd have to do very much—

Wait. Why did a lot of my futures end in a black void?

A tremor seemed to go through the bubble realm, and I thought I could sense a sound on the edge of hearing, something that made me think of something buckling. An image flashed through my head of water pressing against a ship's hull. I didn't understand what was going on. I was alone in this place, especially now that . . .

'Oh crap,' I said out loud. This place had been made as a prison for Abithriax. And now he was gone.

The creaking sound echoed through the bubble realm again, and I could swear I felt the ground shift. I snatched up my armour and the cube and started hurrying towards the exit. Looking through the futures, I felt a chill. The lines ending in a void were multiplying, and worse, they were completely independent of my actions. At any moment, I could get wiped out of existence, and there was nothing I could do . . .

. . . nothing I could do as a *diviner*. But I wasn't just a diviner any more.

I could feel the futures branching, lines of light in the darkness. I picked one in which I was safe, except this time, instead of looking back along the line to match it with my actions, I *reached* for it. I felt the fateweaver stir and unfold, like a muscle contracting. I touched the line and felt the lights shift, the glows of the other possibilities winking out as their potential flowed into the path I'd chosen.

There were no more branching futures, no possibilities of sudden death. The futures followed a clear, set path.

I blinked. *So easy?* I slowed to a walk – no need to hurry – and studied my immediate futures. They weren't a solid line, more like a flowing river. The water could follow many paths, but it was constrained by the banks. But up ahead I could sense the futures branching. Without my intervention, they were drifting apart again.

As I walked, I kept working on the futures, and with each attempt I learned more about how the fateweaver functioned. It wasn't choosing between options, exactly – more of a decree. I could decide on a future, and make it come to pass. It had limits though, which I didn't fully understand but which I was pretty sure involved probability. The more unlikely the event I chose, the more effort the fateweaver had to expend. If I tried to force a future that was sufficiently improbable, or which was possible but not in the way I decreed, it would fail.

Except that my own magic let me know exactly how probable every possible future was. The two types dovetailed perfectly. Divination showed the possibilities; fate let me choose between them.

Right now, the possibilities in which the bubble realm collapsed were multiplying. It was becoming harder to hold to the future in which the bubble stayed together. I probably didn't have more than a few minutes.

The corridor opened into a small, featureless room. I held up the red cube. 'Abithriax is dead,' I told it. 'Ready for something new?'

The cube seemed to consider, then glowed. A section of the wall shimmered and became a gateway. The last time I'd used it, it had led into a grassy meadow deep in the countryside. This time, the gate was masked by an opaque black screen.

I knew what was waiting on the other side. I looked down, taking inventory. Cube, dreamstone, shoes and socks, tattered trousers, shredded T-shirt, a set of armour too badly injured to use. None would be of use in the coming fight.

The bubble's collapse was drawing near. I let the futures settle into one with ten seconds remaining, then stepped through the gate and back to Earth.

12

I came down onto a stone floor. Behind me, the gate winked out, and an instant later I felt something shift and tear. The statue didn't break or shatter, but the life seemed to go out of it. No one was going to be using it as a gateway any more.

'Well, well,' a voice said. 'Look who's here.'

I was back in the mansion storeroom. I turned and saw Onyx.

And Pyre.

And half a dozen other guys standing around them.

And even *more* standing around *them*.

The storeroom was packed, Onyx's gang filling it to standing room only. They formed a semicircle around me, the closest no more than ten feet away. They ranged from teens to as old as their thirties, some showing tattoos and jewellery, hairstyles ranging from dreadlocks to shaven. They carried an assortment of weapons from handguns to knives to AK-47s to a hand grenade; one held a steel chain and another a sawn-off shotgun. Those with no visible weapons radiated magic instead: one had claws growing from his hands and another was juggling a fireball. The looks on their faces were hungry, predators eyeing a meal.

'Surprised?' Onyx said. The Dark mage was slender and whip-quick, dressed in black with gold flashes. He wore an unpleasant smile, and his eyes were cold. 'We put in a sink ward. Guess you're staying.'

I finished my count. Seven adepts with one type or another of combat magic: four elemental, two living and an illusionist. Seventeen normals, sensitives or non-combat adepts, all armed. Onyx and Pyre. And one more. Pyre had Selene at his feet, one hand tangled in her hair.

Pyre met my gaze and smiled. He was good-looking, with blue eyes and messy blond hair. 'Hey, Verus.' He yanked on Selene's hair, pulling her head back; she flinched but didn't make a sound. 'Found your little helper.'

'Give me the fateweaver,' Onyx told me.

I looked back at him silently.

'I'm tired of your shit, Verus,' Onyx said. 'Every time this happens you run away. Well, this time you're in a room that's warded and sealed. You aren't gating and your elemental isn't getting through the doors. So I'm only going to ask one more time. Give me that fateweaver.'

'Don't kill him yet,' Pyre said. 'I want him to call Cinder's boy. I knew he'd—'

'Shut up,' Onyx said clearly, and Pyre did. Onyx didn't take his eyes off me. 'You've got five seconds.'

I looked around and addressed the crowd. 'Lay down your weapons and you can leave.'

The room burst into laughter. The adepts and normals jeered, shouted insults. It was apparently the best joke they'd heard in a long time. Pyre was laughing too. Only three people stayed silent. Onyx, Selene and me.

As the laughter died away, Pyre's eyes fell on my arm. 'Hey, look at his hand. That's it, isn't it?'

Onyx didn't take his eyes off me. 'Cut it off.'

'Wait!' someone called, and one of the boys stepped out. It was Trey. His ear was bloody, and his expression as he looked at me was ugly. 'I owe him.' He pulled out a machete, the blade nearly a foot and a half, gleaming in the light.

I crouched and laid my armour down on the floor, folding it neatly and setting the cube on top of it. Trey stalked towards me. 'You ripped out my rings, you piece of shit,' he told me. I could see the bloody marks on his right ear, and his fingers were bandaged where I'd bitten him. He bared his teeth, lifting the machete for a downward strike.

I blocked, hit the weapon open-handed on the hilt. It flew out of Trey's grip, making two complete circles before I caught it and turned the motion into a spin. Trey was still staring up when I slashed open his throat.

'Kill him!' Pyre shouted.

The room erupted, shouts and gunfire echoing in the confined space. I was already moving, darting away from the dying Trey and into the middle of the people surrounding me. The first one made the mistake of trying to stand and fire. I slashed his hand and kept moving.

Relying on divination for fights is dangerous. You can look ahead, see immediate threats, but it's chaotic: everything is changing and you can't reliably see more than a few seconds ahead. With the fateweaver, everything was different. I could pick out a reasonably probable future and decide that this was what *would* happen. I didn't need to keep checking to see what my opponents would do: I could choose what they'd do and pick a counter at my leisure.

Three of Onyx's gang surrounded me, two wielding a switchblade and a combat chain and an adept using force-enhanced punches. The knifer came in for a grab and I chose an angle of attack that would expose his arm, then pivoted into a cut that half-severed his hand. He went down screaming; the adept tried for a blow that would have broken my spine and I twisted away and stabbed on the reverse. My back was to him but I'd already decided exactly where he was going to be. The machete went through his stomach and he collapsed, pulling the weapon out of my hand as he fell.

The guy with the combat chain advanced, links whirring in an arc. He was joined by another adept, this one bare-handed with death magic at his fingers. Behind I could see half a dozen more levelling guns and spells, but they were blocked by their allies. I analysed the incoming attack pattern in a fraction of a second, identified the point of greatest vulnerability and manipulated the futures to ensure I'd be in a position to exploit it. The first two swings of the chain missed; I caught the third and pivoted to kick the death adept centre mass. He slammed against the statue, and I tangled the chain wielder with his own weapon, then tripped him to let him fall against me with the chain taut around his neck. Trey's body was near my feet and I used the chain wielder as a shield while pulling Trey's handgun from its holster. The death adept was just getting back to his feet when I shot him through the chest.

'Shoot him!' Pyre shouted.

The chain wielder thrashed frantically, reaching out towards the people aiming guns and trying to say something that could have been 'no'. A couple hesitated; most didn't. I let go and spun behind the statue as the chain wielder died under a hail of gunfire.

The chatter of automatic weapon fire filled the room, bullets sparking off the statue and whining past my ears. I checked Trey's pistol calmly as the bullets flew past. Two rounds in the magazine, one in the chamber. Six gun users: four on the left, two on the right. The one on the far left was firing wildly and I noted his ammo expenditure. *Three, two, one, go.*

The rifle clicked on an empty chamber, and I was already stepping out from behind the statue, taking a marksman's stance. The guy with the rifle was looking down at his weapon when my shot exploded his head. Fire tracked in on me; I selected a future where the shots missed and aimed carefully as the bullets whined past. Headshot the second guy, reacquire, track, headshot the third. The fourth scrambled for cover as I stepped back behind the statue.

Magic surged from the other side of the room: Pyre and the fire adept were bracketing me with flame blasts. I twisted the futures, broke into a sprint, heat washing over my back as I burst into the open. Pyre and the adept tried to track my movements; I threw the empty gun at Pyre, rolled and snatched up a knife, threw that too. Pyre threw up a shield that deflected the gun. The adept couldn't shield and the knife took him in the eye. He twisted as he fell; fire gouted from his hands and turned the gunman next to him into a blazing torch.

The roar of a shotgun echoed through the room; the guy with the sawn-off was firing. I managed to push away the futures in which I was hit, but only barely. The cone from the second shot was too broad, and I dived behind a crate. The guy pumped the action on the shotgun and started advancing. The one I'd disarmed earlier had retrieved his gun and was circling to my right, aiming left-handed. I lunged out of cover, closing the distance before he could fire, twisting his hand behind his back in a wrist-lock and putting him between me and the shotgun user. The guy with the shotgun hesitated. Pyre didn't. I shoved the gunman away, letting him take Pyre's fire blast in the chest, then broke left. The shotgun user didn't react fast enough: his first blast hit air, he worked the action, then I caught the barrel before he could fire again. I kicked him in the crotch, twisted the shotgun to break his fingers, fired into him at point-blank range.

A kid with rasta plaits who radiated earth magic came rushing for me, fingers hooked. I worked the action on the shotgun, fired into his chest, aimed left, shot another who'd been about to open up with a machine pistol. Another fire blast from Pyre forced me to roll, and I came up to see that the earth magic adept was still standing and glaring at me. I frowned, lowered the shotgun, blasted his legs out from under him.

Another of Onyx's gang charged me with a short-sword, yelling. I leant away from the first swipe but couldn't bring the shotgun to bear; two more were pressing in with a pickaxe handle and a Stanley knife. I pushed the knifer into the club-man, giving me a second to focus on the guy with the sword. It was a cheap wakizashi, painted black. I blocked the slash with the barrel of the shotgun, shattering the blade, then hit the guy across the jaw with the shotgun butt. He went down and the knifer tried to get me in the back; I let him catch me, put the shotgun against his body, fired. It was the last shell; I let the shotgun go, moved into the guy with the pickaxe handle, threw him, ripped the club out of his hands as he went down, then pivoted with a full-body swing to bring the handle down on his head with a crack of splintering bone.

The earth adept was up again and swinging. I ducked, hit him in the face with the handle, then slugged him across the jaw. It didn't seem to do much but piss him off.

He swung again and I leant back, took a windup and hit him in the side of the head.

The pickaxe handle broke. The earth adept shook his head, glaring, then kept coming. I looked at him in annoyance, stepped back from his punch, saw that the guy with the wakizashi was trying to get up, and stamped on the hand with the broken sword, making him yell and drop it. I scooped up the wakizashi, jerked its owner's head back, cut his throat with the jagged blade, then rose to face the earth adept. He came in with a straight punch and I stepped into the attack, letting his fist brush my hair as I rammed the broken sword through his eye and into his brain.

The earth adept's death gave Pyre a clear line of fire. I turned and ran, following a curving arc as bolts of flame flashed past, yanking the machete from the body of the dying force adept and bending to scoop up a handgun. Another adept blocked my path, this one carrying a longsword that blazed with fire. I leant away from his strike, cut his arm, then had to jump aside from another of Pyre's bolts, snapping off a shot as I did. Pyre's shield flared red, sparks flashing as he deflected the bullet. Before he could recover, I was on him.

I pressured Pyre, machete in my right hand, handgun in my left, trying to find a way through his defences. Pyre backed away, shooting hurriedly aimed blasts. I watched the flow of his movements, studying his shield in my magesight; a weak point appeared and I aimed my gun, trying to force a future where the bullet broke through. At the last second, I realised it wasn't going to work and I had to jump aside, shooting at Pyre's face to make him flinch. The kinetic component of Pyre's shield was slipshod, but a bullet didn't carry enough mass to destabilise it.

The adept with the sword attacked from behind, flames roaring around his blade. I ducked, fired again at Pyre, twisted to dodge the follow-up. Futures opened up and I chose the one I wanted. Pyre aimed a fire blast at the same time that the adept tried a downward slash; I spun aside and Pyre's spell hit the adept, giving him time for one agonised scream before his head and chest were burnt away. Pyre turned on me, snarling, and I fired my second-to-last bullet to make him miss, then lunged in with the machete held low.

Pyre saw me coming, strengthened his shield, and I picked the future where the weak points aligned. The machete sank into the shield, destabilising it: the shield ruptured in an explosion and a flash of flame, and the machete flew apart into red-hot shards. Pyre stumbled back, his shield renewing itself almost instantly.

Almost, but not quite. I'd already dropped the broken machete and was aiming my gun. Time seemed to slow. I could see Pyre, his face narrowed in concentration as he worked to repair the shield. My finger tightened on the trigger and the bullet left the barrel with a bang. The hole in the shield shrank as the bullet flew; I found the future I wanted, pushed and the bullet threaded the needle, reaching Pyre's body just as the shield closed behind it.

A hole opened up under Pyre's ribcage. He staggered, coughed, threw up a wall of flame that forced me to jump back. 'Kill him!' he shouted.

The last half dozen thugs were between me and Onyx. They hesitated.

Pyre spat blood, glared at them. 'Get in there or you're dead!'

The three at the front looked at each other, then charged.

I was getting faster with the fateweaver the more I used it, and I had all three categorised before they'd taken their second step. An adept with curved claws growing from his fingers, an illusionist with a butterfly knife, a normal with a hatchet. By the time the claw user slashed and missed, I had one of their deaths plotted and was setting up the second and third. It felt so inevitable that I almost couldn't understand why they were still coming.

I drove the claw adept back with a kick to the stomach. The hatchet user came in from behind as the illusionist engaged me from the front, butterfly knife whirling. The illusion he was using was a displacement trick, appearing a few feet from where he actually was; it might have worked on someone who couldn't see the future. The visible knife passed harmlessly through my chest as I caught his arm and spun him, choosing the future in which the hatchet user's swing met his. The illusionist screamed as the hatchet sank into his back; the hatchet user let go of his weapon and backed away wide-eyed. I hit the illusionist in the throat, reached past him as he fell to yank the hatchet out, and turned to meet the claw adept's rush.

The remaining guy with an AK-47 was aiming it at me: he'd reloaded but now the claw adept was between us. 'Get out of the way!' he shouted. 'Let me shoot!'

The claw adept was tunnel-visioning on me and didn't react. He attacked, and I pulled my stomach away from a swipe that would have spilled my guts out. I slashed at him but the hatchet was clumsy; he dodged and the future I was trying for wisped away.

'Get down!' the guy with the AK shouted. 'Let me—!'

The claw adept and the AK user's heads came in line and I threw the hatchet, the weapon spinning through the air with an eerie whickering. The claw adept had enough time to dodge. The AK user didn't. The blade sank into his head with a *thunk* as the claw user charged, and the now-hatchetless thug tried to grab me from behind. I spun him around, let the claws go through his stomach, then while the adept was still struggling to pull his claws free, I hit him in the gut, then again on the back of the neck. He went down and I grabbed the illusionist's butterfly knife and rammed it into him, stabbing over and over as he struggled to rise.

Pyre threw another fireball. I dived and rolled, heat washing over me, a scream from behind dying away in a gurgle, then I came up in a run, aiming for the fallen AK. I caught up the assault rifle, worked the action, then opened fire, short controlled bursts. Pyre fell back, staggering, one hand held up before him to focus his shield, the other clutched to the blood leaking from his body. Bullets sparked off his shield, melting and bouncing away, but the assault rifle had far more power than the pistol, and Pyre was hurt. The shield weakened, fracturing under the hail of bullets. I held Pyre's gaze and saw the dawning realisation in his eyes. 'Wait!' he shouted, throwing up his other hand. 'Wait! I'm done!'

The futures aligned and I picked out the one I needed. A three-round burst shattered Pyre's shield, then another went through his chest. Pyre jerked and fell. I emptied what was left of the magazine into him just to make sure.

Turning, I saw that only three others were still standing. A guy with a handgun, another with a combat knife and behind them, Onyx. I started walking.

The two boys looked at me wide-eyed, then raised their hands. 'Don't shoot!' the one with the gun called.

'We give up!' the other shouted. 'Okay? We give up!'
I kept walking.

'You said we could go if we dropped our weapons,' the guy with the gun said, the words spilling out hurriedly. He dropped his handgun. 'I'm going.'

'Yeah.' The other guy dropped his knife. 'I'm done. We're both done.'

I walked up and they backed off to the wall. I dropped the empty AK-47, bent and picked up the handgun. It was an old-model 9mm, scuffed and damaged. Five bullets left.

'Just let us go. Okay?' The first guy glanced fearfully at Onyx, but when Onyx didn't react, he looked at me. 'We won't do nothing.'

I looked back at him, then raised the gun. His eyes went wide and his voice rose to a scream. 'No, wait, don't—!'

I shot him through the head. His friend tried to bolt for the door and I shot him too.

All of a sudden, the room was quiet. After the shouts, screams, gunfire and explosions, the silence was eerie. The only noise was the quiet crackle of fires and the moaning of the last of my attackers still alive and conscious. It was the one whose hand I'd half severed, and he was curled up on the floor whimpering. Without turning to look, I put a bullet through his head and he went still. Now the only sound was the fires.

Two others were left alive. One was Selene. Pyre had dropped her early in the fight and she'd scrambled away into the corner: she was staring at the carnage with eyes wide in horror. And there was Onyx, standing in front of the door, arms folded.

I looked around. The floor was covered in bodies, killed

by fire and bullets and blades. Blood was everywhere. I studied the slaughterhouse for a moment, then turned to Onyx.

'Well,' Onyx said. 'Guess Morden was right about one thing. You want a job done right, you got to do it yourself.'

I glanced down at the 9mm and tossed the pistol aside. It clattered to the floor and I walked to the body of the adept with the sword.

'Had a feeling it'd be this way,' Onyx said. He walked forward into the room, kicking aside the 9mm. He turned his head to watch me as he moved. 'I've been waiting for this a long time.'

Without taking my eyes off Onyx, I bent down and took hold of the weapon's handle. Most of the gang's equipment had been junk, but this wasn't. It was a focus item, well-crafted, designed to channel the wielder's magic through the metal. Not really meant for a diviner, but it would resist spells better than a normal sword and had a slight ability to pierce shields.

'So let's do it,' Onyx said. 'You and me.' A plane of force sprang out from his right hand, the length and shape of my own weapon. He held his left hand out towards me and beckoned.

I advanced, studying Onyx's shield. Onyx wasn't Pyre; his shield was a shimmering weave of force, planes meshing and overlapping. It was optimised against ranged attacks, but effective in mêlée as well. Futures of the next few seconds unfolded, a thousand Veruses attacking a thousand Onyxes from every position and angle. None broke through.

I did a short lunge, testing Onyx's defences. Onyx blocked the first attack, let the second glance off his shield.

He stabbed for my eyes and I leant away, the thrust stopping an inch from my face.

'Come on, Verus,' Onyx said. 'Show me what you got.'

I attacked, careful not to overextend. My bladework was better than Onyx's and more than half of my strikes got through. None broke his shield. The planes of force shifted to block the incoming blade, the focus item's magic meeting Onyx's with a tiny flash at each contact. Onyx counterattacked from time to time but his strikes were casual, almost careless; he was feeling me out.

One of my thrusts glanced off Onyx's shield, and his face twisted in disgust. 'Come on!' He walked towards me, his arms spread wide. His shield glowed brightly in my magesight as he reinforced it. 'Hit me!'

I backed away. Onyx swiped his blade through the air in short cutting arcs, pushing me into the middle of the room. 'Hit me!' Onyx said again. 'You beat me with that fateweaver once. Made me run. It was the first time, you know that? After I became Morden's Chosen, I never lost a battle until you. So hit me with everything you got!'

I kept backing up, watching Onyx warily. The last time we'd done this, I'd used the fateweaver to redirect Onyx's attacks, turning one back into him. He was being more careful this time.

'Morden never treated me the same after that,' Onyx said. 'When I found out you were going to Fountain Reach, I was ready. It was going to be a rematch, just you and me. Except you didn't, did you? You ran away.'

I was still studying Onyx's shield. It was strong – very strong – but there were gaps between the planes of force, chinks where an attack might slip through if he were distracted.

'Pissed me off so much when I learnt what you did,' Onyx said. He slashed as he advanced; each time I skipped away. 'Yeah, I could kill you, but I wanted to face you full strength. That was half the reason I took that statue. Pyre thought he was going to get the fateweaver for himself, but I didn't give a shit. I knew if I waited long enough, you'd come. So bring it, Verus. Give me your best shot. I want to take you on with that fateweaver and kill you with it!'

Onyx had backed me up against the statue and with the last words he lunged. I stepped aside and brought my sword up, picking out the future I wanted. Onyx's blade drove into the statue just as my own sword slid through a chink in his shields and scored his arm.

Onyx jumped back with a snarl, raising his left hand. I dived aside as the statue exploded into a hundred pieces, shards of stone cutting my back and pinging off the walls. Onyx came on again, teeth bared; blood was dripping from his right hand but he was obviously more angry than hurt.

I parried, backed away. There were no futures where I broke Onyx's defence, and I had to give ground. Onyx forced me into a corner, then raised his free hand: blades of force appeared from every direction and arrowed in. I saw myself die in a hundred futures, found one in which Onyx made a slight mistake, pushed. It was close. Two of the blades were too accurate to dodge and I had to block with the sword, the impact jarring it out of my hand.

Onyx slashed and I rolled under his blow, jumping over a body and snatching up a machine pistol. I fired at Onyx blind, the automatic weapon chattering; Onyx advanced through the hail of fire, bullets glancing off his shield until the gun clicked empty. The combat chain was lying near the ruins of the statue and I caught it up.

'Come on!' Onyx snarled. 'Room's sealed, only way out is through me, so stop running and *fight*!' He slashed for my head and I leant away, lashed the chain against his arm to deflect his next strike. I took the second's breather to step back into a ready stance.

Onyx kicked a body out of his way and kept coming. 'Morden wouldn't shut up about you, you know that?' The sword whipped out and I dodged back. '"You should get on with Verus." "You should work things out with Verus." "You and Verus could learn from each other."' Another slash; again I dodged. 'Without the fateweaver, you're nothing. I beat you every time. *You* were the one who kept running away. And then Morden picks you for his aide. I was his Chosen.' He slashed again. 'It should have been me!'

This time I stepped into the blow, ducking down. Onyx's blade snipped a few strands of my hair as the chain whipped out to coil around his leg. Force shields are good at absorbing blows, but they don't do much to stop a pull. I jerked Onyx's leg out and he hit the floor, the blade vanishing as his concentration wavered.

I struck down, using the chain as a whip. Onyx threw up his arms, and the steel links glanced off his shield. I hit once, twice, then Onyx lashed out, force blades exploding upwards.

I was already stepping away, curving the futures to a point. The blades hit the ceiling above, tearing through a support beam, and with a groan a section of ceiling collapsed, burying Onyx in debris. I ran to the corner, snatched up the sword.

Onyx was pulling himself out of the rubble, covered in dust. Force shards sprayed from his hands but he was too angry to keep tight control any more and I easily opened up a channel, walking through unharmed. I struck at Onyx's head, and the force blade sprang back to his hand as he parried.

'I'm going to rip off your face and send it to Morden in a fucking *envelope*!' Onyx slashed high and low; I ducked the first and parried the second. Onyx clambered over another body and kept coming. He was breathing heavily, and it wasn't just anger any more. Onyx might be a battle mage, but he'd spent the last few years living in a mansion with lackeys to do his fighting and slaves to do his chores, and he was slowing down.

Onyx tried to ram his blade through my chest and I stepped in, hitting him with the sword's pommel, then followed up as he stumbled. He aimed a spell that would have torn me in half, but it hit only air and I stabbed down through a gap in his shield, gashing his leg. Onyx tried to blast me again but I was already jumping away.

'Going to kill you,' Onyx said. He was short of breath, having trouble talking. 'Morden shouldn't have . . . Going to show him.'

I studied Onyx's movements in the present and futures. They were getting sluggish, but his shield was still strong. I widened my focus, searching for options.

Onyx came in again, slashing, and this time I stepped aside, striking his leg. It glanced off but made Onyx stumble, and before he could recover I was on top of him, switching hands. Onyx slashed wildly; I parried left-handed, feeling the sword crack under Onyx's blade, and rammed my fist into his shield.

Magic flashed white, the energy of the fateweaver attacking Onyx's shield, planes of forces splintering and breaking. Onyx couldn't reach me with his blade; he let it vanish and thrust his hand at me, trying to tear me apart point-blank. I ducked under his arm, used a shoulder throw. Onyx hit the floor on his back; his concentration wavered and in the instant before it recovered, I drove the sword down two-handed through the weakened section of shield.

The blade went through Onyx's stomach with a *shthunk*, pinning him to the floor. His eyes went wide and he lost his breath in a huff. I met Onyx's gaze, staring down at him as I leant on the sword. 'Morden left you,' I told him clearly, 'because you were stupid.'

Onyx's face twisted in rage and I jumped back. Shards and beams of force lashed out, smashing holes in the ceiling and exploding crates into splinters. I ran back, picking out the futures in which I was safe, looking for the item I needed. It was lying near the door, clipped to one of the bodies, and I caught it up.

'You're dead!' Onyx screamed. He couldn't get up with the sword pinning him to the floor, but he still lashed out, spells tearing apart the walls. He twisted his head to try to see me, feet scrabbling and murder in his face.

I rose, standing calmly side-on as force blades hissed past. Behind me, the door blew out in a spray of splinters. I pulled the pin from the grenade, waited a second, tossed it.

Onyx saw it coming and threw up a barrier, but my throw had been high. The grenade arced over Onyx, hit the shattered legs of the statue, bounced back. The sword was still piercing Onyx, blocking his shield from fully regenerating. The grenade hit the gap between the edge of his shield and the blade, rattled back and forth, dropped through. Onyx had just enough time to look down before it went off.

I was already ducking for cover. The explosion was muffled, with an odd echo to it, wet and splattering.

And then everything was quiet.

I stood up, studied my handiwork. Onyx's shield had contained the explosion, focusing it inwards. What was left of his body was barely recognisable. The snapped-off blade of the sword still pinned the red mess to the floor. All around were the bodies of his men. Smoke and dust hung in the air. The air smelt metallic, gunsmoke and blood.

Well, I thought, looking down at my hand. *Not bad for a first try.*

I walked to the ruins of the statue, brushed rubble and dust off my folded armour, picked it up along with my dreamstone and the cube. Then I looked over at Selene.

Selene flinched at my gaze. She was pressed into the corner of the room, dust coating her hair and clothes. 'Are there any more?' I asked.

Selene swallowed, speaking carefully. 'No.'

I nodded. 'Come with me.'

Slowly, Selene rose. She was clearly terrified, but more terrified of what I might do if she disobeyed. She stopped as far away as she dared, avoiding looking down at the bodies.

I walked out the door and down the corridor, Selene following at a distance. *Luna*, I said through the dreamstone. *You're clear to gate.*

You're back? Are you okay? Where are Onyx and Pyre?

I'm fine. As for Onyx and Pyre, you can come see for yourself.

I turned the corner to see the two girls from the kitchens.

They were hovering in the main hall. The fat-faced one who'd tried to raise the alarm saw me and her eyes went wide. 'Hey!' she shouted. 'It's him!'

I looked back at her.

The girl opened a side door and ran off in the direction of the storeroom, shouting. 'Hey! It's that Verus guy! He's here! Hey!'

As her voice trailed away, I looked at the other girl. 'Your masters are dead. You can stay, or go.'

She looked back at me uncertainly.

The shouts for help in the distance cut off abruptly, followed by shrieks. Apparently the first girl had reached the storeroom. The shrieks continued, and the other girl looked in that direction, eyes wide, and bolted.

I carried on walking. Selene trailed me at a careful distance. 'Kyle and my friends are coming,' I told her. 'You can stay with him, or I can take you somewhere else. What do you want?'

Selene hesitated.

'It's not a trick question.'

'Could I . . . think about it?'

I nodded. 'We'll be leaving in an hour or so. You've got until then.'

We'd reached the front door. I opened it, walked out onto the patio, sat down on the steps. Light pooled around me from the windows and outside lamps of the mansion; all around was darkness. Selene hung back in the doorway. Off to the left, in the black shadow of the hill, I felt a gate spell and knew it was Vari. I laid my armour and items down and sat on the steps, the summer air warm against my bare skin, and waited for my friends.

* * *

Luna, Variam and Kyle were relieved to see me, though in Kyle's case he seemed more happy about Selene. The three of them went in to check the building. When they came out again, they were more subdued.

'You did all that?' Luna asked.

'Yes,' I told her.

Variam shook his head. 'When I said you might be too nice, I didn't expect you to take it this far.'

'Someone told me that being nice didn't work,' I said. I glanced over at Kyle; he was standing next to Selene, talking quietly. 'I decided to listen.'

'Can I see it?' Luna asked.

I held up my right hand, and Luna and Variam bent in to look. 'It's like it's part of you,' Luna said.

'More of a symbiote,' I said. The fateweaver was a steady presence in the back of my mind, ready to be called upon when needed. 'Abithriax told me that these items were always unstable. He managed to link with it mentally. I needed something more direct.'

'What's with the streaks?' Variam asked.

'Connection points,' I said. The thin lines of white running into my forearm seemed a little deeper than they had been an hour ago, but it was a bit late to be worrying about things like that.

'Oh right,' Luna said. 'Shouldn't we be getting out of here?'

'No hurry.'

'You're back out of the bubble realm. The Council can track you again.'

'They're trying,' I said. I'd attended to that while waiting on the steps. 'Their tracking spell isn't working very well.'

'You can do that?' Variam asked.

'I can do pretty much anything, as long as it's a future I can see.' The futures of the Council's tracking attempts failing took a little effort to maintain, but not much. 'Think Luna's curse, but the emphasis is on selection. Which reminds me.' I picked up the red cube and tossed it to Luna. 'Here.'

Luna caught it. 'It's okay?'

'Seems to be.' The cube had been quiet since my return. 'I'm not sure what an imbued item does once the purpose for its existence has gone. Maybe you can help it find something new.'

Kyle exchanged a last few words with Selene, then walked over. 'Hey,' he told me. His weapons were hidden away in his dimensional storage again. 'You sticking around?'

'No.'

'You left a pretty big mess back there.'

I knew Kyle didn't just mean literally. Killing someone like Onyx has consequences. 'Sorry, but I'm not going to be here to clean it up,' I said. 'I don't have the time, and even if I did, you aren't going to want the consequences of having me around.'

'I figured,' Kyle said. He hesitated, gave me a challenging look. 'I'm staying.'

'Okay.'

'You going to give me any trouble?'

'I hired you for a job,' I said. 'You've done it. How's she doing?'

Kyle glanced back at Selene. 'Pretty traumatised.'

It wasn't really surprising. Selene might have been a slave, but the people in that mansion would have been most of her human contact for the past few years. 'Keep

an eye on the other girls. Some might decide it's the time
to go settling old grudges.'

'Yeah, I think I've learnt my lesson as far as that goes.'
Kyle started to turn.

'Kyle.'

Kyle stopped, looked back at me.

'I'm going to say we're even,' I said. 'You agree?'

Kyle studied me for a moment, then shrugged. 'Fine.'

I held out my hand.

Kyle looked askance, then shook it before turning
away and heading back to Selene. I stretched, wincing
slightly at the stiffness in my muscles. 'Okay, guys,' I told
Luna and Variam. 'Time to go.'

Up on the hillside, Variam left to call Landis and check
that no one was after him, leaving me and Luna alone.
'Are you okay?' Luna asked once he was gone.

'I'm not injured, if that's what you mean.'

'It's not.'

'Didn't think so.' I leant against a tree, the bark rough
against my skin, and looked across the valley at Onyx's
mansion. Or what had been Onyx's mansion – I'd have to
come up with a new name for it now. Its windows glowed
against the night sky, a network of light in the darkness.
'I lost more than a hand back there.'

'Was it the fight with Abithriax?' Luna asked. 'I kind
of forgot about that in everything else. I mean, I can tell
you're not possessed this time. But it's like you're . . .'

Luna trailed off and I waited for her to finish. She didn't.
'Like I'm what?'

'Different.'

'Arachne told me I'd have to make sacrifices,' I said.

'Back then, I didn't understand what she meant. You know what I did with Abithriax?'

Luna shook her head.

'I killed him. Just like Onyx and the others.'

'I suppose they didn't give us much of a choice,' Luna said with a grimace. 'Don't tell Vari, but I'm starting to feel like I've seen too much of this.'

'If you're feeling that way, you're probably right,' I said. 'But as for the first part, you're wrong. I did have a choice.'

'Not the best one.'

'I just broke into someone's house to steal something and killed them when they tried to take it back. That *was* my choice.'

'I think they deserved it.'

'They didn't die because they deserved it.'

Luna looked troubled but didn't reply. Variam reappeared out of the darkness, a slim shadow against the trees. I left the mansion behind me and walked away.

13

The Hollow was quiet in the darkness. Both Luna and Vari had gone home to sleep and I was alone. I should have been tired but instead I felt wide awake and full of energy. I walked through the Hollow's woods, listening to the wind in the trees.

The fateweaver seemed to pulse in my hand, singing a song that only I could hear. I traced the futures, flicking from one possibility to another. There was a bird roosting in the branches just above, and I climbed the tree, going hand over foot in pitch-dark. I crawled out along the branch, pushing away the futures in which the bird woke, until I was close enough to reach out and brush its feathers. The bird stirred drowsily, carried on sleeping. I dropped lightly to the grass below and kept walking. I'd just wanted to see if I could do it.

A presence appeared in the futures ahead and I turned towards it. I walked into a clearing, moonlight shining down from above, picking out the blades of grass and fallen leaves. At the other side of the clearing, barely visible in the darkness, the light glinted off a pair of eyes.

I stopped a little distance away and crouched down. 'Hey, Hermes. How's it going?'

Hermes moved cautiously forward and stopped just beyond arm's reach. I held out my right hand. The blink fox leant forward and sniffed. His tail flicked from side to side.

'What do you think?' I asked.

Hermes looked up at me, down at my hand, then backed away and disappeared into the shadows. He gave me a final glance over his shoulder, then was gone.

'I guess I'll put you down as a maybe,' I said to the darkness.

It was a couple of hours before dawn. There were two people I needed to talk to, and looking through the futures, I saw that they were finally asleep. I turned back towards my bed.

I slipped through Elsewhere like a fish through water, feeling the currents and eddies pulling me this way and that. Funnily enough, this was one place where the fate-weaver didn't make things any easier – in Elsewhere, your mind is a better tool than any magic. I found the door I was looking for and opened it.

I stepped through into a darkened gym. Scattered patches of white light illuminated heavy bags, floor mats and a boxing ring. At the far end, a door stood half-open, light spilling out around the edges: whether it led deeper into the building or out into the night, I couldn't say. The sounds of city traffic drifted in from outside, and under that, just audible at the edge of hearing, a woman's laughter.

There was someone else in the gym with me. I couldn't see him, but I could hear impacts, blows thudding into a punchbag. They were rhythmic, steady; one, one-two, one-two, one-two-three. With the end of each combination, there would be a faint metallic clinking as the support chain swung back.

'Got a minute?' I said into the darkness.

The sounds of impact cut off. The punchbag swung for

a second or two longer, creaking, then was still. Seconds ticked by. I could feel myself being watched, but didn't move.

Cinder stepped out of the blackness. He was wearing shorts and a white sleeveless T-shirt, and looked younger than I remembered. Sweat glistened on his bare arms. He looked at me for a moment, then walked past me to the side of the room, disappearing back into the darkness. There was the squeak of a faucet, followed by the splash of running water.

'I'm guessing Kyle gave you an update,' I said to the shadows.

Cinder reappeared. Water dripped from his hair, and he had a towel slung around his neck. He studied me without comment.

'A while ago, we made a deal,' I said. 'You'd help me out, and in exchange, you wanted me to split Deleo away from Richard. You changed your mind about that?'

Cinder looked at me, then folded his arms. 'No.'

I nodded. 'I think I know how to do it.'

'When?'

'As soon as I get the opportunity,' I said. 'Most likely, Richard's next operation. If you can give me any notice, it'd be helpful.'

Cinder nodded.

'One other thing,' I said. 'If what I'm planning works, Richard is not going to be happy with her. Personally, this doesn't bother me very much. But if you still want to help her, she'll probably need it.'

'Anything else?'

'No.'

Cinder turned to go.

'Wait,' I said.

Cinder paused, looked back at me.

'I'm not going to ask what happened between the two of you,' I said. 'I figure it's your business. But when you fought your way out of Richard's shadow realm, Deleo stayed behind.'

'So?'

'So why do you still care about helping her?'

Cinder studied me for a moment. 'You lost a hand,' he said.

'Yeah.'

'Kyle said it was your girlfriend,' Cinder said.

'Yeah.'

'You giving up on her?'

I looked back at Cinder, then gave a short laugh.

Cinder walked away, the darkness swallowing him up. I turned and walked back to the door. *Guess we've got more in common than I thought.*

The better you know someone, and the more history you have with them, the easier it is to find their dreams through Elsewhere. It had taken me a little while to reach Cinder. Finding my next target was easier.

The door opened up into a room with a high arched ceiling and painted white walls. It could have been a palace but the proportions were off, more like a scaled-up doll's house. People were scattered throughout the room, talking among themselves; they wore fine clothes but there was something insubstantial about them. I walked through the crowd, listening with half an ear to the muffled voices, searching for the presence ahead.

At the end of the room was a dais with a gilded throne,

and sitting on the throne was Rachel. She wore clothes of purple and gold, trimmed with white fur, and she sat leaning forward, her brows drawn down in a frown. She tapped her fingers on the throne as she stared down at the boy addressing her from in front of the dais. He was young and plainly dressed; something about him looked familiar and it took me a moment to place him. He looked like Zander, one of the slaves from Richard's mansion, back when Rachel and I had been apprentices.

Rachel asked Zander something. Zander responded slowly, and Rachel snapped at him, her voice sharp. Others were watching from around the walls, dressed in courtiers' outfits; they gestured with fans, pointed and laughed. The murmur of their words never grew quite loud enough to be understandable, but it was a distraction, drowning out what Zander was saying.

Rachel was growing angry. She pointed at Zander, giving him orders; Zander responded sluggishly, as if confused. Rachel rose to her feet, her face a mask of anger. A green ray stabbed out and Zander disintegrated into dust.

'There!' Rachel shouted. 'You see?'

The audience giggled and laughed. No one seemed upset or shocked; they reacted like schoolchildren to a teacher they didn't respect. Rachel screamed at them and they slipped away, turning and ducking into the crowd. I saw other faces I recognised, shifting and changing: Tobruk and Morden, Vihaela and Onyx. From all around, the murmur of conversation continued unabated. Some of the crowd were drinking; I saw a woman who looked like Crystal lower a goblet, a red stain around her lips.

Rachel had sat back down on her throne and was giving orders. A couple of servants nodded and listened with half an ear: they didn't seem to be paying attention. I could see Rachel getting angrier and angrier. Apparently, even now, she wasn't getting the respect she wanted.

She doesn't seem very happy, I thought coldly. I watched Rachel a moment longer.

Then I blew her throne into a million pieces.

Rachel came tumbling out of the explosion, a shield of green light glowing around her, eyes snapping from side to side. Bits of throne came showering down. 'Hey, Rachel,' I called, stepping out of the crowd and into plain view. 'I'm back.'

A green ray flashed out at me. I bent it aside and it hit the figure who might have been Crystal. The phantom shape thinned and faded, the goblet shattering to splatter its contents on the floor. The watching audience pointed and laughed. Rachel fired another disintegrate spell, and again I bent it aside. A statue between the windows puffed into dust. 'Not this time, Rachel,' I said.

'Don't call me that!' Rachel shouted.

'Why?'

Rachel attacked again. It wasn't even close. It was harder for me to change reality here in Rachel's dreams than it would have been in Elsewhere, but I'd been practising for a long time and Rachel couldn't hurt me. Of course, I couldn't do anything to her either, but I was pretty sure she didn't know that.

'So,' I said. I created a grey-blue sofa in the middle of the room and sat, leaning back against the cushions. 'Want to guess why I'm here?'

'Get out,' Rachel said through clenched teeth.

'I'll give you a hint. It's to do with what happened at the Tiger's Palace.'

'What the hell are you talking about?'

'Don't remember? Well, I suppose I shouldn't be surprised. It probably didn't make much of an impression on you.' I crossed my legs, settling back comfortably. 'It was that evening last year. While we were waiting for the Council to kick in the door, we had a chat up there on the balcony.'

'I don't care.'

'So anyway, I asked you why you hated me. Well, I got my answer, and you *really* didn't hold back. You told me that I was a hypocrite, that I was just as power-hungry as any Dark mage, that I wanted the same things as you, I just wasn't willing to pay the price for it. That I'd always known who Richard really was, and that the only reason I'd left was because I couldn't handle taking orders. Remember?'

'Jesus,' Rachel said. 'You're justifying yourself in my *dreams* now?'

'Oh, Rachel, you've got it all wrong. I'm here to say thank you.'

Rachel stared.

'I had a talk with Shireen a few years ago, and she told me something that stuck with me,' I said. 'Back when I was still Richard's prisoner, right at the end, she came down to the dungeons to talk. She was having second thoughts by then – I guess she'd seen what you were turning into and it was making her nervous. Well, at that point I liked her about as much as you like me, so I really let her have it. Funny thing was, it turned out to be the most helpful thing I could have done. If we'd been friends, I would have tried to sugar-coat it and spare her feelings, but instead I was the one person in that mansion who told her the truth.'

'Don't talk about her,' Rachel said, her voice low and dangerous.

'What, painful memory? That's your problem, not mine. Anyway, like I was saying, it took me a while to realise that you were basically doing the same thing to me. You were the one person I could count on to be completely honest, because you hated me so much.'

'You're welcome. Now get out of my head!'

'Why? We're getting to the good part.' I leant forward, looking at Rachel intently. 'You spent all that time telling me all the ways in which I was a loser and a hypocrite. You know the funny thing? I'm pretty sure you never considered I might decide you were *right*.'

'What are you talking about?'

'I'm congratulating you, Rachel. You've won. All these years, and you've finally convinced me that you were right and I was wrong. Except I don't think you're going to enjoy it very much, because the next thing I'm going to do is come after you and Richard. And you know what I'm going to do then? I'm going to take Richard up on his offer.'

'Bullshit.'

'He's been wanting both Anne and me for a long time. Now he gets the complete set.'

'Too late,' Rachel said. 'You already said no.'

'I've changed my mind.'

'You don't get to change your mind!'

'Why?'

'You betrayed Richard. He's not giving you another chance.'

'Richard didn't become the most powerful Dark mage in the country by being inflexible.'

'He doesn't need you any more.'

'You really don't understand, do you?' I said. 'Now that Richard's got Anne, he wants me twice as badly. He can control Anne with his dreamstone, but having me around will make everything so much easier.'

'You can't do this!' I could see the anger on Rachel's face. Good. 'You stopped being a Dark mage! You can't just turn around and come back!'

'But that's what it means to be a Dark mage,' I said. 'I can do whatever I want. The fact that you never got that is why you've been left behind while Richard's promoted everyone else over your head. And soon, he'll be promoting *me* over your head as well.'

Rachel's face was drawn and white. 'I'll kill you first.'

'You're welcome to try. I'm a lot more powerful now.' I gave Rachel a smile. 'But even if I wasn't, Richard would still choose me over you. You know why? Because as far as Richard is concerned, this has always been about Anne. He's put up with your screw-ups and general insanity for this long because he's needed you. But the last couple of years he's needed you less and less. And once he has Anne fully under his control? He won't need you at all.'

Rachel snapped. Green light flashed out and I leapt backwards, alighting on the floor as the sofa turned to dust. Rachel screamed in anger and went for me, but I slipped away, flitting with the speed of thought from cover to cover as disintegration rays exploded chunks of the palace hall. A final blast took out the floor at my feet as I flew through the door I'd entered from and back into Elsewhere.

I alighted and turned to face Rachel. She was striding towards the door, face set in fury. Rachel aimed another green ray at me: it reached the doorway and fizzled. She came to a halt.

Only a few steps separated Rachel from the doorway. Once she crossed that line, she'd be out of her dreams and into Elsewhere. I spread my hands invitingly. 'Coming?'

Rachel stared murder at me but didn't move.

'Didn't think so.' I let my hands fall to my side. 'I want you to tell Richard. Let him know that I'm coming to take up my old place. Tell him, Rachel. Because if you don't, I will.' I turned and walked away.

Rachel didn't follow. I could sense her eyes on me, but she stayed, safe in her own dreams, watching until I disappeared behind a building and vanished from her sight.

I heard a voice calling from behind me. Not Rachel, Shireen. 'Alex! Wait!'

I didn't want to talk to Shireen. I stepped out of Elsewhere, Shireen's voice fading away as I slipped back into my own dreams.

'I do not even know where to start,' Klara said.

It was the next day. The Hollow was peaceful, birds singing in the trees and the midday sun shining down from above. Klara had come to check up on me as promised, and the visit was going a little differently from last time. For one thing, instead of being sprawled out on my mattress, I was sitting at my desk, my right arm laid out on the table. Klara was leaning over it, frowning in concentration, her hair tied up out of the way of her eyes. Luna was leaning against the wall, staying quiet but obviously anxious. Landis wasn't here, which concerned me slightly, but I had bigger problems to worry about.

'Are there any problems?' I asked.

'Problems would imply solutions,' Klara said. 'I have no idea what I am looking at. The last I saw of you, your hand had been severed from your pattern. Now you have replaced it. How did this happen?'

'It's complicated.'

'So I see. The thing on your arm is not a hand. It looks like a hand, it functions like a hand, but it clearly is not. It is an imbued item of some design I do not recognise at all, and whatever it was designed for, it was not to be a body part. Except that something *has* changed it into a body part, and now it has formed a symbiotic bond.'

'So what does that mean?'

'I have absolutely no idea,' Klara said. 'For now, at least, it is functioning. The item has linked into your nervous system and even your circulation. But it has done so by overwriting your body's pattern in the respective areas. It was clearly never designed for anything such as this, and I would not expect it to be stable.'

'Can you stabilise it?'

'Are you listening to me?' Klara said. 'I have no idea how this works or what to expect. It could remain exactly like this for years. It could continue overwriting your pattern until you turn into a construct. It could feed off your blood until you drop dead from desiccation. I would not be surprised by any of these things.'

'Okay,' I said. 'What do you recommend?'

'If I was only concerned with preserving your life, the recommended course of action would be amputation,' Klara said. 'That would of course kill the item. A less hasty approach would be to study it, and you, in intensive care. That still runs the risk of exposing you to negative consequences, but we would have the chance to study the nature of the bond under controlled conditions, and determine whether it was developing, degenerating or remaining stable.'

'I'm afraid neither of those are options.'

Klara looked frustrated but not surprised. 'Very well. Then at the very least you must refrain from using the imbued item's powers.'

'Why?'

'The item is tied into your body's pattern. Each time you use it, it will adapt. The longer this goes on, the more difficult it will be to reverse.'

I nodded. 'Unfortunately, I need to keep using it.'

'There is a good chance that doing so will kill you.'

'I'll just have to see how it turns out.'

Klara threw up her hands and muttered something in German, then switched back to English. 'I cannot help you if you will not cooperate. I will come back to check on you in three days, assuming you haven't killed yourself by then.'

Klara left. 'Don't you think you should be listening to her?' Luna asked once she was gone.

'I am listening. I just have different priorities than she does.' I stretched, flexing my muscles. 'Come on, let's walk.'

I set off along one of the paths in the Hollow, enjoying the feel of the breeze on my face. Luna followed, looking unconvinced. 'Have you heard from Vari?' I asked.

'No,' Luna said. 'I was about to tell you when Klara arrived. When I woke up this morning, I had a text from him saying that there was a problem and he'd been called in. I haven't been able to get in touch since.'

'Was the text from the early hours of the morning?' I said. 'Around two or three a.m.?'

'Maybe?'

I nodded. 'I think something's happened with the Council.'

'Why?'

'I've been using the fateweaver to block their tracking spells,' I said. 'I woke up around dawn to keep that going and found that I didn't need to.'

Luna frowned. 'So what does that mean?'

'Put together with Vari being called in and Landis not showing up? I think they've just been distracted by other problems.'

'I'm still worried about what Klara was saying,' Luna said. 'Maybe you *should* stop using it.'

'You don't understand how big a game-changer this is,' I said. I held up my right hand, the smooth ivory of the fateweaver bright in the midday sun. 'I could never stand up against any of the really powerful mages before. Now, I can.'

'You've gone up against lots of powerful mages without the fateweaver,' Luna pointed out. 'You seemed to do pretty well.'

'I really didn't,' I said. 'You have no idea how many times in the past five years I've been one mistake away from death. Over and over again, I get into situations where I have to do everything perfectly just to survive. And sometimes even that's not enough. I use all of my skill and all of my knowledge and the best I can do is set things up and hope that my enemy will fall for a trick, or someone else will come to the rescue. I don't want to keep living because of other people's slip-ups. I want to control my own fate.'

'Even if it kills you?'

'Trying to go up against Levistus and Richard without something like this *will* kill me,' I said. 'Divination alone isn't enough. You have to be on guard all the time, always watching, because you don't have any safety margin. With this, I can actually make plans of my own, because I know . . .' I stopped.

Luna walked another few steps, then halted and looked back at me. 'What?'

I stared into the trees. 'I just figured out what Richard's magic type is.'

'How?'

'I always thought he acted too confident,' I said. My thoughts were whirling, putting the pieces together. 'That was why I thought it couldn't be . . . But that's it, isn't it? He had the same problem as me, he just solved it a different way. My answer was the fateweaver, his was getting a jinn of his own. But he wanted *all* the power that a jinn could provide, the strongest possible jinn with the strongest possible bond.'

'Wait. Richard's got a jinn?'

'Yeah, but it's not enough,' I said absently. 'Not for everything he wants. Probably he couldn't bond a really powerful jinn without losing more control than he was willing to give up. That's why he needed Anne.'

'Then what—?' Luna cut off as her phone beeped. She pulled it out, then stuffed it back into her pocket. 'I have to go. I told Vari I'd call him now.' She pointed at me. 'Don't leave!'

'I'm not going anywhere.'

Luna disappeared and I sat on a fallen tree, my thoughts turning back to Richard's magic type. Everything made so much more sense now. That was why Richard had always been one step ahead of me.

And he'll always be one step ahead of me. For a moment, I felt overwhelmed. If I was right, Richard had every possible advantage. How could I beat *that?*

Shireen's prophecy had given me an answer. Rachel. If she turned, then Richard would lose.

But how would that help? Rachel was powerful, but not *that* powerful. The only reason she'd been such a problem for so long was because she hated me so much. Well, that and the fact that she was so batshit crazy that—

I stopped.

That divination works really badly on her.

I sat quite still.

I felt the gate spell ten minutes later as Luna returned to the Hollow. She'd come straight back after talking to Variam, and she made a beeline for me through the trees. 'Richard launched an attack last night,' Luna said as she walked into view.

'Where?'

'Vari says there were two. The first one was on the ground-floor offices of the War Rooms in Westminster. Mixed force, mostly adepts. The guards managed to hold out long enough for a response team to arrive and when it did they surrounded them. A few of Richard's mages escaped through a gate, the rest were wiped out.'

'The ground floor of the War Rooms?' I said. 'What were they going for?'

'Fighting was around the security checkpoints, I think?'

I frowned. 'But all the important places in the War Rooms are below ground. Taking the security checkpoints doesn't get you anywhere.'

'The way Vari talked about it, they seemed to think it

was the first stage of an actual attack and they aborted midway through.'

'Mm. You said there were two attacks.'

'Other one was on some place called the Eyrie,' Luna said. 'I've never heard of it, but Vari seemed to know what it was.'

'It's the Council's main monitoring centre,' I said. 'Tracks calls and video feeds, runs surveillance, sends dispatch requests to Keeper HQ. Back when I was in the Keepers, most of our comms were routed through there.'

'Well, it's not going to be doing that any more. According to Vari, they wiped the place clean. Killed all the staff, then set off an EMP that fried every computer in a city block.'

I stared down at the grass, then turned away from Luna and began pacing. 'What are they doing now?'

'The Council? Figuring out what happened and calling up their reserves. All the Keepers are on standby right now, waiting while Council intelligence tries to track down Richard's forces for a counterstrike. As soon as they find something, Vari says they're going all in.'

I thought for a moment. 'Was there any connection between the two attacks?'

'They think hitting the Eyrie was meant to cut the War Rooms off from reinforcements.'

'The War Rooms are too well guarded for that. All it'd do would be slow down the Keeper response teams. And it wouldn't even do that very well.'

Luna shrugged. 'Can only tell you what I heard. What do you think's going on?'

'I'm not sure,' I said slowly. 'Something feels off.'

'You don't think it was Richard?'

'Oh, it was Richard all right. But attacking two targets at the same time doesn't make sense. Even with the jinn, Anne can't be in two places at once.'

'You think one was a fake?'

I nodded. 'He's done it before. In which case, the real target must be the attack that succeeded, on the Eyrie. Question is what he was trying to do. Wiping the computers makes it sound as though he was trying to take out their records, but it's hard to see what they could have on there that would be worth that much.'

'Something they didn't know they had?'

'Or he could be setting up for a different attack. With the Eyrie gone, the Council's response time's going to be lengthened.'

'The War Rooms again?'

'Maybe,' I said dubiously. Taking out the War Rooms would end the war, full stop. But for that exact reason it was the most heavily defended fortress in Britain. Even with Anne, I didn't think Richard had the firepower to break it.

'Well, Vari thinks we should get ready to move,' Luna said. 'They're going after Richard as soon as they manage to follow the attacker's trail. Vari says he'll tell us as soon as they have a lead.'

I hesitated, then shook my head. 'No.'

'You know they're not just after Richard, right?' Luna said. 'Anne's right at the top of their list, too. Vari says their orders are to kill her on sight.'

'I can believe it, but I don't think they're going to find her,' I said. 'Not unless Richard wants her found.' I thought for moment. 'We're going to have to split up. Go out of the Hollow and stay in contact with Vari.'

'I thought you just said you didn't think they were going to find her?'

'I might be wrong.'

'What are you going to do, then?'

'I'm waiting to hear back from Chalice,' I said. 'She's got one last piece of the puzzle that I need before I can move.'

Luna disappeared, and I waited in the Hollow, checking every ten minutes to see if Chalice would be in contact. I was tense now – I didn't know how much longer I had before Richard would strike.

But luck was with me. After less than an hour, my search through the futures found what I was looking for, and I gated out of the Hollow to find a text message on my phone. It contained an address and nothing more. Chalice hadn't added a signature; she didn't need to.

Buenos Aires, I thought. *Feels right.* I sent a message out through the dreamstone calling Starbreeze. I didn't have much time.

Starbreeze set me down in an out-of-the way street in one of Buenos Aires's suburbs before darting off. White-painted houses were nestled behind walls and gardens, and in the distance, down the slope of the hill, I could see the blue sparkle of the river. I checked my phone for the address Chalice had given me, and started walking.

It was winter here, but to me, the Buenos Aires winter felt more like spring. The neighbourhood was pretty but not hospitable – trees lined the road and climbing plants bloomed red and violet on the walls, but the gates were made of thick metal bars and more than one wall was topped with razor wire.

I stopped in front of a house that looked much the same as all the others, two storeys high and painted white, with a black iron fence blocking off access to the garden. There was nothing from outside that marked it out, but with my magesight I could feel the faint signature of wards. The rectangular box of an alarm system was mounted on the outside wall.

I glanced around, scaled the fence at the corner and dropped down on the other side. You really don't appreciate having two working hands until you've had to do without for a while. On the other side was a path of paving stones that led me into a back garden. A stone fountain bubbled away in the middle of a well-tended lawn, with a pagoda on the far side of a goldfish pond. The back of the house held a veranda, French windows leading into a living room. A minute's work got the French windows unlocked and I stepped inside. An alarm panel to my left blinked red; I typed in the code and the light settled obediently on green.

The inside of the house smelt of woodwork and expensive carpets. A grandfather clock ticked, the sound echoing in the quiet. In the kitchen, a light lunch and a jug of orange juice had been laid out on the counter. I climbed the stairs, checking for traps and tell-tales and finding nothing. The bedroom was light and airy, with a balcony overlooking the garden. A double bed held rumpled sheets, as well as two or three outfits lying in roughly the place someone would have tossed them after trying them on in front of the mirror.

I path-walked through the futures in which I hung around, and got a hit between thirty minutes and an hour. I settled down to wait.

The futures narrowed as I waited, focusing until I knew

precisely who would be arriving and when. When the sound of the front door opening drifted up from down below, I was ready. Voices echoed from the hallway, a man and a woman. The language was Spanish, but I could recognise the tones of voice. The man was pushing, entreating; the woman wasn't quite saying yes, but wasn't turning him away. A last exchange of words, then the man's footsteps were moving towards the kitchen, while the woman's shoes clattered on the wooden steps as she headed upstairs.

I moved out onto the balcony, letting the blinds shield me from view. Footsteps sounded from the landing, then the woman was walking into the bedroom. I stayed out of view, studying her through the futures.

Meredith is small and delicate, only a little over five feet tall, with long flowing dark hair. She wore a black blouse and skirt with brown-and-gold highlights, and moved with the confidence of someone who knew that people would find her attractive. And if they didn't, well, she could change that. Meredith is an enchantress, able to manipulate emotions, and she's good at it. She's less skilled when it comes to politics. In the time I'd known her, she'd worked for both the Council and for Richard, without siding with either, and had ended up giving them both good reason to distrust her. Apparently she'd decided to hide out here while things calmed down.

The man called up something from downstairs: I caught the word '*noche*'. Meredith glanced down in annoyance, but her tone as she called back to him was sweet and welcoming. She dropped her handbag onto the bed and was just starting to open it when she paused, frowning. She looked up towards the balcony.

Looks like we're done hiding. I'd been using the fateweaver to push away the futures in which Meredith detected me, but you can't keep people careless for ever. I strode into the bedroom. 'Meredith,' I said. 'We need to talk.'

Meredith's eyes went as big as dinner plates. 'Mateo!' she screamed.

I heard the clatter of something falling followed by footsteps racing up the stairs. The door slammed open and a young man burst in. He was dressed in a tight-fitting outfit of black, decorated in silver thread, and he had a long knife drawn in one hand. With two strides he put himself between me and Meredith.

'Tell your boy-toy to wait outside,' I told Meredith.

Mateo said something in Spanish, not taking his eyes off me. The knife stayed pointed towards my chest.

'No,' Meredith said. 'He's one of the ones—from before, the ones I was telling you about. Mateo, be careful, he's been hunting for me.'

Mateo replied confidently, then switched to accented English, addressing me. 'Leave now, Dark mage. While you still can.'

'Mateo, or whatever your name is, right now I have no particular intention of hurting either you or your mistress. Keep pointing that knife at me and that's going to change. Now, I'm not going to ask again. Go wait outside.'

'I don't know who you are or where you came from,' Mateo said, 'but I'm sure of one thing. No man of honour would enter a lady's bedchamber and threaten her like this.' He drew back his knife in a combat stance, flourishing his free hand; blue energy glowed at his fingertips. 'Come dance with me, if you dare.'

I looked at Meredith in annoyance. 'Where did you find this clown?'

'Catalina, stay behind me,' Mateo announced, glancing back towards Meredith. 'I'll handle—'

I strode towards Mateo. He stepped forward to meet me, light flashing on the blade.

There was a flurry of movement.

The hilt of the knife slammed into Mateo's chin with a solid *thud*. Mateo's eyes rolled back into his skull and he collapsed to the floor. I flipped the knife in my hand and thrust it towards Meredith. 'Stay!'

Meredith froze. She'd started to back towards the door when the fighting had started, but had only made it two steps before it was over. 'Now,' I said. 'You owe me. I'm here to collect.'

'Owe you?' Meredith's eyes flickered down to Mateo, lying unconscious, then from side to side. I knew she was sizing up escape routes. 'What do you—?'

'Six years ago, you sold me and Luna out,' I said. 'I haven't come after you because quite frankly I've had better things to do. But right now, I've got a job that needs doing, and I need a charm mage. You're it.'

'I don't— I can't do anything like that.'

'Oh yes, you can.'

'I can't go back to Britain. The Council will kill me!'

'I'm a member of the Council, and I've seen their most-wanted list. You're not on it.'

'They'll still pull me in for questioning.'

'Right now, they've got bigger things to worry about. And even if they didn't, it wouldn't matter, because you don't get a vote.'

Meredith looked at me nervously. Her attention was all

on me; besides an initial glance when he fell, she hadn't looked at Mateo at all. 'This thing you want me to do. It's dangerous, isn't it?'

'Depends on how well you can do your job.'

'How dangerous?'

'A lot *less* dangerous than turning me down.'

Meredith took a breath; the possibilities of her turning and fleeing flickered, then vanished as the futures bent towards a different path. 'You have to understand,' she said. Her dark eyes rested on me, imploring. 'What happened in the Tiger's Palace . . . it changed things. Those people dying . . .' She took a shaky breath. 'I ran away. I couldn't go back, not after . . . It was too horrible.' There was open fear on her face, and I could feel her terror. 'I can't be a part of something like that. Not again.' Her words vibrated with emotion. I could sense she was on the verge of tears, and I felt a wave of sympathy. It would be too cruel to force her to—

The knife flew past Meredith's hair to sink into the door-frame with a solid *tchunk*. Meredith screamed and the emotions rolling over me suddenly vanished. I was on her in two strides; Meredith flinched, shielding her head, and I slammed my hand into the door-frame behind her, leaning in so that our faces were close. 'Rule number one,' I said clearly. 'Use your magic on me again and I will make you regret it.'

'What do you even need me for?' Meredith cried. 'What do you want?'

'I need you to make someone do something stupid and impulsive that goes against their self-interest. And that is something I know from personal experience that you are very good at.'

'Someone? Who?'

I told her. As I kept talking, Meredith's face grew pale.

I told Meredith that I'd be back later that evening. Reluctantly, she promised to be there and not to try to run away.

As soon as I was out of sight, Meredith tried to run away. I intervened and gave her a reason not to do it again. Once we were done, I gated back to the Hollow.

I'd already checked in with Luna and my other contacts and come up dry. There were reports of skirmishes between Council forces and adepts, but neither the Council nor Richard had made their move. In the meantime, there was one more person I needed to talk to. I went back to my bed, lay down and closed my eyes. It took me longer than it should have to fall asleep.

I walked through Elsewhere, landscapes shifting and changing around me. Once upon a time, just visiting this place would have been dangerous. Now it felt like a refuge before the battle ahead. My progress slowed as I drew closer to my destination, and when the city came to an end, the buildings falling away to be replaced with towering trees, I came to a halt. I stood between the pillars at the end of a colonnade, looking at the forest ahead. Dark green leaves rose up into an overcast sky, the wind hissing through the branches and making the tree trunks creak and sway. I couldn't see the tower in the middle of the forest, but I knew it was there.

I was on the border between my Elsewhere and Anne's. I could cross into her realm, but as soon as I did, she'd know I was there. And then she'd come to meet me, and that was something I didn't want. Not yet.

Ever since taking up the fateweaver, I'd felt strong, powerful. I hadn't been worried when facing Rachel or Meredith. Onyx and Pyre had been a threat, but one I'd approached coolly and calmly. Even when I'd been pressured during the battle, I'd never felt afraid.

But I was afraid of facing Anne. Deep down, I still wanted to plead with her, tell her how sorry I was in the hope that things could go back to how they once were . . . and I knew it was a terrible idea. All my instincts told me that Anne's dark side would react to that *very* badly. I had to meet her from a position of strength.

I didn't feel like I was in a position of strength. I felt horribly vulnerable.

I sensed movement, a presence. Dark Anne had detected me, and she was coming. I fought back the impulse to run away, took a deep breath and stood with my arms folded.

Dark Anne came walking out from between the trees, the undergrowth rustling beneath her feet. She was dressed in grey this time, a drably coloured dress that matched the muted tones of the sky above. 'Well, well,' she called out as she approached. 'Look who's back.'

She doesn't sound angry. I felt a flash of hope, and squashed it; it was more than I could afford. I tried to sound confident. 'Long time no see.'

Dark Anne stopped at the edge of the tree cover, the leaves at the tips of the branches just barely overhanging her head. I stayed where I was at the edge of the colonnade, yellow-grey stone darkened with age. Between us was the border between the two realms, cracked paving stones giving way to tufts of grass.

'I'm sorry about what happened.' I managed to keep my voice steady, but only just. 'It wasn't my choice.'

'Yeah, I know, it was Crystal,' Dark Anne said. 'I figured it out as soon as she and Richard came through that door.'

'Would have been nice if you'd figured it out before killing my right hand.'

'So don't get possessed next time.'

We stood looking at each other for a minute. 'Let's take a walk,' I suggested.

Dark Anne considered for a moment, then shrugged. 'Why not?'

I began walking to the right, and Dark Anne paced me, the two of us following the border of the two realms. To my right were the buildings of my cityscape; to the left Anne's forest. 'Where's your other half?' I asked.

'Somewhere safe,' Dark Anne said. 'For me, that is. And no, before you ask, you don't get to see her. I learned my lesson last time, thank you very much.'

'How is she?'

'No worse off than she treated me. Is she all you wanted to talk about?'

'No, right now I'm more interested in you. How's Richard treating you?'

'I suppose it could be worse,' Dark Anne said. 'At least I get a better room than I had with Sagash.'

'I meant more as in whether he's having Crystal mind-control you.'

'Oh, that. No. I mean, she could – probably – but it wouldn't be much good for combat. No, it's that dream-stone. He can't use it to control me, but apparently he *can* use it to control the jinn. Which really sucks, by the way. I spent so long working out an arrangement with that thing, and then Richard comes along and surprise! Turns out he's been studying jinn for, like, his entire *life*, and he knows literally everything there is to know about them. He's figured out some way to use that dreamstone of his to shut down that jinn completely, at least when it comes to using its powers. So I can do what I want, except if I don't do what Richard says, then he snaps his fingers and suddenly I have to deal with a pissed-off jinn and all of Richard's gang as well. So yeah, I'm pretty much stuck.'

'Were you expecting working for Richard to go any other way?'

'So are you going to do anything to help?'

'What, I'm supposed to sort out your problems now? You *wanted* this. Don't come crying now that it turns out Richard's keeping you on a short leash.'

'It would have worked out just fine if you hadn't messed it up.' Dark Anne waved a hand. 'Fine, whatever, mistakes were made. Water under the bridge and all that. What are you going to do about it?'

We'd drawn closer as we walked, until now we were pacing side by side, almost within arm's reach. 'If I wanted to break you free,' I said, 'what's the best way to do it?'

'Destroy that dreamstone,' Dark Anne said. 'It's messing everything up. And I do mean *destroy* it, just in case you're getting any cute ideas about taking it for yourself. Richard's bonded to it, and as long as it's there, he can call the shots. If I'd known the trouble that stupid thing would cause, I'd have thrown it away back in that shadow realm.'

'Even if the dreamstone's gone, there's still Crystal. She can use that imbued item and dominate you the old-fashioned way.'

'She can't dominate anyone if she's dead,' Dark Anne said flatly. 'I've been wanting to settle the score with that bitch for a *long* time. Trust me, you get rid of the dreamstone, and Crystal will stop being a problem really fast.'

'All right,' I said. 'So the next question is how to find him.'

'Yeah, somehow I don't think that's the biggest thing you have to worry about.'

'Richard keeps the dreamstone on him. If I want to get rid of it, I have to catch him first.'

'*You* are going to catch *him*?' Dark Anne looked at me with raised eyebrows. 'Someone got two spoonfuls of self-esteem in their Corn Flakes this morning. I hope you're bringing a lot of friends.'

'Just me.'

'Were you not listening or something?' Dark Anne stopped, turning to face me. 'I can not pull your feet out of the fire on this one. I can stop Richard from just wishing you out of existence, but when it comes to you and him, you'll be on your own. And it *won't* be just you and him, because Richard doesn't go out on his own these days. There's Morden, Vihaela, Deleo, Crystal, some air mage assassin guy who never talks, a radiation mage called Tenebrous . . . you're going to be dealing with at least two or three out of those guys, plus however many he decides to bring along from his adept army. Did I mention the adept army? Morden's been training them up in some shadow realm he calls Arcadia. You want to stand a chance, you're going to need firepower and lots of it.'

'Not really an option.'

'Argh.' Dark Anne covered her eyes. 'Look, it's cute that you're trying to impress me here, but in case you haven't noticed, all of those mages I just listed are ones who either *can* mop the floor with you, or already *have*.

You are not winning this on your own, so either call in some favours or find some people who hate Richard badly enough and point them at him.'

'I've gone through some changes since we last met.'

'What, you're missing a hand?'

I just looked at her.

'Say you find him,' Dark Anne said. 'What are you going to do, talk him to death?'

'No, I have a plan,' I told her. 'I just don't trust you enough to tell it to you. You went behind my back to make a deal with Morden and Richard once. I don't feel like giving you the ammo to do it again.'

'Well, look who's acting alpha male all of a sudden.' Dark Anne folded her arms and studied me, tapping one finger on her upper arm, then shrugged. 'Fine, it's not like I'm swimming in options. Shoot.'

'I need to know where and when Richard's going to be next.'

'He doesn't brief me,' Dark Anne said. 'I get told when he's launching an attack, and that's it.'

'What about if I spoke to you through the dreamstone the next time you move out?'

'They watch me too closely for that. I try to talk to you like this and Crystal will know. It'll be hard enough stopping her from seeing these memories.'

'He has to talk to Morden and Vihaela at least.'

'Not while I'm around. They discuss the current mission and that's it.' Dark Anne paused. 'There's one thing though. I think Richard's tracking the Senior Council.'

'Are you sure?'

'All through the attack, Deleo was giving Richard updates,' Dark Anne said. 'Saying "they've moved", or "they haven't moved", stuff like that. No names, but right at the end, Richard asked her about something, and she dropped Bahamus's name. Richard gave her a look and she shut up.' Dark Anne shrugged. 'That's all I've got.'

'I guess it'll have to do.'

Dark Anne glanced back towards the forest. 'Time for me to go.'

'All right.'

But she didn't move, and neither did I. We stood within arm's reach, looking at each other. 'I miss you,' I said.

Dark Anne grinned. 'Come see me once that dreamstone's gone. I'll be waiting.' She turned and walked away.

I watched Dark Anne go. She disappeared into the trees without looking back, the wind swaying the branches above. Only when I was sure that she was gone did I step out of Elsewhere and wake, opening my eyes to see the ceiling of my cottage in the Hollow. Anne's side of the bed was empty and I was alone once more.

It was just after eleven when Luna found me. 'It's on,' she said simply.

I was ready and waiting. I was thin on gear – my armour was still repairing itself, and I hadn't had a chance to restock my one-shots – but I had my dreamstone and the fateweaver. 'Where?' I asked, buckling on my webbing belt.

'The Council's got a lead on Richard's shadow realm,' Luna said. 'Vari says they're gearing up to move right now.'

I holstered my gun. 'Let's go.'

We stepped out from the gate and onto the roof of the Arcana Emporium. Luna had had some extensions done to the chimney when she'd had the place rebuilt, and I had to step around the brickwork to get a view of the street.

Luna had one hand to her ear and was talking into her communicator. 'Yeah,' she was saying. 'You sure? . . . Okay.' She turned to me. 'Okay, it might not be Richard's home base. New intel is that it's the adept training camp. They're trying to force entry right now.'

'Okay.'

Luna waited for me to go on. When I didn't, she looked at me. 'So?' she said.

'Give me a second,' I said absently. I walked to the edge of the roof, looking out over the Camden rooftops. The sounds and smells of the city drifted up from the street below: shouts and yells from a party somewhere nearby, the scent of Indian food from the restaurant opposite, a siren rising and falling in the far distance, fading away. I'd often come up here to think, back in the old days.

'Are we going?' Luna asked.

'No.'

'Vari says there's one hundred per cent going to be a fight.'

'I don't care if there's a fight. I care about Richard and Anne.'

Minutes ticked by. I path-walked, searching the futures for any trace of Richard and not finding one. I was certain I'd be able to find one if I waited long enough – the further things developed, the easier it would be to find his trace – but that would take time I didn't have.

Luna put a hand to her ear, listening, then looked at me. 'They're trying to break in through combat gates.'

I nodded.

'You still might be able to make it if you go now.'

I tapped a knuckle to my lips, then shook my head. 'Wait.'

'This is going to be the biggest fight in this war so far,' Luna said.

'I'm not buying it,' I said. 'So far, every time Richard's engaged the Council, he's done it on his own terms.'

'Okay, look,' Luna said. 'You haven't told me much about what you're planning here. From what you've been saying, I'm guessing it has something to do with Deleo. But once you find Richard, you do actually *have* a plan, right? You're not trying to go out in a blaze of glory?'

'No, both of us are going to be walking away from this one.'

'How?'

'The times you've gone out gambling, did you ever try poker?'

Luna looked at me in surprise, her face faintly illuminated in the orange of the street lights below. 'Not much. Too little luck once the cards are dealt. Why?'

'Your play style in poker falls on a scale,' I said. 'Tight versus loose. No one's a hundred per cent one or the other, but the longer you play, the more you find the point on the scale where you're most comfortable. So most of the time, when you first sit down at a table, you want to play your natural style because it's what you're best at. But once someone gets to know you? Then you'll usually find you make the most money when you take your natural style and play the opposite.'

Luna frowned. 'I don't get it.'

'I've tried talking to Rachel a lot of times the past few years,' I said. 'I've tried persuading her, tried probing for a weakness, but I've never pretended to be anything I'm not.'

'How's that going to—?' Luna paused, as if listening to something. 'They've broken in. Keeper teams are entering the shadow realm. Vari says the fighting's already started.'

'All right,' I said. If Richard was going to make a move, this was when he'd do it.

Seconds ticked by. I searched through futures, picking through possibilities of me making calls, checking on contacts, scouting in person. It was slow-going; too much variation between the futures.

Maybe I should play a hunch. Assume I was right and Richard was going after one of the Council. Who would he pick? No, that was the wrong question. If I were Richard, and I wanted to weaken the Council's resolve, make it more willing to come to terms, who would I want removed?

I'd go after Levistus or Sal Sarque. I narrowed my focus to those two but widened the trace. Nothing, nothing . . . wait.

There.

'It's Sal Sarque,' I said. 'Richard's going to make a move on him while the Council forces attack Arcadia.'

Luna frowned. 'Are you sure? If you wait, we can—'

'Can't,' I called over my shoulder. I was already sending out a call to Starbreeze. 'Keep in touch with Vari. I'll call you with the dreamstone.'

14

Two minutes later, I was in the air and soaring. The lights of London had disappeared behind us, and the English countryside was opening up ahead, glowing lines marking the roads and sparkling orange webs the towns. Starbreeze rode the winds at lightning speed, spiralling as she went for the sheer fun of it.

So wait, Luna said. *Sal Sarque isn't in the War Rooms?*

He's got a command centre in that island fortress of his, I said. *Whenever there's a major op, he runs it from there. Means he can funnel all the intel through him and choose what does and doesn't get reported to the Council.*

Island fortress. Sounds great.

The Midlands were racing below us; a city swept past to our left that might have been Leeds. We passed an airliner, its lights blinking white-red-green, there and gone in a flash. *I'm not storming it single-handed*, I said. *I'm going to slip in while the two groups are busy fighting. This is the biggest and most important attack that Richard's launched, which means Anne's going to be at the spearhead. I just need to catch up.*

Don't you want to take someone?

I am. Just not someone I care about.

While I'd been talking, we'd passed over the coastline and swept out over the sea. Starbreeze veered from side to side, dodging clouds before zipping right through a big one. My vision greyed out; when we emerged on the other side, I could make out a few black spots in the distance, visible against the moonlit waters.

I checked the futures quickly, remembering my mental map. Sal Sarque's island was at the south end of a small chain. *There*, I said to Starbreeze. *Angle that way.*

Starbreeze came down in a shallow dive, losing height until she was skimming the waves. The smell of salt water surrounded me, the moonlight a bright reflection off to the right and its light casting a white glow over each wave. Up ahead, the island was getting bigger fast. Very fast. *Not too close*, I said to Starbreeze. *We need to circle around, find a safe place to set—*

Boring. I want to see!

No, wait, don't—

We pulled up just in front of the cliffs and sped upwards at lightning speed, shooting out past the cliff edge and up into the sky right above the south end of the island.

It gave us a great view of the battle.

Sal Sarque's fortress was built on and around a rock outcropping at the island's southern end, and it was under attack. Flashes of coloured light sparkled on the fortress walls and roof and in the rocks nearby. The fortress itself was squat and massive, the walls thick and heavy with covered guard towers, and emplacements on the top were hurling fire into the darkness below.

Ooh, Starbreeze said in fascination. *Pretty.* She angled in for a closer look.

Pull back! Starbreeze! Back!

Why? Starbreeze asked. She'd drifted close enough that I could pick out movement on the roof.

They have anti-air, that's why!

What's anti-air?

A bolt of energy lit the night, joining the rooftop with Starbreeze's position. I shoved frantically at the futures and made it miss by a hair, the heat scorching my airborne body as Starbreeze veered away. *That!*

Oh, okay. Starbreeze didn't seem particularly worried. She swept down and right, putting a ridgeline between us and the fortress. *Didn't look scary.*

Maybe not to you! Held aloft by Starbreeze, I had no way of dodging. *It would have vaporised me.*

Well, you're going to die really soon anyway.

Which was jarring to hear. I think of Starbreeze as my friend, and she *is* my friend, as much as she can be. But she's also very far away from being human. Right now, she was helping me, and as far as I could tell, she was going to keep helping me – right up until I died, at which point she'd promptly forget me the same way she's forgotten the countless other mortals she's known. When she said I was going to die 'really soon', she could mean tomorrow or in fifty years. To Starbreeze, there's not much difference.

Starbreeze dived into a small ravine and turned me solid again. My shoes scraped on rock and I shifted to keep my balance. I could hear the sounds of battle from over the ridge, the stammer of machine-gunfire mixing with the *whoom* of fire spells. 'Can you wait here? A lift would—'

'Boring,' Starbreeze announced. 'Want to see the lights.' She sped up into the night sky and was gone.

'Or I could walk,' I said to the rocks. I took out the gate stone that I'd taken from Meredith's house, and channelled. From over the ridge, I could hear the sounds of battle. The gate opened and I stepped through.

Meredith's street in Buenos Aires felt weirdly quiet and calm. The gate stone came out into her back garden; night had fallen here as well, and the lights were on in her windows. I took out my phone and dialled her number.

No answer.

I frowned, took out the focus I'd picked up yesterday – a small rod of black metal – and channelled through it.

Magic sparked, and I heard a faint clatter from inside the house. A minute later, Meredith appeared at the back doorway, looking rattled. 'You didn't have to do that!'

'Yes, I did. Get moving, we're on a schedule.'

Meredith approached the gate uncertainly. She'd changed her outfit, though it still didn't look particularly practical. 'Where *is* that?'

'British Isles.' I stepped through and beckoned.

Meredith hesitated. 'I'm not sure . . .'

'You'll be in and out in less than an hour.'

'You're not going to ask for anything else?'

'Do this and I'll be out of your life for ever.' I smiled slightly. 'Unless you'd rather I stuck around.'

Meredith didn't look convinced, but she stepped through the gate. I let it close behind her and started up the rocks towards the ridgeline.

'I can't see,' Meredith complained.

I sighed inwardly. This would have been so much easier if I could have brought Luna instead. I took Meredith's hand and started leading her. 'Follow in my footsteps,' I told her. 'The ground's solid, so just concentrate on keeping your balance.'

'What's that noise from over that mountain?'

'That's not a mountain. That's a ridge.'

'You know what I mean. It sounds like a battle.'

'That's because it is.'

'Alex!' Meredith tried to stop; I kept my grip on her

hand and she was dragged along. 'You didn't say anything about a battle!'

'Yeah, well, they didn't ask my permission. Relax, I'm not expecting you to win it.'

We reached the edge of the ridgeline and again Meredith tried to stop. The bulk of Sal Sarque's fortress loomed before us, lit up by the flashes of spells and weapon fire. The machine-gunfire was still going, but it seemed to be coming from the other side of the fortress. At least one thing was going our way.

'Wait, we're going down *there*? We can't— Alex! Stop!'

I was already picking us a path down the slope towards the walls. No immediate danger flashed up in the futures; it might be premature, but it looked as though we might be able to make it all the way there without running into anyone. Some possibilities of contact flickered and I adjusted our course to steer away. 'Keep your voice down.'

'We're going to be killed!'

'No, we're not.'

'What happens if they see us?'

'They won't.'

'How do you know?'

'Because I'm a diviner and that's what I do.'

'I don't like this. Please can we go back?'

I wondered if Richard had to deal with stuff like this from his followers. It was giving me a new appreciation for what he had to put up with.

The battle was still raging by the time we reached the walls. There'd been fighting on this side too, but it had apparently moved away, though not without casualties; we'd passed several bodies in the darkness. I was scanning through the futures, looking for ways to gain entry. The main gate was on the far side and moving around would take too long. Maybe another entrance . . . *There*. I changed direction and started walking.

Meredith tripped on the rocks and I held her as she caught her balance. 'Where are we going?' she whispered. The looming shadow of the walls felt a lot more menacing up close.

'Back door,' I said quietly. I could feel the futures I needed; reaching out with the fateweaver, I picked the one I wanted and began feeding it. 'We're going to have to talk our way past a few people. Back me up.'

The futures settled, and I moved up against the wall and waited. I couldn't make out the line of the door, but I knew where it was. Thirty seconds later it opened, light spilling from the crack. The muzzle of a handgun appeared, followed by a young man, peering out cautiously.

I snatched the gun out of the man's hand, caught his arm as he tried to punch me, twisted it behind his back and pushed through the doorway into the fortress before he'd finished his shout. The door led into a guardroom. Half a dozen men were scattered around, ranging in age from teenage years to thirties. They were armed but raggedly equipped; they had the look of Richard's adepts, which was confirmed when fire lit up around the hands of one at the back and another created a force blade. The rest levelled guns.

'I'm here to see Richard Drakh,' I said. I pushed the guy I'd been holding away; he took a few steps, stumbling, then turned on me. 'Where is he?'

'Whose side are you on?' the man with the force blade said. He was light-skinned, standing in a combat stance with his left hand holding a shield; the force blade was a long triangle, stretching from his right hand and narrowing to a point. He was staring at me suspiciously, but he wasn't attacking yet.

'My side.' I ejected the round from the gun, took out the magazine, then tossed the weapon without looking at the man I'd taken it from. He caught it in surprise. The other adepts exchanged glances. 'And I'm here to see Richard.'

Meredith was hanging behind me in the doorway. 'I don't know who you are,' the force adept began, 'but—'

'Wait,' another adept said. 'That's Verus.'

'The one Deleo said—'

'Yeah, that one.'

I saw the force adept's eyes shift. The futures of violence leapt closer and I knew I had seconds before they'd start shooting. I met his gaze and spoke clearly and calmly. 'I have killed twenty-eight normals, adepts and mages in the past two days. Come at me with that force blade, and you'll make twenty-nine.'

The adept hesitated, his futures wavering between life and death. I pushed at them, but the fateweaver wasn't mind control; it couldn't override a direct choice.

Then a wave of emotion rippled through me, fear and horror and nameless dread. I pushed it off with an effort of will, but it had been aimed at the adepts, not at me. Several went pale and one dropped his gun with a clatter, backing up to the wall. The force adept flinched, taking a step back.

'Deleo gave you those orders for her own reasons,' I said. 'You weren't expected to survive them. I'll ask again. Where's Richard?'

'I don't know.' Fear showed in the force adept's eyes; his voice shook. 'He was heading for the control room.'

'Good enough.' I beckoned to Meredith and walked through the room. No one stopped us. Only when we were through the far doorway and walking down the corridor on the other side did I breathe a little easier.

'Good job on that spell,' I told Meredith once we were out of earshot.

Meredith didn't look happy at the praise. 'Why do you want to find *Drakh* of all people?'

'Because he made me an offer. Now stay quiet while I focus.'

The fortress interior was stone and metal, brutally practical. The thick walls muffled sound, but even so I could hear gunfire. As the futures branched ahead, forking and dividing, I saw danger in every direction, but no sign of Richard.

But the only reason for Richard to be here was to come after Sal Sarque, and Sarque would be at the control room at the centre. 'This way,' I said, heading for a set of stairs.

We climbed to the first floor. The corridor at the top had been fortified; a junction had been turned into something like a bunker, with blast shields and weapon racks. It hadn't done the defenders any good. The remains of several constructs were scattered around, along with outlines of black dust.

'They're fighting all around us,' Meredith said. She was looking nervously from side to side at the walls. 'If the Keepers see us—'

'They've got their hands full,' I said. There was a battle going on on the ground floor below us at this very moment. But the corridor we were in was empty, and I was pretty sure I knew why. We were following the same route that Richard and Anne had taken, and they'd blasted their way through anyone who'd tried to stop them. Right now, the path to the control centre was undefended.

Of course, just because a route's undefended doesn't mean it's going to stay that way.

Running footsteps sounded from a side passage up ahead. 'We've got a speed bump,' I said. 'I'll handle it.'

'Wait, a speed bump? What kind—?'

The footsteps grew louder, and a Keeper came running into our corridor just ahead of us, skidding to a halt as she saw us. It was Caldera, dressed in her working clothes and webbing belt with the dust and sweat of combat on her. 'I've found them,' Caldera said into her communicator. 'Moving to engage.' She started towards us. 'Verus, you're under arrest. Stay where you are.'

I came to a halt, picking out possible futures and identifying candidates. One jumped out and I started feeding it, watching it grow. *Force mage. That'll do.*

Caldera came to a halt twenty feet away. Her eyes flicked to Meredith, who took a half-step back behind me. 'And Meredith Blake,' Caldera said. 'You're wanted for questioning as well.'

'You're in my way,' I told Caldera.

'You're here with Richard?' Caldera said. 'Because if—'

'I don't have time for you right now.'

Caldera planted herself. 'Looking for a rematch?'

'I don't have to. There's a Dark force mage one level below you who's a really bad shot.'

Caldera frowned. 'What's that—?'

The force blast tore out the floor under Caldera, destroying a section of corridor about ten feet wide. With a rumble the flooring collapsed, sending Caldera tumbling down in an avalanche of concrete and stone. I saw Caldera's hands fly up, earth magic reinforcing her as she fell, then she was gone.

I walked around the hole in the floor. Dust clouds obscured the view down, but I could hear shouts and the sounds of combat. 'Keep up,' I said over my shoulder.

'This is crazy!' Meredith whispered. 'They're going to be after us!'

A chunk of concrete came flying up through the hole in the floor, shattering against the ceiling and raining fist-sized chunks of stone onto the other side of the hole. 'Like I said, they've got their hands full.' I'd already plotted out the rest of our course. We were clear all the way to the control centre.

Admittedly, part of the reason we had a clear route was because right now, that route was a dead end. The corridor went through two right-angle turns and then ended in what was apparently a mirrored wall, slightly convex.

'We can't get through that,' Meredith said nervously, looking over her shoulder. 'That's a stasis sphere.'

'More likely a barrier,' I said absently. I could feel the time magic radiating from the 'mirror'. There's no way to see how deep a stasis effect goes, but putting a stasis effect on yourself makes no sense as a defence against any kind of prolonged attack. I finished checking the futures and nodded. The wards on the fortress would bar standard gates, but they were less effective against the dreamstone, and the stasis spell had weakened the wards immediately around it. With the fateweaver's help, I could push through. 'Okay, showtime. Once we're inside, there'll be no more talk. You remember what you have to do?'

'Yes . . .'

'Are you going to do it?'

'All right.'

I looked at Meredith. That had been too easy. 'You're afraid of them.'

'Of course I'm afraid of them! They're going to kill me as soon as they see me!'

'You don't need to be seen.' I walked closer to Meredith, forcing her to tilt her head back to meet my eyes. 'Last year at the Tiger's Palace, Deleo tried to disintegrate you. You remember what she said right before she did it?'

Meredith didn't answer.

'There are two ways in which I'm different from Deleo,' I told Meredith. 'The first is that I won't ask you to do anything you aren't capable of. If I give you an order, it means I know it can work, and I'm using my power to make sure it *will* work.' I paused to make sure that Meredith was listening. 'The second way I'm different from Deleo? I'm a lot faster to write off losses. Do you need a demonstration of that?'

'No,' Meredith said quietly.

I nodded. 'Let's do it.'

I reached out through the dreamstone and opened up a gate to Elsewhere, then took Meredith's hand and led her unresisting through it. I don't think she recognised what it was. She certainly didn't have time to look around or notice the trails of light coming from her skin before I opened a second gateway and took us back into the real world.

The control centre of Sal Sarque's fortress was a two-storey room, with a raised gantry running around the second level. We'd arrived on the upper level, and my feet hadn't even touched the floor before I knew we weren't alone. I silently motioned Meredith to a position where she'd be able to look down into the room by craning her neck; her eyes were wide with fear but she nodded. Then I strode out onto the gantry.

The floor of the control centre held desks filled with computer equipment. The far wall was covered with flat-screen monitors, most of them blacked out or showing static. There was only one entrance, a pair of thick steel double doors at ground level.

I'd come in at the aftermath of a battle. Bodies lay unmoving around overturned swivel chairs and broken desks. Some were still recognisable; others were scatterings of black dust, only the magical residue giving away that they'd once been human. There had been casualties on both sides, but from the positioning, most of them had probably been Council.

Six people were still alive and upright: four from Richard's side, and two from the defenders'. Richard was standing close to the entrance. He'd glanced up as I appeared, registering my appearance with no sign of surprise, then turned back to what he'd been looking at before. By his side was Anne. The jinn formed a flickering black aura about her, looming up and behind her like a vast shadow. Behind them was Crystal, hanging back where she could watch everyone, and a little ahead of Richard to the other side was Rachel.

Facing them was Sal Sarque. The Senior Council member had been backed up nearly to the far wall, but he looked uninjured and he was holding a remote control of some kind above his head. Hiding behind him was Solace, eyes darting left to right as she tried to look for a way out. Sal Sarque was standing in plain view – he didn't even have a shield up – but none of Richard's cabal were making a move to attack.

Several pairs of eyes glanced at me as I appeared on the gantry, though most of them flicked right back again. Only two people kept their eyes on me. Rachel, and Anne.

For just an instant I hesitated. This was way, *way* too many enemies together in one place, and my old instincts – the ones that had kept me alive for so long – were shouting at me to back off and leave them to it. But then I shook the feeling off and walked forward to rest one hand on the railing. 'I'm sorry,' I said, pitching my voice to carry. 'Am I interrupting something?'

'Calling in more?' Sal Sarque shouted. 'Bring them on!'

'Oh, Richard didn't call me,' I said. I walked down the gantry, feeling Rachel and Anne's eyes follow me. 'I just decided we should talk.'

'If you wanted a discussion,' Richard said, not taking his eyes off Sal Sarque, 'you could have chosen a more convenient time.'

'What can I say?' I came to a stop at the corner of the room, just above the stairs. 'You're a hard man to track down.'

I'd moved in this direction for a reason. Meredith was still hidden back in the alcove, and I needed to draw as much attention from her as I could. Crystal and Anne would be able to tell that there was someone there, but there was a good chance they wouldn't know who.

'I'm afraid we're a little busy at the moment. Could you wait?'

I made an open-handed gesture. 'Go right ahead.'

'He's going to interfere,' Rachel told Anne. Her eyes flicked to Sal Sarque, then back to me. 'Kill him.'

'I don't take orders from you,' Anne told her.

'Neither of you will attempt to kill him without my express instructions,' Richard said calmly. 'As I was saying, Sarque, your position is lost. It is time you came to terms.'

Sal Sarque laughed. He looked keyed up, ready to die any second. 'You're the one who's fucked, Drakh. Every Light mage in the country is on their way here right now.'

'Most of your combat forces are committed to the assault on Arcadia,' Richard said. 'I expect they'll be successful, but Morden and Vihaela will slow them down significantly. Your remaining reserves are currently attacking this fortress from the outside—' Richard paused for a moment. '—and losing. By the time reinforcements arrive, the battle for this fortress will be over.'

'Bullshit.'

'Why do you think I'm still talking to you?'

''Cause of this.' Sal Sarque gestured with the remote. His eyes flicked to me. 'And as for you, Verus, you piece of shit, after today every last member of the Council will be hunting you down.'

I just looked at him. 'As opposed to the last few days?'

'Now they know you're working with Drakh, your last few days are going to look easy.'

'I wasn't working with Drakh, you fucking idiot,' I told Sal Sarque. 'I was one of the *only* members of the Council giving him any effective opposition. And I would have been happy to keep doing that, if you and Levistus had just been willing to work with me. But you had your heads so far up your collective arses that it apparently never occurred to any of you that making an enemy of me might be a bad idea.'

'You were always the enemy,' Sarque said.

'Always a Dark mage?' I shrugged. 'Probably. But becoming *your* enemy was all you.'

'Just kill him,' Rachel said again. 'He's lying.'

'Glass houses, Rachel,' I said. 'By the way, did you ever pass on my message to Richard?'

'I'm sure these are all fascinating conversations,' Richard said, 'but I would appreciate it if you could table them until Sarque and I have addressed the matter at hand.'

'Yeah, come on, Drakh,' Sarque said invitingly. 'Try it. I'll blow you and your pet monster into dust.'

So how's things? I said through the dreamstone to Dark Anne.

How do you think? Dark Anne said in annoyance. *We took out the small fry but Sarque's claiming he's going to blow the place sky-high if we make a move. Make yourself useful and tell us if he's bluffing.*

I'd already checked the futures in which I attacked. If Sarque pressed the button that his thumb was resting on right now, the entire control centre would be torn apart by demolition charges. The fateweaver could protect me from a lot of things, but fifty tons of concrete collapsing on my head wasn't one of them.

He's not bluffing, I told her.

Well, that's just frigging wonderful.

'As I have already said,' Richard told Sarque, 'your death is not a requirement. That goes also for your aide.' He nodded towards Solace. 'I would much rather have you alive than crushed in the remnants of your fortress.'

'Yeah, I bet you would.'

'I am not going to torture you,' Richard said. 'You will be kept in custody with a view to trading you back to the Council in some sort of exchange.'

'Bullshit.'

'This war isn't going to last for ever, Sarque. I have no intention of wiping the Council out to the last man. I'd rather come to a mutual agreement. To that end, you are far more useful to me as a bargaining chip than as a corpse.'

Crystal still hadn't spoken or looked at me. She was watching Richard, and something told me that she was in telepathic contact with him. She was probably eavesdropping on my conversation with Anne too. *Can you kill Sarque before he pushes that button?* I asked Dark Anne.

Maybe.

Think about doing it and I'll check the futures.

'Yeah, nice offer,' Sal Sarque said. 'I'll make you a better one. You come over here and we see how many of you we can kill.'

Dark Anne was doing as I'd asked, and I watched as the futures branched, her attacks overlapping within a narrow band as she tried to disarm Sarque. In a very few futures, she was able to beat him to the draw. The rest ended in a bang.

'Is this how you want your time on the Council to end?' Richard asked. 'Blowing yourself up in a useless gesture?'

'I get to take you and your cabal with me. Sounds good to me.'

'Maybe we should—' Solace began nervously.

'Shut up,' Sal Sarque said.

I'd kept my mental link with Dark Anne open. *Can you reach Sarque's finger muscles with a spell?*

Not faster than he can push that button.

'Well,' Richard said. 'It appears we are at an impasse.'

The futures in which the bomb went off were growing.

Richard didn't seem inclined to break the stalemate, but Rachel was another story. I needed more time.

Okay, let's kill two birds with one stone. 'So since we're waiting around anyway,' I said to Richard, 'how about a chat?'

Richard raised an eyebrow at me. 'Now?'

I shrugged. 'Well, you don't seem like you're going to be killing Sarque in the next five minutes.' *Come on, Richard. You always seemed to know the next move. Play along.*

Richard paused very briefly, then nodded. 'Very well.'

'Great,' I said. 'I'd like to change my answer to that last offer of yours. I'd like to join your organisation as your fourth in command.'

'No!' Rachel shouted.

Richard waved a hand down. He was keeping Sarque in his peripheral vision, but seemed focused on me. 'That's quite a specific request,' he said. 'But I seem to recall you already turned down that offer.'

Okay, this is the best I can come up with, Dark Anne told me. *How's it look?*

Looking at the futures, I could see that she'd prepared some kind of spell that would attack Sarque's nervous system. *No good. You need to be about half a second faster.* 'I've reevaluated my priorities,' I told Richard.

'I'm curious as to how,' Richard said. 'You gave me quite an emphatic explanation as to why you were unwilling to cooperate.'

'I knew you were a traitor!' Solace shouted at me.

'You and your boss have been trying to drive me off the Council ever since I joined,' I told Solace. 'Congratulations, you've succeeded.' I turned back to Richard. 'Well, that's kind of the thing. If you remember, my big sticking point

wasn't so much to do with you, it was to do with her.' I
nodded towards Anne. 'I don't have any remaining loyalty
to the Council. I didn't have much before, and Sarque and
his friends have managed to destroy what little was left.
But I *am* still loyal to Anne. And as far as I can see, the
way things are now, the only way I can stay with her
involves working with you.'

'I seem to recall you also had issues with my methods.'

All the time that we were talking, I was exploring
futures, trying to find an angle of attack on Sal Sarque.
None of them were working. The best chance came from
distracting him in some way, letting Anne get a shot on
him before he could react, but Sal Sarque was too old and
wily to drop his guard. For all his age, he was fast, and I
couldn't find any avenue that would draw his attention
away from Anne reliably enough.

I was on the wrong track. Sal Sarque was the strongest
link in the chain. What about the explosives themselves?
I changed my focus, looking for futures in which the bomb
failed.

'Well, that's where the change of priorities comes in,' I
told Richard. 'The more time I've had to think about our
last conversation, the more I've come to see your point.
You *have* been the one bailing me out of trouble. And a
lot of the time, it *has* been because I was insufficiently
ruthless. So, as of a couple of days ago, I've started following
your advice. So far it's been working out.'

'Why fourth in command?'

'Well, I assume you, Morden and Vihaela are numbers
one through three. I wouldn't want to make waves.'

'Did you just break into my home for a job interview?'
Sal Sarque demanded.

'More or less,' I told him. *There.* It was possible for Sal Sarque to push that button and for the explosives to not go off. The future was a ghost, a zero per cent chance, but it could happen if certain prerequisites were met. I started feeding it, the faint spark growing brighter.

'Why are we even talking to him?' Rachel said angrily. 'He's had enough chances.'

'She has a valid point,' Richard said.

I shrugged. 'Things change. My attitudes have changed. So have my abilities. I suspect you've had long enough to figure that out for yourself by now.'

He's getting antsy, Dark Anne told me.

Hold off, I said.

You keep this up, he's going to push that button just for the hell of it.

I said hold off. Get ready for a strike, but don't launch it.

'Unfortunately, trust is an issue,' Richard said. 'As you just admitted to Sarque, you've been opposing me for a long time.'

'Not very effectively.'

'I hope you're not trying to use incompetence as an excuse.'

'We could do it the old-fashioned way,' I said. 'Trial by combat. Why not Rachel? You might find it interesting to see how your last two apprentices measure up.'

'Fascinating though that would be,' Richard said, 'as I said, the issue is trust. I'm afraid I'll need something more than words.'

All the time I'd been talking, I'd been applying pressure through the fateweaver, trying to force the future in which the detonation failed. It wasn't easy – modern explosives are well designed – but any mechanical system has points of failure, and it only needs one link in the chain to break. All of a sudden, something gave and the future in which the explosives failed to go off sprang into possibility. Eyeballing it, I put it at around a five per cent chance. I kept pushing.

'Fair enough,' I said. 'How about I help you out with your current problem then? I'll get rid of Sarque, you give me probationary status.'

'No!' Rachel said.

'What makes you think we need the help?' Richard said.

Ten per cent. 'You did say the issue was trust.'

Richard studied me for a long moment. 'Very well.'

I turned to Sal Sarque. 'Sorry, Sarque. Well, actually, I'm not sorry at all. I'd say it was nothing personal, but it really is.'

Sal Sarque looked at me contemptuously. 'Go ahead and try.'

Fifteen per cent, twenty. 'Before I do, there's something I've been wanting to ask,' I said. 'You remember those two Crusader black ops types from a couple of years ago? Zilean and Lightbringer? They tried to kidnap and torture me and they *did* kidnap and torture Anne. Flayed her alive trying to get her to talk.'

'So?'

'Was it you who gave the order?'

'Don't answer him,' Solace said.

Sal Sarque didn't bother to respond to her. 'Why should I tell you?' he asked me.

Forty per cent. The probability curve was speeding up as the electronics came closer to failure. 'In three minutes, either you'll be dead or I will be,' I said. 'So why not?'

'Because you're a piece of shit,' Sal Sarque said. 'I've

been fighting Dark mages my whole life, and I knew what you were the minute I saw you. You were always one of them. You want to know who gave the order? Fuck you, that's who. You can die never knowing.'

Seventy per cent. Now instead of feeding the future in which the explosives didn't work, I was suppressing ones in which they did. 'Oh well,' I said. 'I guess I'll just ask Levistus.'

'And you're going to do what? Divine him to death?' Sarque gave a short, ugly laugh. 'Enough talk.'

Eighty per cent, eighty-five. I stood looking at Sarque, focusing on the fateweaver. It was easy now, like pushing a boulder that's already started rolling. Ninety per cent. Ninety-five. 'You're right,' I said. 'That's enough talk.' Ninety-eight, ninety-nine . . . one hundred. 'Anne, the bomb's disarmed. You can kill him now.'

Anne struck instantly. Black death flashed out in a howling wave.

Sarque pushed the button and nothing happened. He hesitated an instant.

It was too long. Sarque was strong, and I already knew from watching the futures that he could fight, but against someone like Anne there was no room for error. He threw up a shield of fire and force. Anne's spell tore straight through it and stripped the clothes from his skin and the skin from his muscles, his body changing colours as layer after layer was torn away, flesh and veins and tendons dissolving into black dust.

It was over in less than a second. Where Sal Sarque had stood was an upright skeleton, only traces of flesh hanging off the bones. Black energy swirled around Anne's hand as she held the skeleton up by sheer force of will, then she let her hand drop and the bones collapsed with a clatter. The skull bounced and rolled, coming to rest under a swivel chair, eye sockets staring up at the ceiling.

Richard, Rachel, Crystal and Anne looked at the remains. Then, as one, they all turned to me. As they did, I reached out through the dreamstone to Meredith. *Now.*

In the shadows off to my right, Meredith began her spell.

The pattern in the control room had shifted. Before, it had been a triangle, with Sarque, Richard and me as the three points. Now the three had become two. Richard and his three companions on one side, and me alone at the other. Solace cowered against the far wall, ignored by everyone.

A rush of adrenalin filled me. Everything I'd done for the past few days had been for this, to bring these people together in one place. Richard, studying me from the front of his group, calm and inscrutable; Rachel, her eyes glittering with hate; Anne, aloof and contemptuous but compelled to obey. For a moment I saw them not as people but as playing pieces, moving into the endgame.

'That other mage is still there,' Crystal told Richard.

'I am aware.'

Crystal nodded towards me. 'Get rid of him?'

'I'm shocked that you're suggesting going back on your word, Crystal,' I said. 'Really.' I looked at Richard. 'So?'

As I spoke, I reached out delicately with the dreamstone, but this time to Rachel. I brushed against her mind and had to steel myself not to pull away. Her thoughts were jagged, discordant, like walking on broken glass. But overlaid on her mind was something else, like a voice whispering in her ear.

. . . going to say yes. Meredith's magic wasn't quite a voice and wasn't quite words. It was more like a stream of thoughts, shifting and flowing, and to Rachel, they would feel like *her* thoughts. *Missed the chance. Should have killed him. Now it's too late.*

'Strictly speaking, it was Anne who handled him, rather than you,' Richard said.

'What, you wanted me to shoot him through the head myself? You taught us to use the tools available.'

'I suppose I did.' Richard studied me a moment longer, then nodded. 'Very well.'

'No!' Rachel shouted.

'This is not a final commitment,' Richard told Rachel.

'I agree with her,' Crystal said sharply. 'It's too risky.'

. . . he wants Verus. Meredith's whispers were steady, relentless. *Always did. You were the substitute. Now he can have him. Verus and Anne, together. Won't need anyone. Won't need you . . .*

This was why I'd brought Meredith. No other type of mage would have been able to do this, not under Richard's nose. But Meredith was an enchantress, and the one great trump card of charm magic is that it's undetectable. Only Crystal would have a chance of figuring out what was happening, and even then she'd have to be looking directly at Rachel's thoughts.

'It's not your decision, Crystal,' Richard said, turning back to me. While he was still looking away, I met Rachel's gaze and smiled.

Rachel snapped. Her face twisted in rage, and a green beam stabbed towards me.

My precognition gave me no warning – Rachel had made the decision and acted in a split-second – but you don't need a warning if you're the one pushing the buttons. I leant aside, the ray missing my chest by inches and turning a section of wall behind me to dust.

Anne moved in a green-black flash. There was a *crack* of energy and Rachel went flying, her shield half-broken. She hit the floor rolling and Anne took a step, hand raised to finish her off.

'Enough!' Richard shouted. His left hand came out of his pocket, glowing with black-purple light; Anne's back arched and she went rigid. A thin line of darkness darted from his other hand, hitting the floor right in front of Rachel's face.

Rachel froze and suddenly everyone was still. Anne stood like a statue, head tilted and her back curved into a bow, muscles trembling as she held the pose. Her eyes glittered with anger, but she didn't speak. Crystal hadn't moved; I hadn't moved. The five of us stood, watching one another.

'*None* of you are killing each other unless and until I tell you to,' Richard said in a voice of iron. His eyes swept across the four of us. 'Is that clear?'

One by one, the others dropped their gaze, though Anne had a dangerous look in her eyes. Rachel flinched as Richard looked at her. Through the dreamstone, I could still hear Meredith's whispers: . . . *took you out in one move, she's all he needs, all he's wanted. Replaced. All been for nothing, all of it* . . .

Richard's gaze reached me and I looked back at him, my expression calm. We stared at each other for a long moment.

'Your request is accepted,' Richard told me at last. 'Provisionally. You will accompany us to be questioned.

Any signs of deception will result in an immediate response. Is that clear?'

I could see deep purple light glowing from between Richard's fingers: the dreamstone. I didn't let my eyes rest on it. 'Clear.'

'Don't,' Rachel said.

Both Richard and I turned to look at her. Rachel was on her knees, staring up at Richard, and all of a sudden she looked like a different person. The cold menace was gone: it was as if the years had fallen away and she was a young girl again, lost and vulnerable. 'Don't do this,' Rachel said. 'Please.'

Richard frowned. 'We've discussed this, Deleo.'

'Not him. I'll work with anyone else. But not him.'

A flicker of annoyance crossed Richard's face. He didn't like having to do this, especially in front of witnesses. 'You know what is at stake,' Richard told her.

. . . doesn't need you, he'll say no, has to say yes, all because of her, say yes, say yes . . .

'I'm your Chosen,' Rachel said. She sounded like she had to force out the words. 'It should be me.'

. . . could have been, Shireen, now it's Anne, the stone, her and the stone . . .

'Which means you follow my orders,' Richard said. He turned away from her. 'We'll discuss this later.'

I saw Rachel's face fall in despair. And as it did, Meredith's spell sharpened to a point.

He can't do it if he loses Anne.

Crystal looked towards Rachel, starting to frown. 'There's something—'

Rachel's face changed. Green light flashed out.

It was what I'd been waiting for. I threw all my strength

behind the fateweaver, aiming for the future I needed. Richard had been looking away; at Crystal's words, he twisted sharply. His left hand, still holding the dreamstone, came across.

The futures intersected. Rachel's spell hit the dreamstone. There was a brilliant flash and Richard's dreamstone, the one that Anne had brought out of the deep shadow realm two years ago and that was controlling the jinn right now, disintegrated into dust.

For a moment, everyone froze. Richard stared down at his empty hand. The last particles of the dreamstone were trickling from between his fingers. Then he looked at Rachel, and for the first time that I could remember, his face twisted in rage. 'You stupid, *stupid* little—'

Then Anne spoke. It was only a single word but it echoed in stereo, Anne's soft voice mixed with something deeper and darker, filled with a furious triumph.

'*FREE!*'

And everything happened at once.

Solace launched a spell and Crystal started some mind effect of her own, but Anne was faster. The control room flashed dead black as she cut loose. Richard twisted out of the way, a translucent shield coming up, but Anne hadn't been aiming at him: she'd been aiming at Crystal, and she beat Crystal to the draw. A hurricane of death roared through the room and wiped Crystal from existence. Crystal didn't even last long enough to be stripped to the bone the way Sarque had been: before that annihilating wave she simply . . . ceased. And that quickly, there were four instead of five.

Richard and Rachel turned on Anne, reflected light flashing from the walls, light green to dark green to black.

I drew my gun and fired on Solace, who ran for cover, a water shield flaring around her as she threw spells up at the gantry. Everyone fought everyone, the movements too fast to see. Disintegration blasts blew holes in the walls, and black energy from the jinn tore apart desks as though they were tissue.

At such a pace, the fight couldn't last long. A spell from Anne that would have turned Richard into dust missed by a hair, exploding a bank of computers and starting an electrical fire. Richard's counterstrike was something complex I didn't recognise, but whatever it was, it made Anne stagger. She crossed the room with a jump, landing near to Solace. Anne looked at her, a disintegration ray from Rachel glancing off her shield. 'Oh hey. Didn't you send those guys to my flat?'

Panic flashed across Solace's face. 'No! I wasn't even his aide back then!'

Anne shrugged. 'Well, you can die anyway.'

Solace dived for cover, sliding behind a desk just a hair ahead of Anne's death spell. With her concentration broken, her shield wavered; I pushed with the fateweaver, aimed with my 1911, fired. The bullet found a chink in the shield and blew Solace's brains into a red mist.

'Kill-stealer,' Anne called at me, then whirled to face Richard. He'd been coming up behind her, but Anne met him with a storm of magical death. Richard fell back to cover, and Anne jumped lightly thirty feet into the air, landing on the far gantry. 'Well, got to run,' she shouted across at me. 'Catch you later.'

'Wait!' I called back at her, but Anne was already running, flitting into the shadows.

A control console blew out in a shower of sparks. I'd

lost track of Rachel in the fighting, and the only people left in the room were me and Richard. We stared at each other across the burning room. The electrical fires were spreading and the air was filling with a haze.

'You have no idea what you have done.' Richard's voice was tight; he'd regained his self-control, but anger was clear on his face.

I looked back at Richard. There was a surge of magic from somewhere against the far wall, and from outside, I felt the stasis barrier go down. In only minutes, reinforcements were going to come pouring in, and whether they were on Richard's side or Sal Sarque's, I didn't want to meet them.

I turned and ran. Futures flickered in which I had to dodge an attack, but Richard didn't take the shot. *Starbreeze*, I called out through the dreamstone. *Pickup for two.*

Ooh, Starbreeze said with interest. *That was you?*

Meredith was hiding in an alcove; she flinched as she saw me. 'We're leaving,' I told her.

'Leaving *where*? There are—'

I silenced her with a motion. *Anne. Where are you?*

There was no answer, but I had a sense of distant laughter. I cursed; I could try to chase her, but Richard was in the way and reinforcements were coming fast. Besides, I wasn't sure what I'd do if I caught up.

Then Starbreeze was there. Meredith gave a yelp as she was turned into air; I ground my teeth and surrendered to it. Starbreeze shot out down the corridors at blinding speed. I had a confused impression of faces turning up to look at us, then we were out into the night air and soaring, rising up and up into the sky.

The moon was above us, the island below. Sal Sarque's

fortress shrank as we climbed and began angling west. There was no more fire coming from the rooftop: the survivors seemed to be disengaging. In only seconds we were above the cloud cover, and the fortress vanished from sight.

Starbreeze got bored a few minutes into the journey back, and dropped us in some godforsaken spot in the Highlands of Scotland. She was obviously done with being a ferry service. I'd have to be sparing asking her for lifts in the future.

The gate stone took Meredith and me back to her garden, the air changing from the chill of Scotland to the warmth of Argentina. I let out a breath and closed my eyes as the gate closed, feeling a little of the tension go out of my muscles.

I opened my eyes to see that Meredith was watching me. 'Well?' she said. 'I did it, didn't I?'

'You did.' I smiled slightly. 'You know, it's interesting.'

'What is?'

'Back when I met you, I used to get lifts from Starbreeze all the time,' I told her. 'I only stopped when you betrayed me to Belthas and I had to blow up my calling focus getting away. But because you did that, it forced me to stop relying on her, which meant all of my enemies got used to the idea that I *couldn't* rely on her. And so when I finally figured out a way to call her again, Richard and Caldera and Onyx weren't prepared for it at all. If it hadn't been for you, I never could have used her so effectively now. Funny how things work out.'

Meredith didn't answer. It was hard to make out her expression in the shadows, but it didn't look like she thought it was very funny at all.

'Give me your hand,' I ordered, walking towards her. Meredith hesitated, then lifted her right arm, shrinking back slightly as I took her hand and pulled up her sleeve. The light of the house windows revealed the black metal of the death bracelet, the same one that Selene had been wearing. I took the focus from my pocket, touched it to the metal and channelled. The bracelet clicked open and fell to the grass below.

Meredith tried to pull away but I didn't let go. 'Tell me something,' I said. 'If I'd acted this way back when we'd first met, would you still have betrayed me?'

Meredith held very still. I felt the futures flicker. 'I didn't—'

'The truth, Meredith.'

Meredith flinched. 'No,' she said at last, quietly.

'Good,' I said, and leant in close to her. Meredith looked up at me, only inches away, and I could see the fear in her beautiful dark eyes. 'Now one last question. More than anything else, what do you want from me right now?'

I saw Meredith struggle to keep herself under control. She'd never been brave: she could fight if she had to, but only if she was afraid of something worse. I was close enough to smell her perfume, feel the pulse beating at her wrist, and as I looked at her I noticed that under her make-up, there were wrinkles at the corner of her eyes. Time hadn't changed Meredith as it had me, but she hadn't escaped it.

'I want . . .' Meredith took a breath, swallowed. 'I want you to leave me alone.'

I looked down into Meredith's eyes for a long moment, then smiled slightly. 'Suits me.' I let go of her wrist. 'Go away, Meredith. Go back to your house and your boyfriends and your life in the sun. But make sure I don't catch you working for my enemies again.'

Meredith fled, opening the French windows and stepping inside before closing them. She gave me a last quick glance from behind the glass, then pulled the blinds closed, disappearing from view.

I looked at the house for a moment longer, feeling as though a very old piece of unfinished business had just come to an end. Then I picked up the bracelet and walked away into the night.

15

'I can't believe you actually made that work,' Luna told me.

'I can,' I said. It was the next day, and we were walking in the Hollow, the woods alive with the sounds of the summer morning. I'd just finished filling Luna in on the events of last night.

'If I'd told you I was going to do something like that, you'd have said I was suicidal.'

'I figured my chances were around two in three. Maybe a little more.'

Luna gave me a sceptical look. 'How?'

'So it all started with Richard,' I said. It was a relief to be able to talk like this, walking with Luna without any immediate dangers to worry about. 'Back when Anne and I visited him in his mansion two years ago, I looked into the futures to see what would happen if I attacked him. And it was close, really close. I couldn't see who was going to win.'

'Okay.'

'Except that it shouldn't have been,' I said. 'I mean, even if I didn't believe the rumours, I saw what Richard could do later that year, in the Vault. There was *no way* I could have taken him in a fight. Once I noticed that, I started trying to figure out how my divination could have been so wrong. And the most obvious answer I could come up with was that Richard had some kind of ability that worked against it. Like a shroud that worked in the future instead of the past, letting him project false futures. And the most natural way he'd be able to do *that* was if he was some kind of diviner himself. The aftermath of the Vault fight fit with that as well. The one time I landed a punch on him, it was when I acted on impulse without giving him the time to see it coming.'

'But we already talked about whether Richard might be a diviner,' Luna said. 'Lots of times. You were the one who said it didn't feel right.'

I nodded. 'Because it didn't. He was too confident, as though no one could touch him. It didn't fit with someone whose only ability was seeing the future. It wasn't until I realised that he had a jinn as well that it made sense. A jinn's power, mixed with a diviner's knowledge. I couldn't test it, not without tipping my hand, but I was sure. The thing is, it also made me realise just how screwed I was. He could do everything I could do, plus he could *counter* what I could do, and if somehow *that* wasn't enough, he had the jinn to fall back on as well.'

'That was before you had the fateweaver.'

'The fateweaver was big, but it wasn't enough,' I said. 'Sure, it's powerful, but Richard's gone up against plenty of people with raw power and come out ahead. I knew I needed something more. So I turned things around. I started thinking about how I'd beat *myself*. I thought back over all the times that my divination hadn't worked, and looked at all the things they had in common. And there were three. Sometimes I couldn't predict someone's actions at all, either because they were deciding on the spur of the moment or because they were just too unstable. Sometimes I *could* predict what was happening, but didn't have the power to do anything about it. And finally, there were times when I was caught out looking in the wrong place at the wrong time.'

'So which one did you go for?' Luna asked.

'All of them at once,' I said. 'I got Richard to focus on me when he should have been watching Rachel and Meredith. Once Rachel took her shot, I used the fateweaver to make sure it'd hit. And Richard wasn't able to see it coming far enough away, because it was *Rachel*. She's always been a nightmare for me to predict because she's so crazy.'

'So that was what that dragon was getting at with that prophecy.'

I nodded. 'With anyone else, it wouldn't have worked. Either they wouldn't have been unstable enough to snap the way she did, or Richard wouldn't have trusted them enough to turn his back on them. Rachel was just the right combination of close enough and unbalanced enough. And with Meredith's magic, they couldn't see what was happening until it was too late.'

'Can't believe she was actually useful.' Luna thought for a moment. 'I'm still not sure if we won. I mean, on one level, I guess you did. You finally did what the Council's been failing at for years. You screwed up Richard's plans. He's been working towards getting Anne on his side for God knows how long, and when he finally does it, you break her free.'

'But?'

'But . . .' Luna trailed off. 'I don't know. I know it's silly, but I guess I was hoping that once Richard's control was gone, she'd come back.'

I didn't answer. A part of me had been hoping the same thing.

'How did you know you'd have so much time?' Luna said, returning to her original question. 'I mean, the only reason it worked was because Richard let you stand there and talk.'

'Actually, that was the one thing I wasn't worried about. I knew he was going to hear me out.'

'But he had to know you had some kind of agenda.'

'Of course he did,' I said. 'I was being careful not to tell any blatant lies, and I was keeping my surface thoughts focused so Crystal couldn't get wind of what I was doing. But there was no way Richard was going to trust me. He knew I was playing some sort of game.'

'So why did he let you do it?' Luna said.

'Because he was sure he was going to win,' I said. 'Because he'd always won before. When someone loses to you nineteen times in a row, then comes back and sits down at the table yet again, you don't chase him off. You laugh and get ready to take his money for the twentieth time. Every single time I'd tried to outsmart Richard, I'd lost. Except this one.'

'I don't think I'd have had the nerve,' Luna admitted.

'It's a lot easier to face your fears once you've got something you care about more than yourself.' I glanced through the futures. 'We should get moving.'

We changed direction, angling through the woods until the trees parted before us to reveal the clearing with Karyos's cocoon. 'How long?' Luna asked.

'More than two minutes, less than ten,' I said. 'But there's no violence. Whatever kind of state she's going to be in, she'll be willing to talk at least.'

'I wish Vari could be here.'

'Yeah, that's not going to happen,' I said. Variam had

been almost completely out of contact since last night. 'They just had a member of the Senior Council killed in a straight-up attack. I don't think that's happened since the Gate Rune War. They're going to be in full-on emergency mode, and once they figure out I had something to do with it – which they will – then they'll come after me twice as hard. I don't think Vari's going to be able to come back here any time soon.'

'It feels wrong,' Luna said. 'Vari was here when we won this shadow realm. He ought to be here for the end.'

'I think it's going to be more and more dangerous for Vari to have anything to do with me,' I said. 'For him to keep seeing you will be hard enough.'

Luna made a face. 'No Arachne, no Anne, no Vari. Starting to feel a bit lonely around here.'

There was a cracking sound from the cocoon. We both turned to look.

A fracture had appeared in the curved surface, and as we watched there was another *crack* and the fracture widened. Although the cocoon was wood, the way it broke made me think of an egg. The cracks spread across its surface and the top near the trunk began to peel away. A hand appeared, then Karyos stood up, the cocoon unfolding like the petals of a flower.

She didn't look like a hamadryad. She looked like an eight-year-old girl. Maybe her skin was a shade of gold not quite natural for a human, and maybe her brown hair had a suggestion of bark, but there was no trace of the monstrosity of roots and thorns that we'd fought in the Hollow on our first meeting. She swayed on unsteady legs, and had to catch the cocoon to stop herself from falling.

'Welcome back, Karyos,' I said. 'Can you understand us?'

Karyos looked at us both uncertainly. 'Who are you?' she asked in slow, accented English.

'I'm Luna,' Luna said with a friendly smile and a wave. 'Hey.'

'And I'm Alex,' I said. 'We're your . . . well, guardians, I guess. At least for now.'

Karyos looked around, turning her head as if searching for something. 'Is something wrong?' Luna asked.

'There was . . . someone else,' Karyos said haltingly. 'I felt her. When I was growing.'

Luna started to reply, then looked at me. I hesitated a moment before answering. 'She's not here any more.'

Hampstead Heath was warm in the afternoon sun. Carried on the wind, I could hear the sounds of people talking, children playing, the barking of dogs. It felt like a different world.

The ravine where Arachne had lived was cordoned off with blue and white tape marked POLICE LINE DO NOT CROSS, swaying gently in the breeze. I ducked under the tape and climbed down into the ravine. The entrance to Arachne's cave gaped open with more tape blocking it.

The tunnel felt cool and gloomy after the bright daylight outside. I walked blind down the slope, my feet falling automatically into the old familiar path. My footsteps echoed as I came out into the cavern. Guided by my magic, I walked to one of the walls, touched one of the sphere lights and channelled.

Light bloomed, revealing devastation. Arachne's lair had been torn apart, bolts of cloth shaken out and trampled, cushions cut open, furniture overturned and splintered. Everything valuable had been looted, and the debris scattered. I walked slowly through the wreckage until I found the sofa where I used to sit. It had been knocked over, the bottom slashed open with the stuffing pulled out. I bent down and righted it, then sat down in my old place. The springs sagged.

I looked around sadly. After the old Arcana Emporium had been destroyed, Arachne's cave had been the one place I'd felt at home. It had been the last remnant of my old life, back when I'd wake up every morning knowing that the biggest problem I'd be likely to face would be someone wanting me to sell them a love potion. Now it was gone.

I sat waiting for ten minutes, the light behind me flickering occasionally. My right arm itched and I pulled up the sleeve of my coat to look.

The white streaks of the fateweaver reached halfway from my wrist to my elbow. Back when Klara had examined me, I'd had the feeling they were spreading, but I hadn't been sure. There was no room for doubt now. I scratched but the itch didn't go away.

Footsteps sounded from the tunnel. I pulled my sleeve down and turned towards the entrance.

A faint green light showed from the tunnel mouth, then winked out. A moment later Anne stepped out, looking in my direction. 'I had a feeling it was you.'

The black aura surrounding Anne was gone: to a casual glance, she looked a normal girl. 'I would have given you a lift if you'd asked.'

'What, so you can drop me in some prison until you figure out how to change me back? No thanks.' Anne walked across the cavern, kicking aside bits of wreckage.

'Nice job with the dreamstone. I knew Deleo was a nutcase, but I wasn't expecting that.'

'That was the idea.'

'Well, I don't really care how it works so long as it works.' Anne glanced across at me. 'Weird-looking hand. What is it?'

She doesn't know. It was a surprise, but as I thought about it, it made sense. Anne was a life mage, not a diviner. She could tell everything there was to know about someone's physiology, but that wouldn't tell her what the fateweaver did.

Anne tossed a broken chair out of her way and stepped up to the wall. 'Well, while you're here, make yourself useful and tell me how to open this thing.'

I looked briefly at the futures. 'Move your right hand twelve inches higher and six inches to the left.'

Anne did as I said. There was a click, and a crack appeared in the wall, revealing a hidden alcove. 'Thanks,' Anne called over her shoulder. 'I mean, I could have ripped it apart, but it's such a drag . . . Here we go.'

Anne had taken out something black and yielding from where it had been hidden in the shielded compartment. She shook it out and held it up against her, the dark cloth falling against her skin. It was the dress that Arachne had made for her, a few days and a lifetime ago. I wondered if Arachne had known which Anne would be the one to finally wear it.

'Not even torn,' Anne said. 'Nice.' She looked at me. 'Well?'

'Well, what?'

'Going to turn your back?'

I thought for a moment. 'I don't think I'm going to be turning my back on you any time soon.'

Anne laughed. 'What did you do with the old Alex? Well, I think I like the new one better anyway.' She began stripping off her clothes with a complete lack of concern.

I watched as Anne pulled off her top and dropped it on the floor. 'Luna misses you.'

'So tell her to call,' Anne said, kicking off her jeans.

'Do you want her to?'

'Sure, why wouldn't I? I'm still the same person. Just got a slightly different perspective, you know?' Anne pulled Arachne's dress over her head, wiggling her arms through the straps, then smoothed it down before looking around. 'Damn, they broke all the mirrors. How do I look?'

I looked at Anne: she twirled, letting the skirt flare out. 'It suits you,' I said. 'Actually, better than it did before.'

'Well, duh.' Anne walked forward, the black dress swirling around her knees. 'So why'd you come here?'

'Same reason as Luna, really,' I said. 'I wanted to see if I could talk you into coming back.'

'Yeah, I've got a funny feeling your reasons and Luna's might be *slightly* different.' Anne came to a stop ten feet away and looked down with a smile, one hand resting on her hip. 'Anyway, going to have to turn you down. Things to do, places to be.'

'What kind of things?'

'Well, first on the agenda is settling old scores,' Anne said. 'I mean, what's the point of unlimited power if you can't take horrible vengeance on all the people who've screwed you over? Crystal and Sal Sarque were a good start. But right now, there are two others at the top of the list. I think you can guess who they are, right? Only reason I came here instead of going straight after them is that I'm having a *really* hard time figuring out which one I hate most.'

'And then what?' I said. 'You're going to keep working your way down the list?'

'Sure, why not? One of the things that pissed me off most about you guys was that live-and-let-live attitude. We've had so many people try to kill us I've lost track of them all, and you never did a damn thing about it. I figure it's time for some payback.' Anne tilted her head. 'Want to come along?'

'You mean that?'

'Sure, why not?' Anne said. 'I mean, pretty much all of them are your enemies too. It'll be just like when we were on the Council, except instead of going to meetings, we kill people we don't like. Who knows, you might end up deciding you like the new me. Trust me, anything she can do, I can do better.'

It was more tempting than it should have been. 'And what does the jinn get out of all this?'

Anne shrugged. 'Stuff.'

'It's not helping you for free,' I said. 'So what's the price?'

'Nothing you need to worry about.'

'You should have paid more attention to Arachne, Anne,' I said. 'Jinn hate humans, and they hate mages most of all. Whatever it wants, long term, it's not going to end well for you.'

'I don't really care about long term,' Anne said. 'But fine. How about a compromise? I'll start at my end of the list, and you start at yours, and once we've met in the middle we can have a showdown. Or a date. Or both.'

'If you think that jinn's going to serve you, you're a

fool,' I said. 'I've seen these kinds of partnerships, and they never end well for the human. But you're right about one thing. For now at least, we have the same enemies.'

'Sounds good.' Anne gave me a wave and turned to go. 'Later.'

'Anne,' I said.

Anne paused and looked back.

'I didn't do this to settle old scores,' I said. 'I did it for you. And one way or another, I'm going to protect you.'

Anne laughed. 'Oh, Alex. I don't need protecting any more. It's everyone else who needs protecting from me.'

I watched Anne go, listening to her footsteps recede up the tunnel until they faded into silence. I was sure of one thing: in the contest between Anne and the jinn, Anne was going to lose. Right now, the jinn might be giving her everything she wanted, but it could afford to. All it had to do was wait.

I guess we're both on a clock.

I got to my feet. I had work to do.

*Look out for book eleven in the
Alex Verus series!*

extras

www.orbitbooks.net

about the author

Benedict Jacka became a writer almost by accident, when at nineteen he sat in his school library and started a story in the back of an exercise book. Since then he has studied philosophy at Cambridge, lived in China and worked as everything from civil servant to bouncer to teacher before returning to London to take up law.

Find out more about Benedict Jacka and other Orbit authors by registering for the free monthly newsletter at www.orbitbooks.net.

if you enjoyed
FALLEN

look out for

STRANGE PRACTICE

by

Vivian Shaw

Meet Greta Helsing, doctor to the undead.
After inheriting a highly specialised, and highly
peculiar, medical practice, Dr Helsing spends her days
treating London's undead for a host of ills: vocal
strain in banshees, arthritis in barrow-wights and
entropy in mummies. Although barely making ends
meet, this is just the quiet, supernatural-adjacent life
Greta's dreamed of since childhood.

But when a sect of murderous monks emerges, killing
human undead and alike, Greta must use all her
unusual skills to keep her supernatural clients — and
the rest of London — safe.

The sky was fading to ultramarine in the east over the Victoria Embankment when a battered Mini pulled in to the curb, not far from Blackfriars Bridge. Here and there in the maples lining the riverside walk, the morning's first sparrows had begun to sing.

A woman got out of the car and shut the door, swore, put down her bags, and shut the door again with more applied force; some fellow motorist had bashed into the panel at some time in the past and bent it sufficiently to make this a production every damn time. The Mini really needed to be replaced, but even with her inherited Harley Street consulting rooms Greta Helsing was not exactly drowning in cash.

She glowered at the car and then at the world in general, glancing around to make sure no one was watching her from the shadows. Satisfied, she picked up her black working bag and the shapeless oversize monster that was her current handbag and went to ring the doorbell. It was time to replace the handbag, too. The leather on this one was holding up but the lining was beginning to go, and Greta had limited patience regarding the retrieval of items from the mysterious dimension behind the lining itself.

The house to which she had been summoned was one of a row of magnificent old buildings separating Temple Gardens from the Embankment, mostly taken over by lawyers and publishing firms these days. It was a testament to this particular homeowner's rather special powers of persuasion that nobody had succeeded in buying the house out from under him and turning it into offices for over-priced attorneys, she thought, and then had to smile at the idea of anybody dislodging Edmund Ruthven from the lair he'd inhabited these two hundred years or more. He was as much a fixture of London as Lord Nelson on his pillar, albeit less encrusted with birdlime.

'Greta,' said the fixture, opening the door. 'Thanks for coming out on a Sunday. I know it's late.'

She was just about as tall as he was, five foot five and a bit, which made it easy to look right into his eyes and be struck every single time by the fact that they were very large, so pale a grey they looked silver-white except for the dark ring at the edge of the iris, and fringed with heavy soot-black lashes of the sort you saw in advertisements for mascara. He looked tired, she thought. Tired, and older than the fortyish he usually appeared. The extreme pallor was normal, vivid against the pure slicked-back black of his hair, but the worried line between his eyebrows was not.

'It's not Sunday night, it's Monday morning,' she said. 'No worries, Ruthven. Tell me everything; I know you didn't go into lots of detail on the phone.'

'Of course.' He offered to take her coat. 'I'll make you some coffee.'

The entryway of the Embankment house was floored in black-and-white-checkered marble, and a large bronze ibis stood on a little side table where the mail and car keys and shopping lists were to be found. The mirror behind this reflected Greta dimly and greenly, like a woman underwater; she peered into it, making a face at herself, and tucked back her hair. It was pale Scandinavian blonde and cut like Liszt's in an off-the-shoulder bob, fine enough to slither free of whatever she used to pull it back; today it was in the process of escaping from a thoroughly childish headband. She kept meaning to have it all chopped off and be done with it but never seemed to find the time.

Greta Helsing was thirty-four, unmarried, and had taken over her late father's specialized medical practice after a brief stint as an internist at King's College Hospital. For the past five years she had run a bare-bones clinic out of Wilfert Helsing's old rooms in Harley Street, treating a patient base that to the majority of the population did not, technically, when you got right down to it, exist. It was a family thing.

There had never been much doubt which subspecialty of medicine she would pursue, once she began her training: treating the differently alive was not only more interesting than catering to the ordinary human population, it was in many ways a great deal more rewarding. She took a lot of satisfaction in being able to provide help to particularly underserved clients.

Greta's patients could largely be classified under the heading of *monstrous*—in its descriptive, rather than pejorative, sense: vampires, were-creatures, mummies, banshees, ghouls, bogeymen, the occasional arthritic barrow-wight. She herself was solidly and entirely human, with no noticeable eldritch qualities or powers whatsoever, not even a flicker of metaphysical sensitivity. Some of her patients found it difficult to trust a human physician at first, but Greta had built up an extremely good reputation over the five years she had been practicing supernatural medicine, largely by word of mouth: *Go to Helsing, she's reliable.*

And *discreet.* That was the first and fundamental tenet, after all. Keeping her patients safe meant keeping them secret, and Greta was good with secrets. She made sure the magical wards around her doorway in Harley Street were kept up properly, protecting anyone who approached from prying eyes.

Ruthven appeared in the kitchen doorway, outlined by light spilling warm over the black-and-white marble. 'Greta?' he said, and she straightened up, realizing she'd been staring into the mirror without really seeing it for several minutes now. It really *was* late. Fatigue lapped heavily at the pilings of her mind.

'Sorry,' she said, coming to join him, and a little of that heaviness lifted as they passed through into the familiar warmth and brightness of the kitchen. It was all blue tile and blond wood, the cheerful rose-gold of polished copper pots and pans balancing the sleek chill of stainless steel, and right now it was also full of the scent of really *good* coffee. Ruthven's espresso machine was a La Cimbali, and it was serious business.

He handed her a large pottery mug. She recognized it as one of the set he generally used for blood, and had to smile a little, looking down at the contents—and then abruptly had to clamp down on a wave of thoroughly inconvenient emotion. There was no reason that Ruthven doing goddamn *latte art* for her at half-past four in the morning should make her want to cry.

He was *good* at it, too, which was a little infuriating; then again she supposed that with as much free time on her hands as he had on his, and as much disposable income, she might find herself learning and polishing new skills simply to stave off the encroaching spectre of boredom. Ruthven didn't go in for your standard-variety vampire angst, which was refreshing, but Greta knew very well he had bouts of something not unlike depression—especially in the winter—and he needed things to *do*.

She, however, *had* things to do, Greta reminded herself, taking a sip of the latte and closing her eyes for a moment. This was coffee that actually tasted as good as, if not better than, it smelled. *Focus,* she thought. This was not a social call. The lack of urgency in Ruthven's manner led her to believe that the situation was not immediately dire, but she was nonetheless here to do her job.

Greta licked coffee foam from her upper lip. 'So,' she said. 'Tell me what happened.'

'I was—'

Ruthven sighed, leaning against the counter with his arms folded. 'To be honest I was sitting around twiddling my thumbs and writing nasty letters to the *Times* about how much I loathe these execrable skyscrapers somebody keeps allowing vandals to build all over the city. I'd got to a particularly cutting phrase about the one that sets people's cars on fire, when somebody knocked on the door.'

The passive-aggressive-letter stage tended to indicate that his levels of ennui were reaching critical intensity. Greta just nodded, watching him.

'I don't know if you've ever read an ancient penny-dreadful called *Varney the Vampyre, or The Feast of Blood,*' he went on.

'Ages ago,' she said. She'd read practically all the horror

classics, well-known and otherwise, for research purposes rather than to enjoy their literary merit. Most of them were to some extent entertainingly wrong about the individuals they claimed to depict. 'It was quite a lot funnier than your unofficial biography, but I'm not sure it was *meant* to be.'

Ruthven made a face. John Polidori's *The Vampyre* was, he insisted, mostly libel—the very mention of the book was sufficient to bring on indignant protestations that he and the Lord Ruthven featured in the narrative shared little more than a name. 'At least the authors got the spelling right, unlike bloody Polidori,' he said. 'I think probably *Feast of Blood* is about as historically accurate as *The Vampyre*, which is to say *not very*, but it does have the taxonomy right. Varney, unlike me, *is* a vampyre with a *y*.'

'A lunar sensitive? I haven't actually met one before,' she said, clinical interest surfacing through the fatigue. The vampires she knew were all classic draculines, like Ruthven himself and the handful of others in London. Lunar sensitives were rarer than the draculine vampires for a couple of reasons, chief among which was the fact that they were violently—and inconveniently—allergic to the blood of anyone but virgins. They did have the handy characteristic of being resurrected by moonlight every time they got themselves killed, which presumably came as some small comfort in the process of succumbing to violent throes of gastric distress brought on by dietary indiscretion.

'Well,' Ruthven said, 'now's your chance. He showed up on my doorstep, completely unannounced, looking like thirty kinds of warmed-over hell, and collapsed in the hallway. He is at the moment sleeping on the drawing room sofa, and I want you to look at him for me. I don't *think* there's any real danger, but he's been hurt—some maniacs apparently attacked him with a knife—and I'd feel better if you had a look.'

Ruthven had lit a fire, despite the relative mildness of the evening, and the creature lying on the sofa was covered with two blankets. Greta glanced from him to Ruthven, who shrugged a little, that line of worry between his eyebrows very visible.

According to him, Sir Francis Varney, title and all, had come out of his faint quite quickly and perked up after some first aid and the administration of a nice hot mug of suitable and brandy-laced blood. Ruthven kept a selection of the stuff in his expensive fridge and freezer, stocked by Greta via fairly illegal supply chain management—she knew someone who knew someone who worked in a blood bank and was not above rescuing rejected units from the biohazard incinerator.

Sir Francis had drunk the whole of the mug's contents with every evidence of satisfaction and promptly gone to sleep as soon as Ruthven let him, whereupon Ruthven had called Greta and requested a house call. 'I don't really like the look of him,' he said now, standing in the doorway with uncharacteristic awkwardness. 'He was bleeding a little—the wound's in his left shoulder. I cleaned it up and put a dressing on, but it was still sort of oozing. Which isn't like us.'

'No,' Greta agreed, 'it's not. It's possible that lunar sensitives and draculines respond differently to tissue trauma, but even so, I would have expected him to have mostly finished healing already. You were right to call me.'

'Do you need anything?' he asked, still standing in the doorway as Greta pulled over a chair and sat down beside the sofa.

'Possibly more coffee. Go on, Ruthven. I've got this; go and finish your unkind letter to the editor.'

When he had gone she tucked back her hair and leaned over to examine her patient. He took up the entire length of the sofa, head pillowed on one armrest and one narrow foot resting on the other, half-exposed where the blankets had fallen away. She did a bit of rough calculation and guessed he must be at least six inches taller than Ruthven, possibly more.

His hair was tangled, streaky-grey, worn dramatically long—that was aging-rock-frontman hair if Greta had ever seen it, but nothing *else* about him seemed to fit with the Jagger aesthetic. An old-fashioned face, almost Puritan: long, narrow nose, deeply hooded eyes under intense eyebrows, thin mouth bracketed with habitual lines of disapproval.

Or pain, she thought. *That could be pain.*

The shifting of a log in the fireplace behind Greta made her jump a little, and she regathered the wandering edges of her concentration. With a nasty little flicker of surprise she noticed that there was a faint sheen of sweat on Varney's visible skin. That *really* wasn't right.

'Sir Francis?' she said, gently, and leaned over to touch his shoulder through the blankets—and a moment later had retreated halfway across the room, heart racing: Varney had gone from uneasy sleep to *sitting up and snarling viciously* in less than a second.

It was not unheard-of for Greta's patients to threaten her, especially when they were in considerable pain, and on the whole she probably should have thought this out a little better. She'd only got a glimpse before her own instincts had kicked in and got her the hell out of range of those teeth, but it would be a while before she could forget that pattern of dentition, or those mad tin-colored eyes.

He covered his face with his hands, shoulders slumping, and instead of menace was now giving off an air of intense embarrassment.

Greta came back over to the sofa. 'I'm sorry,' she said, tentatively, 'I didn't mean to startle you—'

'I most devoutly apologize,' he said, without taking his hands away. 'I do *try* not to do that, but I am not quite at my best just now—forgive me, I don't believe we have been introduced.'

He was looking at her from behind his fingers, and the eyes really *were* metallic. Even partly hidden she could see the room's reflection in his irises. She wondered if that was a peculiarity of his species, or an individual phenomenon.

'It's all right,' she said, and sat down on the edge of the sofa, judging that he wasn't actually about to tear her throat out just at the moment. 'My name's Greta. I'm a doctor; Ruthven called me to come and take a look at you.'

When Varney finally took his hands away from his face, pushing the damp silvering hair back, his color was frankly terrible. He *was* sweating. That was not something she'd ever seen in sanguivores under any circumstance.

'A doctor?' he asked, blinking at her. 'Are you sure?' She was spared having to answer that. A moment later he squeezed his eyes shut, very faint color coming and going high on each cheek. 'I really am sorry,' he said. 'What a remarkably stupid question. It's just—I tend to think of doctors as looking rather different than you.'

'I left my pinstripe trousers and pocket-watch at home,' she said drily. 'But I've got my black bag, if that helps. Ruthven said you'd been hurt—attacked by somebody with a knife. May I take a look?'

He glanced up at her and then away again, and nodded once, leaning back against the sofa cushions, and Greta reached into her bag for the exam gloves.

The wound was in his left shoulder, as Ruthven had said, about two and a half inches south of the collarbone. It wasn't large—she had seen much nastier injuries from street fights, although in rather different species—but it was undoubtedly the *strangest* wound she'd ever come across.

'What made this?' she asked, looking closer, her gloved fingers careful on his skin. Varney hissed and turned his face away, and she could feel a thrumming tension under her touch. 'I've never seen anything like it. The wound is . . . *cross*-shaped.'

It was. Instead of just the narrow entry mark of a knife, or the bruised puncture of something clumsier, Varney's wound appeared to have been made by something flanged. Not just two but four sharp edges, leaving a hole shaped like an X—or a cross.

'It was a spike,' he said, between his teeth. 'I didn't get a very good look at it. They had—broken into my flat, with garlic. Garlic was everywhere. Smeared on the walls, scattered all over the floor. I was—taken by surprise, and the fumes—I could hardly see or breathe.'

'I'm not surprised,' said Greta, sitting up. 'It's extremely nasty stuff. Are you having any chest pain or trouble breathing now?'

A lot of the organic compounds in *Allium sativum* triggered a severe allergic response in vampires, varying in intensity based on amount and type of exposure. This wasn't garlic shock, or not *just* garlic shock, though. He was definitely running a fever, and the hole in his shoulder should have healed to a shiny pink memory within an hour or so after it happened. Right now it was purple-black and . . . oozing.

'No,' Varney said, 'just—the wound is, ah, really rather painful.' He sounded apologetic. 'As I said, I didn't get a close look at the spike, but it was short and pointed like a rondel dagger, with a round pommel. There were three people there, I don't know if they all had knives, but . . . well, as it turned out, all they needed was one.'

This was so very much not her division. 'Did—do you have any idea why they attacked you?' Or why they'd broken into his flat and poisoned it with garlic. That was a pretty specialized tactic, after all. Greta shivered in sudden unease.

'They were chanting, or . . . reciting something,' he said, his odd eyes drifting shut. 'I couldn't make out much of it, just that it sounded sort of ecclesiastical.'

He had a remarkably beautiful voice, she noticed. The rest of him wasn't tremendously prepossessing, particularly those eyes, but his voice was *lovely*: sweet and warm and clear. It contrasted oddly with the actual content of what he was saying. 'Something about . . . *unclean*,' he continued, '*unclean* and wicked, *wickedness*, foulness, and . . . *demons*. Creatures of darkness.'

He still had his eyes half-closed, and Greta frowned and bent over him again. 'Sir Francis?'

'Hurts,' he murmured, sounding very far away. 'They were dressed . . . strangely.'

She rested two fingers against the pulse in his throat: much too fast, and he couldn't have spiked *that* much in the minutes she had been with him, but he felt noticeably warmer to her touch. She reached into the bag for her thermometer and the BP cuff. 'Strangely how?'

'Like . . . monks,' he said, and blinked up at her, hazy and confused. 'In . . . brown robes. With crosses round their necks. Like *monks*.'

His eyes rolled back slightly, slipping closed, and he gave a little terrible sigh; when Greta took him by the shoulders and gave him a shake he did not rouse at all, head rolling limp against the cushions. *What the hell,* she thought, *what the actual hell is going on here, there's no way a wound like this should be affecting him so badly, this is—it looks like systemic inflammatory response but the garlic should have worn off by now, there's nothing to* cause *it, unless—*

Unless there had been something on the blade. Something *left behind.*

That flicker of visceral unease was much stronger now. She leaned closer, gently drawing apart the edges of the wound—the tissue was swollen, red, warmer than the surrounding skin—and was surprised to notice a faint but present smell. Not the characteristic smell of infection, but something sharper, almost metallic, with a sulfurous edge on it like silver tarnish. It was strangely familiar, but she couldn't seem to place it.

Greta was rather glad he was unconscious just at the moment, because what she was about to do would be quite remarkably painful. She stretched the wound open a little wider, wishing she had her penlight to get a better view, and he shifted a little, his breath catching; as he moved she caught a glimpse of something reflective half-obscured by dark blood. There *was* something still in there. Something that needed to come out right now.

'Ruthven,' she called, sitting up. 'Ruthven, I need you.'

He emerged from the kitchen, looking anxious. 'What is it?'

'Get the green leather instrument case out of my bag,' she said, 'and put a pan of water on to boil. There's a foreign body in here I need to extract.'

Without a word Ruthven took the instrument case and disappeared again. Greta turned her attention back to her patient, noticing for the first time that the pale skin of his chest was crisscrossed by old scarring—*very* old, she thought, looking at the silvery laddered marks of long-healed injuries. She had seen Ruthven without his shirt on, and he had a pretty good collection of scars from four centuries' worth of misadventure, but Varney put him to shame. *A lot of duels,* she thought. *A lot of . . .* lost *duels.*

Greta wondered how much of *Feast of Blood* was actually based on historical events. He had died at least once in the part of it that she remembered, and had spent a lot of time running away from various pitchfork-wielding mobs. None of *them* had been dressed up in monastic drag, as far as she knew, but they had certainly demonstrated the same intent as whoever had hurt Varney tonight.

A cold flicker of something close to fear slipped down her spine, and she turned abruptly to look over her shoulder at the empty room, pushing away a sudden and irrational sensation of being watched.

Don't be ridiculous, she told herself, *and do your damn job.* She was a little grateful for the business of wrapping the

BP cuff around his arm, and less pleased by what it told her. Not critical, but certainly a long way from what she considered normal for sanguivores. She didn't know what was going on in there, but she didn't like it one bit.

When Ruthven returned carrying a tea tray, she felt irrationally relieved to see him—and then had to raise an eyebrow at the contents of the tray. Her probes and forceps and retractors lay on a metal dish Greta recognized after a moment as the one that normally went under the toast rack, dish and instruments steaming gently from the boiling water—and beside them was an empty basin with a clean tea towel draped over it. Everything was very, very neat, as if he had done it many times before. As if he'd had practice.

'Since when are *you* a scrub nurse?' she asked, nodding for him to set the tray down. 'I mean—thank you, this is exactly what I need, I appreciate it, and if you could hold the light for me I'd appreciate that even more.'

'*De rien*,' said Ruthven, and went to fetch her penlight.

A few minutes later, Greta held her breath as she carefully, carefully withdrew her forceps from Varney's shoulder. Held between the steel tips was a piece of something hard and angular, about the size of a pea. That metallic, sharp smell was much stronger now, much more noticeable.

She turned to the tray on the table beside her, dropped the thing into the china basin with a little *rat-tat* sound, and straightened up. The wound was bleeding again; she pressed a gauze pad over it. The blood looked *brighter* now, somehow, which made no sense at all.

Ruthven clicked off the penlight, swallowing hard, and Greta looked up at him. 'What *is* that thing?' he asked, nodding to the basin.

'I've no idea,' she told him. 'I'll have a look at it after I'm happier with him. He's pushing eighty-five degrees and his pulse rate is approaching low human baseline—'

Greta cut herself off and felt the vein in Varney's throat again. 'That's strange,' she said. 'That's *very* strange. It's already coming down.'

The beat was noticeably slower. She had another look at his blood pressure; this time the reading was much more reasonable. 'I'll be damned. In a human I'd be seriously alarmed at that rapid a transient, but all bets are off with regard to hemodynamic stability in sanguivores. It's as if that thing, whatever it is, was directly responsible for the acute inflammatory reaction.'

'And now that it's gone, he's starting to recover?'

'Something like that. *Don't* touch it,' Greta said sharply, as Ruthven reached for the basin. 'Don't even go near it. I have no idea what it would do to you, and I don't want to have two patients on my hands.'

Ruthven backed away a few steps. 'You're quite right,' he said. 'Greta, something about this smells peculiar.'

'In more than one sense,' she said, checking the gauze. The bleeding had almost stopped. 'Did he tell you how it happened?'

'Not really. Just that he'd been jumped by several people armed with a strange kind of knife.'

'Mm. A very strange kind of knife. I've never seen anything like this wound. He didn't mention that these people were dressed up like monks, or that they were reciting something about unclean creatures of darkness?'

'No,' said Ruthven, flopping into a chair. 'He neglected to share that tidbit with me. Monks?'

'So he said,' Greta told him. 'Robes and hoods, big

crosses round their necks, the whole bit. Monks. And some kind of stabby weapon. Remind you of anything?'

'The Ripper,' said Ruthven, slowly. 'You think this has something to do with the murders?'

'I think it's one hell of a coincidence if it *doesn't*,' Greta said. That feeling of unease hadn't gone away with Varney's physical improvement. It really was impossible to ignore. She'd been too busy with the immediate work at hand to consider the similarities before, but now she couldn't help thinking about it.

There had been a series of unsolved murders in London over the past month and a half. Eight people dead, all apparently the work of the same individual, all stabbed to death, all *found with a cheap plastic rosary stuffed into their mouths*. Six of the victims had been prostitutes. The killer had, inevitably, been nicknamed the Rosary Ripper.

The MO didn't exactly match how Varney had described his attack—multiple assailants, a strange-shaped knife—but it was way the hell too close for Greta's taste. 'Unless whoever got Varney was a copycat,' she said. 'Or maybe there isn't just one Ripper. Maybe it's a group of people running around stabbing unsuspecting citizens.'

'There was nothing on the news about the murders that mentioned weird-shaped wounds,' Ruthven said. 'Although I suppose the police might be keeping that to themselves.'

The police had not apparently been able to do much of *anything* about the murders, and as one victim followed another with no end in sight the general confidence in Scotland Yard—never tremendously high—was plummeting. The entire city was both angry and frightened. Conspiracy theories abounded on the Internet, some less believable than others. This, however, was the first time Greta had heard anything about the Ripper branching out into *supernatural* victims. The garlic on the walls of Varney's flat bothered her a great deal.

Varney shifted a little, with a faint moan, and Greta returned her attention to her patient. There was visible improvement; his vitals were stabilizing, much more satisfactory than they had been before the extraction.

'He's beginning to come around,' she said. 'We should get him into a proper bed, but I think he's over the worst of this.'

Ruthven didn't reply at once, and she looked over to see him tapping his fingers on the arm of his chair with a thoughtful expression. 'What?' she asked.

'Nothing. Well, *maybe* nothing. I think I'll call Cranswell at the Museum, see if he can look a few things up for me. I will, however, wait until the morning is a little further advanced, because I am a kind man.'

'What time *is* it?' Greta asked, stripping off her gloves.

'Getting on for six, I'm afraid.'

'Jesus. I need to call in—there's no way I'm going to be able to do clinic hours today. Hopefully Anna or Nadezhda can take an extra shift if I do a bit of groveling.'

'I have faith in your ability to grovel convincingly,' Ruthven said. 'Shall I go and make some more coffee?'

'Yes,' she said. Both of them knew this wasn't over. 'Yes, do precisely that thing, and you will earn my everlasting fealty.'

'I earned your everlasting fealty last time I drove you to the airport,' Ruthven said. 'Or was it when I made you tiramisu a few weeks ago? I can't keep track.'

He smiled, despite the line of worry still between his eyebrows, and Greta found herself smiling wearily in return.